2.50

D0298136

Trojan Odyssey

DIRK PITT® ADVENTURES BY CLIVE CUSSLER

Valhalla Rising	*Cyclops*
Atlantis Found	*Deep Six*
Flood Tide	*Pacific Vortex*
Shock Wave	*Night Probe*
Inca Gold	*Vixen 03*
Sahara	*Raise the Titanic*
Dragon	*Iceberg*
Treasure	*The Mediterranean Caper*

KURT AUSTIN ADVENTURES BY CLIVE CUSSLER
WITH PAUL KEMPRECOS

White Death	*Blue Gold*
Fire Ice	*Serpent*

OREGON FILES ADVENTURES BY CLIVE CUSSLER
WITH CRAIG DIRGO

The Golden Buddha

NONFICTION BY CLIVE CUSSLER AND CRAIG DIRGO

The Sea Hunters II

Clive Cussler and Dirk Pitt Revealed

The Sea Hunters

Trojan

Odyssey

CLIVE
CUSSLER

MICHAEL JOSEPH
an imprint of
PENGUIN BOOKS

MICHAEL JOSEPH

Published by the Penguin Group
Penguin Books Ltd, 80 Strand, London WC2R 0RL, England
Penguin Group (USA), Inc., 375 Hudson Street, New York, New York 10014, USA
Penguin Books Australia Ltd, 250 Camberwell Road, Camberwell, Victoria 3124, Australia
Penguin Books Canada Ltd, 10 Alcorn Avenue, Toronto, Ontario, Canada M4V 3B2
Penguin Books India (P) Ltd, 11 Community Centre, Panchsheel Park, New Delhi - 110 017, India
Penguin Books (NZ) Ltd, Cnr Rosedale and Airborne Roads, Albany, Auckland, New Zealand
Penguin Books (South Africa) (Pty) Ltd, 24 Sturdee Avenue, Rosebank 2196, South Africa

Penguin Books Ltd, Registered Offices: 80 Strand, London WC2R 0RL, England

www.penguin.com

First published in the United States of America by G.P. Putnam's Sons 2003
First published in Great Britain by Michael Joseph 2003
1

Printed in Great Britain by Clays Ltd, St Ives plc

A CIP catalogue record for this book is available from the British Library

HB ISBN 0-718-14702-2
TPB ISBN 0-718-14703-0

In loving memory of my wife, Barbara,
who walks with the angels

ACKNOWLEDGMENTS

I am extremely grateful to Iman Wilkens and his revealing book *Where Troy Once Stood.* He has truly shown the way toward a more practical solution to the mystery of Homer's Trojan War.

I would also like to thank Mike Fletcher and Jeffrey Evan Bozanic for their expertise regarding underwater rebreathers.

Night of Infamy

RAM THAT BECAME A HORSE

THE VOYAGE OF ODYSSEUS

I T WAS A SETUP, created with simplicity and an acute insight into human curiosity. And it fulfilled its function flawlessly. The ugly monstrosity stood twenty feet high on four stout wooden legs propped on a flat platform. The housing, mounted on the legs, sat triangularly with open ends. A rounded hump rose on the front of the peaked housing, with two forward slits for eyes. The sides were covered with cowhides. A platform supporting the legs lay flat on the ground. It looked like nothing the people of the citadel of Ilium had ever seen.

To some with a good imagination, it vaguely resembled a stiff-legged horse.

The Dardanians had awakened in the morning, expecting to see the Achaeans surrounding their fortress city, and ready for battle as they had been for the past ten weeks. But, the plain below was empty. All they could see was a thick haze of smoke drifting over the ashes of what had been the enemy camp. The Achaeans and their fleet had vanished. During the dead of night they had loaded their ships with their supplies, horses, arms and chariots, and sailed away, leaving only the mysterious wooden monster behind. Dardanian scouts returned and reported that the Achaean camp was abandoned.

Overjoyed that the siege of Ilium had ended, the people threw aside the main gate of the citadel and poured across the open plain where both armies had clashed and spilled their blood in a hundred battles. At first they were mystified. Several of them suspected some kind of trick and argued in favor of burning it. But they soon discovered it was simply a harmless housing on four legs crudely constructed of wood. A man climbed one of the wooden legs, entered the structure and found it empty.

"If this is the best the Achaeans can do for a horse," he yelled, "small wonder we won."

The crowd laughed and chanted with glee when King Priam of Ilium arrived in a chariot. He stepped to the ground, and acknowledged the cheers of the onlookers. Then he walked around the odd-looking edifice, trying to make sense of it.

Satisfied it presented no threat, he declared it a spoil of war and decreed that it be dragged on its rollers across the plain to the gate of the city, where it would stand as a monument to the glorious victory over the raiding Achaeans.

The happy event was interrupted as two soldiers escorted an Achaean prisoner through the crowd who had been left behind by his comrades. His name was Sinon, and he was known to be the cousin of the mighty Odysseus, king of Ithaca, and one of the leaders of the great raiding party that had besieged Ilium. At the sight of King Priam, Sinon prostrated himself at the elderly king's feet and pleaded for his life.

"Why were you left behind?" the king demanded.

"My cousin listened to those who were my enemies and cast me out of the camp. If I had not escaped into a grove of trees when they were launching the ships, I would have surely been dragged behind until I drowned or was eaten by the fish."

Priam studied Sinon intently. "What is the story behind this aberration? What purpose does it serve?"

"Because they could not take your fortress and because our mighty hero Achilles was killed in battle, they believed they had fallen from the favor of the gods. The edifice was built as an offering for a safe journey home across the seas."

"Why so large?"

"So you could not take it inside the city as a prize, where it would be a reminder of the greatest Achaean failure of our time."

"Yes, I can understand their vision." Wise old Priam smiled. "What they failed to predict was that it can serve the same purpose outside the city."

A hundred men cut and trimmed logs for rollers. Then another hundred gathered ropes, formed two lines and began dragging their prize across the plain between the city and the sea. For most of the day, they sweated and hauled, more men taking their place on the ropes as they pulled the ungainly monstrosity up the slope leading to the citadel. Late in the afternoon, the effort ended and the great effigy stood before the city's main gate. The populace emerged en masse and for the first time in over two months passed freely outside without fear of their enemy. The crowd stood and stared in awe at what was now called the Dardanian horse.

Excited and jubilant that at last the seeming endless series of battles was over, the women and girls of the city went outside the walls and picked flowers for garlands to decorate the grotesque wooden creature.

"Peace and victory are ours!" they cried joyously.

But Priam's daughter, Cassandra, who was thought to be mentally unbalanced because of her dire predictions and foresight into future events, cried, "Don't you see? It's a trick!"

The bearded priest, Laocoön, agreed. "You are beguiled by rapture. You are fools to trust Achaeans offering gifts."

Laocoön reeled back and with a mighty heave threw his spear into the belly of the horse. The spear pierced the wood up to its shaft and quivered. The crowd laughed at the crazy display of skepticism.

"Cassandra and Laocoön are mad! The monster is harmless. Nothing more than boards and logs tied together."

"Idiots!" Cassandra. "Only a fool would believe Sinon the Achaean."

A warrior stared her in the eyes. "He says because it now belongs to Ilium, our city will never fall."

"He's lying."

"Can you not accept a blessing from the gods?"

"Not if it came from the Achaeans," said Laocoön, pushing his way through the milling throng and striding angrily to the city.

There was no reasoning with the happy mob. Their enemy was gone. To them, the war was over. Now was the time for celebration.

The two skeptics were ignored in the euphoria that swept the crowd. Before an hour passed, their curiosity waned and the people launched a great feast to celebrate their triumph over their Achaean foe. Music from flutes and pipes soared within the citadel walls. Song and dance swept every street. Wine flowed through the houses like streams down a mountain. Laughter rang as they lifted and drained their goblets.

In the temples, the priests and priestesses burned incense, chanted and made offerings to the gods and goddesses in thanksgiving for ending the terrible conflict that had sent so many of their warriors to the underworld.

The joyous people toasted their king and the heroes of their army, the veterans, the wounded and the revered dead who had fought the brave fight. "Hector, O Hector, our great champion. If only you had lived to enjoy our glory."

"For nothing the Achaeans, the fools, attacked our magnificent city," shouted one woman as she whirled and danced wildly.

"Like chastened children they have fled," cried another.

So they babbled as the wine coursed through their blood, the royalty in their palace, the rich in their large houses built on terraces and the poor in their simple hovels huddled against the interior city walls for protection against wind and rain. They feasted throughout Ilium, drinking and eating the rest of their precious food supplies hoarded during the siege and making merry as if time had stopped. By midnight the drunken orgy subsided and old King Priam's subjects fell into a deep sleep, their befogged minds at peace for the first time since the hated Achaeans had laid siege to their city.

Many wanted to leave the great gate open as a symbol of victory, but saner minds prevailed and the gate was closed and bolted.

THEY HAD erupted out of the north and east, ten weeks before, sailing across the green sea in hundreds of ships before landing in the bay surrounded by the great Ilium plain. Seeing much of the lowlands filled with swamps, the Achaeans set up their camp on a headland protruding into the sea and off-loaded their fleet of ships.

Because their keels were tarred, the hulls were black below the waterline but above sported a myriad of colors preferred by the various kings of the fleet. They were propelled by rowers with long oars and steered with large oars mounted astern. With bow and stern virtually identical in symmetry they could be rowed in either direction. Unable to sail into the wind, a large square sail was raised only when the breeze blew from astern. Platforms rose fore and aft while carved birds, mostly hawks and falcons, sat above the bow stem. The number of crewmen varied from one hundred and twenty warriors in the troop ships to twenty in the supply transports. Most were manned by a crew of fifty-two, including the commander and a pilot.

Leaders of small kingdoms formed a loose alliance to pillage and raid coastal towns up and down the coast, much like the Vikings two thousand years later. They came from Argos, Pylos, Arcadia, Ithaca and a dozen other regions. Though considered large men for their time, few stood over five feet four inches. They fought ferociously, protected by cuirasses of beaten bronze, plates covering the front of the body and connected by leather thongs. Bronze helmets fit flush over their head, some with horns, some with pointed topknots, most all of them embossed with the owner's personal crest. Armor called greaves was worn that covered the lower legs and arms.

They were masters of the spear, their preferred weapon, and only used their short swords when their spears were shattered or lost. Fighters of the Bronze Age seldom used the bow and arrow, considering it a coward's weapon. They fought from behind huge shields made from six to eight layers of cowhide sewn with leather thongs to a wicker frame with the outer edges in bronze. Most were round, but many were in the shape of a figure eight.

Strangely, unlike warriors of other kingdoms or cultures, the Achaeans did not use horses as cavalry, nor did they charge with chariots. They employed chariots mostly for transportation, carrying men and supplies back and forth from the battlefield. The Achaeans chose to fight on foot as did the Dardanians of Ilium. But this was not simply a war to conquer and take over a territory as rulers. This was not merely a war for plunder. It was an invasion to gain ownership of a metal almost as precious as gold.

Before beaching their ships at Ilium, the Achaeans had raided a dozen towns and cities up and down the coast, taking a hoard of treasure and many slaves, mostly women and children. But they could only imagine the vast wealth that was guarded by the thick walls of Ilium and its determined defenders.

There was apprehension in their ranks as the warriors stared at the city standing on the end of a rocky promontory and studied its massive stone walls and sturdy towers with the king's palace rising above the center. Now as their objective stood before them it became obvious that unlike the others towns and cities they had sacked, this one would not fall without a long and lengthy campaign.

This fact came home when the Dardanians sallied forth from their fortress city and attacked the Achaeans as they landed, nearly driving off the vanguard of the invading fleet before the rest of the ships arrived and unloaded their main force. The Dardanians, soon outnumbered, retreated to the safety behind the main gate of the city after dealing the Achaeans a bloody nose.

For the next ten weeks the battle raged back and forth across the plain. The Dardanians fought tenaciously. Bodies piled up and were strewn from the Achaean camp to the walls of the Ilium citadel as the great heroes and champions of both sides fought and died. At the end of the day, huge pyres were laid by each side and the fallen were cremated. Mounds were later erected over the burned-out pyres as monuments. Thousands died and the seemingly endless battles never diminished.

Brave Hector, son of King Priam and the greatest warrior of Ilium, fell, as did his brother Paris. Mighty Achilles and his friend Patroclus were among the many Achaean dead. With their greatest hero gone, the leaders of the Achaeans, kings Agamemnon and Menelaus, were ready to give up the siege and sail for home. The citadel walls had proven too formidable to penetrate. Food supplies ran low and they had to scrounge the countryside, soon purging the land of all agricultural growth, while the Dardanians were supplied by their allies outside the kingdom who had joined them in the war.

Depressed with certain defeat, they began making plans to strike their camp and disembark, when wily Odysseus, king of Ithaca, came up with a canny plan for a last-ditch effort.

WHILE ILIUM PARTIED, the Achaean fleet returned under cover of darkness. Swiftly they rowed from the nearby island of Tenedos where they had hidden during the daylight hours. Guided by a beacon fire ignited by the deceitful Sinon, they beached their keels again, donned their armor and marched quietly across the plain, carrying a colossal log in slings of braided rope.

Aided by a pitch-dark night with no hint of a moon, they stopped within a scant hundred yards of the gate without being discovered. Scouts led by Odysseus crept around the huge horselike structure and approached the gate.

In the guard tower above, Sinon slew the two slumbering guards. Never intending to open the gate by himself—it took eight strong men to lift the huge wooden bar securing the thirty-foot-high doors—he quietly called down to Odysseus.

"The guards are dead and the city is either drunk or asleep. There is no better time to break down the gates."

Odysseus quickly ordered the men who were carrying the immense log to tilt up the forward end and place it on a small ramp leading into the interior of the horse. While a team pushed from the bottom, another group of Achaeans climbed inside and pulled it up under the peaked roof. Once inside, it was lifted onto slings until it was suspended in the air. What the Dardanians never realized was that the horse, as Odysseus had conceived it, was not a horse but a battering ram.

The men inside the ram hauled the log back as far as it would go and hurled it forward.

The pointed bronze beak that fitted over the end of the log struck the wooden gate with a dull thud that shuddered the gate in its hinges but did not force it open. Again and again the ram was plunged against the foot-thick beam-supported gate. With each strike it splintered but did not give. The Achaeans were fearful that a Dardanian might hear the pounding, look over the wall, see the army below and alert the warriors sleeping off their premature jubilation. High on the top of the wall, Sinon also kept a wary eye on any townsman who might have heard the noise, but those still awake thought it was the sound of distant thunder.

The exertion began to look like an exercise in futility when suddenly the gate dropped off one hinge. Odysseus urged his crew inside the ram for one more mighty effort, placing his arms around the log and lending his muscle to the thrust. The warriors hurled the beak into the stubborn door with every ounce of strength they possessed.

At first the door seemed unconquerable, but then the Achaeans held their breath as it sagged on its remaining hinge for a few moments before giving a rueful tearing moan and falling backward into the citadel, dropping flat on the stone pavement with a great rumbling thump.

Like famished wolves, the Achaean army surged into Ilium, howling like madmen. Like an unstoppable tide they swept through the streets. The frustration flowing in their breasts from ten weeks of unending battle that had accomplished nothing but the death of their comrades, spilled over in a blood lust of ferocity. No one was safe from their swords and spears. They stormed into houses, slaying left and right, killing the men, looting valuables and abducting the women and children before burning everything in sight.

The beautiful Cassandra ran inside the temple, believing she would be safe in the protection of the guards. But the warrior Ajax felt no such misgiving. He assaulted Cassandra beneath the statue of the temple's goddess. Later, in a fit of remorse, he threw himself on his sword and died.

The warriors of Ilium were no match for their avenging enemies. Stumbling from their beds, muddled and confused because they were drunk with wine, they put up a feeble resistance and were slaughtered where they stood. None could withstand the vicious onslaught. Nothing could hold back the wave of destruction. The streets ran crimson with torrents of blood. The beleaguered Dardanians fought and fell, dying wretchedly, gasping their final breaths as death shrouded them. Few died before seeing their homes blazing and their families being led off by their conquerors, hearing the screams of their women, the cries of their children along with the howls of a thousand city dogs.

King Priam, his attendants and guards were murdered mercilessly.

His wife, Hecuba, was carried off into a life of slavery. The palace was looted of its treasures, the gold stripped from columns and ceilings, the beautiful wall hangings and gilded furniture were all seized before flames gutted the once-magnificent interior.

No Achaean held a spear or sword that was not stained with blood. It was as if a pack of wolves ran amok among a herd of sheep in a pen. Old men and old women failed to escape the slaughter. They were slain as if they were rabbits, too frightened to move or too infirm to flee.

One by one the Dardanian hero warriors of the war fell slain until there was none left to wield a spear against the blood-crazed Achaeans. In the burning homes of the city their bodies lay where they had gone down fighting to protect their possessions and loved ones.

Allies of the Dardanians—the Thracians, Lycians, Ciconians and Mysians—fought bravely, but were quickly overwhelmed. The Amazons, proud female warriors who fought with Ilium's army, gave as well as they took, killing many of the hated invader before they too were overpowered and annihilated.

Every home and hovel in the city was now ablaze with fire that gilded the sky as the Achaeans went about their orgy of self-indulgence, plundering and killing. The horrible spectacle never seemed to end.

Finally the Achaeans, weary from the night's bloody debauchery, began departing the burning city, carrying their loot and prodding their enslaved human spoils toward their ships. The captive women, sick with grief for lost husbands and wailing pitifully as they were led away, shepherded their terrified children toward the fleet, knowing they were facing a dreaded future of slavery in foreign Achaean lands. It was the way of the brutal age in which they lived and though it was abhorred they would eventually come to accept their fate. Some were later taken as wives by their captors, bearing their children and living long and fruitful lives. Some died early, mistreated and abused. No record exists telling what happened to their children.

Behind the retreating army the horror did not die with those killed by the sword. Many of those who had been spared the slaughter were dying in burning homes. Flaming roof beams collapsed, trapping many in a fiery death. The glow of the fire mounted above the misery and turmoil. The red and orange glare stained clouds that were drifting in from the sea with swirling sparks and ashes. It was an atrocity that would be repeated many times through the centuries.

Hundreds were fortunate to have escaped the death and destruction by fleeing inland into the nearby forests, where they hid until the Achaean fleet had disappeared over the northeastern horizon whence they had come. Slowly the survivors of Ilium returned to their once-great citadel city, only to find the massive walls surrounding a smoldering pile of ruins, reeking with the sickening stench of burned flesh.

They could not bring themselves to rebuild their homes, but migrated off to another land to raise a new city. The years passed and the ashes of the burned-out rubble were blown by the sea breeze across the plain while the stone streets and walls were slowly buried in dust.

I N T I M E the city rose again, but never to its former glory. Through earthquakes, drought and pestilence it finally succumbed for the last time and lay deserted and desolate for two thousand years. But its fame burned brightly once more when, seven hundred years later, a writer known as Homer wrote vividly of what became known as the Trojan War and the voyage of the Greek hero Odysseus.

O DYSSEUS, though canny and shrewd and hardly adverse to murder and mayhem, was not as barbaric as his brothers in arms when it came to enslaving captive women. Though he allowed his men the evil, he took only the riches he'd seized during the destruction of the hated people who took the lives of so many of his men. Odysseus was the only one of the Achaeans who did not carry away a member of the fair sex as a concubine. He missed his wife, Penelope, and his son, whom he had not seen in many months, and wanted to return to his kingdom on the isle of Ithaca as quickly as the winds would take him.

Leaving the burned-out city in his wake after making sacrifices to the gods, Odysseus set sail across the great green sea as friendly winds carried his small fleet of ships to the southwest and home.

SEVERAL MONTHS later after a vicious storm at sea, Odysseus, more dead than alive, struggled through the surf and crawled ashore on the island of the Phaeacians. Exhausted, he fell asleep in a pile of leaves near the beach, where he was later discovered by a princess, the daughter of Alcinous, king of the Phaeacians. Curious, she shook him to see if he was still alive.

He woke and stared up at her, fascinated by her beauty. "In Delos once I saw a gorgeous creature such as you."

Smitten, Nausicaa led the castaway to the palace of her father where Odysseus revealed himself as king of Ithaca and was royally received and respected. King Alcinous and his wife, Queen Arete, graciously offered Odysseus a ship to carry him home, but only after he promised to regale the king and his court with a narration of the great war and his adventures since leaving Ilium. A magnificent banquet was held in Odysseus' honor and he readily agreed to tell the tale of his exploits and tragedy.

SOON AFTER leaving Ilium," he began, "the winds turned contrary and my fleet was driven far out to sea. After ten days of turbulent waters we finally made it to shore in a strange land. There, my men and I were treated with great warmth and friendliness by the natives who we called Lotus Eaters, because of the fruit from an unknown tree they ate that kept them in a constant state of euphoria.

Some of my men began to consume the lotus fruit and soon became lethargic, no longer having a desire to sail home. Seeing that the homeward voyage might end then and there, I ordered them dragged back to the ships. We quickly raised our sails and rowed swiftly out to sea.

"Mistakenly believing I was far to the east, I sailed west, steering by the stars at night and the sun during its rise and fall. The fleet came to several islands swept by warm and constant rain that were thickly wooded. The islands were inhabited by a race of people who called themselves the Cyclopses, lazy louts who raised large herds of sheep and goats.

"I took a party of men and searched for food supplies. On the side of a mountain we came across a cave that acted as a stall with railings across the entrance to keep animals inside. Taking advantage of a gift from the gods, we began tying a herd of sheep and goats together for the journey to our ships. Suddenly, we heard the sound of footsteps and soon a huge mountain of a man filled the entrance. He entered and rolled a large rock into the opening before tending to his flock. We hid in the shadows, not daring to breathe.

"In time he blew the smoldering embers of a fire pit into flame and saw us cringing in the rear of the cave. No man had a face uglier than the Cyclops who had only one round eye as dark as the night. 'Who are you?' he demanded. 'Why have you invaded my home?'

" 'We are not invaders,' I answered. 'We came ashore in our boats to fill our casks with water.'

" 'You came to steal my sheep,' the giant thundered. 'I shall call my friends and neighbors. Soon hundreds will come and we will boil and eat you all.'

"Although we were Achaean warriors who had fought a long and hard war, we knew we would soon be vastly outnumbered. I found a long narrow log penning in his sheep and sharpened the end into a sharp point with my sword. Then I held up the goatskin full of wine and said to him, 'Look here, Cyclops, here is a wine offering to let us live.'

" 'What is your name?' he demanded.

" 'My mother and father called me *Noman.*'

" 'What kind of a stupid name is that?' Without a word the ugly monstrosity drank the whole goatskin and became very drunk within a very short time and fell into a drunken stupor.

"I quickly snatched up the long log and ran at the sleeping giant, embedding the sharpened point into his one and only eye.

"Screaming in agony he staggered outside, pulled the point from his eye and shouted for help. His neighboring Cyclopses heard him screaming and came to investigate. They shouted, 'Are you being attacked?'

"He cried in reply, 'I am being attacked by *Noman.*'

"Thinking he was crazy, they went back to their homes. We ran from the cave and to our ships. I shouted insults at the sightless giant.

" 'Thank you for the gift of your sheep, you stupid Cyclops. And when your friends ask you how you injured your eye, tell them it was Odysseus, the king of Ithaca, who outsmarted you.' "

"Were you then shipwrecked before you landed here in Phaeacia?" asked the good king.

Odysseus shook his head. "Not for many long months." He took a drink of wine before continuing. "Carried far to the west by prevailing currents and winds, we found land and dropped anchor off the island called Aeolia. Here lived the good king Aeolus, son of Hippotas and dear to the gods. He had six daughters and six lusty sons, so he induced his sons to marry his daughters. They all live together, constantly feasting and enjoying every conceivable luxury.

"Resupplied by the good king, we soon sailed on into rough seas. On the seventh day, after the seas had calmed, we reached the harbor of the city of the Laestrygonians. Navigating the narrow entrance between two rocky headlands, my fleet dropped anchor. Thankful to be on firm ground again, we began exploring the countryside and met a fair maiden who was fetching water.

"When asked who their king might be, she directed us to her father's house. But when we arrived there, we found the wife to be a huge giantess the size of a great tree and we were dumbstruck at the ghastly sight of her.

"She called her husband, Antiphates, who was even larger than she and twice the size of the Cyclops. Horrified at such a monstrosity, we ran back to our ships. But Antiphates raised the alarm and soon thousands of sturdy Laestrygonians appeared like a forest and cast rocks at us from huge slings atop the cliffs, not mere stones, but boulders almost as large as our ships. My ship was the only one that escaped the onslaught. All the others in my fleet were sunk.

"My men were thrown into the harbor, where the Laestrygonians speared them like fish before dragging their bodies ashore, robbing and then eating them. Within minutes my ship reached open water and safety, but with great sadness. Not only were our friends and comrades gone, but so were the ships carrying all the treasure we had looted from Ilium. The vast amount that was our share of the Dardanian gold lay on the bottom of the Laestrygonian harbor.

"Sick with grief, we sailed ever onward until we came to the Aeaean island of Circe, home of the renowned and lovely queen revered as a goddess. Smitten by the charms of the beautiful and fair-tressed Circe, I became friends with her, lingering in her company for three circuits of the moon. I found myself wanting to stay longer but my men insisted we resume our journey to our homes in Ithaca or they would sail without me.

"Circe tearfully agreed to my leave, but implored me to make one more journey. 'You must sail to the house of Hades and consult those who have passed on. They will guide you in understanding death. And when you continue your voyage beware of the song of the Sirens, for they will surely lure you and your men to death on their islands of rocks. Close your ears so you do not hear their lilting songs. Once free of the Sirens' temptation, you will sail past the rocky crags called the Wanderers. Nothing, not even a bird, can pass over them. Every ship except one that tried to pass the Wanderers met its doom, leaving nothing but wreckage and bodies of sailors.'

" 'And the vessel that got through?' I inquired.

" 'The famous Jason and his ship the *Argonaut*.'

" 'And then we'll sail calm seas?'

"Circe shook her head. 'Then you will come to a second mountain of rocks that runs to the sky, whose sides are as polished as a glazed urn and impossible to climb. There in the middle is a cavern, where Scylla, a dreadful monster, strikes terror on any who come near her. She has six snakelike necks, extremely long, with frightful heads containing jaws with three rows of teeth that can crush a human to death in an instant. Beware that she throws out her heads and snatches members of your crew. Row fast, or all of you will surely die. Then you must pass the waters where the Charybdis lurks, a great whirlpool that will suck your ship into the depths. Time your passage when it is asleep.'

"Bidding Circe a tearful farewell, we took our places in the ship and began beating the sea with our oars."

"You truly sailed to the underworld?" murmured King Alcinous' lovely queen, her face pale.

"Yes, I followed Circe's instructions and we sailed toward Hades and its frightful place of the dead. In five days' time we found ourselves in a thick mist as we entered the waters of the river Oceanus that flowed beside the end of the world. The sky had vanished and we were in a perpetual darkness the rays of the sun can never penetrate. We ran the ship ashore. I disembarked alone and walked through the eerie light until I came to a vast cavern in the side of a mountain. Then I sat back and waited.

"Soon the spirits began assembling, uttering terrible moaning sounds. I was nearly stunned senseless when my mother appeared. I did not know she had died, for she was still alive when I left for Ilium.

" 'My son,' she murmured in a low voice, 'why do you come to the abode of darkness while you are still alive? Have you yet to reach your home in Ithaca?'

"With tears in my eyes, I related to her the nightmare voyages and the terrible loss of my warriors during the voyage home from Ilium.

" 'I died of a broken heart fearing I would never see my son again.'

"I wept at her words and tried to embrace her, but she was like a wisp of nothing and my arms came empty with only a vapor.

"They came in bands, men and women I had once known and respected. They came, recognized me and nodded silently before returning to the cavern. I was surprised to see my old comrade, King Agamemnon, our commander at Ilium. 'Did you die at sea?' I asked.

" 'No, my wife and her lover attacked me with a band of traitors. I fought well, but succumbed from overwhelming numbers. They murdered Cassandra, daughter of Priam, as well.'

"Then came noble Achilles with Patroclus and Ajax, who asked about their families, but I could tell them nothing. We talked of old times, until they too returned to the underworld. The ghosts of other friends and warriors stood beside me, each telling his own tale of melancholy.

"I had seen so many of the dead my heart filled with overflowing sadness. Finally, I could see no more and left that pitiful place and boarded my ship. Without looking back we sailed through the shroud of mist until we were touched by the sun again and set a course for the Sirens."

"Did you sail pass the Sirens without distress?" inquired the king.

"We did," he answered. "But before we attempted to run the gauntlet, I took a large wad of wax and cut it up in pieces with my sword. Then I kneaded the pieces until they were soft and used them to plug the ears of my crew. I ordered them to tie me to the mast and ignore my pleadings to change course or we would surely run ashore onto the rocks.

"The Sirens began their enchanted singing as soon as they saw our ship start to pass their island of rocks. 'Come to us and listen to the sweetness of our song, renowned Ulysses. Hear our melody and come into our arms, for you will be charmed and wiser.'

"The music and the sound of their voices was so hypnotic I begged my men to change course for them, but they only bound me tighter to the mast and quickened their stroke until the Sirens could be heard no more. Only then did they remove the wax from their ears and untie me from the mast.

"Once past the rocky island we encountered great waves and the loud roaring of the sea. I exhorted the men to row harder as I steered the ship through the turbulence. I did not tell them of the terrible monster Scylla or they would have stopped rowing and huddled in fear together in the hold. We came to the rock-bound straits and entered the swirling waters of the Charybdis that swept us into a vortex of misery. We felt as if we were in a cyclone within a cauldron. While we were expecting each moment to be our last, Scylla pounced down from above, her viperous heads snatching six of my finest warriors. I heard their despairing cries as they were pulled into the sky, crushed by jaws filled with sharp teeth, their arms stretched out to me in mortal agony as they screamed in horror. It was the most horrendous sight I witnessed throughout the awful voyage.

"Escaping out to sea, thunderbolts began shattering the sky. Lightning struck the ship, filling it with the smell of sulfur. The terrible force burst the ship into pieces, throwing the crew into the raging waters, where they quickly drowned.

"I managed to find part of the mast with a large leather thong wrapped around it that I used to tie my waist to a section of the fractured keel. Getting astride my makeshift raft, I was carried out to sea, drifting where the wind and current chose to take me. Many days later, barely still alive, my raft became stranded on the island of Ogygia, home of Calypso, a woman of great seductive beauty and intelligence and the sister of Circe. Four of her subjects found me on the beach and carried me to her palace where she took me in and nursed me back to full health.

"For a while I lived happily on Ogygia, lovingly cared for by Calypso, who slept by my side. We dallied in a fabulous garden with four fountains that sent their waters spraying in opposite directions. Lush forests with flocks of colorful birds flying among the branches abounded on the island. Clear pure springs ran through quiet meadows bordered by flourishing grapevines."

"How long did you spend with Calypso?" queried the king.

"Seven long months."

"Why did you not simply find a boat and sail away?" asked Queen Arete.

Odysseus shrugged. "Because there was no boat to be found on the island."

"Then how did you finally leave?"

"Kind, gentle Calypso knew of my sorrow. She woke me one morning and spoke of her wish that I return home. She offered up the tools, took me into the forest and helped me cut the wood to make a seaworthy raft. She sewed sails for me from cowhides and provisioned the raft with food and water. After five days I was ready to depart. I was saddened by her emotional cries of pain in letting me go. She was a woman among women, one all men desire. If I hadn't loved Penelope more, I would have gladly stayed." Odysseus paused and a tear came to one eye. "I fear she died of grief in the lonely days that followed my leave."

"What happened to your raft?" wondered Nausicaa. "You were cast away when I found you."

"Seventeen calm days at sea ended when the sea suddenly raged in wrath. A violent storm with driving rain and sweeping gusts tore the sail away. This disaster was followed by great waves that battered my fragile craft until it barely hung together. I drifted for two days before I was finally washed up on your shore, where you, sweet and lovely Nausicaa, found me." He paused. "And so ends my tale of hardship and woe."

Everyone in the palace had sat enthralled by Odysseus' incredible saga. Presently, King Alcinous rose and addressed his guest. "We are honored to have such a distinguished guest in our midst and owe you a great debt for entertaining us in so wondrous a manner. Therefore, in grateful appreciation, my fastest ship and crew are yours to carry you to your home in Ithaca."

Odysseus expressed his gratitude, and he felt humble for such generosity. But he was anxious to be on his way. "Farewell, good King Alcinous and gracious Queen Arete, and to your daughter Nausicaa, for her kindness. Be happy in your house and may you always be graced by the gods."

Then Odysseus crossed the threshold and was escorted to the ship. With a fair wind and a friendly sea, Odysseus finally arrived in his kingdom on the isle of Ithaca, where he was reunited with son Telemachus. There, too, he found his wife Penelope besieged by suitors, and he slew them all.

A ND SO ENDS the story of the *Odyssey,* an epic that has lived on for centuries, inflaming the wonder and imaginations of all who have read it or listened to it. Except that it isn't quite true. Or at least, only *some* of it is true.

For Homer was not a Greek. Nor did the *Iliad* and the *Odyssey* take place where the legends placed them.

The real story of Odysseus' adventures is something else entirely, and it would not be revealed until much, much later . . .

PART ONE

Hell Hath
No Wrath
Like the Sea

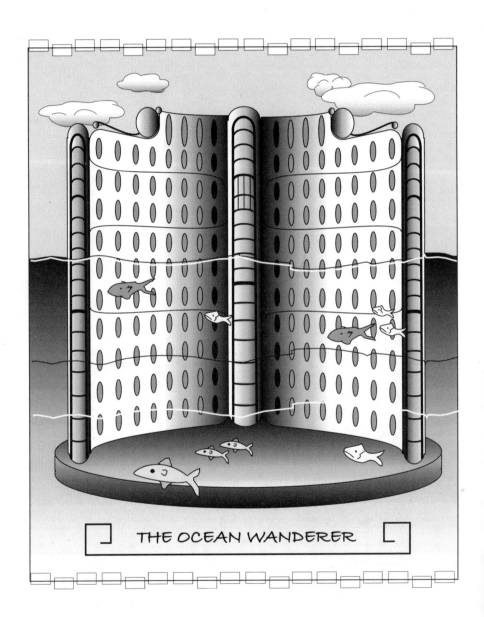

THE OCEAN WANDERER

I

D R. HEIDI LISHERNESS was about to meet her husband for a night out on the town when she took one last cursory glance at the latest imagery collected by a Super Rapid Scan Operations satellite. A full-figured lady with silver-gray hair pulled back in a bun, Heidi sat at her desk in green shorts and matching top as a measure of comfort against the heat and humidity of Florida in August.

She came within a hair of simply shutting down her computer until the following morning. But there was an indiscernible something about the last image that came into her computer from the satellite over the Atlantic Ocean southwest of the Cape Verde Islands off the coast of Africa. She sat down and gazed more intently into the screen of her monitor.

To the untrained eye the picture on the screen simply took on the appearance of a few innocent clouds drifting over an azure blue sea. Heidi saw a view more menacing. She compared the image with one taken only two hours earlier. The mass of cumulus clouds had increased in bulk more rapidly than any spawning storm she could re-member in her eighteen years monitoring and forecasting tropical hur-ricanes in the Atlantic Ocean with the National Underwater and Marine Agency Hurricane Center. She began enlarging the two images of the infant storm formation.

Her husband, Harley, a jolly-looking man with a walrus mustache, bald head and wearing rimless glasses, stepped into her office with an impatient look on his face. Harley was also a meteorologist. But he worked for the National Weather Service as an analyst on clima-tological data that was issued as weather advisories for commercial and private aircraft, boats and ships at sea. "What's keeping you?" he said, pointing impatiently at his watch. "I have reservations at the Crab Pot."

Without looking up, she motioned at the two side-by-side images on her computer. "These were taken two hours apart. Tell me what you see."

Harley examined them for a long moment. Then his brow furrowed and he repositioned his glasses before leaning closer for a more in-depth look. Finally, he looked at his wife and nodded. "One hell of a fast buildup."

"Too fast," said Heidi. "If it continues at the same rate, God only knows how huge a storm it will brew."

"You never know," said Harley thoughtfully. "She might come in like a lion and go out like a lamb. It's happened."

"True, but most storms take days, sometimes weeks, to build to this strength. This has mushroomed within hours."

"Too early to predict her direction or where she'll peak and do the most damage."

"I have a dire feeling this one will be unpredictable."

Harley smiled. "You *will* keep me informed as she builds?"

"The National Weather Service will be the first to know," she said, lightly slapping him on the arm.

"Thought of a name for your new friend yet?"

"If she becomes as nasty as I think she might, I'll call her Lizzie, after the ax murderess Lizzie Borden."

"A bit early in the season for a name beginning with *L* but it sounds fitting." Harley handed his wife her purse. "Time enough tomorrow to see what develops. I'm starved. Let's go eat some crab."

Heidi dutifully followed her husband from her office, switching off the light and closing the door. But the growing apprehension did not diminish as she slid into the seat of their car. Her mind wasn't on food. It dwelled on what she feared was a hurricane in the making that might very well reach horrendous proportions.

A HURRICANE is a hurricane by any other name in the Atlantic Ocean. But not in the Pacific, where it is called a typhoon, nor the Indian, where it is known as a cyclone. A hurricane is the most horrendous force of nature, often exceeding the havoc caused by volcanic eruptions and earthquakes, creating destruction over a far larger territory.

Like the birth of a human or animal, a hurricane requires an array of related circumstances. First, the tropical waters off the west coast of Africa are heated, preferably with temperatures exceeding eighty degrees Fahrenheit. Then, bake the water with the sun, causing vast amounts to evaporate into the atmosphere. This moisture rises into cooler air and condenses into masses of cumulus clouds while giving birth to wide-ranging rain and thunderstorms. This combination provides the heat that fuels the growing tempest and transforms it from infancy to puberty.

Now stir in spiraling air that whips around at speeds up to thirty-eight miles an hour, or thirty-three knots. These growing winds cause the surface air pressure to drop. The lower the drop the more intense the wind circulation as it whirls around in an ever-faster momentum until it forms a vortex. Feeding on the ingredients, the system, as it is called by meteorologists, has created an explosive centrifugal force that spins a solid wall of wind and rain around the eye that is amazingly calm. Inside the eye, the sun shines, the sea lies relatively calm and the only sign of the horrendous energy are the surrounding white frenzied walls reaching fifty thousand feet into the sky.

Until now, the system has been called a tropical depression, but once the winds hit 74 miles an hour it becomes a full-fledged hurricane. Then, depending on the wind velocities it puts out, it is given a scale number. Winds between 74 and 95 miles an hour is a Category 1 and considered minimal. Category 2 is moderate with winds up to 110. Category 3 blows from 111 to 130 and is listed as extensive. Winds up to 155 are extreme, as was Hurricane Hugo that eliminated most of the beach houses north of Charleston, South Carolina, in 1989. And finally, the granddaddy of them all, Category 5 with winds 155-plus. The last is labeled catastrophic, as was Hurricane Camille, which struck Louisiana and Mississippi in 1969. Camille left 256 dead in her wake, a drop in the bucket as compared to the 8,000 who perished in the great hurricane of 1900 that laid complete waste to Galveston, Texas. In terms of sheer numbers, the record is held by the 1970 tropical cyclone that stormed ashore in Bangladesh and left nearly half a million dead.

In terms of damage, the great hurricane of 1926 that devastated Southeast Florida and Alabama left a bill totaling $83 billion, allowing for inflation. Amazingly, only two hundred and forty-three died in that catastrophe.

What no one was counting on, including Heidi Lisherness, was that Hurricane Lizzie had a diabolic mind of her own and her coming fury was about to put the previous recorded Atlantic hurricanes to shame. In a short time, after bulking up on muscle, she would begin her murderous journey toward the Caribbean Sea to wreak chaos and havoc on everything she touched.

2

S WIFT AND POWERFUL, a great hammerhead shark fifteen
feet long glided gracefully through the air-clear water like a gray
cloud drifting over a meadow. Its two bulging eyes gazed from the ends
of a flat stabilizer that spread across its snout. They caught a motion
and swiveled, focusing on a creature swimming through the coral forest below. The thing looked like no fish the hammerhead had ever
seen. It had two parallel fins protruding to the rear and was colored
black with red stripes along the sides. The huge shark saw nothing sa-
vory and continued its never-ending search for more appetizing prey,
not realizing that the odd creature would have made a very tasty morsel
indeed.

Summer Pitt had noticed the shark but ignored it, concentrating on
her study of the coral reefs inside Navidad Bank seventy miles northeast of the Dominican Republic. The bank encompassed a dangerous
stretch of reefs thirty by thirty square miles with depths varying from
three feet to one hundred feet. During the passage of four centuries,
no less than two hundred ships had come to grief on the unforgiving
coral that crowned a seamount soaring from the abyssal depths of
the Atlantic Ocean.

The coral on this section of the bank was pristine and beautiful, rising in some areas as much as fifty feet off the sandy bottom. There were delicate sea fans and huge brain coral, their vivid colors and sculptured contours spreading into the blue void like a majestic garden with a myriad of archways and grottos. It seemed to Summer that she was swimming into a labyrinth of alleyways and tunnels, some becoming dead ends while others opened into canyons and crevasses large enough to drive a large truck through.

Though the water was in excess of eighty degrees, Summer Pitt was fully encased from head to foot in a Viking Pro Turbo 1000 heavy-duty vulcanized rubber dry suit. She wore the black-and-red suit instead of a lighter wet suit because it totally sealed every inch of her body, not so much as protection from the mild water temperature but as a deterrent to the chemical and biological contamination that she had planned to encounter during her assessment and monitoring of the coral.

She glanced at her compass and made a slight turn to the left, kicking her fins while clasping her hands behind and under her twin air tanks to reduce water resistance. Wearing the bulky suit and AGA Mark II full face mask made it seem easier to walk on the bottom than swim over it, but the often sharp and uneven surface of the coral made that nearly impossible.

Her physical contours and facial features were shrouded by the baggy dry suit and full head mask. The only clues to her beauty were the exquisite gray eyes gazing through the face mask lens and a wisp of red hair that showed on her forehead.

Summer loved the sea and diving through its void. Every dive was a new adventure through an unknown world. She often imagined herself as a mermaid with salt water in her veins. Urged by her mother, she had studied ocean sciences. A top student, she graduated from the Scripps Institute of Oceanography, where she had received her master's degree in biological oceanography. At the same time, her twin brother, Dirk, had achieved his degree in ocean engineering at Florida Atlantic University.

Soon after they returned to their home in Hawaii, they were informed by their dying mother that the father they never knew was the special projects director for the National Underwater and Marine Agency in Washington, D.C. Their mother had never talked about him until she was lying on her deathbed. Only then did she describe their love and why she let him believe that she had died in an underwater earthquake twenty-three years before. Badly injured and disfigured, she thought it best that he live his life unencumbered, without her. Several months later she gave birth to twins. In memory of her undying love she had named Summer after herself, and Dirk after his father.

After her funeral, Dirk and Summer flew to Washington to meet Pitt Sr. for the first time. Their sudden appearance came as a total shock to him. Stunned at confronting a son and daughter who he had no idea existed, Dirk Pitt became overjoyed, having believed for more than twenty years that the unforgettable love of his life had long since died. But then he was deeply saddened to learn she had lived all these years as an invalid without telling him and had died only the month previously.

Embracing the family he never knew he had, he immediately moved them into the old aircraft hangar where he lived with his huge classic car collection. When he was told that their mother had insisted they follow in his path and become educated in the ocean sciences, he orchestrated their employment with NUMA.

Now, after two years of working on ocean projects around the world, she and her brother had embarked on a unique journey to investigate and gather data on the strange toxic contamination that was killing the fragile sea life on Navidad Bank and other reefs throughout the Caribbean.

Most parts of the reef system still teemed with healthy fish and coral. Brightly hued snappers mingled with huge parrot fish and groupers while little iridescent yellow-and-purple tropical fish darted around tiny brown-and-red sea horses. Moray eels looking fierce with their heads protruding out of holes in the coral, opened and closed their jaws menacingly, waiting to sink their needle teeth into a meal. Summer knew they looked frightening only because that was their method of breathing since they did not have a set of gills on the back of their necks. They seldom attacked humans unless they were antagonized. To be bitten by a moray eel, one almost had to place a hand in its mouth.

A shadow crossed above a sandy gap in the coral and she looked up, half expecting to see the same shark returning for a closer look, but it was a flight of five spotted eagle rays. One peeled off the formation like an aircraft and cruised around Summer, staring curiously before swooping upward and rejoining the others.

After traveling another forty yards she slipped over a formation of horny gorgonian coral and came within view of a shipwreck. A huge five-foot barracuda hovered over the debris, staring out of cold, black beady eyes at all that took place in its domain.

The steamship *Vandalia* was driven onto Navidad Bank in 1876 during a fierce hurricane. Of her one hundred and eighty passengers and thirty crewmen, none survived. Listed by Lloyd's of London as lost without a trace, her fate remained a mystery until sport divers discovered her coral-encrusted remains in 1982. There was little left to distinguish *Vandalia* as a shipwreck. A hundred and thirty years on, the bank had covered her with anywhere from one to three feet of sea life and coral. The only obvious signs of what was once a proud ship were the boilers and engines that still protruded from the twisted carcass and exposed ribs. Most of the wood was gone, long rotted away by the salt water or eaten by critters of the sea that consumed anything organic.

Built for the West Indies Packet Company in 1864, *Vandalia* was 320 feet from the tip of her bow to the jack staff on her stern, with a

42-foot beam and accommodations for 250 passengers and three holds for a large amount of cargo. She sailed between Liverpool and Panama, where she unloaded her passengers and cargo for the rail trip to the Pacific side of the isthmus where they boarded steamers for the rest of the journey to California.

Very few divers had salvaged artifacts from *Vandalia*. She was difficult to find in her camouflaged position amid the coral. Little was left of the ship after being crushed that horrible night by the mountainous waves of the hurricane that caught her in the open sea before she could reach the safety of the Dominican Republic or nearby Virgin Islands.

Summer roamed over the old wreck, carried by a mild current, looking down and trying to picture the people who had once trod her decks. She sensed a spiritual sensation. It was as if she was flying over a haunted graveyard whose inhabitants were speaking to her from the past.

She kept a wary eye on the great barracuda that hung motionless in the water. Food was no problem for the ferocious-looking fish. There was enough sea life living in and around the old *Vandalia* to fill an encyclopedia on marine ichthyology.

Forcing her mind from visions of the tragedy, she swam warily around the barracuda that never took a beady eye off her. A safe distance away, she paused to check the air left in her tanks on the pressure gauge, mark her position on a Global Positioning System satellite minicomputer, eye the compass needle in relationship to the underwater habitat where she and her brother were living while studying the reef and note the reading on her bottom timer. She felt slightly buoyant and neutralized by venting a bit of air from her back-mounted buoyancy compensator.

Swimming another hundred yards, she saw the bright colors fading and the coral turning colorless. The farther she swam the more the sponges became glazed and diseased, until they died and ceased to exist. The visibility of the water also dropped drastically, until she could see no farther than the extended tip of her hand and fingers.

She felt as if she had entered a dense fog. It was a phenomenon, known as the mysterious "brown crud," that had appeared throughout the Caribbean. The water near the surface was an eerie brown mass that fishermen described as looking like sewage. Until now, no one knew exactly what caused the crud or what triggered it. Ocean scientists thought it was associated with a type of algae, but had yet to prove it.

Strangely, the crud did not appear to kill the fish, like its notorious cousin, the red tide. They avoided contact with the worst of the toxic effects, but soon began to starve after losing their feeding grounds and shelter in the process. Summer noticed that the usually brilliant sea anemone, with their arms extended to feed in the current, also seemed hard hit by the weird invader to their realm. Her immediate project was simply to take a few preliminary samples. Recording the dead zone on Navidad Bank with cameras and chemical analysis instruments to detect and measure its composition would come later, in the hope of eventually finding countermeasures to eradicate it.

The first dive of the project was purely one of exploration, to see firsthand the effects of the crud so she and her fellow marine scientists on board the nearby research ship could evaluate the full scale of the problem and create a precise pattern for future study of the cause.

The first brown crud invasion warning had been sounded by a commercial diver working off Jamaica in 2002. The baffling crud had left a path of underwater destruction unseen and mostly unreported from the surface as it drifted out of the Gulf of Mexico and around the Florida Keys. That outbreak was, Summer was beginning to discover, much different than here. The crud on Navidad Bank was far more toxic. She began to find dead starfish, and shellfish such as shrimp and lobster. She also noted that the fish swimming through the strange discolored water seemed lethargic, almost comatose.

She removed several small glass bottles from a pouch strapped to one thigh and began taking water specimen samples. She also collected dead star- and shellfish and dropped them in a netted bag attached to her weight belt. When the jars were sealed and securely resting in the pouch, she checked her air again. She had over twenty minutes of dive time left. She rechecked her compass readings and began swimming in the direction from which she had come, soon reaching clean and clear water again.

Casually observing the bottom that had turned to a small river of sand, she sighted the opening to a small cavern in the coral, one she hadn't noticed before. At first glance it looked like any one of twenty others she'd passed in the last forty-five minutes. But there was something different about this one. The entrance had a square-cornered, carved look about it. Her imagination visualized a pair of coral-encased columns.

A ribbon of sand led inside. Curious, and with an ample supply of air in reserve, she swam over to the entrance of the cavern and peered into the gloom.

A few feet inside the chamber the indigo of the walls flickered under the shimmering light from the sun's rays above. Summer slowly swam along the sandy bottom as the blue turned dark and became brown after several yards. She nervously turned and looked over her shoulder, reassuring herself at seeing brightness surrounding the opening. Without a dive light there was nothing to see and it didn't take great imagination to picture danger in the inky interior. She nimbly turned and stroked toward the entrance.

Suddenly one of her fins brushed against something half buried in the sand. She was about to simply dismiss it as a lump of coral, but the coral-encrusted object had a seemingly man-made symmetrical contour. She dug into the sand until the thing came free. Moving toward the light, Summer held it aloft and lightly swirled it in the water, cleaning away the sand. It looked to be about the size of an old-fashioned lady's hatbox except that it felt quite heavy, even underwater. Two handles protruded from the upper area, while the bottom gave the impression under the encrustation of having a pedestal base. As near as she could tell, the interior looked hollow, another sign that it wasn't created by nature.

Through the mask, Summer's gray eyes mirrored skeptical interest. She decided to carry it back to the habitat, where she could carefully clean and determine what was to be seen under the accumulated coral sea growth.

The extra weight of the mysterious object and the dead sea life she had collected on the bottom had affected her buoyancy, so she compensated by adding air to her BC. Tightly gripping the object under her arm, she languidly swam toward the habitat oblivious of her air bubbles trailing behind her.

The habitat that she and her brother would call home for the next ten days appeared through the shimmering blue water a short distance ahead.

Pisces was often called an "inner space station," but she was an underwater laboratory designed and dedicated to ocean research. She was a sixty-five-ton rectangular chamber rounded off on the ends, thirty-eight feet long by ten feet wide by eight feet high. The habitat sat on legs attached to a heavy weighted base plate that provided a stable platform on the seafloor fifty feet below the surface. The entry air lock served as a storage unit and a place to don and remove diving equipment. The main lock that maintained a differential pressure between the two compartments contained a small lab working area, a galley, a confined dining area, four bunk beds, and a computer and communications console connected to an outside antenna for contact with the world above the surface.

She removed her air tanks and connected them with a bottom tank filling station next to the habitat. Holding her breath, she swam up and into the entry lock, where she carefully set the pouch and net containing her specimen samples in a small container. The mysterious coral-encrusted object she set on a folded towel. Summer was not about to risk the dangers of contamination. Suffering from the tropical heat and the sweat emerging from her insulated pores for a few more minutes were a small price to pay to avoid a potentially deadly illness.

After swimming in and through brown crud, one drop on her skin could prove fatal. She did not dare remove her Viking dry suit with attached Turbo hood and boots, gloves sealed by locking rings and full face mask, just yet. After unsnapping her weight belt and buoyancy compensator, she turned on two valves that activated a strong sprinkling system, washing down her wet suit and gear with a special decontamination solution to remove any brown crud residue. Certain she was properly sanitized, she turned off the valves and rapped on the door to the main lock.

Although the masculine face that appeared on the other side of the view port belonged to her twin brother, there was little resemblance. Though they were born within minutes of each other, she and her brother Dirk Jr. were about as nonidentical as twins could get. He towered over her at six feet four, and was lean and hard and deeply tanned. Unlike her straight red hair and soft gray eyes, the thick mass of hair on his head was wavy and black, the eyes a mesmeric opaline green that sparkled when the light hit just right.

When she stepped out of the chamber, he removed the yoke and collar seal between the neck of her suit and head mask. By the look in his eyes that were more piercing than usual and the grim expression on his face, she knew she was in big trouble.

Before he could open his mouth, she threw up her hands and said, "I know, I know, I shouldn't have gone off alone without a dive partner."

"You know better," said her brother in exasperation. "If you hadn't sneaked off at the crack of dawn before I was awake, I would have come after and dragged you back to the lab by your ear."

"I apologize," said Summer, feigning remorse, "but I can accomplish more if I don't have to be concerned with another diver."

Dirk helped her undo the heavy, riveted waterproof zippers on her

Viking dry suit. First removing the gloves and pulling the inner hood down behind her head, he began peeling the suit from her torso, arms and then legs and feet, until she could step out of it. Her hair fell in a cascade of copper red. Underneath, Summer wore a skin-tight polypropylene nylon body suit that nicely displayed her curvaceous body.

"Did you enter the crud?" asked Dirk with concern in his tone.

She nodded. "I brought back samples."

"You certain there was no leakage inside your suit?"

Holding her arms over her head, she did a pirouette. "See for yourself. Not a drop of toxic slime to be seen."

Pitt put a hand on her shoulder. "Words to remember: 'Don't ever dive alone again.' Certainly not without me if I'm in the neighborhood."

"Yes, brother," she said with a condescending smile.

"Let's get your samples in a sealed case. Captain Barnum can take them back to the ship's lab for analysis."

"The captain is coming to the habitat?" she asked in mild surprise.

"He invited himself for lunch," Pitt answered. "He insisted on delivering our food supplies himself. Said it will give him a break from playing ship's commander."

"Tell him he can't come if he doesn't bring a bottle of wine."

"Let us hope he got the message by osmosis," Dirk said with a grin.

A CADAVEROUSLY built man, Captain Paul T. Barnum might have been taken for a brother to the legendary Jacques Cousteau, except that his head was almost desolate of hair. He wore a shorty wet suit and left it on after entering the main lock. Dirk helped him lift a metal box containing two days of food onto the galley counter where Summer began stowing the various supplies in a little cupboard and refrigerator.

"I brought you a present," Barnum announced, holding up a bottle of Jamaican wine. "Not only that, the ship's cook made you lobster thermidor with creamed spinach for dinner."

"That explains your presence," Pitt said, slapping the captain on the back.

"Spirits on a NUMA project," Summer murmured mockingly. "What would our esteemed leader, Admiral Sandecker, have to say about breaking his golden rule of no booze during working hours?"

"Your father was a bad influence on me," said Barnum. "He never came aboard ship without a case of vintage wine while his buddy Al Giordino always showed up with a humidor filled with the admiral's private stock of cigars."

"It seems everybody but the admiral knows that Al secretly buys the cigars from the same source," said Dirk, smiling.

"What's for a side dish?" asked Barnum.

"Fresh fish chowder and crab salad."

"Who's doing the honors?"

"Me," muttered Dirk. "The only seafood Summer can prepare is a tuna sandwich."

"That's not so," she pouted. "I'm a good cook."

Dirk gazed at her cynically. "Then why does your coffee taste like battery acid?"

Panfried in butter, the lobster and creamed spinach were washed down with the bottle of Jamaican wine, accompanied by tales of Barnum's seafaring adventures. Summer made a nasty face at her brother as she presented them with a lemon meringue pie she had baked in the microwave. Dirk was the first to admit she had performed a gourmet wonder, since baking and microwave ovens were not suited to one another.

Barnum stood to take his leave, when Summer touched his arm. "I have an enigma for you."

Barnum's eyes narrowed. "What kind of enigma?"

She handed him the object she'd found in the cavern.

"What is it?"

"I think it's some kind of pot or urn. We won't know until we clean off the encrustation. I was hoping you'd take it back to the ship and have someone in the lab give it a good scrubbing."

"I'm sure someone will volunteer for the job." He hoisted it in both hands as if weighing it. "Feels too heavy for terra-cotta."

Dirk pointed to the base of the object. "There's an open space free of growth where you can see that it's formed out of metal."

"Strange, there doesn't appear to be any rust."

"Don't hold me to it, but my guess is it's bronze."

"The configuration is too graceful for native manufacture," added Summer. "Though it's badly encrusted, it appears to have figures molded around the middle."

Barnum peered at the urn. "You have more imagination than I do. Maybe an archaeologist can solve the riddle after we return to port, if they don't go into hysterics because you removed it from the site."

"You won't have to wait that long," said Dirk. "Why not transmit photos of it to Hiram Yaeger in NUMA's computer headquarters in Washington? He should be able to come up with a date and where it was produced. Chances are it fell off a passing ship or came from a shipwreck."

"The *Vandalia* lies nearby," offered Summer.

"There's your probable source," said Barnum.

"But how did it get inside a cavern a hundred yards away?" Summer asked no one in particular.

Her brother smiled foxlike and murmured, "Magic, lovely lady, voodoo island magic."

D ARKNESS HAD SETTLED over the sea when Barnum finally bid good night.

As he slipped through the entry lock door, Pitt asked, "How does the weather look?"

"Pretty calm for the next couple of days," replied Barnum. "But a hurricane is building up off the Azores. The ship's meteorologist will keep a sharp eye on it. If it looks like it's heading this way, I'll evacuate the two of you and we'll make full speed out of its path."

"Let's hope it misses us," said Summer.

Barnum placed the urn in a net bag and took the pouch of water samples Summer had collected before he dropped out of the entry lock into the night-blackened water. Dirk switched on the outside lights, revealing schools of vivid green parrot fish swimming in circles, seemingly indifferent to the humans living in their midst.

Without bothering to don air tanks, Barnum took a deep breath, beamed a dive light ahead of him and stroked to the surface in a free ascent fifty feet away, exhaling as he rose. His little aluminum rigid-hull inflatable boat bobbed on its anchor that he'd dropped earlier a safe distance from the habitat. He swam over, climbed in and pulled up the anchor. Then he turned the ignition and started the two one-hundred-and-fifty-horsepower Mercury outboard motors and skimmed across the water toward his ship, whose superstructure was brightly illuminated with an array of floodlights embellished with red and green navigation lamps.

Most oceangoing vessels were usually painted white with red, black or blue trim. A few cargo ships sported an orange color scheme. Not the *Sea Sprite*. As with all the other ships in the National Underwater and Marine Agency fleet, she was painted a bright turquoise from stem to stern. It was the hue the agency's feisty director, Admiral James Sandecker, had chosen to set his ships apart from the other vessels that roamed the seas. There were few mariners who didn't recognize a NUMA vessel when they passed one at sea or in port.

Sea Sprite was large, as her type of vessel went. She measured 308 feet in length with a 65-foot beam. State of the art in every detail, she had started life as an icebreaker tug and spent her first ten years stationed in and around the north polar seas, battling frigid storms while towing damaged ships out of ice floes and around icebergs. She could

4 2   C L I V E   C U S S L E R

bulldoze her way through six-foot-thick ice and tow an aircraft carrier through rough seas and do it with motion stability.

Still in her prime when purchased by Sandecker for NUMA, he ordered her refitted into an ultra-multipurpose ocean research and dive support vessel. Nothing was spared in the major refurbishment. Her electronics were designed by NUMA engineers as were her automated computerized systems and communications. She also possessed high-quality laboratories, adequate work space and low vibration. Her computer networks could monitor, collect and pass processed data to the NUMA laboratories in Washington for immediate investigation that turned the results into vital ocean knowledge.

Sea Sprite was powered by the most advanced engines modern technology could create. Her two big magnetohydrodynamic engines could move her through the water at nearly forty knots. And, if she could tow an aircraft carrier through turbulent seas before, she could now pull two without breathing hard. No research ship in any country in the world could match her rugged sophistication.

Barnum was proud of his ship. She was one of only thirty research ships in the NUMA fleet but easily the most unique. Admiral Sandecker had placed him in charge of her refit and Barnum was more than happy to oblige, especially when the admiral told him cost was no problem. No corner was cut and Barnum never doubted that this command was the pinnacle of his marine career.

Deployed a full nine months a year overseas, her scientists were rotated with every new project. The other three months were spent in voyaging to and from study sites, dock maintenance and upgrading equipment and instruments with newer technical advances.

As he approached, he gazed at the eight-story superstructure, the great crane on the stern that had lowered *Pisces* to the bottom and was used to lift and retrieve robotic vehicles and manned submersibles from the water. He studied the huge helicopter platform mounted over the bow and the array of communications and satellite equipment growing like trees around a large dome containing a full range of radar systems.

Barnum turned his attention to steering alongside the hull. As he shut down the engines, a small crane swung out from above and lowered a cable with a hook. He attached the hook to a lift strap and relaxed as the little boat was lifted aboard.

Once he stepped onto the deck, Barnum immediately carried the enigmatic object to the ship's spacious laboratory. He handed it to two intern students from the Texas A&M School of Nautical Archaeology.

"Clean it up the best you can," said Barnum. "But be very careful. It just might be a very valuable artifact."

"Looks like an old pot covered with crud," said a blond-haired girl, wearing a tight Texas A&M T-shirt and cutoff shorts. It was obvious that she didn't relish the job of cleaning it.

"Not at all," said Barnum with icy menace. "You never know what vile secrets are hidden in a coral reef. So beware of the evil genie inside."

Happy to have the last word, Barnum turned and walked toward his cabin, leaving the students staring suspiciously at his back before turning and contemplating the urn.

By ten o'clock that evening, the urn was on a helicopter heading toward the airport at Santo Domingo in the Dominican Republic, where it would be put on a jetliner whose destination was Washington, D.C.

3

THE NUMA HEADQUARTERS building rose thirty stories beside the east bank of the Potomac River overlooking the Capitol. Its computer network on the tenth floor looked like a sound-stage from a Hollywood science fiction movie. The remarkable setting was the domain of Hiram Yaeger, NUMA's chief computer wizard. Sandecker had given Yaeger free rein to design and create the world's largest library on the sea, without interference or budget restraints. The amount of data Yaeger had accumulated, assembled and cataloged was massive, covering every known scientific research study, investigation and analysis, dating from the earliest ancient records to the present. There was none like it anywhere in the world.

The spacious setting was open. Yaeger felt that, unlike most government and corporate computer centers, cubicles were a nemesis to efficient work habits. He orchestrated the vast complex from a large circular console set on a raised platform at its center. Except for a conference room and the bathrooms, the only enclosure was a transparent circular tube the size of a closet that stood off to one side of an array of monitors spread around Yaeger's console.

Never quite making the transition from hippie to pin-striped suit, Yaeger still dressed in Levi's with matching jacket and very old, worn cowboy boots. His graying hair was pulled back in a ponytail and he peered at his adored monitors through granny glasses. Peculiarly, the NUMA computer wizard did not lead the life he exhibited in his appearance.

Yaeger had a lovely wife who was an acclaimed artist. They lived on a farm in Sharpsburg, Maryland, where they raised horses. Their two daughters attended private school and were making plans to attend the college of their choice after graduation. Yaeger drove an expensive V-12 BMW to and from NUMA headquarters while his wife preferred a Cadillac Esplanade to haul the girls and their friends to school and parties.

Intrigued by the urn that had been air-shipped from Captain Barnum on *Sea Sprite,* he lifted it out of its box and set it in the tubular enclosure a few feet from his leather swivel chair. Then he punched in a code on his keyboard. In a few moments the three-dimensional figure of an attractive woman wearing a floral-patterned blouse with matching skirt materialized in the chamber. A creation of Yaeger's, the ethereal lady was an image of his own wife and was a talking and self-thinking computerized manifestation that had a personality all its own.

"Hello, Max," greeted Yaeger. "Ready to do a little research?"

"I'm at your beck and call," Max replied in a husky voice.

"You see the object I placed at your feet?"

"I do."

"I'd like you to identify it with an approximate date and culture."

"We're doing archaeology now, are we?"

Yaeger nodded. "The object was found in a coral cavern on Navidad Reef by a NUMA biologist."

"They could have done a better job of dressing it up," Max said dryly, looking down at the encrusted urn.

"It was a rush job."

"That's obvious."

"Circulate through university archaeological data networks until you find a close match."

She looked at him slyly. "You're coercing me into a criminal act, you know."

"Hacking into other files of historical purposes is not a criminal act."

"I never fail to be impressed with the way you legitimize your nefarious activities."

"I do it out of sheer benevolence."

Max rolled her eyes. "Spare me."

Yaeger's index finger touched a key, and Max slowly disappeared as though she was in a state of vaporization while the urn sank into a receptacle beneath the floor of the tube.

In that instant the blue phone amid a row of colored receivers buzzed. Yaeger held the earpiece against his ear as he continued typing on his keyboard. "Yes, Admiral."

"Hiram," came the voice of Admiral James Sandecker, "I need the file on that floating monstrosity that's moored off Cabo San Rafael in the Dominican Republic."

"I'll bring it right up to your office."

JAMES SANDECKER, age sixty-one, was doing push-ups when Yaeger was ushered into the office by the admiral's secretary. A short man a few inches over five feet, he had a thick carpet of red hair matched by a red Vandyke beard. He glanced up at Yaeger through cool assertive blue eyes. A health addict, he jogged every morning, worked out in the NUMA gym every afternoon and ate vegetarian. His only vice was a penchant for huge custom cigars, rolled to his special order. A longtime member of the Beltway crowd, he had built NUMA into the most efficient bureaucracy in government. Though most presidents he had served under during his long term as director of NUMA did not find him a team player, his impressive record of achievement and admiration by Congress assured him of a lifetime job.

He literally jumped to his feet as he motioned Yaeger to a chair across from his desk that had once belonged in the captain's cabin of the French luxury liner *Normandie* before it burned in New York Harbor in 1942.

They were joined by Rudi Gunn, Sandecker's deputy director of the agency. Gunn was less than an inch taller than the admiral. A highly intelligent individual and a former commander in the navy who had served under Sandecker, Gunn stared at the world through thick-lensed horn-rim glasses. Gunn's main job was to oversee NUMA's many scientific ocean projects operating around the world. He nodded at Hiram and sat down in an adjacent chair.

Yaeger half stood and laid a thick folder in front of the admiral. "Here is everything we have on the *Ocean Wanderer*."

Sandecker opened the folder and stared at the plans for the luxury hotel that was designed and constructed as a floating resort. Self-contained, it could be towed to any one of several exotic locations throughout the world, where it would be moored for a month until it was hauled to its next picturesque site. After a minute of studying the specifications, he looked up at Yaeger, his expression grim. "This thing is a catastrophe waiting to happen."

"I have to agree," said Gunn. "Our engineering staff carefully scrutinized the interior structure and came to the conclusion that the hotel was inadequately designed to survive a violent storm."

"What brought you to that conclusion?" asked Yaeger innocently.

Gunn stood and leaned over the desk, unrolling plans of the anchor cables that were attached to pilings driven into the seabed to anchor the hotel. He pointed with a pencil at the cables where they were secured to huge fasteners beneath the lower floors of the hotel. "A strong hurricane could rip it off its moorings."

"According to the specs, it's built to withstand one-hundred-and-fifty-mile-an-hour winds," pointed out Yaeger.

"Not the winds we're concerned about," said Sandecker. "Because the hotel is moored out to sea instead of firmly embedded on hard ground, it's at the mercy of high waves that could build up as they approach shallow water and beat the structure to pieces, along with all the guests and employees inside."

"Wasn't any of this taken into consideration by the architects?" asked Yaeger.

Sandecker scowled. "We pointed out the problem to them, but were ignored by the founder of the resort corporation who owns it."

"He was satisfied that an international team of marine engineers pronounced it safe," added Gunn. "And because the United States has no jurisdiction over a foreign enterprise, it was out of our hands to interfere with its construction."

Sandecker put the specifications back in the file and closed it. "Let us hope the hurricane building off West Africa will either bypass the hotel or fail to build to a Category Five with winds exceeding a hundred and fifty miles an hour."

"I've already alerted Captain Barnum," said Gunn, "who is supporting the *Pisces* coral investigation not far from the *Ocean Wanderer,* to keep a wary eye on any hurricane warnings that might put them in the path of a coming storm."

"Our center in Key West is watching the birth of one now," said Yaeger.

"Keep me informed as well," advised Sandecker. "The last thing we need is a double disaster in the making."

WHEN YAEGER returned to his computer console, he found a green light blinking on the panel. He sat down and typed in the code that prompted Max to put in an appearance, along with the urn that rose from inside the floor.

When she fully appeared, he asked, "Have you analyzed the urn from *Pisces?*"

"I have," Max answered without hesitation.

"What did you find out?"

"The people on board *Sea Sprite* did a poor job of scouring away the growth," Max complained. "The surface still had a calcareous scale adhering to it. They didn't even bother to clean the interior. It was still filled with accretions. I had to apply every imagery system I could tap to get a relevant reading. Magnetic resonance imaging, digital X rays, 3-D laser scanner and Pulse-Coupled Neural Networks, whatever it took to obtain decent image segmentation."

"Spare me the technical details," Yaeger sighed patiently. "What are the results?"

"To begin with, it is not an urn. It is an amphor because it has small handles on the neck. It was cast from bronze during the Middle to Late Bronze Age."

"That's old."

"Very old," Max said confidently.

"Are you certain?"

"Have I ever been wrong?"

"No," said Yaeger. "I freely admit, you've never let me down."

"Then trust me on this one. I ran a very meticulous chemical analysis of the metal. Early hardening of copper began about thirty-five hundred B.C., with the copper enriched with arsenic. The only problem was that the old miners and coppersmiths died young from the arsenic vapors. Much later, probably through an accident sometime after twenty-two hundred B.C., it was discovered that mixing ninety percent copper with ten percent tin produced a very tough and durable metal. This was the beginning of the Bronze Age. Fortunately, copper was found throughout Europe and the Middle East in great supply. But tin was fairly rare in nature and more difficult to find."

"So tin was an expensive commodity."

"It was then," said Max. "Tin traders roamed the ancient world buying ore from the mines and selling it to the people who manned the forges. Bronze produced a very advanced economy and made many of the early ancients rich. Everything was forged, from weapons—bronze spearheads, knives and swords—to small necklaces, bracelets, belts and pins for the ladies. Bronze axes and chisels greatly advanced the art of woodworking. Artisans began casting pots, urns and jars. Taken in proper perspective, the Bronze Age greatly advanced civilization."

"So what's the amphor's story?"

"It was cast between twelve hundred and eleven hundred B.C. And in case you're interested it was cast using the lost-wax method to produce the mold."

Yaeger sat up in his chair. "That puts it over three thousand years old."

Max smiled sarcastically. "You're very astute."

"Where was it cast?"

"In Gaul by ancient Celts, specifically in a region known as Egypt."

"Egypt," Yaeger echoed skeptically.

"Three thousand years ago the land of the pharaohs was not called Egypt, but rather L-Khem or Kemi. Not until Alexander the Great marched through the country did he name it Egypt, after the description in the *Iliad* by Homer."

"I didn't know the Celts went back that far," said Yaeger.

"The Celts were a loose collection of tribes who were involved with trade and art as far back as two thousand B.C."

"But you say the amphor originated in Gaul. Where do the Celts come into the picture?"

"Invading Romans gave Celtic lands the name Gaul," explained Max. "My analysis showed the copper came from mines near Hallstatt, Austria, while the tin was mined in Cornwall, England, but the style of artwork is suggestive of a tribe of Celts in southwestern France. The figures cast on the outer diameter of the amphor are almost an exact match to those found on a cauldron dug up by a French farmer in the region in nineteen seventy-two."

"I suppose you can tell me the name of the sculptor who cast it."

Max gave Yaeger an icy stare. "You didn't ask me to probe genealogical records."

Yaeger thoughtfully soaked in the data Max reported. "Any ideas how a Bronze Age relic from Gaul came to be in a coral cavern on the Navidad Bank off the Dominican Republic?"

"I was not programmed to deal in generalities," answered Max haughtily. "I haven't the foggiest notion how it got there."

"Speculate, Max," asked Yaeger nicely. "Did it fall off a ship or perhaps become scattered cargo from a shipwreck?"

"The latter is a possibility, since ships had no reason to sail over the Navidad Bank unless they had a death wish. It might have been part of a cargo of ancient artifacts going to a rich merchant or a museum in Latin America."

"That's probably as good a guess as any."

"Not even close, actually," Max said indifferently. "According to my analysis the encrustation around the exterior is too old for any shipwreck since Columbus sailed the ocean blue. I dated the organic composition in excess of twenty-eight hundred years."

"That's not possible. There were no shipwrecks in the Western Hemisphere before fifteen hundred."

Max threw up her hands. "Have you no faith in me?"

"You have to admit that your time scale borders on the ridiculous."

"Take or leave it. I stand by my findings."

Yaeger leaned back in his chair, wondering where to take the project and Max's conclusions. "Print up ten copies of your findings, Max. I'll take it from here."

"Before you send me back to Never-Never Land," said Max, "there is one more thing."

Yaeger looked at her guardedly. "Which is?"

"When the glop is cleaned out from the interior of the amphor, you'll find a gold figurine in the shape of a goat."

"A what?"

"Bye-bye, Hiram."

Yaeger sat there, totally lost, as Max vanished back into her circuits. His mind ran toward the abstract. He tried to picture an ancient crewman on a three-thousand-year-old ship throwing a bronze pot overboard four thousand miles from Europe but the image would not unfold.

He reached over and picked up the amphor and peered inside, turning away at the awful stench of decaying sea life. He put it back in its box and sat there for a long time, unable to accept what Max had discovered.

He decided to run a check of Max's systems first thing in the morning before sharing the report with Sandecker. He wasn't about to take a chance on Max somehow becoming misguided.

4

THE AVERAGE HURRICANE takes an average of six days to mature to its full magnitude. Hurricane Lizzie did it in four.

Her winds spiraled at greater and greater speeds. She quickly passed the stage of "Tropical Depression" with wind speeds of thirty-nine miles per hour. Soon as they sustained seventy-four miles an hour, she became a full-fledged, certified, Category 1 hurricane on the Saffir-Simpson scale. Not content to simply become a lower-end tempest, Lizzie soon increased her winds to one hundred and thirty miles an hour, quickly passing Category 2 and charging into a Category 3 system.

In NUMA's Hurricane Center, Heidi Lisherness studied the latest images transmitted down from the geostationary satellites orbiting the earth twenty-two thousand miles above the equator. The data was transmitted into a computer, using one of several numerical models to forecast speed, path and the growing strength of Lizzie. Satellite pictures were not the most accurate. She would have preferred to study more detailed photos, but it was too early to send out a storm-tracking Air Force plane that far into the ocean. She would have to wait before obtaining more detailed images.

Early reports were far from encouraging.

This storm had all the characteristics of crossing the threshold of Category 5, with winds in excess of one hundred and sixty miles an hour. Heidi could only hope and pray that Lizzie would not touch the populated coast of the United States. Only two Category 5 hurricanes held that appalling distinction: the Great Labor Day Hurricane of 1935 that had charged across the Florida Keys and Hurricane Camille that struck Alabama and Mississippi in 1969, taking down entire twenty-story condominiums.

Heidi took a few minutes to type a fax to her husband, Harley, at the National Weather Service to alert him to the hurricane's latest numbers.

Harley,

Hurricane Lizzie is moving due east and accelerating. As we suspected, she has already developed into a dangerous storm. Computer model predicts winds of 150 knots with 40- to 50-foot seas within a radius 350 miles. She's moving at an incredible 20 knots.

Will keep you informed.
Heidi

She turned back to the images coming in from the satellites. Looking down on an enlarged image of the hurricane, Heidi never ceased to be impressed with the evil beauty of the thick, spiraling white clouds called the central dense overcast, the cirrus cloud shield that evolves from the thunderstorms in the surrounding walls of the eye. There was nothing up nature's sleeve that could match the horrendous energy of a full-blown hurricane. The eye had formed early, looking like a crater on a white planet. Hurricane eyes could range in size from five miles to over a hundred miles in diameter. Lizzie's eye was fifty miles across.

What gripped Heidi's concentration was the atmospheric pressure as measured in millibars. The lower the reading, the worse the storm. Hurricane Hugo in 1989 and Andrew in 1992 registered 934 and 922, respectively. Lizzie was already at 945 and rapidly dropping, forming a vacuum in her center that was intensifying by the hour. Bit by bit, millibar by foreboding millibar, the atmospheric pressure fell down the barometric scale.

Lizzie was also moving at a record pace westward across the ocean.

Hurricanes move slowly, usually no more than twelve miles an hour, about the average speed of someone riding a bicycle. But Lizzie was not following the rules laid down by those storms that went before her. She was hurtling across the sea at a very respectable twenty miles an hour. And contrary to earlier hurricanes that zigged and zagged their way toward the Western Hemisphere, Lizzie was traveling in a straight line as if her mind was on a specific target.

Quite often, storms spin around and head in a totally different direction. Again, Lizzie wasn't going by the book. If ever a hurricane had a one-track mind, thought Heidi, it was this one.

Heidi never knew who on what island coined the term *hurricane*. But it was a Caribbean word that meant "Big Wind." Bursting with enough energy to match the largest nuclear bomb, Lizzie was running wild with thunder, lightning and driving rain.

Already, ships in that part of the ocean were feeling her wrath.

I T WAS NOON NOW, a crazy, wild, insane noon. The seas had built from a relatively flat surface to thirty-foot waves in what seemed to the captain of the containership, the Nicaraguan-registered *Mona Lisa,* the blink of an eye. He felt as though he'd thrown open a door to the desert and had a tankful of water thrown at him. The seas had gone steep in a matter of minutes and the light breeze had turned into a full-blown gale. In all his years at sea, he'd never seen a storm come up so fast.

There was no nearby port to head toward for shelter, so he steered

Mona Lisa directly into the teeth of the gale in the calculated gamble that the faster he steamed through the heart of the storm, the better his chances of coming through without damage to his cargo.

Thirty miles north, just over the horizon from the *Mona Lisa,* the Egyptian super oil tanker *Rameses II* found herself overtaken by the surging turbulence. Captain Warren Meade stood in horror as a ninety-foot wave traveling at an incredible speed surged up over his ship's stern, tearing off the railings and sending tons of water smashing through hatches and flooding the crew's quarters and storerooms. The crew in the pilothouse watched dumbstruck as the wave passed around the superstructure and swept over the huge seven-hundred-foot-long deck of the hull whose waterline was sixty feet below, mangling fittings and pipes before it passed over the bow.

An eighty-foot yacht owned by the founder of a computer software company, carrying ten passengers and five crew on a cruise to Dakar, simply vanished, overwhelmed by huge seas without time to send a Mayday.

Before night fell, a dozen other ships would suffer Lizzie's destructive violence.

H EIDI AND fellow meteorologists at the NUMA center began hovering in conferences and studying the data on the latest system sweeping in from the east. They saw no slackening of Lizzie as she swept past longitude 40 west in mid-Atlantic, still throwing all previous predictions out the window by running straight with barely a wobble.

At three o'clock, Heidi took a call from Harley. "How's it looking?" he asked.

"Our ground data processing system is disseminating the data to your center now," she answered. "Marine advisories began going out last night."

"What does Lizzie's path look like?"

"Believe it or not, she's running straight as an arrow."

There was a pause. "That's a new twist."

"She hasn't deviated as much as ten miles in the last twelve hours."

Harley was dubious. "That's unheard-of."

"You'll see when you get our data," said Heidi firmly. "Lizzie is a record breaker. Ships are already reporting ninety-foot waves."

"Good lord! What about your computer forecasts?"

"We throw them in the trash as soon as they're printed. Lizzie is not conforming to the modus operandi of her predecessors. Our computers can't project her path and ultimate power with any degree of accuracy."

"So this is the hundred-year event."

"I fear this is more like the one that comes every thousand."

"Can you give me any indication, anything at all, on where she might strike, so my center can began sending out advisories?" Harley's tone became serious.

"She can come ashore anywhere between Cuba and Puerto Rico. At the moment, I'm betting on the Dominican Republic. But there is no way of knowing for certain for another twenty-four hours."

"Then it's time to issue preliminary alerts and warnings."

"At the speed Lizzie is traveling it won't be too soon."

"My weather service coworkers and I will get right on it."

"Harley."

"Yes, love."

"I won't make it home for dinner tonight."

Heidi's mind could picture Harley's jovial smile over the phone as he replied, "Neither will I, love. Neither will I."

After she hung up, Heidi sat at her desk for a few moments, staring up at a giant chart of the North Atlantic active hurricane region. As she scanned the Caribbean islands closest to the approaching monster, something tugged at the back of her mind. She typed in a program on her computer that brought up a list depicting the name of the ships, a brief description and their position in a specific area of the

North Atlantic. There were over twenty-two in position to suffer the full effects of the storm. Apprehensive that there might be a huge cruise ship with thousands of passengers and crew sailing in the path of the hurricane, she scanned the list. No cruise ships were shown near the worst of the tumult, but one name caught her eye. At first she thought it was a ship, then the old fact dawned on her. It was not a ship.

"Oh lord," she moaned.

Sam Moore, a bespectacled meteorologist working at a nearby desk, looked up. "Are you all right? Is anything wrong?"

Heidi sagged in her chair. "The *Ocean Wanderer.*"

"Is that a cruise ship?"

Heidi shook her head. "No, it's a floating hotel that's moored directly in the path of the system. There is no way she can be moved in time. She's a sitting duck."

"That ship that reported a ninety-foot wave," said Moore. "If one that huge strikes the hotel . . ." His voice trailed off.

"We've got to warn their management to evacuate the hotel."

Heidi jumped to her feet and ran toward the communications room, hoping against hope that the hotel management would act without hesitation. If not, over a thousand guests and employees were facing an unspeakable death.

5

NEVER HAD SUCH ELEGANCE, such grandeur, risen from the sea. Nothing remotely approaching its unique design and creative distinction had ever been built. The *Ocean Wanderer* underwater resort hotel was an adventure waiting to be experienced, an exciting opportunity for its guests to view the wonders beneath the sea. She rose above the waves in wondrous splendor two miles off the tip of Cabo Cabron peninsula that jutted from the southeastern shore of the Dominican Republic.

Acknowledged by the travel industry as the world's most extraordinary hotel, it was built in Sweden to exacting standards never before achieved. The highest degree of craftsmanship, using the ultimate in materials combined with a daring exploitation of lavish textures that illustrated life in the sea. Wild exuberant greens, blues and golds, all came together to create one lavish ensemble, magnificent outside, breathtaking inside. Above the surface, the outer structure was configured to resemble the soft, graceful lines of a low drifting cloud. Soaring over two hundred feet into the sky, the upper five stories housed the quarters and offices of the four hundred management staff and crew, the expansive storerooms, kitchen galleys, and heating and air-conditioning systems.

Ocean Wanderer also offered endless upscale gourmet dining options. Five restaurants, run by five world-class chefs. Exotic seafood dishes only minutes fresh from the sea in superb settings. And then there was the sunset catamaran dinner cruise for intimate romance.

Three levels held two lounges featuring celebrity artists and entertainers, an opulent ballroom featuring a full orchestra, and unparalleled shopping with designer boutiques and variety shops filled with exciting and exquisite merchandise rarely found in the guests' malls at home. And it was all duty-free.

There was a movie theater featuring plush seating and satellite feeds of the latest motion pictures. The casino, though smaller in scale, surpassed anything Las Vegas had to offer. Fish swam in contoured aquariums that snaked in and around the gaming tables and slot machines. The glass ceilings also held a variety of sea life that glided lazily above the gambling action below.

The middle levels housed a world-class spa with complimentary professional trainers. A full menu of massages, facials and luxurious body treatments were available, as were saunas and steam rooms decorated like tropical jungle gardens filled with exotic plants and flowers. For the active set, the roof over the spa featured tennis courts and a mini golf course that wound around the deck, with a driving range where guests could drive balls far out into the sea at floating targets spaced at fifty-yard intervals.

For the more adventurous, there were several spectacular water slides with entries at different levels reached by elevators. One wild ride began at the roof of the hotel and spiraled down into the water from fifteen stories below. Other water sports were available that included windsurfing, jetskiing, waterskiing and of course a myriad of free scuba-diving activities directed by certified instructors. Guests could also experience submarine tours in and around the reefs and into the upper reaches of the deeper abyss, as well as a fish's-eye view of the underwater levels of the hotel. Fish identification classes and educational lectures on the sea were given by university teachers of the ocean sciences.

But the magic guests truly experienced was a liquid adventure in the huge pod-shaped structure beneath the surface. Like a man-made iceberg, the *Ocean Wanderer* did not have rooms; it had suites, four hundred and ten of them, all under the surface of the sea, with floor-to-ceiling viewing ports of thick pressurized glass with stunning views of life underwater. Artistic decor in hues of rich blues and greens filled the suites, while selectable colored mood lighting enhanced the feeling that guests were truly living under the sea.

Visually spectacular, guests could come face-to-face with the predators of the sea, the sharks and barracudas, as they moved through the fluid void. Colorful tropical angelfish, parrot fish and friendly dolphins schooled around outside the suites. Giant groupers and manta rays swam through graceful jellyfish as they frolicked amid the vividly colored coral. At night guests could lie in bed and watch the ballet of fish under an array of colored lights.

Unlike the opulent fleet of cruise ships that sailed the seven seas, *Ocean Wanderer* had no engines. It was a floating island moored into position by giant steel pins that were driven deep into the bottom sediment. Stretching from the pins, four heavy cables ran to links that could be automatically coupled or uncoupled.

But it was not a permanent mooring. Mindful of how the wealthy traveler seldom repeats vacations in the same spot, the designers of *Ocean Wanderer* cleverly built mooring facilities in more than a dozen scenic locations around the world. Five times a year, a pair of one-hundred-and-twenty-foot tugboats would rendezvous with the floating hotel. Giant buoyancy tanks were pumped dry, raising the hotel until only two levels remained underwater, the mooring cables were released and the tugs, each mounting three-thousand-horsepower Hunnewell diesel engines, would tow the floating hotel to a new tropical setting, where she would be remoored. Guests could depart for home or stay aboard for the voyage as they chose.

Life raft drills were mandatory for guests and crew alike every four days. Special elevators with their own energy source, in the event all generator power was lost, could evacuate the entire hotel to the deck running around the second level, where the latest state-of-the-art enclosed life rafts were mounted that could maintain buoyancy in extreme sea conditions.

Because of her unique experience and larger-than-life ambience, the *Ocean Wanderer* was booked solid two years in advance.

Today, however, was a special occasion. The man who was the driving force behind the creation of the *Ocean Wanderer* was arriving for a four-day stay for the first time since the floating hotel's lavish opening the month before. A man as mysterious as the sea itself. A man who was photographed only from a distance, and who never revealed lips and chin below the nose while the eyes remained hidden under dark glasses. His nationality was unknown. He was a man with no name, as enigmatic as a specter, Specter being the name given him by the news media. Reporters from newspapers and television news bureaus and stations had failed to penetrate even one layer of his anonymity. His age and history had yet to be revealed. All that was known about him for certain was that he headed and directed Odyssey, a giant scientific research and construction empire with tentacles in thirty countries that made him one of the richest and most powerful men in the civilized world.

There were no stockholders of Odyssey. There were no annual reports or profit-and-loss statements to be examined. The Odyssey empire and the man in control stood alone in cryptic secrecy.

A T FOUR in the afternoon the silence of the aquamarine sea and azure sky was shattered by the shriek of an overhead jet aircraft. A large passenger plane painted in the trademark lavender color of Odyssey appeared from the west. Curious hotel guests gazed up at the unusual aircraft as its pilot gently banked the jet around the

Ocean Wanderer to give his passengers a bird's-eye view of the floating spectacle.

The plane was unlike any of them had seen before. The Russian-built Beriev Be-200 was originally designed as an amphibious fire-fighting aircraft. But this one was built to carry eighteen passengers and a crew of four in regal luxury. It was powered by two BMW–Rolls-Royce turbofan engines mounted on the overhead wing. Capable of speeds of over four hundred miles an hour, the rugged craft could easily handle water takeoffs and landings in four-foot seas.

The pilot banked the high-performance amphibian and made his approach in front of the hotel. The big hull kissed the waves in unison with the outer pontoons and settled into the water like an overweight swan. Then it taxied up to a floating dock that extended from the main entrance of the hotel. Mooring lines were thrown and the aircraft was tied alongside the dock by its crew.

A welcoming party led by a bespectacled bald-headed man wearing a crisp blue blazer stood on the dock that was edged with golden velvet cords. Hobson Morton was the executive director of the *Ocean Wanderer*. A fastidious man totally dedicated to his job and employer, Morton stood six feet six inches tall and weighed only one hundred and seventy-five pounds. Morton had been personally lured away by Specter, whose philosophy was to surround himself with men who were smarter than he was. Behind Morton's back, his associates referred to the tall man as "the stick." Distinguished, with graying temples below a thick mass of neatly brushed blond hair, he stood straight as a light post while a six-man team of attendants exited the aircraft's main hatch, followed by four security men in blue jumpsuits who stationed themselves at strategic locations along the dock.

Several minutes passed before Specter stepped off the plane. In contrast to Morton he might have reached a height of five feet five inches if he had stood up straight, but settled inside a grossly overweight body, standing rigid was an impossibility. As he walked— actually, more of a waddle—he looked like a pregnant bullfrog in search of a swamp. His enormous belly stretched a trademark white tailored suit far beyond its double-threaded limits. His head was swathed in a white silk turban whose lower sash covered his chin and mouth. There was no way to read the face, even the eyes were covered by the impenetrable lenses of heavily coated dark sunglasses. The men and women who were closely associated with Specter could never fathom how he was able to see through them, never knowing that the lenses were like a one-way mirror. The wearer could see perfectly from his side while his eyes remained impenetrable.

Morton stepped forward and formally bowed. "Welcome to the *Ocean Wanderer,* sir."

There was no shaking of hands. Specter tilted his head back and stared up at the magnificent structure. Though he had taken a personal interest in its design from conception to construction, he had yet to see it fully completed and moored in the sea.

"The appearance exceeds my most optimistic expectations," Specter said in a soft melodious voice with the barest hint of an American southern accent that did not fit his appearance. When Morton first met Specter he expected him to speak in high-pitched, scratchy sounds.

"I'm sure you will be more than pleased with the interior as well," said Morton in a patronizing tone. "If you will please follow me, I will give you the grand tour before escorting you to the royal penthouse suite."

Specter merely nodded in reply, and began trundling across the deck to the hotel with his retinue bringing up the rear.

IN THE communications room across a wide hallway from the executive offices, an operator was monitoring and relaying the satellite calls that were coming in from Specter's main headquarters at his company-built city in Laguna, Brazil, and offices around the world. A light blinked on his console and he answered the call.

"*Ocean Wanderer,* how may I direct your call?"

"This is Heidi Lisherness from the NUMA Hurricane Center in Key West. May I speak to the director of your resort?"

"I'm sorry, but he is busy escorting the owner and founder of *Ocean Wanderer* on a private tour of the hotel."

"This is extremely urgent. Let me talk to his assistant."

"Everyone in the executive office is on the tour also."

"Then will you please," Heidi pleaded, "please, inform them that a Category Five hurricane is headed in the direction of the *Ocean Wanderer.* It is traveling at incredible speed and could strike the hotel as soon as dawn tomorrow. You must, I repeat, you *must* begin evacuating your hotel. I will give you frequent updates and will stand by at this number for any questions your director may have."

The operator dutifully jotted down the Hurricane Center's number and then answered several other calls that came in while he was talking with Heidi. Not taking the warning seriously, he waited until he was relieved two hours later before he tracked down Morton and relayed the message.

Morton stared at the message typed out by the operator's voice printer and reread it thoughtfully before handing it to Specter. "A weather warning from Key West. They report that a hurricane is heading in our direction and suggest we evacuate everyone in the hotel."

Specter scanned the warning message and lumbered to a large view window and gazed toward the east across the sea. The sky was free of clouds and the water surface looked quite calm, the wave crests reaching no more than a foot or two in height. "We'll make no hasty decisions. If the storm follows the usual hurricane track, it should veer north and miss us by hundreds of miles."

Morton was not so sure. A cautious and conscientious man, he preferred to be safe rather than sorry. "I do not believe, sir, it would be in our best interest to risk the lives of our guests or employees. I respectfully suggest that we instruct everyone to begin evacuation procedures and arrange transportation to a safe haven in the Dominican Republic as soon as possible. We should also alert the tugboats to launch an operation to tow us from the worst of the storm."

Specter stared out the window again at the serene weather as if reassuring himself. "We'll wait another three hours. I do not wish to harm the image of *Ocean Wanderer* with stories of a mass flight the news media will blow out of proportion and compare to the abandonment of a sinking ship. Besides," he said, throwing up his arms as if embracing the magnificent floating edifice like a balloon with long thin ears, "my hotel was built to resist any violence the sea can throw at her."

Morton briefly considered mentioning the *Titanic,* but thought better of it. He left Specter in the penthouse suite and returned to his office to begin preparations for the evacuation he was sure would come.

FIFTY MILES north of *Ocean Wanderer,* Captain Barnum studied the meteorological reports coming in from Heidi Lisherness and unconsciously stared toward the east the way Specter had. Unlike landsmen, Barnum was wily to the ways of the sea. He was aware of the slowly increasing breeze and the rising waves. He had weathered many storms during his long career at sea and knew how they could creep up on an unsuspecting ship and crew and engulf them in less than an hour.

He picked up the phone and hailed *Pisces.* An indistinct, garbled voice answered from under the water. "Summer?"

"No, this is the brother," Dirk replied humorously as he adjusted the frequency. "What can I do for you, Captain?"

"Is Summer inside *Pisces* with you?"

"No, she's outside, checking the hydrolab oxygen tanks."

"We have a storm warning from Key West. A Category Five hurricane is coming down our throats."

"Category Five? That's a brutal one."

"As ferocious as they come. I saw a Category Four in the Pacific twenty years ago. I can't imagine anything worse."

"How much time do we have before it's on us?" asked Dirk.

"The center predicted six in the morning. But updates show it's coming on much faster. We have to get you and Summer out of *Pisces* and onto *Sea Sprite* as soon as possible."

"I don't have to tell you about saturation dives, Captain. My sister and I have been down here four days. It will take us at least fifteen hours of decompression before we can be recompressed to ambient water pressure and come to the surface. We'll never make it before the hurricane is on us."

Barnum was well aware of the threatening situation. "We may have to terminate our topside support and run for it."

"At this depth, we should be able to weather the storm comfortably," Dirk said confidently.

"I don't like leaving you," Barnum spoke grimly.

"We may have to go on a diet, but we have generating power and enough oxygen to last us four days. By then the worst of the storm should have passed."

"I wish it was more."

There was a pause from *Pisces*. Then, "Do we have an option?"

"No," Barnum sighed heavily. "I guess not." He looked up at the big digital clock above the pilothouse's automated ship's console. His greatest fear was that if *Sea Sprite* was driven far off its position by the storm, he might not get back in time to save Dirk and Summer. He feared he was faced with a no-win situation. If he lost Dirk Pitt's children to the sea, there was no telling the wrath that would explode from NUMA's special projects director. "Take every precaution to extend your air supply."

"Not to worry, Captain. Summer and I will be snug as bugs in a rug in our little shack down in coral gulch."

Barnum felt uneasy. The odds were also long that *Pisces* could survive intact if the reef was pounded by hundred-foot waves generated by a Category 5 hurricane. He stared through the bridge windows to the east. Already the sky was filling with threatening clouds and the seas had risen to five feet.

With much regret and a deepening sense of foreboding, he gave orders for *Sea Sprite* to pull up the anchor and lay a course away from the predicted path of the storm.

W HEN S U M M E R reentered the main lock, Dirk gave her a rundown on the nasty weather coming their way over the horizon. He ran through instructions for conserving food and air. "We should also batten down any loose objects in case high seas knock us around down here."

"How soon before the worst of the storm reaches us?" asked Summer.

"According to the captain, sometime before morning."

"Then you have time for a final dive with me before we're cooped up in here until the weather clears."

Dirk looked at his sister. A lesser man, captivated by her beauty, would have fallen under her spell, but as her twin brother he was immune to her Machiavellian wiles. "What's on your mind?" he asked casually.

"I want to take a closer look inside the cavern where I found the urn."

"Can you find it again in the dark?"

"Like a fox to its lair," she said, cocksure. "Besides, you always enjoy seeing different species of fish on a night dive that you can't see during the day."

Dirk was hooked. "Then let's make it quick. We have a lot of work to do before the storm hits."

Summer put her arm through his. "You won't regret it!"

"Why do you say that?"

She stared up at her brother from those soft gray eyes. "Because the more I think about it, I believe there is a greater mystery than the urn waiting to be found inside the cave."

6

WITH SUMMER IN THE LEAD, they dropped out of the
entry lock, checked each other's equipment and then moved
into the sea that was as black as deep space. Together, they switched
on their dive lights and startled the nearby night fish who had emerged
after dark to feed in their coral domain. Above, there was no moon to
sweep the surface with shimmering silver. The stars were cloaked by
ominous clouds, the precursors of the vicious storm soon to come.

Dirk stroked his fins behind his sister, following her into the dark
void. He knew she enjoyed the underwater world by her graceful, languid movements. Her bubbles rose in clusters of balloons indicating
the comfortable breathing of an expert diver. She looked back at him
through her mask and smiled. Then she pointed to her right and kicked
off over the coral illuminated by her dive light in a maze of muted
colors.

There was nothing sinister about the silent sea beneath the surface
at night. Curious fish were attracted by the dive lights and came out
of their coral hiding places to study the unfamiliar and awkward swimming creatures intruding in their midst who were carrying sealed hous-
ings that beamed like the sun. A huge parrot fish swam at Dirk's side,

staring at him like a curious cat. Six four-foot barracudas materialized out of the gloom, their lower jaws protruding beyond their noses and displaying rows of needle-sharp teeth. They ignored the divers and glided past without the slightest sign of interest.

Summer finned through the coral canyons as if she was following a road map. A little blowfish, startled by the glare of the light, puffed its body into a round ball with spikes protruding from its sides like a cactus, making it impossible or extremely unlikely a big predator would be dumb enough to attempt to swallow such a throat-ripping morsel.

Their lights threw eerie, flickering shadows against the distorted coral whose surface varied from jagged sharpness to round and globular. To Dirk, the complex hues and shapes took on the look of a continuous abstract painting. He glanced at his depth gauge. It read forty-five feet. He glanced ahead as Summer suddenly dropped down into a narrow coral canyon with steep sides. He descended in her wake, noticing a number of openings in the coral leading to shallow caves and wondering which one had attracted her the day before.

Finally, she hesitated before a vertical opening with squared corners sandwiched between a pair of unnatural-looking columns. Turning briefly to see that her brother was still following, Summer swam unhesitatingly into the cavern beyond. This time, with a dive light in hand and the security of her brother beside her, Summer penetrated deeper into the cavern, past the place in the bottom sand where she had discovered the urn.

The cave was not crooked or irregular. The walls, ceiling and floor were almost perfectly flat, stretching into the darkness like a corridor without twists and turns. Deeper and deeper it led them on.

Becoming lost in a cave system is the number one cause of cave-diving fatalities. Mistakes prove deadly. Here, fortunately, there was no problem of orientation. This was not a dangerous cave dive, nor was there a fear of becoming lost in a complex system of adjoining caves. The chamber had no side openings or separate shafts that could cause them to lose their way. To regain the entrance, they had only to reverse their course. They were thankful there was no fine silt on the bottom that when disturbed could cloud vision for an hour before it settled again. The floor of the coral shaft was covered with coarse sand too heavy to swirl in the water if disturbed by their fins.

Abruptly, the shaft ended in what teased Summer's imagination. Though infested with marine growth, it seemed as if the shaft rose with a flight of steps. A school of angelfish twirled in a corkscrew above her head, then darted past as she began to ascend. Her skin and the nape of her neck suddenly tingled with expectation. Her earlier feeling that there was more to the cavern than met the eye came back with a rush.

The coral thinned this far under the reef. With no light to encourage marine growth the encrustation on the walls of the shaft was less than an inch thick and consisted more of slimy growth than hard coral. Dirk took his gloved hand and brushed away the greasy coating and felt his heart quicken as he recognized grooves in granite rock that he theorized were put there by ancient hands when the sea was lower.

Then, through the water, he heard Summer utter a distorted squeal. He kicked upward and was stunned when he broke the surface of the water into an air pocket. He looked up as Summer's light swept over a domed ceiling of seemingly chiseled stones fit tightly together without mortar.

"What have we got here?" Dirk spoke through his underwater communications system.

"It's either a freak of nature or an ancient man-made vault," Summer murmured in awe.

"This is no freak of nature."

"It must have been submerged after the melting of the Ice Age."

"That was ten thousand years ago. Impossible to be that ancient. More likely, the vault sank during an earthquake like the one that struck Port Royal, Jamaica, the pirate haven that slipped into the sea after a massive tremor in sixteen ninety-two."

"Could it be a forgotten ghost city?" asked Summer, her excitement mounting.

Dirk shook his head. "Unless there is much more buried under the surrounding coral, my gut instinct is this was some sort of temple."

"Built by ancient natives of the Caribbean?"

"I doubt it. Archaeologists have found no evidence of stone masonry in the West Indies before Columbus. And the local natives certainly didn't know how to forge a bronze urn. This was built by a different culture, a lost and unknown civilization."

"Not another Atlantis myth," Summer said sarcastically.

"No, Dad and Al put that to rest in the Antarctic several years ago."

"Seems incredible that ancient peoples of Europe sailed across the ocean and built a temple on a coral reef."

Dirk slowly ran his gloved hand on one wall. "Navidad Reef was probably an island back then."

"When you think about it," said Summer, "we must be breathing air thousands of years old."

Dirk deeply inhaled and then exhaled. "Smells and tastes good to me."

Summer pointed over her shoulder. "Help me with the camera. We must get a photo record."

Dirk moved behind her and removed an aluminum carrying case attached to a clip beneath her air tanks. He pulled out a minidigital Sony PC-100 camcorder mounted inside a compact Ikelite clear-acrylic housing. Setting the controls on manual mode, he attached the arms for the floodlights. Since there was no ambient light there was no need for a light meter.

There was an illusive grandeur to the submarine chamber and Summer was more than proficient enough with a camera to capture it. The instant she flicked on the floodlights the bleak cave came alive in a montage of green, yellow, red and purple hues from the growth on the sheer walls. Except for a mild distortion, the water was nearly as clear as glass.

While Summer photographed the vault below and above the water, Dirk dove down and began exploring the floor along the walls. The lights from Summer's camera cast weird quivering images in the water as he slowly worked his way around the perimeter.

He almost passed by without seeing a space that opened up between two walls. It was a corner entrance no more than two feet wide. Dirk barely shouldered through with his air tanks, keeping the hand gripping the dive light extended in front of him. He entered another chamber slightly larger than the outer one. This one had recessed seats in the walls and what looked like a large stone bed in the center. At first he thought it was empty of artifacts but then his light revealed a round object with two large holes on the sides and one smaller hole at the top lying on the bed, like armor that covered the torso. A gold necklace rested on the stone above the object with two coiled armbands placed on each side. What looked like an intricate metal lace headpiece sat above the necklace and above it an ornate diadem.

Dirk began to imagine that a body once lay inside the relics. Where the legs might have been were a pair of bronze greaves, ancient armor worn below the knees. A sword blade and dagger blade were situated on the left side while a socketed spearhead without its shaft lay on the right. If there was a body, it was long ago dissolved or consumed by sea creatures that devoured anything organic.

Sitting at the foot of the bed was a large cauldron.

Rising a few inches over four feet, the circumference of the cauldron was too large for him to circle his arms around and touch his fingertips. He rapped the hilt of his dive knife against the side and heard a dull metallic thud. Bronze, he thought to himself. He smeared away the growth on the surface and revealed the figure of a warrior throwing a spear. Using his glove to brush his way around the cauldron, he discovered an army of sculpted men and women wearing armor and posed as if fighting a battle. They carried man-sized shields and long swords. Several held spears with short shafts but extremely long heads in a spiral form. Some fought in body armor that covered their torso.

Others fought naked, but most all wore huge helmets, many with horns protruding out the top.

He swam above the rim, shined his light through the wide neck and peered inside.

The interior of the big cauldron was filled almost to the top with jumbled, intermingled but still recognizable artifacts. Dirk identified bronze spearheads, dagger blades with the hilts eroded away, edged and winged axes, coiled bracelets and chain waist belts. He left the relics as he had found them, all but one. He gently picked it out of the cauldron and held it between his fingers. Then he moved through an archway that loomed on the opposite side of what he now supposed was an ancient bedroom used as a tomb.

He quickly identified the chamber beyond as a kitchen. There was no air pocket here and his bubbles trailed to the ceiling and flowed outward in confused streams like quicksilver. Bronze cooking tureens, amphors, urns and jars lay scattered on the floor along with broken clay pots. Beside what appeared to be a fireplace he found bronze tongs and a large ladle, all partially buried in the silt that had filtered into the chamber over thousands of years. He swam over the debris and examined the artifacts closely, trying to find distinguishing artwork or markings, but they were half buried in the silt and covered with little hard-shell crustaceans that had made their way over the centuries into the room.

Satisfied there were no more doorways or side rooms to explore, he returned through the bedroom chamber and approached Summer, who was focusing and furiously recording every dimension of the arched vault below the water surface.

He touched her arm and pointed up. After they surfaced, he said excitedly, "I found two more chambers."

"This gets more intriguing by the minute," Summer said, without taking her eye from the viewfinder.

He grinned and held up a bronze lady's hair comb. "Run the comb through your hair and try to imagine the last woman to use it."

Summer lowered her camera and stared at the object in Dirk's hand. Her eyes widened as she delicately took the comb and held it between her fingers. "It's lovely," she murmured. She was about to run the comb through a few strands of her flame-red hair that trailed past her ears when she stopped and suddenly looked at him seriously. "You should put it back where you found it. When archaeologists examine this place, and they will, you'll be condemned as a relic thief."

"If I had a girlfriend, I bet she'd keep it."

"The last of your long string of women would have stolen the charity box from a church."

Dirk feigned looking hurt. "Sara's streak of larceny made her irresistible."

"You're just lucky Dad is a better judge of women than you are."

"What's he got to do with it?"

"He gave Sara the boot when she showed up at his hangar looking for you."

"I wondered why she never returned my calls," said Dirk, without a hint of distress.

She gave him a baleful glare and studied the comb, trying to conjure up an image of the last woman to touch it, wondering what style and color her hair might have been. After a few moments, she carefully laid the ancient relic in her brother's open hands so she could photograph it.

As soon as Summer took several close-up photos, Dirk returned the comb to the cauldron. He was soon followed by Summer, who recorded more than thirty images of the bedroom chamber and the ancient artifacts on her digital camera before entering and shooting the ancient kitchen. Satisfied that she had achieved a detailed photographic inventory of the three chambers and their artifacts, she passed the camera to Dirk, who disassembled the lights and slipped it back into its aluminum container. Rather than reattaching it to Summer's back, he held the grip handle tightly in one hand as insurance against losing or damaging the case.

He made a final check of both their air gauges and determined they had more than an ample air reserve for the journey back to their habitat. Well trained by their father, Dirk and his sister were cautious divers who had yet to come remotely close to the fatal danger of empty air tanks. He led the way this time, having memorized the bends and curves in the coral they had passed through earlier.

When they finally reached the comfort of *Pisces* and passed into the main lock, the waves above were rising, driven by a mushrooming wind that forced the waves to build and pound the reef like a jackhammer against a piling. As Dirk took his turn at fixing dinner, he and Summer looked forward to discovering the riddle of the underwater ghost temple. They relaxed and ate dinner under a false security. Neither had any conception of how vulnerable they were fifty feet beneath the surface of a vicious sea, certainly not with waves that were about to reach a hundred feet high, with troughs that would expose the habitat to the full force of the horrendous killer storm.

7

P UNCHING INTO THE WHIRLING wall of the hurricane,
scourged by screaming winds, blankets of hail and rain, and
tossed by downdrafts and updrafts through unimaginable turbulence,
the twenty-nine-year-old Orion P-3 Hurricane Hunter aircraft took the
beating in stride. Her wings flexed and fluttered like blades on a
fencer's sword. The big propellers on her four Allison forty-six-
hundred-horsepower engines chopped her through the deluge at three
hundred knots. Built in 1976, the Navy, NOAA and NUMA had never
found a better aircraft that could stand up to the punishment of violent weather.

Remarkably stable, *Galloping Gertie,* as she was affectionately named,
with an animated painting of a cowgirl riding a bucking bronco on her
bow, carried a crew of twenty: two pilots, a navigator and flight meteorologist, three engineering and electronic communication special-
ists, twelve scientists and a media passenger from a local TV station
who asked to come aboard when he learned that Hurricane Lizzie
was building into a record-setting storm.

Jeff Barrett sat relaxed in the pilot seat, his eyes sweeping the instrument panel every other minute. Six hours into a ten-hour flight,

the gauges and lights were all he had to look at, since the only thing to be seen through the windshield was a view similar to peering inside a washing machine on the soap cycle. With a wife and three children, Barrett saw no more danger in his job than if he were driving a trash truck through a downtown alley.

But danger and death lurked in the swirling cloud of moisture smothering the Orion, especially when Barrett made passes so low over the water that salt spray spun off the propellers and glazed the windows with a frostlike film before he spiraled up to seven thousand feet, flying in and out of the worst part of the storm. Corkscrew penetration was the most efficient way to record and analyze the hurricane's strength.

It was not a job for the unintrepid. Those who flew into hurricanes and typhoons were a special breed of scientists. There could be no observing storms from a distance. They had to get down and dirty, flying directly through the aerial maelstrom, not once but as many as ten times.

They flew without complaint under incredibly appalling conditions to sample wind speeds and direction, rain, air pressure and data on a hundred other measurements they sent to the hurricane center. There, the information was fed into computer models so meteorologists could forecast the strength of the storm and issue warnings for people living in the predicted track to evacuate the shoreline in an effort to save countless lives.

Barrett wrestled easily with the controls that were modified to endure extreme turbulence and checked the numbers on his Global Positioning satellite instrument before making a slight course adjustment. He turned to his copilot. "This is a real bad one," he said, as the Orion was jolted by a sudden wind surge.

The crew spoke through microphones and listened through headsets. Any conversation without the radio had to be shouted into an upturned ear. The shriek of the wind was so piercing it drowned out the exhaust roar of the engines.

The rangy man slouched in the copilot's seat was sipping coffee from a covered cup through a straw. Neat and fastidious, Jerry Boozer prided himself on never spilling a drop of liquid or a sandwich crumb in the cockpit during a hurricane stalk. He nodded in agreement. "The worst I've seen in the eight years I've been chasing these things."

"I'd hate to be living in her path when she reaches land."

Boozer picked up his microphone and spoke into it. "Hey, Charlie, what's your magic department reading of the storm's wind?"

Back in the science compartment packed with an array of instruments and consoles crammed with meteorological electronic systems, Charlie Mahoney, a research scientist from Stanford University, sat strapped in a chair facing a matrix of sensors that measured temperature, humidity, pressure, winds and fluxes. "You ain't gonna believe this," he answered in a Georgia accent, "but the last dropwindsonde profiling system I released recorded horizontal wind speeds of up to two hundred and twenty miles an hour as it fell through the storm toward the sea."

"No wonder poor old *Gertie* is taking a beating." Boozer had hardly mouthed the words when the aircraft soared into calm air and the sun glittered on the shiny aluminum fuselage and wings.

They had entered Lizzie's eye. Below, a restless sea reflected the blue of the sky. It was like flying into a giant tube whose circular walls were forged with swirling, impenetrable clouds. Boozer felt as if he was flying inside a vast whirlpool whose pit led to Hades.

Barrett banked and circled within the eye while the meteorologists behind gathered their data. After nearly ten minutes, he turned the Orion and headed into the tortured gray wall. Again, the aircraft shuddered as if it was under attack by all the furies of the gods. Abruptly, it felt like a giant's fist had smashed into the starboard, sending the plane over on one wing. Anything that wasn't tied down in the cockpit—papers, folders, coffee cups, briefcases—was hurled against the starboard bulkhead. No sooner had the gust passed than a blast of even increased force hurled the aircraft through the turmoil like a balsa wood glider tied to a fan, sending all that loose debris crashing against the opposite side of the cockpit. The double shock came like the blow of a tennis ball from a racket against a backstop. Barrett and Boozer were nearly frozen in shock. Neither had ever experienced a collision with a wind gust of that magnitude, and not one but two in almost as many seconds. It was unheard of.

The Orion shuddered and fell off in an uncontrolled bank to the port.

Barrett felt a sudden loss of power and his eyes immediately swept the instrument panel as he struggled to level out the aircraft. "I'm getting no readings on number four engine. Can you see if she's still turning?"

"Oh God!" muttered Boozer, staring through his side window. "Number four engine is gone!"

"Then shut it down!" Barrett snapped.

"There's nothing left to shut down. It's fallen away."

His mind and strength fully concentrating on righting the Orion, Barrett twisted the wheel on the control column and fought the pedals, not comprehending Boozer's dire report. He sensed something terribly wrong with the aerodynamics. The plane was not responding to his physical commands. All response was extremely sluggish. It was as if a giant rope with a weight was pulling the starboard wing from behind.

At last he brought *Gertie* into level flight. Only then did Boozer's words come home to him. It was the loss of the engine, torn from its mountings by the violent assault of the storm that threw the Orion out of control and was causing the starboard drag. He leaned forward and stared past Boozer.

Where the Allison turboprop engine had been attached to the wing was now an empty gap with twisted and torn mountings, severed hydraulic, oil and fuel lines, mangled pumps and electrical wiring. It shouldn't have happened, thought Barrett, incredulous. Engines simply did not drop off aircraft, not even under the worst turbulence.

Then he counted nearly thirty empty, tiny holes in the wing where the rivets had popped out. His foreboding grew as he saw several cracks in the stressed aluminum skin.

A voice from the main compartment came over his headphones. "We have injuries back here and most of the equipment is damaged and malfunctioning."

"Those who are able, tend to the injured. We're heading for home."

"If we can make it," Boozer said pessimistically. He pointed out Barrett's side window. "We have a fire in number three."

"Shut it down!"

"In the process," Boozer answered calmly.

Barrett was tempted to call his wife and say goodbye, but he was far from giving up. Getting sorely wounded *Gertie* and her scientists out of the storm and safely back to land would take a miracle. He began to mutter a prayer under his breath as he used every fraction of his experience to fly the Orion through the vortex into calm air. If they escaped the worst of the chaos the rest would take care of itself.

After twenty minutes the wind and rain began to diminish and the clouds lighten. Then, just as he thought they were through the clouds, Lizzie threw one more punch and sent a wind blast that struck the Orion's rudder a punishing blow and crippled what little control Barrett and Boozer had.

All bets on a successful attempt to reach home were now off.

8

OST OF THE TIME, the oceans appear to be at rest. Unending waves no higher than the head of a German shepherd give the image of a sleeping giant, the surface of his chest slowly rising and falling with each breath. It is an illusion that beguiles the unwary. Sailors could fall asleep in their berths with clear skies and calm seas and wake up to a frenzied sea that quickly swept over thousands of square miles, engulfing every vessel in its path.

Hurricane Lizzie had all the ingredients for unmitigated disaster. If she looked nasty by morning, she was downright rotten by noon, and a shrieking hellion by evening. Two-hundred-and-twenty-mile-an-hour winds soon passed two hundred and fifty. They hurled and whipped the once-flat water into a giant turmoil that rose and fell a hundred feet between crest and trough as it advanced relentlessly toward Navidad Bank and the Dominican Republic, its first landfall.

The anchor was barely up and the *Sea Sprite* under way when Paul Barnum turned for perhaps the twentieth time and stared over the sea to the east. Earlier he noted no change. But this time the horizon where the tanzanite blue water met a sapphire blue sky was smudged by a dark gray streak like a distant chinook dust storm rolling over the prairie.

Barnum gazed at the advancing nightmare, stunned by how rapidly it grew and began filling the sky. He had never experienced nor had he conceived that a storm could move with what seemed the speed of an express train. Even before he could program the computerized automated controls for course and speed, the storm was covering the sun in a death shroud while painting the sky the lead gray on the bottom of a well-used skillet.

For the next eight hours *Sea Sprite* ran hard, as Barnum drove her in what seemed a futile attempt to put as much distance as possible between her hull and the sharp coral of Navidad Reef. But when he realized the worst of the storm was about to overtake him, he knew the most efficient way to survive was to head right into it, relying on *Sea Sprite* to fight her way through. He patted her helm affectionately, as if she was flesh and blood instead of cold steel. She was a staunch ship that had taken everything the sea could throw at her in her years of rigorous sailing in the polar regions. She might be mauled and hammered but Barnum didn't doubt she would survive.

He turned to his first officer, Sam Maverick, who looked like a high school dropout with his long red hair, shaggy beard and gold pendant dangling from his left ear. "Program a new course, Mr. Maverick. Bring her around on a heading of eighty-five degrees east. We can't outrun the storm so we'll ride into her bow-on."

Maverick looked at the seas that were cresting a good fifty feet over the stern and shook his head. He stared balefully at Barnum as if his captain had lost half his gray matter. "You want to bring her around in this sea?" he asked slowly.

"No time like the present," replied Barnum. "Better now than when the rogue waves hit."

It was ship handling at its most frightening. For an agonizing length of time, the ship's hull would swing and face the waves along her entire beam, leaving her vulnerable to a massive wave that would roll her over. Many a ship through the centuries was capsized by attempting the maneuver, going to the bottom without leaving a trace.

"When I see an interval between the swells, at my command, give her full speed." Then he spoke into the ship's radio. "We're coming around in a heavy sea. Everyone brace yourselves and hold on for dear life."

Hunched over the console in front of the bridge window, Barnum gazed unblinkingly through the windshield and waited with the patience of a rock until he saw a wave coming that was higher than any that had passed.

"Full speed, if you please, Mr. Maverick."

Maverick instantly obeyed Barnum's order, but was horrified, certain of disaster, as an enormous wave bore down on the research ship. He was about to curse Barnum for turning too soon, but realized what the captain had in mind. There were no timely intervals. The monstrous waves almost seemed to mesh on one another, like soldiers marching in close formation. Barnum had jumped the gun and begun the turn early, gaining a precious minute while the ship took the blunt of the wave on an angle.

The implacable wave tossed the bow up and shoved *Sea Sprite* almost over to her port side before sweeping her over and around. For fifteen seconds the ship was overwhelmed by a seething white mass of water as she struggled partially through the crest that towered above the bridge. Then she was fishtailing viciously down the other side, rolling heavily to port, the sea inundating her deck railings. Almost miraculously, with agonizing slowness, she righted in the trough and took the next sea bow-on, plunging through on an even keel.

Maverick had walked ships' decks for eighteen years, but he had never seen a more professional, more intuitive, display of seamanship. He stared at Barnum and was amazed to see a smile, perhaps a grim smile, but a smile nonetheless, on the captain's face. My God, Maverick thought, the man is actually enjoying himself.

. . .

F IFTY MILES to the south of *Sea Sprite,* the outer edge of Hurricane Lizzie was within minutes of slamming into the *Ocean Wanderer.* The forward edge of the menacing clouds swept past, cutting off the sun and plunging the sea into an eerie gray darkness. A dense sheet of rain followed, pelting the windows of the floating hotel like the blast from a thousand machine guns.

"Too late!" Morton moaned to himself while standing in his office staring at the tumult that was headed directly for the hotel as if it was an enraged *Tyrannosaurus rex* with a vendetta. Despite the warnings and updates from Heidi Lisherness at the Hurricane Center, he did not conceive the incredible speed and distance the rampage had traveled since morning. Though Heidi Lisherness had given him up-to-date forecasts on the magnitude and speed, it didn't seem possible that calm seas and quiet skies could turn so fast. He could not believe Lizzie's forward fringe was already assaulting the building.

"Inform every staff director to assemble in the conference room immediately!" he snapped to his executive secretary as he marched into his office.

His anger at Specter's indecision to evacuate eleven hundred guests and employees when there was still of chance of transporting them to safety in the Dominican Republic only a few scant miles away bordered on fury. He became even more infuriated as the sound of aircraft engines warming up vibrated the windows. He walked over and stared below just in time to see Specter and his entourage board the Beriev Be-210 executive jet. The entry hatch was barely closed before the engines revved up and the plane began gathering speed, planing over the rising waves, throwing great billowing sheets of spray before lifting into the air and banking on a course toward the Dominican Republic.

"You rotten cowardly scum," Morton hissed at seeing Specter flee for his life without the least concern for the eleven hundred souls he left behind.

He watched until the plane was lost in the menacing clouds, and turned as his staff entered and gathered around the conference table. It was obvious by the expressions of apprehension on their faces that they were standing on the fine line between calm and panic.

"We underestimated the speed of the hurricane," he began. "Its full force is less than an hour away. Since it's too late to evacuate, we must move all guests and employees to the upper level of the hotel, where it's the safest."

"Can't the tugboats pull us out of harm's way?" inquired the reservation's director, a tall, perfectly groomed lady of thirty-five.

"The tugs were alerted early and should arrive shortly, but a rising sea will make it extremely difficult for them to make a connection with our towing capstans. If the procedure proves impossible then we have no choice but to weather the storm."

The concierge raised his hand. "Wouldn't it be safer to ride out the storm on the guest floors below the surface?" asked the concierge.

Morton slowly shook his head. "If the worst happens and the crush of the storm waves break our mooring lines, and the hotel drifts . . ." he paused and shrugged his shoulders. "I don't want to think about what would happen if we are driven onto Navidad Bank forty miles to the east or onto a rocky shoreline of the Dominican Republic that would tear out the glass walls of the lower floors."

The concierge nodded. "We understand. Once the water flooded into the lower levels the ballast tanks could not keep the hotel afloat and the waves would bash her to pieces on the rocks."

"And if it looks like that will happen?" asked Morton's assistant manager.

Morton's face turned very solemn indeed as he looked around the conference table. "Then we abandon the hotel, enter the life rafts and pray to God a few will survive."

9

BATTERED AND LASHED by Hurricane Lizzie, Barrett and Boozer fought to keep the plane on a level flight path. The double satanic gusts coming from flip-side directions and slamming into *Galloping Gertie* at almost the same time nearly tore her out of the air. Both pilots struggled with the controls together, fighting to keep *Gertie* on a straight course. With the rudder slack, they angled direction by reducing or increasing the rpms of their remaining two engines in unison with the ailerons.

Never in their combined years of chasing tropical storms had they ever encountered one that unleashed such incredible strength as Hurricane Lizzie. It was as though she was trying to twist the world apart.

Finally, after what seemed thirty hours but was closer to thirty minutes, the sky gradually turned from solid gray to dirty white to brilliant blue, as the badly pounded Orion escaped the fringes of the storm and staggered into calm weather.

"We'll never make it back to Miami," said Boozer, studying a navigation chart.

"A long shot with only two engines, a fuselage barely hanging together and our rudder frozen," Barrett said grimly. "Better divert to San Juan."

"San Juan, Puerto Rico, it is."

"She's all yours," said Barrett, taking his hands off the controls. "I'm going to check the science guys. No telling what I'll find back there."

He released his safety harness and stepped through the cockpit door into the main cabin of the Orion. The interior was a shambles. Computers, monitors and the racks of electronic instruments were scattered and piled as if thrown off a truck at a salvage yard. Equipment that had been mounted to sustain the worst turbulence had sheared from their bolts and screws as if ripped apart by a giant hand. Bodies were sprawled in different positions, a few unconscious and badly injured, lying against bulkheads, a few still on their feet tending to those who needed medical attention the most.

But that was not the most horrendous sight that met Barrett's eyes. The Orion's fuselage was cracked in a hundred places, rivets having popped out like bullets from a gun. In some areas he could actually see daylight. It was obvious that if they had lingered in the worst of the storm another five minutes, the plane would have ripped apart and crashed in a thousand pieces into the waiting arms of the murderous sea.

Weather scientist Steve Miller looked up from caring for an electrical engineer with a compound fracture of the lower arm. "Can you believe this?" he said, motioning around the destruction. "We were smashed by a wind blast of two hundred and ten miles an hour on the starboard side only seconds before an even stronger gust struck the port."

"I've never heard of wind driving that hard," muttered Barrett in awe.

"Take my word for it. Nothing like this has ever been measured. Two opposing gusts colliding in the same storm is a meteorological rarity, yet it happened. Somewhere in this mess we've got the records to prove it."

"*Galloping Gertie* is in no condition to make Miami," said Barrett, nodding at the fuselage that was barely hanging together. "We'll try for San Juan instead. I'll ask for emergency vehicles to stand ready."

"Don't forget to make a request for extra paramedics and ambulances," said Miller. "No one got off with less than cuts and bruises. The injuries on Delbert and Morris are serious, but no one is critical."

"I've got to get back to the cockpit and help Boozer. If there's anything . . ."

"We'll manage," answered Miller. "Just keep us in the air and not in the ocean."

"Don't think we won't work at it."

Two hours later they sighted the San Juan airport. Handling the controls with a masterful touch, Barrett flew the plane barely above stalling speed to reduce all the stress possible on the weakened aircraft. With flaps lowered, he took a long sweeping approach toward the runway. There would be one attempt and one attempt only. He knew his chances were slim for another approach if he botched this one.

"Gear down," he said, as the runway lined up through the windshield.

Boozer dropped the landing gear. Mercifully, the wheels came down and locked. Fire engines and ambulances lined the strip in expectation of a disaster, the emergency crews having heard the extent of the damage over the radio.

Staring through binoculars at the plane as it grew from a speck into full view, no one in the control tower could believe what they saw. With one engine dead and trailing smoke and one completely missing from the wing, it seemed impossible the Orion could still claw the air. They diverted all commercial traffic into holding patterns until the final curtain on the drama dropped. Then they watched and waited in hushed apprehension.

The Orion came in low and slow. Boozer worked the throttles, maintaining a straight flight while Barrett finessed the controls. He flared out and touched down as gently as humanly possible all too close to the end of the runway. There was just the slightest indication of a bounce when the tires screeched and settled onto the asphalt. There was no reversing the two props. Boozer pulled the throttles back to the stops and let the remaining engines idle as the plane sped down the runway.

Barrett gently tapped the brake pedals, staring at the fence just beyond the runway that loomed ahead. If worse came to worst, he could stand on the left brake and cut a sharp turn into the grass. But everything worked in his favor and *Gertie* dragged her feet and slowed down, rolling to a stop with less than two hundred feet of runway left to go.

Barrett and Boozer sat back in their seats and sighed with relief just as the aircraft shuddered and shook. They threw off the safety harnesses and rushed back into the science compartment. On the opposite end of the trashed instruments and injured scientists, they stared through a huge opening in the fuselage at the runway they'd just covered.

The entire tail section had twisted off and fallen to the ground.

THE WIND hurled itself at the flat-angled ocean side of the *Ocean Wanderer*. The engineers had done their job well. Though designed to take a one-hundred-and-fifty-mile-an-hour wind, the structure with its heavy plate windows was sustaining gusts up to two hundred without breakage. The only damage sustained in the early hours of the hurricane came on the roof where the sports center, with its golf greens, basketball and tennis courts, and dining tables and chairs, was swept away until there was nothing left but a freshwater swimming pool that overflowed, its water spilling down the slides to the sea far below.

Morton was proud of his staff. They had performed admirably. His worst initial fear was panic. But the managers, desk clerks, concierge and maids all worked together in moving the guests from their suites below the waterline and accommodating them in the ballroom, spas, theater and restaurants on the upper levels. Life jackets were passed out along with directions to the life rafts and instructions on which ones to enter.

What no one knew, not even Morton, because none of the employees had risked stepping out on the roof in the two-hundred-mile-an-hour gale, was that the life rafts had been swept away along with the sports facilities twenty minutes after the hurricane struck the floating hotel.

Morton kept in constant touch with his maintenance people, who roamed the hotel reporting on any damage and organizing repairs. So far the stout structure was holding its own. It was a horrifying experience for the guests to watch a monstrous wave rear up as high as the tenth floor and break against the angled side of the hotel, hearing the groan from below of the mooring cables and the shriek of the framework as it was stretched and twisted against its riveted steel joints.

So far there were only a few reports of minor leakage. All the generators and electrical and plumbing systems were still functioning. The *Ocean Wanderer* might shake off the assault for another hour, but Morton knew the beautiful structure was only stalling off the inevitable.

The guests and those of the hotel employees who were released from their regular work assignments stared in hypnotic horror at the maelstrom of confused water whipped by gale winds into swirling white vapor and spray. They watched helplessly as gigantic hundred-foot-tall waves thousands of feet in length and impelled by a two-hundred-mile-an-hour wind rushed toward the hotel, knowing that the only barrier separating them from millions of tons of water was a thin pane of reinforced glass. It was unnerving, to say the least.

The spectacular height of the waves defied comprehension. They could only stand and watch, men clutching women, women clutching children, gazing in rapt fear and fascination as the wave engulfed the hotel, then staring into a massive liquid void until the trough appeared.

Their shocked minds could not grasp the immensity of it all. Every-one hoped and prayed the next wave would be smaller, but it was not to be. If anything, they seemed to grow taller.

Morton took a momentary break and sat at his desk, his back to the windows, not wishing to be distracted from the responsibilities falling like an avalanche on his narrow shoulders. But mostly he faced away from the windows because he couldn't bear to watch the massive green seas surging against his exposed hotel. He sent frantic messages requesting immediate assistance in evacuating the guests and employ-ees, begging for rescue before it was too late.

His pleas were answered and yet they were ignored.

Every ship within a hundred miles was worse off than the hotel. Al-ready, a six-hundred-foot containership's Maydays had stopped trans-mitting. An ominous sign. Two other ships also failed to respond to radio signals. All hope was gone of nearly ten fishing vessels that had the misfortune of being caught in the path of Hurricane Lizzie.

All Dominican Republic military and sea rescue aircraft were grounded. All naval vessels were kept in port to brave out the storm. All Morton heard was "Sorry, *Ocean Wanderer,* you're on your own. We will respond as soon as the storm abates."

He kept in contact with Heidi Lisherness at the NUMA Hurricane Center, giving her reports on the magnitude of the storm.

"Are you certain about the height of the waves?" she asked, disbe-lieving his description.

"Believe me. I'm sitting a hundred feet above the waterline of the hotel and every ninth wave sweeps over the roof of the hotel."

"It's unheard-of."

"Take my word for it."

"I will," said Heidi, now in deep concern. "Is there anything I can do?"

"Just keep me informed as to when you think the sea and winds will decrease."

"According to our storm-hunter aircraft and satellite reports, not anytime soon."

"If you don't hear from me again," said Morton, finally turning and staring through a wall of water outside, "you'll know the worst has happened."

Before Heidi could reply, he switched off as another call came in. "Mr. Morton?"

"Speaking."

"Sir, this is Captain Rick Tapp of the Odyssey tug fleet."

"Go ahead, Captain. The storm is causing interference, but I can hear you."

"Sir, I regret to inform you that the tugs *Albatross* and *Pelican* cannot come to your aid. The seas are far too rough. No one has ever experienced a storm of this magnitude. We could never reach you. As sturdy as our vessels are, they weren't built to make way through a sea this violent. Any attempt would be inviting suicide."

"Yes, I understand," Morton said heavily. "Come when you can. I don't know how much longer our mooring cables can withstand the strain. It's a miracle the hotel structure has stood up to the waves as long as it has."

"We'll do everything humanly possible to reach you the minute the worst of the storm passes the harbor."

Then as an afterthought, "Have you received any instructions from Specter?"

"No, sir, we've heard no word from him or his directors."

"Thank you, Captain."

Can it be that Specter, with a heart of cold stone, has already written off the *Ocean Wanderer* and all the people inside her? Morton could not help wondering. The man was a bigger monster than he ever imagined. He could envision the fat man meeting with his advisors and directors to make plans distancing the company from a disaster in the making.

He was about to leave his office and inspect the battered hotel and to reassure the guests that they would survive the storm. He had never acted on a stage but he was about to give the performance of his life.

Abruptly, he heard a loud ripping sound and felt the floor lurch beneath his feet as the room twisted on a slight angle.

In almost the same instant, his portable communicator buzzed.

"Yes, yes, what is it?"

The familiar voice of his chief maintenance superintendent came over the little speaker. "This is Emlyn Brown, Mr. Morton. I'm down in the number two winch room. I'm looking at the frayed end of the mooring cable. It snapped a hundred yards out."

Morton's worst fear was rapidly becoming a reality. "Will the others hold?"

"With one gone and the rest taking up excess stress, I doubt if they can anchor us for long."

Each time a huge wave struck, the hotel shuddered, was buried in green raging waters and emerged like a fortress under siege, rock steady and immovable. Gradually, morale among the guests escalated as their confidence grew in the *Ocean Wanderer* when she emerged seemingly unscathed after every gigantic wave. The guests were mostly affluent and had reserved their holiday on the floating resort in search of adventure. They all became mentally attuned to the menace threatening them and appeared to take it all in stride. Even the children eventually shook off their initial fright and began to enjoy watching the colossal mass of water smash into and flow over the luxury hotel.

Rising to the occasion, the chefs and kitchen workers somehow managed to turn out meals, served by waiters with impeccable manners throughout the crowded theater and ballroom.

During the ordeal, Morton could feel a growing sickness inside him. He became convinced that disaster was only minutes away and there was nothing any mere human could achieve against the incredible onslaught nature had created.

One by one, the cables parted, the final two within less than a minute of one another. Unleashed, the hotel began her precipitous drift toward the rocks along the shore of the Dominican Republic, driven unmercifully by a sea turned cruel beyond any that had been recorded by man.

IN TIMES PAST, the helmsman, or in many cases the captain of the ship, stood with legs firmly planted on the deck, hands locked around the spokes of the wheel in a death grip, battling the sea by steering with every ounce of his strength for long hours on end.

No more.

Barnum had but to program the ship's course into the computer, then he strapped himself into his raised leather chair in the pilothouse and waited as the electronic brain took over the *Sea Sprite*'s destiny.

Fed a constant stream of data from the vast array of meteorological instruments and systems on board, the computer instantly analyzed the most efficient method of attacking the storm. Then it took command of the automated control system and began maneuvering the ship, measuring and anticipating the towering crests and cavernous troughs while critically judging time and distance for the best angle and speed to plunge through the brutal chaos.

Visibility was measured in inches. Driven crazy by the wind, salt spray and foam lashed the pilothouse windows during the short interval the ship wasn't buried under incalculable tons of water. The horrendous wave and wind conditions were enough to daunt any man who was not bred to the sea. But Barnum sat there like a rock, his eyes seemingly penetrating the treacherous waves and locking on some maddened god of the oceans but totally preoccupied with the problem of survival. Though he placed his explicit trust in the ship's computerized automated control system to battle the storm, an emergency could very well come up when he would have to take command.

He studied the waves as they rolled over his ship, gazing at the crest far above the pilothouse, staring into the solid mass of water until the

Sea Sprite struggled through to the other side and dipped down into the trough.

The hours passed with no relief. A few of the crew and most all the scientists were seasick, yet none complained. There was no thought of coming out on the decks that were continuously swept clean by the great seas. One look at the immense sea was enough to send them to their cabins where they tied themselves to their bunks and prayed they would be alive to see tomorrow.

Their only measure of comfort was the mild tropical temperature. Those who peered through the ports saw waves as high as ten-story buildings. They watched in awe as the crests were blown away by the frightful winds into great clouds of foaming spray before disappearing within the demented rain.

To those below in the crew's quarters and engine room, the motion was not quite as extreme as that experienced by Barnum and his officers up in the pilothouse. He began to get aptly concerned at the way the seas were throwing *Sea Sprite* around like a car on a roller coaster. As the research ship took a steep roll to starboard, he watched the digital numbers on the clinometer. They showed that she heeled and hung at thirty-four degrees before the numbers gradually drifted back between five and zero.

"Another roll like that," he muttered to himself, "and we'll be living under the water permanently."

How the ship could sustain such wild and savage seas, he could not imagine. Then, almost as if it was an ordained blessing, the numbers on the wind speed instrument began to drop with increasing swiftness until it indicated less than fifty miles an hour.

Sam Maverick shook his head in wonder. "Looks like we're about to enter the eye of the hurricane, and yet the water seems more berserk than ever."

Barnum shrugged. "Who said it's darkest before the dawn?"

The communications officer, Mason Jar, a short dumpling of a man with bleached white hair and a large earring dangling from his left ear, approached Barnum and handed him a message.

Barnum scanned the wording and looked up. "This just come in?

"Less than two minutes ago," answered Jar.

Barnum passed the message to Maverick, who read it aloud: "Hotel Ocean Wanderer suffering extreme sea conditions. Mooring cables have parted. Hotel is now adrift and being swept toward the rocks of the Dominican Republic shore. Any ships in the area please respond. Over a thousand souls on board."

He handed the message back to Barnum. "Judging from the Mayday calls, we're the only ship still afloat that can attempt a rescue."

"They didn't give a position," said the communications officer.

Barnum looked grim. "They're not seamen, they're innkeepers."

Maverick leaned over the chart table and manipulated a pair of dividers. "She was fifty miles south of our position when we pulled up anchor to tackle the storm. Won't be easy coming around inside Navidad Reef to effect a rescue."

Jar reappeared with another message. This one read . . .

TO SEA SPRITE FROM NUMA HEADQUARTERS, WASH-
INGTON. IF POSSIBLE, TRY TO EFFECT A RESCUE OF
THE PEOPLE ABOARD OCEAN WANDERER FLOATING
HOTEL. I WILL RELY ON YOUR JUDGMENT AND BACK
YOUR DECISION. SANDECKER

"Well, at least we now have official authorization," said Maverick.

"We only have forty people on board *Sea Sprite*," said Barnum. "The *Ocean Wanderer* has over a thousand. I can't in good conscience run away."

"What about Dirk and Summer down in *Pisces*?"

"They should be able to tough out the storm underwater protected by the reef."

"How's their air supply?" asked Maverick.

"Enough for four more days," replied Barnum.

"If this bloody storm passes, we should be back on station in two."

"Providing we can hook up with the *Ocean Wanderer* and tow her a safe distance from shore."

Maverick looked out the windshield. "Once we enter the eye of the storm, we should be able to make good headway."

"Program the hotel's last position and predicted drift into the computer," ordered Barnum. "Then set a course for a rendezvous."

Barnum started to rise from his chair to order his radio operator to report his decision to attempt a rescue of the *Ocean Wanderer* to Admiral Sandecker, when to his horror a monstrous wave, more towering than any before, rose nearly eighty feet above the pilothouse that was already nearly fifty feet above the waterline, and came crashing down with unimaginable force that hammered and engulfed the entire vessel. The *Sea Sprite* bravely surged through the watery mountain, plunging into what seemed a bottomless trough before rising again.

Barnum and Maverick looked into each other's eyes in stunned astonishment when another wave of even more staggering dimensions smashed and immersed the research ship, plunging her into its depths.

Crushed by millions of tons of water, the *Sea Sprite*'s bow dove down, down, deeper and deeper, as if she never intended to stop.

10

OCEAN WANDERER was now totally helpless. Free of her moorings, the floating hotel was at the full mercy of the hurricane's assault. There was nothing left the men could do to save the guests and the hotel.

Morton was becoming more desperate by the minute. He faced one critical decision after another. He could either order the ballast tanks filled to higher levels, settling the hotel lower in the water to lessen the rate of drift under the vicious gale, or empty the tanks and allow the waves to toss the luxury structure and its passengers about like a house in a Kansas tornado.

On the face of it the first option seemed the most practical. But that meant a battering by an irresistible force against a nearly immovable object. Already, sections of the hotel were giving way, allowing flooding into the lower levels that pushed the pumps to their limits. The second option would mean extreme discomfort for everyone on board and speed up the inevitable impact on the Caribbean island's rocky coast.

He was about to opt for filling the tanks to the brim when the wind suddenly began to slacken. After half an hour it almost died away completely and the sun beamed down on the hotel. People in the ballroom and theater started to cheer, believing the worst of the storm was over.

Morton knew better. True gale winds had decreased but the sea was still rough. Looking through the salt-stained windows, he could see the gray inner walls of the hurricane soaring into the sky. The storm was moving directly over them and they were now in the hurricane's eye.

The worst was yet to come.

In the few short hours remaining before the eye passed, Morton called together all his maintenance people and every able male employee and passenger. Then he divided them up into work parties, assigning some to repair the damage and others to shore up the lower-level windows that were badly leaking and ready to give way. They labored heroically and soon their efforts paid off. The flooding decreased and the pumps began to gain on the leaks.

Morton realized they had merely gleaned a temporary reprieve as long they remained in the eye, but it was vital to keep up morale and assure everyone they had a fighting chance of survival, even though he didn't believe it himself.

He returned to his office and began studying charts of the Dominican Republic shoreline, attempting to predict where the *Ocean Wanderer* might be driven ashore. With luck they could be forced onto one of the many beaches, but most were too small, some even blasted out of the rock to build hotel resorts. His best estimate was that they had a ninety percent chance of striking rocks created out of volcanic lava many millions of years ago.

In his worst nightmare Morton could not conceive how he could remove a thousand human beings from the battered hotel and transport them safely to land while it was being bashed by giant waves against unyielding rocks.

There seemed no way of avoiding a terrible fate.

He had never felt so vulnerable, so impotent. He was rubbing his tired and reddened eyes when his communications operator burst through the door.

"Mr. Morton, help has come!" he shouted.

Morton looked at him blankly. "A rescue ship?"

The operator shook his head. "No, sir, a helicopter."

Morton's brief optimism sank. "What good is a single helicopter?"

"They radioed that they were going to lower two men onto the roof."

"Impossible." Then he realized that it *was* possible as long as they were in the hurricane's eye. He rushed past the operator and stepped into his private elevator, taking it to the roof of the hotel. As the doors opened and he walked out onto the roof, he was dismayed to find the entire sporting complex had been swept away, leaving nothing but the swimming pool. He was especially horrified to see that the life rafts had all vanished.

Now that he had a clear three-hundred-and-sixty-degree view of the inner hurricane, he stood awestruck at the sheer malevolent beauty of it all. Then he looked straight up and saw a turquoise-colored helicopter descending down on the hotel. He could see the word NUMA in bold letters painted on the fuselage. The aircraft paused and hovered twenty feet above the deck, as two men in turquoise jumpsuits and crash helmets were lowered by cables to the roof of the hotel. Once they disengaged, two large bundles wrapped in orange plastic came down on another cable. They quickly disconnected the hook and signaled an all clear.

A man inside the helicopter pulled up the cables on a winch and gave a thumbs-up sign as the pilot banked away from the hotel and ascended up through the hurricane's eye. Seeing Morton, the two visitors approached, easily carrying the bulky bundles.

The taller of the two removed his helmet, revealing a thick head of black hair, graying on the temples. His face was craggy from a life in the elements and his opaline green eyes, edged in mirth lines, seemed to bore into Morton's brain.

"Please take us to Mr. Hobson Morton," he said in a voice strangely calm under the circumstances.

"I'm Morton. Who are you and why are you here?"

A glove was removed and a hand extended. "My name is Dirk Pitt. I'm special projects director for the National Underwater and Marine Agency." He turned to a short man with dark curly hair and heavy eyebrows who looked to be descended from a Roman gladiator. "This is my assistant director, Al Giordino. We came to effect a tow for the hotel."

"I was told the company tugs could not leave port."

"Not Odyssey tugs, but a NUMA research ship capable of towing a vessel the size of your hotel."

Willing to snatch at any straw, Morton motioned Pitt and Giordino into his private elevator and escorted them down to his office.

"Forgive the cold reception," he said, offering them a chair. "I was given no warning of your arrival."

"We haven't had much time to prepare," Pitt answered indifferently. "What is your current status?"

Morton shook his head bleakly. "Not good. Our pumps are barely staying ahead of the flooding, the structure is in danger of collapsing, and once we run onto the rocks surrounding the Dominican Republic"—he paused and shrugged—"then a thousand people, including yourselves, are going to die."

Pitt's face became as hard as granite. "We're not running on any rocks."

"We'll need the services of your maintenance personnel to assist us in hooking up with our ship," said Giordino.

"Where is this ship?" Morton questioned, his voice suggesting doubt.

"Our helicopter's radar put her less than thirty miles away."

Morton looked out the window at the ominous walls surrounding the hurricane's eye. "Your ship will never get here before the storm closes in again."

"Our NUMA Hurricane Center measured the eye at sixty miles in diameter and her speed at twenty miles an hour. With a little luck, she'll get here in time."

"Two hours to reach us and one to make the hookup," said Giordino, glancing at his watch.

"There is, I believe," said Morton in an official tone, "a matter of marine salvage to discuss."

"There is nothing to discuss," said Pitt, annoyed at being delayed. "NUMA is a United States government agency dedicated to ocean research. We are not a salvage company. This is not a no-cure, no-pay arrangement. If successful, our boss, Admiral James Sandecker, won't charge your boss, Mr. Specter, one thin dime."

Giordino grinned. "I might mention, the admiral has a love of expensive cigars."

Morton simply stared at Giordino. He was at a loss over how to deal with these men who had dropped from the sky unannounced and calmly informed him that they were going to save the hotel and everyone in it. They hardly looked like his salvation.

Finally, he acquiesced. "Please tell me what you gentlemen need."

THE *Sea Sprite* refused to die.

She went deeper than anyone could have believed a ship would dive and live. Totally immersed, her bow and stern buried deeply in the water, no one thought she could come back. For agonizing seconds, she seemed to hang suspended in the gray-green void. Then slowly, laboriously, her bow began to rise fractionally as she struggled defiantly back toward the surface. Then her thrashing screws dug in and propelled her forward. At last she burst into the fury of the storm again, her bow thrusting above the water like a porpoise. Her keel crashed down, jolting every plate in her hull that was weighted down with tons of water that flowed across her decks and cascaded back into the sea.

The demonic gale had thrown her worst punch at the tough little ship and she had survived the boiling cauldron. Time and again she had suffered the great swirling mass of wind and water. It was almost as if *Sea Sprite* had a human determination about her, knowing without reservation that there was nothing left the sea could throw at her that she couldn't brush aside.

Marverick stared through the pilothouse windshield that had miraculously failed to shatter, his face white as a lily. "That was macabre," he said in a classic understatement. "I had no idea I'd signed aboard a submarine."

No other ship could have withstood such a freak occurrence and survived without sinking to the seabed. But *Sea Sprite* was no ordinary ship. She had been built tough to tolerate massive polar seas. The steel on her hull was far thicker than average to fight the solid mass of ice floes. But she did not escape unscathed. All but one boat had been swept away.

Gazing astern, Barnum was amazed that his communications gear had somehow survived. Those who suffered belowdecks had no inkling how close they came to ending up forever on the bottom of the sea.

Suddenly, sunlight beamed into the pilothouse. *Sea Sprite* had broken into Hurricane Lizzie's giant eye. It appeared paradoxical, with a blue sky above and maniacal sea below. To Barnum it seemed evil that a sight so tantalizing could still be so menacing.

Barnum glanced at his communications officer, Mason Jar, who was standing braced against the chart table, gripping the railing with ivory knuckles, looking like he'd seen an army of ghosts. "If you can come back on keel, Mason, contact the *Ocean Wanderer* and tell whoever is in charge that we're coming as quickly as possible through heavy seas."

Still dazed by what he had experienced, Jar slowly emerged from shock, nodded without speaking and walked off toward the communications room as if he was in a trance.

Barnum scanned his radar system and studied the blip that he was certain was the hotel twenty-six miles to the east. Then he programmed his course into the computer and again turned over command to the computerized automated controls. When he finished, he wiped his forehead with an old red bandana and muttered, "Even if we reach her before they go on the rocks, what then? We have no boats to cross over, and if we had they'd be swamped by the heavy seas. Nor do we have a big tow winch with thick cable."

"Not a pretty thought," said Maverick. "Watching helplessly as the hotel crashes into the rocks with all those women and children on board."

"No," said Barnum heavily. "Not a pretty thought at all."

II

HEIDI HADN'T BEEN HOME in three days. She caught cat-naps on a cot in her office, drank gallons of black coffee and ate little but baloney-and-cheese sandwiches. If she was walking around the Hurricane Center like a somnambulist, it wasn't from lack of sleep but from the stress and anguish of working amid a colossal catastrophe that was about to cause death and destruction on an unheard-of scale. Though she had correctly forecast Hurricane Lizzie's horrifying power from her birth and sent out warnings early, she still felt a sense of guilt that she might have done more.

She watched the projections and images on her monitors with great trepidation as Lizzie raced toward the nearest land.

Because of her early warnings, more than three hundred thousand people had been evacuated to the mountainous hills in the center of the Dominican Republic and its neighbor, Haiti. Still, the death toll would be staggering. Heidi also feared that the storm might veer north and strike Cuba before crashing into southern Florida.

Her phone rang and she wearily picked it up.

"Any change in your forecast as to direction?" asked her husband Harley at the National Weather Service.

"No, Lizzie is still heading due east as if she's traveling on a railroad track."

"Most unusual to travel thousands of miles in a straight line."

"More than unusual. It's unheard-of. Every hurricane on record meandered."

"A perfect storm?"

"Not Lizzie," said Heidi. "She's far from being perfect. I'd class her as a deadly cataclysm of the highest magnitude. An entire fishing fleet has gone missing. Another eight ships—oil tankers, cargo ships and private yachts—have stopped transmitting. Their distress signals are no longer being received, only silence. We have to expect the worst."

"What's the latest word on the floating hotel?" asked Harley.

"At last reports, she broke her moorings and was being driven by gale-force winds and high seas toward the rocky coast of the Dominican Republic. Admiral Sandecker sent one of NUMA's research ships to its position in an effort to tow it to safety."

"Sounds like a lost cause."

"I fear that we're looking at a sea disaster beyond any in the past," said Heidi grimly.

"I'm going to head home for a few hours. Why don't you take a break and come too? I'll fix us a nice dinner."

"I can't, Harley. Not just yet. Not until I can predict Lizzie's next mood."

"With her infinite strength, that could be days, even weeks."

"I know," said Heidi slowly. "That's what scares me. If her energy doesn't begin to diminish as she passes over the Dominican Republic and Haiti, she'll strike the mainland in full force."

SUMMER HAD a fascination with the sea beginning when her mother insisted she learn to dive when she was only six years old. A small tank and air regulator was custom made for her small body and she was given lessons by the finest instructors, as was her brother

Dirk. She became a creature of the sea, studying its inhabitants, its caprices and spirits. She came to understand it after swimming in its waters serene and blue. She also experienced its monumental power during a typhoon in the Pacific. But like a wife with a husband of twenty years who suddenly sees a man with a hateful and sadistic streak, she was witnessing firsthand just how cruel and malicious the sea could be.

Sitting in the front of *Pisces,* brother and sister stared up through the big transparent bubble at the boiling turmoil above. As the hurricane's outer rim slashed across Navidad Bank, the fury seemed remote and distant, but as its strength increased it soon became apparent that their cozy little habitat was in dire danger and ill-prepared to protect them.

The crests of the waves easily passed over them at their forty-foot depth, but soon the waves grew to towering dimensions, and when the troughs dropped down to the seabed, Dirk and Summer found the habitat completely exposed to the surface rain before the next sea swept over them.

Time after time *Pisces* was battered and buffeted by the unending march of the huge waves. The inner-space station was built to take the pressure of the deep and her steel shell had no problem in repelling the besieging waters. But the terrible force exerted on her outer surface soon began to move her across the bottom. The four support legs were not connected to a base. They sat individually embedded only a few inches in the coral. Only *Pisces*'s sixty-five-ton mass kept the chamber from being lifted and hurled across the reef like an empty bottle.

Then the same pair of enormous waves that had buried *Sea Sprite* only twenty miles distant struck Navidad Bank, relentlessly crushing the coral and shattering its delicate infrastructure into millions of fragments. The first one pitched *Pisces* over on her side and sent her tumbling round and round like a barrel rolling across a rocky desert. Despite the occupants' attempts to hang on to anything solid, they were tossed about as if they were rag dolls in a blender.

The habitat was pitched and tossed for nearly two hundred yards before it came to rest, perched precariously on the edge of a narrow coral crevasse. Then the second monstrous wave struck and threw the habitat over the edge.

Pisces dropped one hundred and twenty feet to the floor of the crevasse, bumping and grinding against the coral walls during its fall, striking the bottom in a great explosion of sand particles. *Pisces* landed flat on its right side and lay wedged between the walls of the crevasse. Inside, everything that wasn't tied down had been thrown in a dozen different directions. Dishes, food supplies, dive equipment, bedding, personal clothing was strewn in mad confusion.

Ignoring the pain from a dozen bruises and a sprained ankle, Dirk immediately crawled to the side of his sister, who lay in a ball between the upended bunk beds. He looked into her wide gray eyes and for the first time since they were old enough to walk he saw sheer fright. He gently took her head in his hands and smiled tightly.

"How was that for a wild ride?"

She looked up into his face, saw the game smile and slowly breathed deeply as her fear subsided. "During the chaos I kept thinking that we were born together and we would die together."

"My sister the pessimist. We've got another seventy years to tease each other." Then he asked with concern, "Are you injured?"

She shook her head. "I wedged myself under the bunks and wasn't bounced around as badly as you." Then she looked outside the viewing bubble at the cauldron above. "The habitat?"

"Still sound- and leakproof. No wave, no matter how gigantic, could break up *Pisces*. She's got a four-inch steel skin."

"The storm?"

"Still raging, but we'll be safe down here. The waves are passing over the canyon without causing turbulence."

Her gaze swept the jumbled clutter. "God, what a mess."

Pleased that Summer had survived the ordeal without injury, Dirk made an inspection of the life-support systems while his sister began tackling the debris. There was no hope of putting everything back where it belonged, not with the habitat lying on its side. She simply stacked everything into neat piles and laid blankets over sharp protrusions from instruments, valves, gauges and systems mountings. Without a floor, they had to climb over it all to move around. She felt strange to be existing in an environment where everything was turned on a ninety-degree angle.

She felt more secure knowing they had survived up until now. The storm could no longer threaten them in their coral canyon with its steep walls. Down deep, there was no howling wind to hear, no beating wind when the trough of a wave exposed the chamber to the atmosphere. Her fear and suspense of what might happen next began to fade. They were safe until *Sea Sprite* braved the hurricane and returned. And there was the warmth and comfort of her brother, who had the courage and strength of their legendary father.

But the expression of confidence she had come to expect was not in his face when he came and sat on the wall beside her, favoring the bruises on his body that were turning black and blue.

"You look glum," she said. "What is it?"

"The fall into the crevasse tore off the lines connecting the air bottles to our life-support system. According to the air pressure gauges, the four tanks that were undamaged will supply us with only fourteen hours of air before they run dry."

"What about the dive tanks we left in the entry lock?"

"Only one was left inside for a valve repair. It contains only enough to last the two of us for forty-five minutes at best."

"We could use it to go outside and bring back the others," Summer said hopefully. "Then wait a day or two until the storm deteriorates before abandoning the habitat, and use our inflatable raft to drift on the surface until rescued."

He shook his head solemnly. "The bad news is we're trapped. The hatch on the entry lock is jammed against the coral. Nothing short of dynamite could force it open far enough for us to slip outside."

Summer sighed very deeply and then said, "It looks like our fate is in Captain Barnum's hands."

"I'm sure we're still on his mind. He won't forget us."

"He should be informed of our situation."

Dirk straightened and put his hands on her shoulders. "The radio was smashed when we plunged into the crevasse."

"We could still release our homing device so they know we're alive," she said hopefully.

His voice came in a soft, controlled tone. "It was mounted on the side of the habitat that fell against the bottom. It must have been crushed. Even if it survived, there is no way to release it."

"When they come looking for us," she said tensely, "they won't have an easy time finding us down here in the crevasse."

"You can bet Barnum will send every boat and diver on board *Sea Sprite* to scour the reef."

"You're talking as if we had enough air for days instead of hours."

"Not to worry, sis," Dirk said confidently. "For the moment, we're safe and secure from the storm. The minute the sea flattens, the crew aboard *Sea Sprite* will come for us like a drunk after a case of Scotch that fell off a liquor truck." Then he added, "After all, we're their number one priority."

12

AT THAT MOMENT the *Pisces* and her two crew members were the last thing on Barnum's mind. Anxiously, he fidgeted in his chair as his gaze ceaselessly turned from the radar monitor to the windshield and back again. The titan-sized waves had dropped from gigantic to merely huge. Like clockwork they marched in formation against *Sea Sprite*, pitching her up and down in a continuous motion that became monotonous. No longer did they climb more than a hundred feet. Now the distance between crest and trough averaged only forty. Still heavy, but a lake compared to the goliaths earlier. It was almost as if the sea knew it had thrown its best punch against the research ship and failed to sink her. Frustrated, it relented and admitted defeat, dwindling to little more than a nuisance.

The hours passed, with *Sea Sprite* making headway with as much speed as Barnum dared to push her. Normally a humorous and friendly captain, he became cold and serious as he contemplated the hopeless task staring him in the face. He saw no way he could get a towline on the *Ocean Wanderer*. The great tow winch and its arm-thick cable had been removed long ago when the *Sea Sprite* had been converted to a NUMA research ship. Now the primary winch and cable on board the ship was for lowering and lifting deepwater submersibles. Installed on the stern deck behind the big crane, it was grossly inadequate for towing a floating hotel with a displacement tonnage more than that of a battleship.

Barnum's eyes tried to drill through the blowing sheets of rain. "We'd have her in sight if we could see through this muck," he said.

"According to the radar she's less than two miles away," advised Maverick.

Barnum stepped into the communications compartment and spoke to Mason Jar. "Have you heard anything from the hotel?"

"Nothing, sir. She's silent as a tomb."

"God, I hope we're not too late."

"I don't want to believe that."

"See if you can raise them again. The satellite communications. The guests and management are most likely to communicate with shore stations via phone than ship-to-shore radio."

"Let me try maritime radio first, Captain. At this distance there should be less interference. The hotel must have top-of-the-line equipment for communicating with other vessels when she's towed around the seas like a barge."

"Patch onto the bridge speakers so I can speak to them when they respond."

"Yes, sir."

Barnum returned to the pilothouse in time to hear Jar's voice through the speakers.

"This is *Sea Sprite* to *Ocean Wanderer*. We are two miles southeast of you and closing. Please respond."

There was half a minute of crackling static. Then a voice boomed through the speakers.

"Paul, are you ready to go to work?"

Because of the interference, Barnum did not recognize the voice at first. He picked up the bridge radio receiver and spoke into it. "Who is speaking?"

"Your old shipmate, Dirk Pitt. I'm in the hotel along with Al Giordino."

Barnum was stunned at putting a face with the voice. "How in God's name did you two come to be on a floating hotel in a hurricane?"

"It sounded like such a swell party, we didn't want to miss it."

"You must know we don't have the equipment to tow the *Wanderer.*"

"All we need are your big engines."

Barnum had come to learn during their years with NUMA that Pitt and Giordino wouldn't be where they were without a plan. "What's on your devious mind?"

"We've already formed work crews to help us use the hotel's mooring cables for tow cables. Once you take them aboard *Sea Sprite,* you can join them together, then secure them to your stern capstan where they will form a bride for towing."

"Your plan sounds crazy," said Barnum, disbelieving. "How do you expect to send tons of cable that's dragging across the seabed under a hurricane-maddened sea over to my ship?"

There was a pause, and when the reply came Barnum could almost see the devilish grin on Pitt's face.

"We have apple-pie high-in-the-sky hopes."

The rain abated and visibility increased from two hundred yards to nearly a mile. Suddenly the *Ocean Wanderer* loomed through the storm dead ahead.

"God, just look at her," said Maverick. "She looks like a glass castle in a fairy tale."

The hotel seemed regal and magnificent amid the raging sea surrounding it. The crew and scientists, who were swept up in mounting excitement, had left their cabins and crowded onto the bridge to witness the spectacle of a modern edifice where none should have existed.

"It's so beautiful," murmured a blond, petite woman who was a marine chemist. "I never expected such creative architecture."

"Nor I," agreed a tall ocean chemist. "Coated with so much salt spray, she could pass for an iceberg."

Barnum trained a pair of binoculars on the hotel, whose mass swayed back and forth under the trouncing from the waves. "Her roof deck looks like it was swept clean."

"A miracle she survived," muttered Maverick in wonder. "Certainly beyond all expectations."

Barnum lowered his glasses. "Bring us around and set our stern on her windward side."

"After we take another battering getting in position to take on a towline, Captain, what then?"

Barnum stared pensively at the *Ocean Wanderer*. "We wait," he said slowly. "We wait and see what Pitt has up his sleeve after he waves his magic wand."

PITT STUDIED the detailed plans of the mooring cables given him by Morton. He, Giordino, Morton and Emlyn Brown, the hotel's chief maintenance superintendent, were standing around a table in Morton's office.

"The cables will have to be reeled in before we know their length after parting."

Brown, who had the wiry build of a college track-and-field miler, ran a hand through a bush of jet-black hair. "We've already reeled in what was left of them right after they snapped. I was afraid that if they snagged in the rocks it might cause the hotel to twist around under the devil's waves and cause damage."

"How far out did cables three and four break from their moorings?"

"I can only guess, mind you, but I'd say they both gave up the ghost about two hundred, maybe two hundred and twenty yards out."

Pitt looked at Giordino. "That doesn't leave Barnum enough safe latitude for maneuver. And if the *Ocean Wanderer* should sink, Barnum's crew will have no time to cut the cable. The *Sea Sprite* will be dragged down to the bottom along with the hotel."

"If I know Paul," said Giordino, "he won't hesitate to take the gamble with so many lives at stake."

"Am I to understand, you intend to use the mooring cables as towing lines?" inquired Morton, who stood on the opposite side of the table. "I was told your NUMA vessel is an oceangoing tugboat."

"She was once," replied Pitt. "But no more. She was converted from an icebreaker tug into a research ship. The big winch and tow cable were removed when she was refitted. All she has now is a crane for lifting submersibles. We'll have to improvise and make do with what we've got."

"Then what good is she?" Morton demanded angrily.

"Trust me." Pitt looked him in the eye. "If we can make a hookup, *Sprite* has enough power in her engines to tow this hotel."

"How will you get the ends of the cables over to the *Sea Sprite*?" Brown queried. "Once they're unreeled, they'll sink to the bottom."

Pitt looked at him. "We float them over."

"Float?"

"You must have fifty-gallon drums on board?"

"Very clever, Mr. Pitt. I see what you're aiming at." Brown paused and thought a moment. "We have quite a few that contain oil for the generators, cooking oil for the kitchens and liquid soap for cleaning personnel."

"We can use as many empty drums as you can scrape up."

Brown turned to four of his maintenance crew, who were standing nearby. "Assemble all the empties and drain the rest as quick as you can."

"As you and your people unreel the cables," Pitt explained, "I want you to tie a drum every twenty feet. By making the cables buoyant, they can float and be hauled over to *Sea Sprite*."

Brown nodded. "Consider it done—"

"If four of our cables snapped earlier," interrupted Morton, "what makes you think these two will stand up to the stress?"

"For one thing," Pitt rationalized patiently, "the storm has abated considerably. Two, the lines will be shorter and less prone to excessive strain. And last, we'll be towing the hotel on her narrowest beam. When she was moored, her entire front face took the brunt of the storm."

Without waiting for a comment from Morton, Pitt turned back to Brown.

"Next, I'll need a good mechanic or machinist to splice loops or eyes to the ends of the cables, so they can be shackled together once they're wound around the *Sprite*'s tow bit."

"I'll handle that chore myself," Brown assured him. Then he said, "I hope you have a plan for transporting the cables over to your NUMA ship? They won't float there on their own, certainly not in this sea."

"That's the fun part," answered Pitt. "We'll require a few hundred feet of line, preferably a thin diameter but with the tensile strength of a steel cable."

"I have two five-hundred-foot spools of Falcron line in the storeroom. It's finely woven, thin, lightweight and could lift a Patton tank."

"Tie two hundred-yard lengths of the Falcron line to each end of the cables."

"I understand using the Falcron lines to pull the heavy cables to your ship, but how do you intend to get them there?"

Pitt and Giordino exchanged knowing glances.

"That will be our chore," said Pitt with a grim smile.

"I hope it won't take long," Morton said darkly, pointing out the window. "Time is a commodity we've little left."

As if they were spectators at a tennis match, all heads turned in unison and saw that the menacing shoreline was little more than two miles away. And as far as they could see in either direction, an immense surf was pounding on what seemed a never-ending ridge of rocks.

. . .

JUST INSIDE an air-conditioning equipment room in one corner of the hotel, Pitt spread the contents of his large bundle across the floor. First he slipped on his custom shorty neoprene wet suit. He preferred this abbreviated suit for the job at hand because the water was blessed with tropical temperatures and he saw no need for a heavy suit, wet or dry. He also enjoyed the ease of movement because the arms above the elbows and legs below the knees were open. Then came his buoyancy compensator, followed by a ScubaPro dive mask. He cinched his weight belt and checked the quick-release safety snap.

Next he sat down as one of the hotel maintenance men helped mount a closed-circuit rebreather on his back. He and Giordino agreed that a compact rebreathing unit offered greater freedom of movement than two bulky steel air tanks. As with regular scuba gear, the diver inhales through a regulator, breathing compressed gas from a tank. But then the expired air is saved and recycled back through canisters that remove the carbon dioxide while replenishing the oxygen in the tank. The SIVA-55 unit they were using was developed for military underwater covert operations.

His final check was the underwater communications system from Ocean Technology Systems. A receiver was attached to the strap of his mask. "Al, do you hear me?"

Giordino, who was going through the same procedure on the opposite corner of the hotel, answered in a voice that seemed wrapped in cotton. "Every word."

"You sound unusually coherent."

"Give me a hard time and I'll resign and head up to the cocktail lounge."

Pitt smiled at his friend's ever-constant sense of humor. If he could rely on anyone in the world, it was Giordino. "Ready when you are."

"Say when."

"Mr. Brown."

"Emlyn."

"Okay, Emlyn, have your people stand by the winches until we give the signal to pay out the cables and drums."

Answering from the rooms where the great mooring cable winches were mounted, Brown acknowledged, "Just say the word."

"Keep your fingers crossed," said Pitt, as he pulled on his dive fins.

"Bless you, boys, and good luck," replied Brown.

Pitt nodded at one of Brown's maintenance men, who was standing beside a reel containing the Falcron line. He was short and husky and insisted on being called "Critter." "Pay out a little at a time. If you feel any tension, release it quickly or you'll halt my progress."

"I'll send it along nice and easy," Critter assured him.

Then Pitt hailed *Sea Sprite*. "Paul, are you ready to take the lines?"

"Soon as you hand them to me," came Barnum's firm voice over Pitt's receiver. His words were transmitted from a transducer he had lowered in the water off the stern of *Sea Sprite*.

"Al and I can only drag two hundred feet of line underwater. You'll have to move in closer to reach us."

In these seas both Pitt and Barnum knew that one monstrous wave could sweep *Sea Sprite* into the hotel, taking them both to the bottom. Yet Barnum didn't hesitate to risk the dice on one throw. "All right, let's do it."

Pitt slung a loop of the Falcron line over one shoulder line as a harness. He stood and tried to push open the door leading to a small balcony that hung twenty feet above the water, but the force of the wind beat against it from the other side. Before he could ask for help, the hotel maintenance man was beside him.

Together they rammed their weight and shoulders against the door. The second it was cracked, the wind cut through the opening and hurled the door back against its stops as though it was kicked by a mule. Now exposed in the open doorway, the maintenance man was blown back into the equipment room as if he was flung there by a catapult.

Pitt managed to stay on his feet under the onslaught. But when he looked up and saw an enormous wave heading his way, he leaped over the balcony hand railing and somersaulted into the water.

THE WORST OF the furies had passed. The hurricane's eye was hours gone and the *Ocean Wanderer* had somehow survived Lizzie's final fury. The winds had decreased to forty knots and the seas had dropped to an average of thirty feet. The water surface was still vicious, but not nearly as angered as earlier. Hurricane Lizzie had moved westward to continue casting her death and destruction on the island of the Dominican Republic and Haiti before spilling over into the Caribbean Sea. In another twenty-four hours the sea would flatten in the trail of history's greatest storm.

The crashing surf looked ominously closer with each passing minute. The hotel had drifted close enough for the hundreds of guests and employees to see the spray hurled into the sky in great clouds as the swells piled up and smashed into the rocky cliffs. They struck with the force of a mountainous avalanche. The foam swirled into the air in sheets as it met the backwash of the previous wave. Death was no more than a mile away and the *Ocean Wanderer*'s rate of drift was close to a mile an hour.

Everyone's eyes swept back and forth from the shore to *Sea Sprite*, riding in the swells like a fat duck only a few hundred yards away.

Covered head to toe in yellow oilskins, Barnum braved the downpour, still lashed by heavy winds on the stern of his ship, and stood beneath the big crane. He looked down on the deck where the great winch used to sit and imagined the difference it would have made. But the tow bit would have to do. Somehow the cable would have to be shackled manually.

Barnum stood in the shelter of the crane, ignored the soaking breeze and peered through his binoculars at the base of the hotel. He and four of his crew were tied to the railings to keep from being washed overboard. He observed Pitt and Giordino enter the water and disappear beneath the rolling surface. He could just make out men standing in the doorways, battered by the seas, paying out the red Falcron line to the divers struggling below the wild waves.

"Throw out a pair of lines with buoys," he ordered without lowering the glasses, "and prepare the grappling hooks."

Barnum prayed he would not have to use the grappling hooks on the divers' bodies in an extreme crisis should they become unconscious or unable to reach the high stern of the ship. The grappling hooks were connected to eight-foot aluminum shafts that had been inserted into pipes, giving them an extra length of thirty feet.

They watched expectantly but doubtfully, unable to see Pitt or Giordino under the swirling seas nor spot their bubbles floating to the surface, since their rebreathing apparatus did not expel the diver's breath.

"Stop engines," he ordered his chief engineer.

"You did say stop engines, Captain," came back the chief of the engine room.

"Yes, there are divers bringing over the cable lines. We have to let the seas carry us within two hundred yards and narrow the gap so they can reach us with the cable lines."

Then he trained his binoculars on the murderous coastline that seemed to be approaching with unearthly swiftness.

AFTER HE SWAM a hundred feet from the hotel, Pitt briefly surfaced to get his bearings. The *Ocean Wanderer,* whose mass was implacably coerced by the wind and waves away from him, rose like a skyscraper in Manhattan. *Sea Sprite* showed herself only when Pitt rose on the crest of a wave. She rolled in the sea what seemed like a mile away but was actually less than a hundred yards. He noted her position on his compass and ducked back under the surface and dove deep below the confusion above.

The line in his wake quickly became awkward to pull as the drag increased with each foot it was paid out. He was thankful the Falcron line was not heavy or bulky, which would have made it too unwieldy. To move with the least hydrodynamic drag as possible, he kept his head down and his hands clasped behind his back under the oxygen rebreathing apparatus.

He tried to stay just deep enough below the wave troughs so his progress wouldn't be hindered by the heavy seas. More than once he became disoriented, but a quick glance at his compass set him on the right course again. He kicked his fins with all the strength in his legs, doggedly dragging the line that was digging into his shoulder, gaining two feet and losing one from the strong current.

Pitt's leg muscles began to ache and his progress became sluggish. His mind was becoming giddy from deeply inhaling too much oxygen. His heart was beginning to pound from the heavy exertion and his lungs began to heave. He dared not pause or rest or the current would have wiped out all his gains. There could be no delay. Every minute counted as the *Ocean Wanderer* was impelled toward disaster by an uncaring sea.

Another ten minutes of all-out effort, his strength began to ebb. He sensed that his body was about played out. His mind urged him to try even harder, but there was only so much that muscle and flesh could be called on to achieve. Out of desperation he began to stroke with his hands and arms in an attempt to take the strain from his legs, whose numbness was growing by the minute.

He wondered if Giordino was in the same fix, but he knew Al would die before giving up, not with all those women's and children's lives at stake. Besides, his friend was built like a Brahma bull. If anyone could swim across a wild ocean with one hand tied behind him, Al could.

Pitt did not waste a breath to inquire of his friend's condition over the intercom. There were sickening moments when he felt as if he might not make it. The defeatist thought was brushed aside, and he reached deep within himself to tap his inner reserves.

His breath was coming in great heaves now. The escalating drag on the line made it feel as if he was in a tug-of-war against a herd of elephants. He started to recall the old ads of the muscleman Charles Atlas pulling a steam locomotive down the track. Thinking he might have been carried away from his goal, he spared another glance at his compass. Miraculously, he had managed to stay on a straight course toward *Sea Sprite*.

The dark cloud of total exhaustion was beginning to creep over the edge of his vision, when he heard a voice speak his name.

"Keep coming, Dirk," Barnum shouted through his headphone. "We can see you under the water. Surface now!"

Pitt obediently swam upward and broke the surface.

Then Barnum shouted again, "Look to your left."

Pitt turned. No more than ten feet away was an orange buoy on the end of a line leading to the *Sea Sprite*. Pitt didn't bother acknowledging. He had about five good strong kicks of his fins left in him, and he gave them to the cause. With a physical relief he had never known, he grasped the safety line, threw his arm over it so that it was firmly embedded under his armpit with the buoy lodged against his back shoulder.

At last he could relax as Barnum and his crew pulled him up to the stern. Then they cautiously placed the grappling hook under the line three feet behind Pitt and carefully lifted him onto the deck.

Pitt raised his hands and Barnum deftly removed the looped end of the Falcron line from his shoulder and connected it to the winch on the crane along with the line already brought aboard by Giordino. Two of the crew removed Pitt's mouthpiece and full head mask. Taking a deep breath of pure ocean salt air, he found himself looking up into the grinning face of Giordino.

"Slowpoke," muttered Giordino, still in the throes of exhaustion. "I beat you on board by a good two minutes."

"I'm lucky to be here," Pitt muttered back between gasps.

Now merely bystanders, they sagged to the deck under the gunwales and out of the water that blew over the deck, waiting for their heartbeats to slow and their breathing to come back to normal. They watched as Barnum gave the signal to Brown and the fifty-gallon drums that supported the mooring cables unseen below the surface began to spit out from beneath the hotel. The crane's winch turned, the thin Falcron line took up the slack and the drums began moving. The cable hanging under its steel floats was whipped by the current like a withering snake. Ten minutes later, the leading drums were bumping against the hull. The crane lifted them onto the stern deck along with the ends of both cables. The crew quickly moved in and shackled the ends together through the eyes spliced by Brown. Then, with the added muscle from Pitt and Giordino, who had recovered from their ordeal, they wrapped them around the big tow bit mounted in front of the crane.

"Ready for tow, *Ocean Wanderer*?" announced Barnum between heavy breaths.

"Ready as we'll ever be on this end," came back Brown.

Barnum hailed his chief engineer. "Ready in the engine room?"

"Aye, Captain," came back a heavily Scots-accented brogue.

Then to his first officer in the pilothouse, "Mr. Maverick, I will control from here."

"Acknowledged, Captain. She's all yours."

Barnum stood at a control console mounted forward of the big crane, legs spread apart, a set look on his face. He gripped the two chrome throttle levers and gently eased them ahead while he half turned and stared at the hotel that loomed over the seemingly midget research ship.

Pitt and Giordino stood on opposite sides of Barnum. Every member of the crew and scientific team was standing in the rain on the bridge wing above the waves now, staring at the *Ocean Wanderer* in hushed suspense laced with expectation. The two huge magnetohydrodynamic engines were not connected to shafts leading to propellers. They produced an energy force that pumped water through thrusters for propulsion. Instead of a churning mass of green water thrashing from under the stern, the surface was only stirred by twin rivers of water that roiled the water like horizontal tornadoes.

Sea Sprite's stern dug in and she shuddered under the strain from the tow, the blasting wind and the still-agonized sea. She began to fishtail, but Barnum quickly adjusted the angle of the thrusters and she straightened. For tortured minutes that seemed to last forever, nothing seemed to happen. The hotel appeared as if she was stubbornly continuing her journey toward a tumultuous death.

Below their feet on the stern deck, the engines did not throb and pound like diesels. The pumps that provided power for the thrusters whined like banshees. Barnum scanned the gauges and dials that registered the stress on the engines, not happy at what he saw.

Pitt came over and stood next to Barnum, whose hands bled white as he gripped the throttles and shoved them to their stops and beyond if it had been possible.

"I don't know how much more the engines can take," shouted Barnum above the noise from the wind and shriek from below in the engine room.

"Run the guts out of them," said Pitt, his tone cold and hard as glacial ice. "If they blow, I'll take responsibility."

There was no question of Barnum being the captain of his ship, but Pitt far outranked him in the NUMA hierarchy.

"That's easy for you to say," warned Barnum. "But if they blow, we end up on the rocks, too."

Pitt threw him a grin that was hard as granite. "We'll worry about that when the time comes."

To those on board *Sea Sprite*, the cause was becoming more hopeless with each passing second. It looked as if she was standing dead still in the water.

"Do it!" Pitt pleaded with *Sprite*. "You can do it!"

. . .

O N BOARD the hotel, deep anxiety was creeping over the passengers, followed by a growing panic as they stared in frozen fear at the surf crashing on the nearby rocks in a catastrophic display of raging water and exploding spray. Their mounting terror was accelerated by a sudden tremor as the bottom level of the hotel nudged into the rising seafloor. There was no insane rush to exits as in the event of a fire or an earthquake. There was no place to run. Jumping into the water was more than a simple act of suicide. It meant a horrible and painful death, either by drowning or being smashed to pieces on the jagged black lava rocks.

Morton tried to move about the hotel, calming and reassuring the passengers and his employees, but few paid any heed to him. He felt waves of frustration and defeat. One look out the windows was enough to turn the stoutest heart to paste. Children easily picked up on the fear written on their parents' faces and began crying. A few women screamed, some sobbed, others maintained a stony and blank exterior. The men for the most part were silent in their personal fear, holding their loved ones in their arms and trying to act brave.

The waves beating on the rocks below now came like thunder, but to many it was the toll of drums in a funeral procession.

I N THE pilothouse, Maverick anxiously studied the digital speed indicator. The red numerals seemed frozen on zero. He saw the cables stretch out of the water with their fifty-gallon drums dangling like scales on a sea monster. He was not the only one mentally urging the ship to move. He turned his attention to the Global Positioning System readouts that recorded the exact position of the unit itself within a few feet. The numbers remained static. He glanced down through the rear windows at Barnum standing like a statue at the stern control console, then up at the *Ocean Wanderer*, still beset by the angry sea.

He glanced at the digital anemometer and noted the wind had dropped substantially in the last half hour. "That's a blessing," he muttered to himself.

Then, when he looked at the GPS again, the numbers had altered.

He rubbed his eyes, making sure he wasn't simply imagining a change. The numbers had slowly clicked over. Then he stared at the speed indicator. The digit on the far right was ticking back and forth between zero and one knot.

He stood numbed, wanting desperately to believe what he saw but not sure if it wasn't purely the harvest of an overly optimistic imagination. But the speed indicator didn't lie. There *was* forward movement, no matter how minuscule.

Maverick snatched up a bullhorn and ran out on the bridge wing. "She moved!" he shouted, half mad with excitement. "She's under way!"

Nobody cheered, not yet. Passage through the swirling waves was unreadable to the naked eye, so infinitesimal that they had no way of determining movement. They only had Maverick's word for it. Insufferable minutes passed as hope and excitement mounted as one. Then Maverick shouted again.

"One knot! We're moving at one knot!"

It was not illusory. With crawling awareness, it became apparent that the distance between *Ocean Wanderer* and the frenzied coastline was slowly but steadily widening.

There would be no death or disaster on these rocks this day.

13

SEA SPRITE STRAINED against the mooring cables, driving forward with her engines spinning wildly beyond limits never imagined by her designers. No one on the stern deck was looking at the murderous coastline or the endangered hotel. All eyes were locked on the capstan and the big mooring cables that creaked and groaned under extreme stress. If they snapped, the show was over. There would be no saving the *Ocean Wanderer* and all those within her glass walls.

But inconceivably in everyone's minds, the big cables remained in one piece just as Pitt had calculated.

Very slowly, almost imperceptibly, *Sprite* worked up to a speed of two knots, her bow bucking the great clouds of spray that swept the length of the ship. Only after the hotel had been towed nearly two miles off the cliffs did Barnum ease back on the throttles to relieve the overburdened engines. The danger diminished with each yard gained until the menacing rocks and the wild sea had been solidly cheated out of a major catastrophe.

. . .

THE CREW of *Sea Sprite* waved back at the joyous passengers of *Ocean Wanderer,* who were wildly waving and cheering behind the glass walls. With all fears of death lifted, pandemonium broke loose. Morton ordered the wine cellars opened and champagne was soon flowing in rivers throughout the hotel. To the passengers and his employees, he was the man of the hour. Hotel guests constantly surrounded and thanked him for his efforts in saving them from a horrible death, fully deserved or not.

Stealing away from the joyous bedlam, he returned to his office and sat at his desk in happy exhaustion. As waves of relief swept over him, his mind turned to his future. Though he hated to leave his position as manager of the *Ocean Wanderer,* he knew that any relationship with Specter was a thing of the past. He could never work again for the mysterious character who abandoned so many people who were fundamentally his responsibility.

Morton thought long and hard. There wasn't an international luxury hotel chain in the world that wouldn't hire him once his part in the drama became known. But becoming known and respected for his achievement was a problem.

It didn't take a Nostradamus to predict that once Specter realized the hotel had survived, he would order publicity and public relations people to grind out press releases, set up news conferences and arrange television interviews for the story of how he, Specter, had masterminded the rescue and was the savior of the famed hotel and everyone in it.

Morton decided to grasp his time advantage and leap first. With the hotel phones back in service without interference from the hurricane, he called an old college roommate who owned a public relations company in Washington, D.C., and gave him his rendition of the fabulous saga, graciously giving credit to NUMA and the men who engineered the tow, nor did he fail to mention the brave acts of Emlyn Brown and his maintenance crew. Morton's description of his direction of events during the excitement, however, was not exactly modest.

Forty-five minutes later, he set the receiver back in its cradle, placed his hands behind his head and smiled like the famed Cheshire Cat. Specter would counterpunch, to be sure. But once the lead story swept the media and the rescued passengers were interviewed, any follow-up would be diluted.

He downed another glass of champagne and promptly fell asleep.

G OD, that was close," said Barnum quietly.
"Nice work, Paul," said Pitt, slapping him on the back.

"I'm reading two knots," shouted Maverick from the pilothouse bridge wing to the gathering, cheering crowd below.

The rain had let up and the sea, whose surface was carpeted by a heavy chop embellished with a pattern of whitecaps, now lay down with waves of less than ten feet. Hurricane Lizzie, seemingly bored endangering and sinking ships at sea, was now taking out her rage on the town and cities of the Dominican Republic and its neighboring nation of Haiti. Trees were leveled in the Dominican Republic, but the vast majority of the people survived the gale winds in the interior that was still forested. The death toll was less than three hundred.

But the poorer Haitians, burdened with the worst poverty of any nation in the Western Hemisphere, had denuded their countryside of forested growth to make shacks and burn as firewood. Their buildings, run-down from neglect, offered them little protection, and nearly three thousand died before Hurricane Lizzie crossed the island and swept into open water again.

"Shame on you, Captain," Pitt said, laughing.

Barnum looked at him quizzically, so mentally and physically exhausted he could barely mutter, "What's that you say?"

"You're the only one of your crew not wearing a life jacket."

He looked down at his unhindered oil slickers and smiled. "I guess

I got too carried away by the excitement to think of putting one on." He turned and faced forward and spoke through his headset. "Mr. Maverick."

"Sir?"

"The ship is yours. You have control."

"Aye, Captain, the bridge has command."

Barnum turned to Pitt and Giordino. "Well, gentlemen, you saved a lot of lives today. That was a brave thing you did, pulling those cable lines over to *Sprite*."

Both Pitt and Giordino looked genuinely embarrassed.

Then Pitt grinned and said dryly, "It was nothing, really. Just another one of our many accomplishments."

Barnum wasn't fooled by the sarcastic wit. He knew both men well enough to know that they would go to their graves in silence before they ever boasted of what they did this day. "You can make light of the magnitude of your actions if you wish, but I for one think you did a damn fine job. Now, enough talk. Let's go up to the pilothouse and get out of the wet. I could use a cup of coffee."

"Got anything stronger?" asked Giordino.

"I think I can accommodate you. I picked up a bottle of rum for my brother-in-law when we were last in port."

Pitt looked at him. "When did *you* get married?"

Barnum didn't answer, merely smiled and began walking toward the ladder to the bridge.

B EFORE HE TOOK a well-deserved rest, Pitt stepped into the communications room and asked Jar to call young Dirk and Summer. After repeated attempts, Jar looked up and shook his head. "Sorry, Mr. Pitt. They don't respond."

"I don't like the sound of that," Pitt said pensively.

"Could be any number of minor problems," Jar said optimistically. "The storm probably damaged their antennas."

"Let's hope that's all it is."

Pitt walked down a passageway to Barnum's cabin. He and Giordino were sitting at a table enjoying a glass of Gosling's Rum.

"I can't raise *Pisces*," said Pitt.

Barnum and Giordino exchanged concerned glances. Suddenly the happy mood faded. Then Giordino reassured Pitt.

"The habitat is built like a tank. Joe Zavala and I designed her. We built in every possible safety device. No way her hull could be punctured. Not at fifty feet below the storm's surface. Not when we built her to reach a depth of five hundred."

"You're forgetting the hundred-foot waves," said Pitt. "*Pisces* might have sat high and dry during the passing of a trough, but then she could have been smashed off her mounts by a solid wall of water into exposed rock amid the coral. An impact that strong could easily have shattered her view port."

"Possible," Giordino admitted, "but not likely. I specified a reinforced plastic for the view port that could repel a mortar shell."

Barnum's phone buzzed and he took the call from Jar. He rang off and sat down. "We just heard from the captain of one of the *Ocean Wanderer*'s tugs. They left port and should arrive on station in another hour and a half."

Pitt stepped to the chart table and picked up a pair of dividers. He measured the distance between their current position and the *X* marked on the chart that depicted *Pisces*. "An hour and a half for the tugs," he said thoughtfully. "Another half hour to release the mooring cables and be on our way. Then two hours, maybe less at full speed, to the habitat. Slightly more than four hours to reach the site. I pray to God the kids are all right."

"You sound like a distressed father whose daughter is out after midnight," said Giordino, trying to ease Pitt's fears.

"I must agree," added Barnum. "The coral reef would have protected them from the worst of the storm."

Pitt wasn't fully convinced. He began to pace the deck of the pilothouse. "You may both be right," he said quietly. "But the next few hours are going to be the longest of my life."

S UMMER RECLINED on the mattress from her bunk that she had laid on the angled wall of the habitat. Her breath was shallow as she inhaled and exhaled slowly. She made no attempt at exertion in an effort to conserve as much air as possible. She could not help staring out the view port at the brightly colored fish that returned after the turbulence and darted around the habitat, gazing curiously at the creatures inside. She could not help but wonder if this was to be her final vision before death took her by asphyxiation.

Dirk was trying every imaginable scenario for escape. Nothing panned out. Using the remaining air tank to reach the surface was not a practical idea. Even if he could somehow break the main portal, which was doubtful even with a sledgehammer, the water pressure at one hundred and twenty feet was sixty pounds per square inch. It would explode into the interior of the habitat with the force of a cannon blast and assault their bodies with deadly results.

"How much air do we have left?" asked Summer softly.

Dirk looked at the array of gauges. "Two hours, maybe a few minutes more."

"What happened to *Sea Sprite*? Why hasn't Paul come looking for us?"

"The ship is probably out there right now," said Dirk without conviction. "They're searching, but just haven't found us in the crevasse yet."

"Do you think they were lost in the hurricane?"

"Not the *Sprite*," said Dirk in a comforting tone. "No hurricane ever born could send her to the bottom."

They went silent as Dirk turned his attention to repairing the smashed underwater radio transmitter in a futile attempt to get it operational again. There was nothing frenzied about the manner in which he began reassembling the damaged connections. He moved with a steady purpose, coldly concentrating on his work. There was no further talk as they conserved their remaining air, relying on the strength they drew from each other.

It seemed a lifetime passed as the next two hours dragged on endlessly. Above, they could see the sun had returned to sparkle the sea that brushed restlessly over Navidad Bank. Despite Dirk's obstinacy he simply could not repair their communications equipment. Finally, he was forced to give up in defeat.

He felt his breathing become more labored. For the hundredth time he scanned the gauges registering the remaining air in the undamaged tanks. All needles stood fixed on zero. Dirk moved over and gently shook Summer, who had drifted off into a light sleep brought on by the diminishing oxygen left inside *Pisces*.

"Wake up, sis."

Her gray eyes fluttered open and she stared up at him with a calm serenity that raised a quick flare of fraternal love within him that was classic among twins.

"Wake up, sleepyhead. We have to start breathing from the dive tank." He placed the tank between them and passed the mouthpiece of the regulator to her. "Ladies first."

Summer was achingly aware that she and Dirk were facing a situation they could not influence. Helplessness was alien to her. She had always maintained a measure of control throughout her life. This time she was totally powerless and it was pushing her into despondency.

Dirk, on the other hand, was more frustrated than helpless. He felt as though the Fates were undermining his every effort to escape their prison and eventual execution. He kept thinking there had to be a way out before they took their final breath, but he met a dead end with every plan he conceived.

The end, he came to realize, was rapidly crystallizing into dead certainty.

14

THE TOP ARC OF THE SUN was falling below the horizon
and dusk was only minutes away. The winds had fallen from a
violent to a brisk breeze from the east, caressing and darkening the sea.
The tension that had been building up among the crew when they
learned that all communication had been lost with *Pisces* seemed to spill
over *Sea Sprite* like a black cloud. The fear that harm had come to Dirk
and Summer nagged at their minds.

Only one seriously damaged rigid-hull inflatable boat had survived
the hurricane. The other three usually carried by *Sea Sprite* had been
swept away by massive seas. During the high-speed run back to the
original anchorage site off Navidad Bank, the boat was repaired just
enough to carry three divers. Pitt, Giordino and Cristiano Lelasi, a
master diver and equipment engineer from Italy who was aboard *Sprite*
testing a new robotic vehicle, would conduct the search-and-rescue
operation.

The three men were gathered in the ship's conference room along
with most of the crew and concerned scientists. They listened intently
as Barnum described the underwater geology to Pitt and Giordino. He

paused to glance at a big twenty-four-hour clock on one bulkhead. "We should be on site in another hour."

"Since there has been no radio contact," said Giordino, "we must proceed under the belief that *Pisces* was damaged in the hurricane. And if Dirk's theory is correct, there is every reason to believe gigantic waves may have carried the habitat away from her last known position."

Pitt took over. "When we arrive at the habitat's position and it's gone, we'll launch our search using the grids programmed into our GPS computers. We'll fan out, with me in the middle, Al on my right and Cristiano to my left, and comb the bank toward the east."

"Why east?" asked Lelasi.

"The direction the storm was moving when it struck Navidad Bank," answered Pitt.

"I'll bring *Sprite* as close as I dare to the reef," advised Barnum. "I won't anchor, so I can move swiftly if the need arises. As soon as you spot the habitat and assess the position, report her condition."

"Are there any questions?" Pitt asked Lelasi.

The burly Italian shook his head.

Everyone looked at Pitt with deep compassion in their eyes and hearts. This was not a search for strangers. Dirk and Summer had been their shipmates for the past two months and were regarded as much more than simply passing acquaintances or temporary friends. They were all allied in a quest to study and protect the sea. None dared entertain the thought that the brother and sister might have been lost.

"Then let's get started," said Pitt, adding, "God bless you all for your support."

Pitt wanted one thing and one thing only, to find his son and daughter alive and unharmed. Though he had not known they existed the first twenty-two years of their lives, he had nourished a love that had mushroomed in the short time since they had shown up on his doorstep. His only regret, and a deep one, was that he was not present during their childhood. He was also deeply saddened he had not known their mother had been alive those many years.

The only other person in the world who had come to love the children as much as Pitt was Giordino. He was like a loving uncle to them, a sounding board and a hardy plank for them to lean on when their father proved stubborn or overly protective.

The dive team filed out and made their way to the boarding ladder ramp that hung over the hull into the water. A crewman had lowered the battered inflatable boat into the water and set the twin outboard motors popping away at idle.

Pitt and Giordino pulled on full wet suits this time, with reinforced padding at the knees, elbows and shoulders for protection against the sharp coral. They also decided to use air tanks instead of the re-breathing apparatus. Their full face masks were settled over their heads and a check made of their communication phones. Then, carrying their fins in one hand, they descended the ramp and climbed into the boat with their gear. As they boarded, the crewman jumped out and held the boat firmly against the ramp. Pitt stood at the console, took the wheel and eased the twin throttles forward as soon as the crewman cast off the lines.

Pitt had programmed *Pisces*'s last known coordinates into his Global Positioning System instrument and set a direct course for the site less than a quarter of a mile away. Anxious to get there and almost afraid of what he might find, Pitt leaned on the throttles, sending the little boat whipping over the waves at nearly forty knots. When the GPS numbers indicated he was getting close, he slowed and approached their target with the motors idling.

"We should be on it," he announced.

Almost before the words were out of his mouth, Lelasi slipped over the side with a small splash and disappeared. In three minutes he was back on the surface. Gripping a hand rope on the gunwale, he hoisted himself into the boat, air tanks and all, with one hand and rolled onto the bottom.

Giordino surveyed the feat with amused interest. "I wonder if I can still do that."

"I know I can't," said Pitt. Then he knelt beside Lelasi, who shook his head and spoke through his headphone.

"Sorry, *signore*," he spoke in accented Italian. "The habitat is gone. I saw nothing but a few scattered tanks and some small debris."

"No way of telling their exact position," said Giordino soberly. "Giant waves could have carried them more than a mile."

"Then we follow," Cristiano said hopefully. "You were right, Signor Pitt. The coral appears crushed and broken in a trail toward the east."

"To save time, we'll search from the surface. Stick your heads over the sides. Al, you take the starboard. Cristiano, the port. Guide me by voice and point toward the trail of broken coral. I'll steer by your directions."

Hanging over the rounded hull of the inflatable, Giordino and Lelasi peered through their face masks into the water and traced the path of the storm-swept habitat. Pitt steered as if in a trance. Subconsciously, he aimed the bow toward the course pointed out by Giordino and Lelasi. Consciously, his mind wandered over the past two years since his son and daughter had entered his adventurous but sometimes lonely existence. He recalled the moment he met their mother in the venerable old Ala Moana Hotel on Waikiki Beach. He had been seated in the cocktail lounge in conversation with Admiral Sandecker's daughter when she appeared like a vision, her long flaming red hair cascading down her back. Her perfect body was encased in a tight, green silk Chinese-style dress split up the legs on the sides. The contrast was breathtaking. A solid bachelor who never believed in love at first sight, he knew in an instant that he was ready to die for love. Sadly, he thought she had drowned when her father's underwater dwelling off the north shore of Hawaii collapsed in an earthquake. She swam to the surface with him, but then, before he could stop her, she returned beneath the sea in an attempt to rescue her father.

He never saw her again.

"The smashed coral ends fifty feet dead ahead!" Giordino yelled, lifting his head from the water.

"Have you spotted the habitat?" Pitt demanded.

"There's no sign of it."

Pitt refused to believe him. "It couldn't have disappeared. It has to be there."

In another minute it was Lelasi's turn to shout. "I have it! I have it!"

"I see it too," said Giordino. "It's fallen into a narrow canyon. Looks like it's lying at a depth of about a hundred and ten feet."

Pitt turned off the ignition and shut the motors down. He nodded at Lelasi. "Throw out a buoy to mark the position, and mind the boat. Al and I are going down."

Already geared up, all he needed to do was slip on his fins. He pulled them over his boots and went over the side without wasting another moment. He raised his feet and eased downward through a cloud of bubbles that burst with his entry into the water. The walls of the crevasse were so narrow he found it astonishing that the habitat had fallen to the bottom without becoming lodged against the narrow walls.

The old familiar fingers of foreboding started clawing at his stomach until he stopped all movement for a moment and drew a deep breath to prepare himself for what he hoped he wouldn't find. But he couldn't shake the thought from his mind that he might arrive too late to save them.

From above as he approached, the habitat appeared to be intact. Not surprising, considering its substantial construction. Giordino arrived and motioned toward the damaged entry lock that was smashed and jammed against the coral. Pitt gestured that he saw it too. Then his breath stopped for an instant and his heart increased its beat when he spied the badly damaged tanks that supplied air to the interior. Oh God, no, he thought as he kicked down and swung around to face the big view portal. Please may they not have run out of air.

Fearful that they were not in time, he pressed his face mask against the thick plastic, his eyes trying to penetrate the gloom inside. There was a weird half-light that filtered down through the crevasse from the surface and it was like looking into a mist-shrouded cave.

He could just make out Summer lying inert on blankets on the bottom side of the habitat. It looked to him as though Dirk was leaning against the upturned floor beside her, but propped on his elbows, leaning over her. Pitt's heart leaped when he saw Dirk move. He was in the act of passing an air regulator from his mouth to hers. Overjoyed at finding his children alive, he rapped the hilt of his dive knife wildly against the view port.

T HE PRESSURE GAUGE on the tank was in the red. The end was now only a few short minutes away.

Summer and Dirk inhaled and exhaled slowly in measured breaths to stretch their diminishing air supply as long as they could. The water outside had turned from blue-green to a gray-green as the light from the setting sun faded. He glanced at his SUB 300T orange-faced Doxa dive watch given to him by his father—7:47 P.M. They had been alone in the habitat without communication from the outside world for nearly sixteen hours.

Summer lay in a semisleep. She opened her eyes only when it was her turn to take a few breaths from the tank through the regulator, while Dirk held his, absorbing every molecule of air in his lungs. She thought she saw a movement beyond the view port. At first her fogged mind thought it was merely a large fish, but then she heard a rapping sound on the hard transparent surface. Abruptly, she sat up and stared over Dirk's shoulder.

A diver was hovering outside. He pressed his face mask against the port and waved excitedly. Seconds later, he was joined by another diver, who made happy animated motions at finding life inside the habitat.

Summer thought that she had entered a happy mood of twilight delirium but then she became aware that the men she saw in the water were real. "Dirk!" she cried. "They're here, they've found us!"

He turned and blinked in dazed relief. Then a wild realization set in as he recognized the two divers outside the port. "Oh my God, it's Dad and Uncle Al!"

They both placed their hands on the view port and laughed in exhilaration as Pitt held his gloved hands in the same position outside. Then he took a slate from his belt and wrote two words before holding it up:

YOUR AIR?

Dirk frantically searched through the jumbled mess inside *Pisces* until he found a felt pen and a pad of paper. He wrote in large letters and pressed the pad against the port:

10 MAYBE 15 MINUTES LEFT.

THAT'S CUTTING IT pretty fine," Giordino said over his headphone.

"Damned fine," Pitt agreed.

"No way we can break the view port before their air runs out." Giordino spoke words that sickened him but had to be said. "Nothing short of a missile could blast through the view port. And even if it was possible, the water pressure at this depth would erupt into the habitat like dynamite exploding inside a pipe. The surge would crush them."

Giordino never ceased to be amazed at Pitt's cold, calculating mind. Another man might have panicked at knowing his son and daughter had only minutes before dying an agonizing death. Not Pitt. He hung poised in the water as if he was contemplating the languid movements of a tropical fish. For several seconds he seemed placid and unmotivated. When he spoke, it was in an even, distinct tone.

"Paul, are you reading me?"

"I hear and understand your dilemma. What can I do from this end?"

"I assume your tool locker is equipped with a Morphon underwater bore."

"Yes, I'm pretty sure we have one on board."

"Have it ready at the ramp when we arrive and make sure the drill is fitted with its largest circular cutting bit."

"Anything else?"

"We could use an extra pair of air tanks with regulators."

"All will be waiting when you arrive."

Then Pitt wrote on his slate and held it up in front of the view port:

HANG IN. BACK IN 10 MINUTES.

Then he and Giordino rose out of sight and vanished above.

WHEN PITT and Giordino ascended to the surface and vanished from view, it was as though a rainstorm had fallen on a surprise birthday party out on a lawn. Their hopes had soared at seeing their father and his best friend, but with them gone everything turned bleak again.

"I wish they hadn't left," Summer said softly.

"Not to worry. They know the score on our air. They'll be back before you know it."

"How do you suppose they're going to get us out?" Summer wondered aloud.

"If anybody can pull off a miracle, Dad and Al can."

She looked at the needle on the air tank gauge. It was quivering agonizingly closer to the end. "They'd better do it quick," she murmured softly.

B ARNUM HAD the spare tanks and the Morphon underwater drill waiting as Pitt rushed back to the ship. Expertly turning the speeding boat on a dime, Pitt brought the boat to an abrupt stop beside the ramp.

"Thank you, Paul," he said.

"I aim to please," Barnum replied, with a tight smile.

No sooner was the gear stowed on board than Pitt jammed the throttles forward and charged back to the buoy floating over *Pisces*.

Lelasi threw out an anchor, as Pitt and Giordino adjusted their full face masks and fell over backward into the water. Pitt had not inflated his buoyancy compensator to obtain neutral buoyancy with the heavy twenty-pound Morphon drill. He allowed its mass to drag him to the bottom in little less than a minute, equalizing his ears as he descended. As soon as his feet were firmly planted in the sandy bottom of the crevasse, he pressed the circular cutting edge of the drill against the view port.

Before he switched the drill to rotate, he peered inside. Summer looked like she was semiconscious. Dirk waved feebly. Swiftly, Pitt laid aside the drill and wrote on his slate:

WILL DRILL HOLE FOR AIR
TANKS. STAY CLEAR OF
INCOMING TORRENT.

With precious few minutes to spare, Pitt pushed the drill against the view port and squeezed the trigger, hoping against hope the bit would penetrate the transparent material with nearly the tensile strength of steel. The whirring sound of the drill motor, magnified underwater, and the rasp of the bit as it attacked the view port startled every fish within a hundred yards and sent them darting throughout the reef.

Pitt leaned against the drill and pushed with every muscle in his legs and arms. He was thankful when Giordino dug his knees into the sand, hunched beneath Pitt and placed his hands on the forward, cylindrical section of the drill, adding his strength to the effort.

Minute crawled after minute as the two men leaned against the drill with all their might. They didn't talk to each other. They didn't have to. Each had read the other's mind for more than forty years. They worked like a matched pair of draft horses.

Pitt bordered on frantic when he could see no more movement within the habitat. The deeper into the view port the bit bored, the faster it penetrated. At last Pitt and Giordino felt it burst through. They instantly jerked the drill back. Almost before Pitt could switch it off, Giordino was shoving an air tank and a regulator through the ten-inch-diameter round hole, helped by the water that forced it into the lower air pressure inside.

Pitt wanted to shout for his kids to react, but they could not have heard him. He could see that Summer made no effort to move. He was starting to retrieve the drill to enlarge the hole enough to crawl through, when Dirk weakly reached out for the regulator and clamped his teeth on the mouthpiece. Two deep breaths and he became aroused to normalcy again. He immediately and gently eased the mouthpiece between Summer's lips.

Pitt wanted to cheer in euphoria when he saw Summer's eyes flutter open and her chest began to rise and fall. Though the inrush of water was rapidly filling the interior of the habitat, they now had more than enough air to breathe. He and Giordino picked up the drill again and attacked the view port in an effort to enlarge the hole big enough for the two inside to escape. There was no feverish effort this time. They took turns widening the opening until the circular cuts had grown into a four-leaf clover broad enough for a body to slip through.

"Paul," Pitt called on his headphone.

"I'm listening," Barnum answered.

"The hyperbaric chamber?"

"Ready to receive them the minute they come on board."

"At what depth and how long have they been down on *Pisces*?"

"They've been pressurized at sixty feet for three days and four-teen hours."

"Then they'll need at least fifteen hours of decompression."

"Whatever time it takes," said Barnum. "I have an expert on hy-perbaric medicine on board. He'll compute their decompression time."

Giordino signaled that he had finished drilling the final hole. The interior of the habitat was nearly filled with water now, the condensed air pressure restricting the flow. He reached in, took Summer by the hand and pulled her outside. Dirk passed through one of the air tanks. Summer started to wrap her arms around it and inhale through the mouthpiece of the regulator. Then, suddenly, she waved her hands in a wait signal and disappeared back inside the habitat. She quickly reap-peared, clutching her notebooks, computer disks and the digital cam-era in a watertight plastic bag. Giordino took her by the arm and led her up to the surface.

Dirk came next with the second spare tank. Pitt gave him a quick embrace before they ascended together toward the only remaining in-flatable. No sooner were the brother and sister pulled safely into the boat than Cristiano pushed the throttles forward and sped off toward the research ship. Pitt and Giordino, saving a couple of minutes by not climbing aboard too, remained in the water and pushed themselves clear before being chopped by the spinning propellers.

When Lelasi returned and picked them up, Pitt's son and daughter were already inside the hyperbaric chamber. The basis behind de-compression sickness, or what is known as the bends, is that under normal air pressure the body respires most of its excess nitrogen. However, under increasing pressure as a diver descends, nitrogen in-creases in the bloodstream. As a diver ascends and the surrounding water pressure decreases, pure nitrogen bubbles form in the blood and eventually become too large to pass through tissue. In order for the bubbles to diffuse and pass through lung tissue, the diver must sit inside a chamber that very slowly decreases pressure while breathing one hundred percent oxygen.

Dirk and Summer passed the long hours inside the chamber reading and writing reports on their findings about the dying coral and the brown crud, as well as recording their impressions of the cavern with the ancient artifacts, all while being monitored by the hyperbaric physician.

THE STARS glittered like diamonds and the lights of the high-rise condominiums beamed as *Sea Sprite* sailed into Fort Lauderdale's Port Everglades, one of the busiest deepwater ports in the world. The research ship's deck lights blazed as she slowly sailed past a long line of luxury cruise ships loading passengers and supplies for a morning departure. Alerted by the Coast Guard, every ship in the harbor blew three blasts of their whistles and air horns in salute as *Sprite* passed on her way to the NUMA dock facilities.

Her epic rescue of the *Ocean Wanderer* and her thousand guests forty-eight hours earlier was worldwide news. Pitt dreaded the media reception that would be waiting at the dock. He leaned over the railing on the bow and watched the black water, streaked by flashes of light that sparkled white off the bow. He became aware of a figure beside him, and he turned and looked into the smiling face of his son. It never ceased to amaze him that it was like looking into a mirror of himself twenty-five years ago.

"What do you think they'll do with her?" Dirk asked.

Pitt's eyebrows raised. "Do with what?"

"*Pisces.*"

"The decision whether to salvage her or not rests with Admiral Sandecker. Getting a barge with a crane over the coral might prove impossible. And even if it could be done, pulling sixty-five tons of dead-weight up through the narrow confines of the crevasse might prove cost-prohibitive. Chances are the admiral may simply write it off."

"I wish I could have been there to see you and Al drag the lines tied to the hotel's mooring cables to *Sea Sprite*."

Pitt smiled. "I doubt if either one of us would volunteer to attempt it again."

It was Dirk's turn to smile. "I'd have to bet against you on that one."

Pitt turned and leaned his back against the railing. "Are you and Summer fully recuperated?"

"We passed our balance and comparative sensitivity tests with flying colors and have no sign of aftereffects."

"Different symptoms can turn up days or weeks later. Better you and your sister take it easy for a while. In the meantime, if you're so anxious for something to do, I'll give you a chore."

Dirk gave his dad a suspicious look. "Like what?"

"I'll arrange a meeting with St. Julien Perlmutter. You two can work with him to come up with answers about those ancient artifacts you found on Navidad Bank."

"We really need to go back and further investigate what we found in the cavern."

"That can also be arranged," Pitt assured him. "But all in good time. There's no deadline."

"And the brown crud that's killing the sea life around the bank?" Dirk persisted. "It can't be ignored."

"Another NUMA expedition with a new crew and different research ship will be assembled to return and study the scourge."

Dirk turned and looked across the port at the lights dancing on the water. "I wish we had more time to spend together," he said wistfully.

"How about a fishing trip in the north woods of Canada?" Pitt suggested.

"Sounds good to me."

"I'll work on Sandecker. After what we all achieved in the past few days, I don't think he'll deny us a little time off for pleasure."

Giordino and Summer came and joined them at the railing, waving to the ships they passed that signaled their praise for a job well done. The *Sprite* rounded a bend and the NUMA dock came into view. As Pitt feared, it was crowded with TV vans and reporters.

Barnum eased the ship alongside the dock, the lines were thrown down and looped on the bollards. Then the boarding ramp was lowered. Admiral James Sandecker charged onto the ship like a fox chasing a chicken. He almost looked like a fox with his narrow features, flaming red hair and Vandyke beard. He was followed by the deputy director of NUMA, Rudi Gunn, the administrative genius behind the agency.

Barnum greeted the admiral as he stepped on board. "Welcome aboard, Admiral. I didn't expect to see you."

Sandecker waved an arm airily over the dock and mob of newspeople and beamed. "I wouldn't have missed this for the world." Then he vigorously shook Barnum's hand. "A magnificent job, Captain. All NUMA is proud of you and your crew."

"It was a team effort," Barnum said humbly. "Without the heroic transfer of the mooring cables by Pitt and Giordino, the *Ocean Wanderer* would have surely smashed onto the rocks."

Sandecker spotted Pitt and Giordino and walked over to them. "Well," he said testily, "another day, another dollar. You two never seem able to stay out of trouble."

Pitt knew that was the finest compliment the admiral would pay him. "Let's just say that we were lucky to have been on a project off Puerto Rico when Heidi Lisherness called from our hurricane center in Key West and described the situation."

"Thank God you were able fly to the scene in time to help avert a major tragedy," said Gunn. He was a short little man with thick horn-rim glasses, blessed with a friendly disposition, a man whom everyone immediately liked.

"Luck played a major role," Giordino said unpretentiously.

Dirk and Summer approached and were greeted by Sandecker. "You two seem fit after your ordeal."

"If Dad and Al hadn't gotten us out of *Pisces* when they did," said Summer, "we wouldn't be standing here."

Sandecker's smile seemed cynical, but his eyes were filled with pride. "Yes, it seems that good-deed-doer's work never ends."

"Which brings me to a request," said Pitt.

"Request denied," replied Sandecker, reading his mind. "You people can put in for a restful vacation as soon as you finish the next project."

Giordino stared sullenly at the admiral. "You're an evil old man."

Sandecker ignored the slur. "Soon as you all get your things together, Rudi will drive you to the airport. I have a NUMA jet waiting to fly you to Washington. It's pressurized, so Dirk and Summer shouldn't have any complications from their recent decompression. We'll all meet in my office at noon tomorrow."

"I hope you have beds on the airplane, because that's the only sleep we're going to get," Giordino came back.

"Are you flying with us, Admiral?" asked Summer.

He grinned craftily. "Me? No, I'll follow on another plane." He motioned toward the waiting reporters. "Somebody has to sacrifice himself on the altar of the news media."

Giordino pulled a cigar from his breast pocket that looked suspiciously like one of Sandecker's private brand. He gazed cagily at the admiral as he lit the end. "Make sure they spell our names right."

H EIDI LISHERNESS sat staring unseeing at the array of monitors showing a dying Hurricane Lizzie. After swinging southeast and causing havoc with ships traveling through the Caribbean, she slammed into the east coast of Nicaragua between Puerto Cabezas and Punta Gorda. Fortunately, her strength had dropped by half and there were few inhabitants living along the coastline. Before Lizzie traveled fifty miles across the lowland swamps and into the foothills, she had sputtered and finally died, but not before eighteen ships were lost with all hands and three thousand people had been killed, with another ten thousand injured and homeless.

She could only imagine how the death toll might have mushroomed if her forecasts and warnings hadn't been sent out soon after Lizzie was born. She was sitting there, slouched at her desk that was littered with photos, computer analysis reports and a forest of paper coffee cups, when her husband Harley approached through the empty office that looked as though Lizzie had swept through it, leaving an absolute mess for the cleaning people.

"Heidi," he said as he gently placed his hand on her shoulder.

She looked up through reddened eyes. "Oh, Harley. I'm glad you came."

"Come along, old girl, you've done an extraordinary job. Now it's time to let me take you home."

Wearily, thankfully, Heidi came to her feet and leaned on her husband as he walked her out of the paper-strewn offices of the Hurricane Center. At the door she turned and took a last look, focusing on a large strip of paper pinned on one wall that someone had written on. The block lettering read: IF YOU KNEW LIZZIE LIKE WE KNOW LIZZIE, OH, OH, OH WHAT A STORM.

She smiled to herself and switched off the lights, sending the big storm center room into darkness.

PART TWO

What Now?

THE WHITE HORSE OF UFFINGTON

15

THE AIR WAS HOT and damp with humidity that hung heavy
without a breeze. The sky was cobalt blue with white clouds
marching across it like a herd of sheep. Except for the tourists, the city
simmered at a slow pace in the middle of summer. Congress used any
excuse for a recess to escape the heat and soggy air, holding sessions
only when it thought it was either absolutely necessary or when it polished its members' image, as busy bees in the voters' eyes. To Pitt, as
he stepped off the NUMA Citation jet, the atmosphere was little different from the tropics he'd come from. The private government airport a few miles north of the city was empty of other aircraft, as
Giordino, Dirk and Summer followed him down the boarding stairs
to the black asphalt that felt hot enough to fry Spam.

The only vehicle waiting on the aircraft parking strip was a prodi-
gious 1931 Marmon town car with a V-16 engine. It was a wondrous
vehicle with style and class, technically superior in its time, noble and
elegant. One of only 390 Marmon V-16s built, it was magically

smooth and silent, its big engine putting out 192 horsepower with 407 foot-pounds of torque. Painted a dusty rose, the coachwork was perfectly in tune with Marmon's advertising as "The World's Most Advanced Motor Car."

Every bit as lovely and stylish as the car was the woman standing beside it. Tall and captivating, cinnamon hair glinting in the sun and falling to her shoulders, framing a soft beautiful face with a model's high cheekbones that were enhanced by soft violet eyes, Congresswoman Loren Smith stood cool and radiant. She was wearing a white lace patch blouse cut to show off her natural curves over matching asana pants cut loose with flared legs that dropped slightly over white canvas sneakers. She waved, smiled and ran over to Pitt. She looked up at him and kissed him lightly on the lips. Then stood back.

"Welcome home, sailor."

"I wish I had a dollar for every time you've said that."

"You'd be a rich man," she said with a cute laugh. Then she hugged Giordino, Summer and Dirk. "I hear you all had a big adventure."

"If not for Dad and Al," said Dirk, "Summer and I would be wearing wings."

"After you settle in, I want you to tell me all about it."

They carried their luggage and duffel bags to the car, threw some in the humpbacked trunk and the rest on the floor of the rear seat. Loren slipped behind the wheel that sat in the open air while Pitt moved into the passenger's side. The rest shared the enclosed rear compartment behind the divider window.

"Are we dropping Al off at his condo in Alexandria?" she asked.

Pitt nodded. "Then we can head for the hangar and clean up. The admiral wants us in his office by noon."

Loren looked down at the clock on the instrument panel. The hands read: 10:25. Frowning as she expertly, smoothly, shifted through the gears, she said caustically, "No time to relax before going back to work? After what the four of you have been through, isn't he crowding you a bit?"

"You know as well as I that beneath his sandpaper exterior beats the heart of a considerate man. He wouldn't insist on a deadline unless it was important."

"Still," Loren said, as the car was waved through the armed security guard at the airport gate, "he could have given you twenty-four hours to rejuvenate."

"We'll know soon enough what's on his mind," Pitt muttered, doing his best to keep from dozing off.

Fifteen minutes later, Loren drove up to the gated condominium complex where Giordino lived. A bachelor who had yet to marry, he seemed in no hurry to take the big step, preferring to spread his frosting on the cake, as he put it. Loren had seldom seen him with the same lady twice. She had introduced him to her lady friends, who all found him charming and interesting, but after a while he always drifted off to someone else. Pitt always likened him to a prospector wandering a tropical paradise for gold but never finding it on the beach under the palm trees.

Giordino retrieved his duffel bag and waved. "See you again soon . . . too soon."

The drive to Pitt's aircraft hangar apartment at one deserted end of Ronald Reagan National Airport was traffic-free. Again, they were waved through a security gate when the guard recognized Pitt. Loren stopped at the old hangar once used by a long-extinct airline in the nineteen thirties and forties. Pitt had purchased it to store his old-car collection and remodeled the upper offices into an apartment. Dirk and Summer lived on the main floor that also housed his fifty-car collection, a pair of old aircraft and a railroad Pullman car that he'd found in a cave in New York.

Loren braked the Marmon in front of the main door as Pitt used his remote to disengage his complicated alarm system. Then the door raised and she drove inside and parked in the middle of the incredible array of beautiful old classic automobiles dating from the earliest, a 1918 V-8 Cadillac, to a 1955 Rolls-Royce Hooper-bodied Silver

Dawn. Sitting on a white epoxy floor and illuminated by skylights above, the old cars radiated a dazzling rainbow of colors.

Dirk and Summer retired to their separate compartments in the Pullman car while Pitt and Loren went up to his apartment, where he showered and shaved as she fixed a light brunch for the four of them. Thirty minutes later, Pitt exited his bedroom, dressed in casual slacks and golf shirt. He sat down at his kitchen table as Loren handed him a Ramos Fizz.

"Have you ever heard of a big corporation called Odyssey?" he asked Loren out of the blue.

She looked at him for a moment. "Yes, I'm on a congressional committee that has looked into its operations. It's not an agenda that's being covered by the news media. What do you know about our investigation?"

He shrugged casually. "Absolutely nothing. I wasn't aware of your congressional involvement with Specter."

"The corporation's nebulous founder? Then why did you ask?"

"Curiosity. Nothing more. Specter owned the hotel Al and I helped save from being carried onto the rocks by Hurricane Lizzie."

"Other than the fact he heads a vast scientific research facility in Nicaragua and is involved with huge construction projects and mining operations around the world, very little is known about him. Some of his international dealings are legitimate, others are very shady."

"What are his projects in the U.S.?"

"Water canals through the southwest deserts and a few dams. That's the extent of it."

"What sort of scientific research projects does Odyssey conduct?" Pitt asked.

Loren shrugged. "Their activities are heavily veiled, and since their facility is in Nicaragua, they aren't bound by any laws to report their experiments. Rumor has it they're involved with fuel cell research, but no one knows for certain. Our intelligence people don't see Odyssey as a priority investigation."

"And their construction operations?"

"Mostly underground vaults and warehouse excavation," answered Loren. "The CIA has heard rumors that he's hollowed out caverns for clandestine nuclear and biological weapons manufactured in countries such as North Korea, but there's no proof. A number of their projects are with the Chinese, who want their military research programs and weapons supplies kept secret. Odyssey seems to have made a speciality of building below-the-surface vault warehouses that hide military activity and arms assembly plants from spy satellites."

"Yet Specter built and operated a floating hotel."

"A toy he uses to entertain clients," explained Loren. "He's only in the resort business for the fun of it."

"Who is Specter? The operation's manager for the *Ocean Wanderer* had nothing good to say about him."

"He must not like his job."

"Not that. He told me he would no longer work for Specter, because he ran from the hotel and flew off in his private plane before the hurricane struck, abandoning the guests and employees, not caring whether they might all die."

"Specter is a very mysterious person. Probably the only corporate executive officer of a giant business who doesn't have a personal publicity agent or public relations firm. He's never given an interview and is rarely seen in public. There are no records of his history, family or schooling."

"Not even a birth record?"

Loren shook her head. "No record of his birth has been found in the U.S. or in any other nation's archives around the world. His true identity has yet to be revealed despite the best efforts of our intelligence agencies. The FBI tried to get a handle on him a few years ago, but came up empty. There are no revealing photographs because his face is always covered by a scarf and heavy sunglasses. They tried to obtain fingerprints, but he wears gloves. Even his closest business

aides have never seen his face. All that is obvious is that he is very
obese, probably weighing more than four hundred pounds."

"Nobody's life or business can remain *that* veiled."

Loren made a helpless gesture with her hands.

Pitt poured himself a cup of coffee. "Where are his corporate headquarters located?"

"Brazil," replied Loren. "He also has a huge office center in
Panama. And because he has made a large investment in the country,
the president of the republic made him a citizen. He also appointed
Specter as a director of the Panama Canal Authority."

"So what is the justification for your congressional probe?" asked
Pitt.

"His dealings with the Chinese. Specter's connection with the People's Republic of China's is a long-standing relationship that goes back
fifteen years. As a director of the Canal Authority, he was instrumen-
tal in helping the Hong Kong–based Whampoa Limited company,
which is tied in with the People's Liberation Army, to obtain a twenty-
five-year option for control of the canal's Atlantic and Pacific Ocean
ports of Balboa and Cristobal. Whampoa will also be in charge of all
loading and unloading of ship cargoes, and the railroad that transports
cargo between the ports, and will soon begin construction on a new
suspension bridge that will be used to truck oversized cargo containers north and south over the Canal Zone."

"What is our government doing about this?"

Loren shook her head. "Nothing that I'm aware of. President Clinton gave the Chinese carte blanche for their influence and expansion
throughout Central America." Then she added, "Another intriguing
thing about the Odyssey Corporation is that its top management is almost entirely staffed by women."

Pitt smiled. "Specter must be idolized by the feminist movement."

Dirk and Summer joined them for a brief late breakfast before they
left for Sandecker's office. This time, Pitt drove one of the turquoise

NUMA Navigators that were part of the fleet of agency vehicles. He stopped at Loren's town house to drop her off.

"Dinner tonight?" he queried.

"Are Dirk and Summer coming too?"

"I might drag the kids," Pitt said, smiling, "but only if you insist."

"I insist." Loren gave his hand a squeeze and elegantly exited the Navigator, stepped lightly to the driveway and walked up the steps to her door.

THE NUMA headquarters building rose thirty stories on a hill above the Potomac River and had a commanding view of the city. Sandecker had personally chosen the site when Congress provided him with the funding to construct the building. It was far more magnificent than officials had originally conceived and ran several million dollars over budget. Because it was on the east side of the river just out of the District of Columbia, the admiral had unaccountably found a skyline free from the building height restrictions and erected a magnificent green glass tubular structure that could be seen from miles around.

Pitt drove into the crowded underground parking and pulled into his reserved slot. They took the elevator up to Sandecker's office on the top floor and exited the elevator into an anteroom paneled with teak decking from old shipwrecks. The admiral's secretary asked if they wouldn't mind waiting a minute since he was in a meeting.

Almost before the words left her lips, the door to the admiral's office opened and two old friends stepped into the anteroom. Kurt Austin, with a premature forest of gray hair, who was Pitt's counterpart as director of special projects, and Joe Zavala, the wiry engineer who often worked on submersible designs and construction with Giordino, stepped forward and shook hands.

"Where is the old geezer sending you two?" asked Giordino.

"Heading for the Canadian north country. There's rumors of mutant fish in some of the lakes. The admiral asked us to check it out."

"We heard about your rescue of the *Ocean Wanderer* in the middle of Hurricane Lizzie," said Zavala. "I didn't expect to see you back in the harness so soon."

"No rest for the weary in Sandecker's book," Pitt said with a half grin.

Austin nodded at Dirk and Summer. "One of these days I'll have you and the kids over for a barbecue."

"I'd like that," accepted Pitt. "I've always wanted to see your antique gun collection."

"And I've yet to see your auto collection."

"Why not arrange a tour? We'll have cocktails and hors d'oeuvres at my place and then drive to your house for the barbecue."

"Consider it a done deal."

Sandecker's secretary approached. "The admiral is ready for you now."

They bid their goodbyes, as Austin and Zavala headed toward the elevators and Pitt's group was ushered into Sandecker's office, where the admiral sat behind an immense desk fashioned from the salvaged hatch cover from a Confederate blockade runner.

A gentleman of the old school, he rose as Summer entered, and motioned her to a chair across from the desk. Amazingly, Giordino had arrived early. He was dressed in casual slacks and a Hawaiian flowered-print shirt. Rudi Gunn came up from his office on the twenty-eighth floor and joined them.

Without prelude, Sandecker launched the meeting. "We have two intriguing problems to deal with. The most important is the brown crud which is spreading throughout the Caribbean, which I'll come to later." He looked across his desk with piercing eyes, first at Summer and then at Dirk. "You two certainly opened up a Pandora's box with your discoveries on Navidad Bank."

"I haven't heard of the test results since Captain Barnum sent the amphor to the lab," said Summer.

"The lab is still in the process of cleaning it," clarified Gunn. "It was Hiram Yaeger and his computer magic that established a date and culture."

Before Summer could ask, Sandecker said, "Hiram dated the amphor sometime prior to eleven hundred B.C. He also established that it was Celtic."

"Celtic?" Summer echoed. "Is he sure?"

"It matches every other amphor known to have been created by ancient Celts around three thousand years ago."

"What about the comb we photographed?" asked Summer.

"Without having the actual objects to study," answered Sandecker, "Hiram's computer could only make an approximation as to the date. However, his best guess is they're also three thousand years old."

"Where does Yaeger think the artifact came from?" queried Pitt.

Sandecker stared at the ceiling. "Since the Celts weren't a seafaring people and are not known to have sailed across the Atlantic to the new world, it must have been thrown or lost off a passing ship."

"No ships sailed over Navidad Bank unless they wanted to have their hulls ripped apart by shallow coral and file a phony insurance claim," said Pitt. "The only other possibility is that the ship was driven onto the bank by a storm."

Gunn gazed down at the carpet as if something had entered his mind. "According to insurance records, an old steamer called *Vandalia* smashed onto the reef."

"I surveyed her remains," said Summer, looking at her brother expectantly.

Dirk nodded at her and grinned. "The amphor was not all we found."

"What Dirk is hinting is that we also discovered a labyrinth of caverns or rooms carved from rock that is now covered with the coral." She reached into her purse and retrieved the digital camera. "We took pictures of the architecture and a large cauldron sculpted with images of ancient warriors. It was filled with small, everyday artifacts."

Sandecker looked at her in disbelief. "A city beneath the sea in the Western Hemisphere predating the Olmecs, Mayans and Incas? It doesn't seem possible."

"We won't have answers until a thorough exploration is conducted." Summer held the camera as if it was a piece of expensive jewelry. "The structure we observed looked like some sort of temple."

Sandecker turned to Gunn. "Rudi?"

Gunn nodded in understanding, took the camera from Summer's hand and pushed a switch on the wall that raised a panel, revealing a large digital television. He then connected the cable into the TV, picked up the remote and began running through the images recorded by Dirk and Summer of the sunken temple.

There were more than thirty images, beginning with the entry arch and the steps leading to the interior with what looked like a large stone bed. The cauldron and its contents were in another chamber.

Dirk and Summer narrated as Gunn moved from one picture to the next. When the last image flashed on the monitor, they all sat silently for a few moments.

Finally, Pitt spoke first. "I think we should get St. Julien Perlmutter in on this."

Gunn looked skeptical. "St. Julien isn't an archaeologist."

"True, but if anyone has theories on early seafarers and navigators sailing to this side of the ocean three thousand years ago, he would."

"Worth a shot," Sandecker agreed. He looked at Dirk and Summer. "Your research project for the next two weeks. Find answers. Consider it a working vacation." He swung in his big leather executive's chair until he faced Pitt and Giordino. "And now to the matter of the brown crud. All we know at this moment is that it is not associated with a diatom or a form of algae. Nor is it a biotoxin linked to the red tide phenomenon. What we *do* know is that it leaves a swath of devastation as it is carried out into the open Atlantic and swept north by the southern equatorial current toward the Gulf and Florida. Ocean scientists believe the crud has already reached American waters. Reports coming in from Key West say sponge beds are suffering from an unknown source of devastation."

"I'm sorry the glass jars containing my water samples and dead sea life specimens were destroyed when the waves tumbled *Pisces* into the crevasse," said Summer.

"Don't concern yourself. We have samples and specimens coming in daily from fifty different locations throughout the Caribbean."

"Any indications where the crud might originate?" asked Pitt.

Gunn pulled off his glasses and wiped the lenses with a small cloth. "Not really. Our scientists have sorted through water samples, wind and current data, satellite images and ship sightings. Their best guess at the moment is that the crud is spawned somewhere off the coast of Nicaragua. But that's all it is, a guess."

"Could it be some kind of chemical flushed from a river?" inquired Dirk.

Sandecker rolled one of his immense cigars in his fingers without lighting it. "Possible, but we have yet to discover a trail to its source."

"Something nasty is going on," said Gunn. "This stuff is deadly to most sea life and the coral. We've got to find a solution soon before it spreads out of control throughout the entire Caribbean and creates a sea of sludge and a dead zone for all water life."

Pitt stared at Gunn. "You don't paint a very pretty picture."

"The source must be found and a counteraction developed," added Sandecker. "That's where you and Al come in. Your mission is to investigate the waters off the west coast of Nicaragua. I've lined up one of NUMA's Neptune-class research vessels. I don't have to tell you that she's small, requiring no more than a five-man crew. She carries the latest state-of-the-art research equipment and instrumentation for specialized projects such as this one. Unlike our other ocean research and survey ships, she's as fast as anything in the oceans, with speed to spare."

"Like the *Calliope* we were forced to destroy several years ago on the Niger River?" said Pitt without looking up as he took notes on a yellow pad.

"I should have taken the cost of losing her out of your paychecks."

"If it's all the same to you, Admiral, Al and I would rather not be quite so conspicuous this time."

"You won't be," Sandecker said, ignoring the nonsmokers and finally lighting his cigar. "The *Poco Bonito* is my pride and joy. She's seventy-five feet in length and her appearance is misleading. No one will find her conspicuous, because her hull, deck and wheelhouse was based on a Buckie, Scotland–built fishing trawler."

Pitt was continually taken in by Sandecker's fascination with odd and creative vessels. "An oceanographic research vessel disguised like a fishing boat. That has to be a new first."

"A Scots-built fishing trawler will stand out in the Caribbean like a street derelict at a debutante ball," said Giordino dubiously.

"Not to worry," replied Sandecker. "The superstructure of *Poco Bonito* is electronically designed to automatically alter her appearance to fit in with any fishing fleet in the world."

Pitt stared at the carpet, trying to visualize such a vessel. "If my high school Spanish serves me correctly, *Poco Bonita* means 'little tuna.'"

Sandecker nodded. "I thought it appropriate."

"Why all the subterfuge?" asked Pitt. "We're not entering a war zone."

Sandecker gave him a cagey look that Pitt knew too well. "You never know when you might cross paths with a ghost ship full of phantom pirates."

Pitt and Giordino both gazed at the admiral as if he'd just claimed to have flown to Mars and back. "A ghost ship," Pitt repeated sardonically.

"You've never heard of the legend of the Wandering Buccaneer?"

"Not lately."

"Leigh Hunt was an unscrupulous freebooter and pirate who ravaged the West Indies in the late seventeenth century, preying on every ship he came upon, be it Spanish, English or French. A giant of a man, he made Blackbeard look like a sissy. Tales of his brutality were legend throughout the Spanish Main. Crews of merchant ships he captured were known to have killed themselves before surrendering to Hunt. His favorite pastime was dragging unfortunate captives behind his ship until the ropes were pulled in empty after the sharks took them."

"He sounds like an old salt I know," muttered Giordino testily.

Sandecker continued as if he hadn't heard the gibe. "Hunt's reign of terror lasted fifteen years until he attempted to capture a British warship disguised to look like a helpless merchantman. Taken in, Hunt raised his Jolly Roger flag with a black background and skull with blood streaming from the eyes and teeth and sent a shot across the Britishers' bow. Then, just as he pulled alongside, the British raised their gunports and poured a series of murderous broadsides into Hunt's ship, which was named the *Scourge*. After a furious battle the pirates were decimated. A company of British marines then swarmed aboard the pirate vessel and made short work of its crew."

"Was Hunt still alive after the battle?" asked Summer.

"Unfortunately for him, yes."

Dirk ran his fingers over Sandecker's old worn desk. "Did the British treat him in kind and drag him behind their ship?" asked Dirk.

"No," replied Sandecker. "The captain had lost a brother to Hunt two years before, so he was set on revenge. He ordered Hunt's feet cut off. Then he was strung up by a rope and lowered over the side until his bloody stumps were only a foot from the water. It was only a matter of time before the sharks got the scent of blood and leaped out of the water, jaws snapping until only Hunt's hands and arms were left hanging by the rope."

Summer's pretty face altered to an expression of repulsion. "That's disgusting."

Dirk disagreed. "Sounds to me like he got what he deserved."

"Enlighten me, Admiral," said Giordino, fighting to keep awake. "What has this pirate got to do with anything?"

Sandecker smiled crookedly. "Like the *Flying Dutchman*, Leigh Hunt and his crew of bloodthirsty pirates still roam the waters you'll be working."

"Sez who?"

"Over the past three years there has been any number of sightings by ships, pleasure craft and fishing boats. Some radioed that they were being attacked by a haunted sailing ship with a ghostly crew before they disappeared with all hands."

Pitt looked at Sandecker. "You've got to be joking."

"I'm not." The admiral was decisive. "Since you have a doubting mind, I'll send you the reports."

"Make a note," Giordino said acidly, "to stock up on wooden stakes and silver bullets."

"A phantom ship with a skeletal crew sailing through a sea of brown crud." Pitt gazed pensively out the window at the Potomac River below. Then he shrugged resignedly. "Now there's a sight to take to the grave."

16

PITT DECIDED TO DRIVE everyone to the restaurant in the elegant old Marmon. It was a warm evening, so the three men sat together in the open front seat while the women sat in the back to keep their hair from getting windblown. The men wore light sport coats over slacks. The women dressed in a variety of light summery dresses.

Giordino brought his current lady friend, Micky Levy, who worked for a Washington-based mining company. She had soft facial features with dark skin and wide brown eyes. Her long black hair was done in curled strands wound into a crown. She wore a small hibiscus blossom behind her left ear. She spoke in a soft voice that had a slight trace of an Israeli accent.

"What a marvelous car," she said after Giordino made the introductions. She entered through the rear door held open by Giordino and sat next to Summer.

"You'll have to bear with my friend," said Giordino dryly. "He can't go anywhere without pomp and circumstance."

"Sorry, no trumpets or drumroll," Pitt retorted. "My band has the night off."

With the divider window between the seats rolled up to shield the breeze, the women chatted on the way to the restaurant. Loren and Summer learned that Micky was born and raised in Jerusalem and that she had obtained her master's degree at the Colorado School of Mines.

"So you're a geologist," said Summer.

"A structural geologist," replied Micky. "I specialize in conducting analysis for engineers who have plans for an excavation project. I investigate water seepage and underground channels into deeper zones and aquifers, so they can be aware of possible flooding while boring their tunnels."

"Sounds positively dull," said Loren in a nice way. "I took a geology course in college to satisfy the scientific requirements for a degree in social economics. I thought it would be interesting. Was I ever wrong. Geology is about as fascinating as bookkeeping."

Micky laughed. "Fortunately, working in the field is not quite as banal."

"Did Dad say where he's taking us to dinner?" Summer asked.

Loren shook her head. "He didn't say anything to me."

TWENTY-FIVE minutes later, Pitt turned into the driveway of L'Auberge Chez François restaurant in Great Falls, Virginia. The Alsatian architecture and interior decor exuded a warm, comfortable atmosphere. He parked the car and they walked through the front door, where one of the family who owned the restaurant checked Pitt's name off on the reservation sheet and escorted them to a table for six in a small alcove.

Pitt spotted some old friends—Clyde Smith and his lovely wife, Paula—and conversed briefly. Smith had been with NUMA almost as long as Pitt, but in the financial section of the agency. After everyone was seated, the waiter arrived and announced the evening's specials. Skipping cocktails, Pitt went right to the wine, ordering a hearty Sparr Pinot Noir. He then ordered a game platter for the table as an appetizer consisting of deer, antelope, breast of pheasant, rabbit and quail with wild mushrooms and chestnuts.

While they savored the wine and enjoyed the huge game appetizer, Loren reported on the latest buzz in Washington politics. They all listened in rapt attention at hearing the inside gossip from a member of Congress. She was followed by Dirk and Summer, who told of their discovery of the ancient temple and artifacts, ending with their near-death experience on Navidad Bank during the hurricane. Pitt interrupted to notify them that he had called St. Julien Perlmutter and let him know that his son and daughter would be stopping by to tap his vast knowledge of ships and the sea.

The entrees came that any lover of French cooking would heartily approve. Pitt ordered the kidneys and mushrooms in a sauce of sherry and mustard. Calves' brain and exotic veal tongue were also on the menu, but the women weren't up to it. Giordino and Micky shared the rack of lamb while Dirk and Summer tried the *choucroute garni,* a large platter of sauerkraut with sausages, pheasant, duck confit, squab and foie gras, which was a specialty of the house. Loren settled for the *petite choucroute* with the sauerkraut, smoked trout, salmon, monkfish and shrimp.

Most of the couples shared a rich dessert followed by a glass of fine port. Afterward, they voted unanimously that everyone would begin dieting the next day. While relaxing after the sumptuous meal, Summer asked Micky what part of the world her geological expeditions had taken her to. She described immense caverns in Brazil and Mexico and the often difficult penetration into their deepest reaches.

"Ever find any gold?" asked Summer jokingly.

"Only once. I discovered faint trace elements in an underground river that runs beneath the lower California desert into the Gulf of California." As soon as she spoke of the river, Pitt, Giordino and Loren began laughing. Micky was quite surprised to learn how Pitt and Giordino had discovered the river and saved Loren from a gang of artifact thieves during the Inca Gold project.

"Rio Pitt," said Micky, impressed. "I should have made the connection." She continued describing her travels around the world. "One of my most fascinating projects was to investigate water levels in the limestone caverns in Nicaragua."

"I knew Nicaragua had bat caves," said Summer, "but not limestone caverns."

"They were discovered ten years ago and are quite extensive. Some run for miles. The development corporation that hired me for the study has plans for building a dry canal between the oceans."

"A dry canal across Nicaragua?" questioned Loren. "That's a new one."

"Actually, the engineers called it an 'underground bridge.' "

"A canal that runs underground?" Loren said skeptically. "I'm still trying to figure it out."

"Deepwater container ports and free-trade zones on the Caribbean and Pacific, yet to be constructed, would be linked by a high-speed, magnetic levitation railroad running through huge bores beneath the mountains and Lake Nicaragua, with trains capable of speeds up to three hundred and fifty miles an hour."

"The idea is sound," Pitt admitted. "If practical, it could conceivably cut shipping costs by a wide margin."

"You're talking heavy bucks," said Giordino.

Micky nodded in agreement. "The estimated budget was seven billion dollars."

Loren still looked doubtful. "I find it strange that no reports of such a vast undertaking have been circulated by the Department of Transportation."

"Or mentioned in the news media," Dirk added.

"That's because it never got off the ground," said Micky. "I was told the development company behind the project decided to pull out. Why, I never found out. I signed a confidential agreement never to mention my work or reveal any information on the project, but that was four years ago. And since it has apparently died, I don't mind ignoring the agreement and telling my friends the story over a lovely dinner."

"A fascinating tale," Loren acknowledged. "I wonder who was going to put up the financial backing?"

Micky took a sip of her port. "My understanding was that part of the funding was to come from the Republic of China. They've heavily invested in Central America. If the underground transportation system had been completed, it would have given them great economic power throughout North and South America."

Pitt and Loren looked at each other, a growing understanding in their eyes. Then Loren asked Micky, "Who was the construction firm that hired you?"

"A huge international development outfit called Odyssey."

"Yes," Pitt said softly, squeezing Loren's knee under the table. "Yes, it seems to me I've heard of it."

"There's coincidence for you," said Loren. "Dirk and I were discussing Odyssey not more than a few hours ago."

"An odd name for a construction company," said Summer.

Loren smiled faintly and paraphrased Winston Churchill. "A puzzle wrapped in a maze of secret business dealings inside an enigma. The founder and chairman, who calls himself Specter, is as far out as the formula for time travel."

Dirk looked thoughtful. "Why do you think he broke off the project? Lack of money?"

"Certainly not the money," Loren answered. "British economic journalists estimate his personal assets upward of fifty billion dollars."

"Makes you wonder," Pitt murmured, "why he didn't complete the tunnels, with so much at stake."

Loren hesitated; not so Giordino. "How do you know he threw in the towel? How do you know he isn't secretly digging away under Nicaragua while we enjoy our port?"

"Not possible." Loren was blunt. "Satellite photos would show construction activity. There's no way he could hide an excavation of such immense magnitude."

Giordino studied his empty glass. "A neat trick if he could hide millions of tons of excavated rock and muck."

Pitt looked across the table at Micky. "Could you supply me with a map of the area where the tunnel was supposed to begin and end?"

Micky was only too happy to oblige. "You've piqued my curiosity. Let me have your fax number and I'll send you the site plans."

"What's on your mind, Dad?" asked Dirk.

"Al and I will be cruising down Nicaragua way in a few days," Pitt said with a crafty grin. "We just might drop in and browse the neighborhood."

17

D IRK AND SUMMER DROVE to St. Julien's residence in
Georgetown with the top down on Dirk's 1952 Meteor, a
California custom-built fiberglass-bodied hot rod with a DeSoto Fire-
Dome V-8 that was souped up from the stock one hundred and sixty
horsepower to two hundred and seventy. The body was painted in
American racing colors, white with a blue stripe running down the
middle. Actually, the car never had a top. When it rained, Dirk merely
pulled a piece of plastic from under one seat and spread it over the
cockpit with a hole for his head to poke through.

He pulled off a picturesque tree-lined brick street and turned into
the drive circling a large, old, three-story manor house with eight
gables. He continued around the side until he came to a stop in front
of what was the manor's former carriage and stable house. Quite large,
it was once the home of ten horses and five carriages, with rooms up-
stairs for the grooms and drivers. Purchased by St. Julien Perlmutter
forty years earlier, he had remodeled the interior into a homey archive
with miles of shelves crammed with books, documents and private papers, all recording the marine history of nearly three hundred thousand ships and shipwrecks. A gourmand and bon vivant, he maintained

a refrigerated food locker stocked with delicacies from around the world and a four-thousand-bottle wine cellar.

There was no doorbell, only a big door knocker cast in the shape of an anchor. Summer rapped three times and waited. A full three minutes later the door was thrown open by a massive man standing four inches over six feet and weighing four hundred pounds. Perlmutter may have been huge, but he was solid; the sea of flesh was firm and tight.

His gray hair was shaggy and his full beard was enhanced by a long mustache twisted on the ends. Except for his size, children might have taken him for Santa Claus because of his round red face with a tulip nose and blue eyes. Perlmutter was dressed in his customary purple-and-gold paisley silk robe. A little dachshund puppy danced around his legs and yapped at the visitors.

"Summer!" he exclaimed. "Dirk!" He swept the young people up in his huge arms in a great bear hug and lifted both of them off the porch. Summer felt as if her ribs were cracking and Dirk gasped for breath. To their great relief, Perlmutter, who didn't know his own strength, set them down and waved them through the door.

"Come in, come in. You don't know what a joy it is to see you." Then he admonished the dog. "Fritz! Any more barking and I'll cut off your gourmet dog food allowance."

Summer massaged her breast. "I hope Dad told you we were coming?"

"Yes, yes, he did," Perlmutter said cheerfully. "What a pleasure." He paused and his eyes became misty. "Looking at Dirk, I can remember when your father was your age, even a bit younger, when he used to come around and browse my library. It's almost as if time has stood still."

Dirk and Summer had visited Perlmutter with Pitt on several occasions and were always astounded by the vast archives that sagged the shelves and the volumes stacked in hallways and every room of the carriage house, even the bathrooms. It was renowned as the world's largest repository of marine history in the world. Libraries and archives around the nation stood in line, ready to bid whatever price it took should Perlmutter ever decide to sell his immense collection.

Summer was always bewildered at Perlmutter's incredible memory. It would seem that the mass of data should be categorized and indexed onto a computer data file system, but he always claimed he couldn't think abstract and never bought a terminal. Amazingly, he knew where every scrap of information, every book, every author and source and every report was deposited. He liked to boast that he could pick any one out of the maze within sixty seconds.

Perlmutter escorted them into his beautiful sandalwood-paneled dining area, the only room of the house devoid of books. "Sit down, sit down," he fairly boomed, motioning to a thick, round dining table he'd had carved from the rudder of the famous ghost ship *Mary Celeste,* whose remains had been found in Haiti. "I've made a light lunch of my own concoction of guava-sautéed shrimp. We'll wash it down with a Martin Ray Chardonnay."

Fritz sat beside the table, his tail sweeping the floor. Perlmutter reached down every few minutes and gave him a bit of shrimp, which he swallowed without chewing.

Not much later, Dirk patted his flat stomach. "The shrimp was so good I'm afraid I made a pig of myself."

"You weren't alone," Summer groaned softly, fully sated.

"Now then, what can I do for you kids?" said Perlmutter. "Your Dad said something about you finding Celtic artifacts."

Summer opened a briefcase she'd brought with her, retrieved the report she and Dirk had written on the airplane to Washington and photos of the ancient relics. "This pretty well sums up our findings. It also includes Hiram Yaeger's conclusions on the amphor, comb and printed photocopies of the artifacts and chambers."

Perlmutter poured himself another glass of wine, dropped his spectacles over his nose and began reading. "Help yourself to more shrimp. There's plenty."

"I don't think either of us could manage another bite," Dirk muttered, holding his stomach.

Wordlessly, Perlmutter dabbed around his beard that hid most of his mouth. He paused occasionally, staring up at the ceiling in thought before he went back to studying the report. Finally, he laid it on the table and fixed the Pitts with a steady stare.

"Do you realize what you've done?"

Summer shrugged unknowingly. "We think it's an archaeological find of some significance."

"Some significance," Perlmutter parroted, with a slight tone of sarcasm. "If what you've discovered is the genuine article, you've thrown a thousand accepted archaeological theories down the sink."

"Oh dear," said Summer, looking at her brother, who was containing laughter. "Is it all that bad?"

"Depends from what direction you look at it," Perlmutter said between sips of wine. If the report was an earthshaking revelation, he was acting buoyantly calm. "Very little is known about Celtic culture much before five hundred B.C. They didn't keep written records until the Middle Ages. All that is known through the mists of time is that sometime around two thousand B.C., the Celts fanned out from Eastern Europe after originating around the Caspian Sea. Some historians theorize that the Celts and Hindus shared a common ancestry because their language was similar."

"How widespread were their settlements?" asked Dirk.

"They moved into the north of Italy and Switzerland, then on to France, Germany, Britain and Ireland, reaching as far north as Denmark in the Scandinavian region and as far south as Spain and Greece. Archaeologists have even found Celtic artifacts across the Mediterranean in Morocco. Also, graves of well-preserved mummies have been discovered in northern China from a culture called the Urumchi people. They were most certainly Celtic, since they had Caucasian skin and facial features, blond and red hair, and were dressed in tartan-woven cloth."

Dirk leaned back in his chair, lifting the front legs off the floor. "I've read of the Urumchi. But I had no idea the Celts migrated into Greece. I always thought the Greeks were indigenous."

"Though some of them originated in the region, it has generally been accepted that most filtered south from Central Europe." Perlmutter shifted his bulk into a more comfortable position before continuing. "The Celts eventually ruled lands almost as vast as the Roman Empire. Displacing the neolithic people who built megalithic monuments around Europe such as Stonehenge, they continued the traditions of the Druid religion of mysticism. *Druids*, by the way, means 'the very wise ones.' "

"Strange, so little has come down through the ages about them," said Summer.

Perlmutter nodded in agreement. "Unlike the Egyptians, Greeks and Romans, they never built an empire nor formed a national unity. They were made up of a loose confederation of tribes that often fought each other but came together and banded against a common enemy. After fifteen hundred years their village culture eventually gave way to hill forts constructed of earthworks and wooden palisades that evolved into crowded communities. Quite a number of modern cities are built on the sites of old Celt fortresses. Zurich, Paris, Munich and Copenhagen, for example, and half the towns across Europe rest on top of what were once Celtic villages."

"Hard to believe nonbuilders of palaces and citadels became the dominant culture of Western Europe."

"Celtic society leaned mainly toward the pastoral. Their primary endeavor in life was the raising of cattle and sheep. They engaged in agriculture but their yield was small, raised only to feed individual families. But for the fact they were not nomadic, their tribal existence was very similar to that of the American Indian. They often raided other villages for cattle and women. Not until three hundred B.C. did they turn to growing crops to feed their animals during harsh winters. Those who lived along the coasts became traders, dealing in bronze weapons and selling precious tin for other cultures to produce the metal. Most of the gold for the production of exotic adornments for the ruling chieftains and upper-caste classes was imported."

"Strange, a culture with so little going for it grew so strong over such a vast territory."

"You can't say the Celts had nothing going for them," Perlmutter lectured Dirk. "They led the way into the Bronze Age by developing the metal using copper alloyed with the tin found in huge reserves in Britain. They were later credited with smelting iron and ushering in the Iron Age as well. They were superb horsemen and brought to Europe knowledge of the wheel, built war chariots and were the first to use four-wheeled farm wagons and metal implements for plowing and harvesting. They created tools still in use today like pincers and pliers. They were the first to have shod their horses with bronze shoes and made iron rims for chariot and wagon wheels. The Celts educated the ancient world on the use of soap. Their craftsmanship in metal was second to none, and their mastery of gold in the decoration of jewelry, ornaments, warriors' helmets, swords and axes was exquisite. Celtic ceramics and pottery were also creatively designed, and they mastered the art of producing glass. They also taught the art of enameling to the Greeks and Romans. Celts exceled in poetry and music. Their poets were placed in greater esteem than their priests. And their practice of beginning the day at midnight has been passed down to us today."

"What were the causes behind their fading glory," asked Summer.

"Mainly defeats by the invading Romans. The world of the Gauls, as the Romans called the Celts, began to unravel, as other cultures such as the Germans, the Goths and the Saxons began to expand throughout Europe. In a way, the Celts were their own worst enemy. A wild, untamed people who loved adventure and individual freedom, they were mercurial, impetuous and completely undisciplined, factors that hastened their downfall. By the time Rome fell, the Celts had been driven across the North Sea to England and Ireland, where their influence is still felt today."

"What was their appearance—and how did they treat their women?" asked Summer, with a kittenish grin.

Perlmutter sighed. "I wondered when you'd get around to that." He poured the last of the wine in their glasses. "The Celts were a hardy race, tall and fair. Their hair ran from blond to red to brown. They were described as a boisterous lot, with deep-sounding and harsh voices. You'll be happy to know, Summer, that women were held on a pedestal in Celtic society. They could marry whom they desired and inherit property. And unlike most cultures since their time, women could claim damages if they were molested. Celtic women were described as being as large as their men and fought alongside them in battle." Perlmutter hesitated and grinned before continuing. "An army of Celtic men and women must have been quite a sight."

"Why is that?" asked Summer, falling into the trap.

"Because they often went into battle naked."

Summer was too intrepid to blush, but she did roll her eyes and stare at the floor.

"Which brings us back around to the Celtic artifacts we found on Navidad Bank," said Dirk seriously. "If they weren't being transported aboard a ship three thousand years later, where did they come from?"

"And what about the room and chambers we found that were carved from the rock?" added Summer.

"Are you sure they were carved from the rock and not stones laid one on the other?" Perlmutter questioned.

Dirk looked at his sister. "I suppose it's possible. The encrustation could easily have covered the cracks between the stones."

"It wasn't like the Celts to carve chambers out of solid rock. They rarely built structures from stone," said Perlmutter. "It may have been there were no trees to fell as lumber when Navidad Bank rose above the sea. Tropical palms, for example, because of their curved and fiber trunks, were not practical for livable structures."

"But how could they have crossed six thousand miles of ocean in eleven hundred B.C.?"

"A tough question," Perlmutter admitted. "Those who lived on the Atlantic shores were a seafaring people, often called 'people of the oars.' They are known to have sailed into the Mediterranean from ports in the North Sea. But there are no legends of Celts crossing the ⟨ Atlantic, other than possibly Saint Brendan, the Irish priest, whose voyage of seven years is thought by many to have reached the east coast of America."

"When did this the voyage occur?" Dirk asked.

"Sometime between 520 and 530 A.D."

"Fifteen hundred years too late for our find," said Summer.

Dirk reached down and petted Fritz, who promptly sat up and licked his hand. "We seem to strike out with every pitch."

Summer looked down and smoothed her dress. "So where do we go from here?"

"The first item on your list of enigmas to be solved," Perlmutter advised, "is to find out when and if Navidad Bank sat above the surface of the sea three thousand years ago."

"A geomorphologist who studies the origin and age of land surfaces might come up with some theories," Summer suggested knowledgeably.

Perlmutter gazed at the model of the famed Confederate submarine *Hunley*. "You might begin with Hiram Yaeger and his computer wizardry. The world's most extensive accumulation of data on marine sciences is in his library. If any scientific study on the geology of Navidad Bank was ever conducted, he'd have a record of it."

"And if it were compiled by a German or Russian team of scientists?"

"Yaeger will have a translation. You can count on it."

Dirk came to his feet and began pacing the floor. "Our first stop on returning to NUMA headquarters is to meet with Hiram and ask him to probe his files."

Summer smiled. "And then what?"

Dirk didn't hesitate. "Next stop, Admiral Sandecker's office. If we want to get to the bottom of this thing, we must persuade him to loan us a crew, research ship and the necessary equipment to conduct a thorough investigation of the sunken chambers and retrieve their artifacts."

"You mean, go back."

"Is there any other way?"

"I suppose not," she said slowly. For some reason she could not fathom, a fear welled up inside her. "But I don't think I could bring myself to look at *Pisces* again."

"Knowing Sandecker," said Perlmutter, "he'll save NUMA funds by combining your exploration with another project."

"You have to agree that's a reasonable assumption," Dirk said, turning to his sister. "Shall we go? We've taken up enough of St. Julien's time."

Summer gave Perlmutter a cautious hug. "Thank you for the glorious lunch."

"Always a joy for an old bachelor to have a pretty young girl for company."

Dirk shook Perlmutter's hand. "Goodbye and thank you."

"Give your dad my best and tell him to drop by."

"We will."

After the kids had left, Perlmutter sat for a long time lost in his thoughts, until the phone rang. It was Pitt.

"Dirk, your son and daughter just left."

"Did you steer them in the right direction?" asked Pitt.

"I whetted their appetite a bit. Not a great deal I could offer them. There is little recorded history of the seafaring Celts."

"I have a question for you."

"I'm here."

"Ever hear of a pirate named Hunt?"

"Yes, a buccaneer who achieved minor fame in the late sixteen hundreds. Why do you ask?"

"I'm told he's a restless ghost known as the Wandering Buccaneer."

Perlmutter sighed. "I've read the reports. Another *Flying Dutchman* fable. Although, several of the ships and boats that radioed that they'd seen his ship disappeared without a trace."

"So there is cause to be concerned when sailing in Nicaraguan waters?"

"I suppose so. What's your interest?"

"Curiosity."

"Would you like whatever history I have on Hunt?"

"I'd be grateful if you could send it to my hangar by courier," said Pitt. "I've a plane to catch first thing in the morning."

"It's on its way."

"Thank you, St. Julien."

"I'm having a little soiree in two weeks. Can you make it?"

"I never miss one of your fabulous parties."

After he rang off, Perlmutter assembled his papers on Hunt, called a courier service and went to his bedroom, where he stood before a case tightly packed with books. Unerringly, he pulled one from the shelf and walked heavily to his study, where he reclined his bulk on a leather Recamier doctor's couch made in Philadelphia in 1840. Fritz jumped up and lay on Perlmutter's stomach, staring at him through doleful brown eyes.

He opened the book by Iman Wilkens titled *Where Troy Once Stood* and began reading. After an hour, he closed the cover and gazed at Fritz. "Could it be?" he murmured to the dog. "Could it be?"

Then he allowed the lingering effects of the vintage Chardonnay to put him to sleep.

18

P ITT AND GIORDINO LEFT for Nicaragua the next day on
a NUMA Citation jet to Managua. There, they switched to a
commercial Spanish-built Cassa 212 turboprop for the hour-and-ten-
minute flight over the mountains and across the lowlands to the
Caribbean sea and over an area known as the Mosquito Coast. They
could have made the short flight in the NUMA jet, but Sandecker
thought it best they arrive like ordinary tourists, in order to blend in.

The setting sun in the west bathed the mountain peaks gold before
the rays were lost in shadows on the eastern slopes. It was hard for Pitt
to imagine a canal crossing such difficult terrain, and yet throughout
history Nicaragua was always considered the better route for an inter-
oceanic channel than Panama. It had a healthier climate, the surveyed
route was easier to excavate, and the canal would have been three hundred miles closer to the United States; six hundred miles, if you consider the mileage down and up from the Panama passage.

Before the turn of the century, as with too many far-reaching and
historic turning points, politics crawled out of its lair and came to a
bad verdict. Panama had a powerful lobby and worked hard to push
their cause and disrupt relations between Nicaragua and the U.S. gov-

ernment. For a while, it was a toss-up, but with Teddy Roosevelt working behind the scenes to hammer out a sweet deal with the Panama-
nians, the pendulum swung the extra mile away from Nicaragua when
Mount Pelee, a volcano on the Caribbean island of Martinique,
erupted, killing more than thirty thousand people. In a case of incredibly bad timing, the Nicaraguans issued a series of stamps advertising the country as the land of volcanos, one of them depicting an
eruption behind an illustration of a wharf and a railroad. That clinched
it. The Senate voted for Panama as the site of the U.S.-built canal.

Pitt began studying a report on the Mosquito Coast soon after takeoff from Washington. Nicaragua's Caribbean lowlands were isolated
from the more populated western side of the country by the rugged
mountains unfolding below and dense tropical rain forests. The people and the region were never a part of the Spanish empire but came
under British influence until 1905, when the entire coast fell under the
jurisdiction of the Nicaraguan government.

His destination, Bluefields, was Nicaragua's main Caribbean port,
named after the infamous Dutch pirate who used to hide his ship in
the coastal lagoon near the city. The population of the area was made
up of Miskitos, the dominant group whose diverse ancestors came
from Central America, Europe and Africa; the Creoles, who are the
black descendants of colonial-era slaves; and the Mestizos, whose
bloodlines are a mixture of Indian and Spanish.

The economy, based on fishing, was big business along the coast.
The primary catch came mostly from shrimp, lobster and turtle. A
large plant in town processed the fish for export while extensive maintenance facilities serviced, fueled and supplied the international fishing fleets.

When he looked up from the report, the sky had turned as black as
coal. The drone of the propellers, the whine of the engines, took his
mind and sent it on a journey into the land of nostalgia. The face he
was seeing every morning in the mirror no longer revealed the smooth
skin he'd seen twenty-five years earlier without the craggy lines. Time

and adventurous living and the onslaught of the elements had taken its toll.

As he stared through the window into nothingness, his mind traveled back to where it had all begun on that lonely stretch of beach at Kaena Point on the island of Oahu in Hawaii. He was lying on the sand in the sun, gazing idly past the breakers out to sea, when he spotted a yellow cylinder floating in the water. Swimming through treacherous riptides, he retrieved the cylinder and struggled back to shore. Inside was the message from the captain of a missing nuclear submarine. From that moment on, his life took a new turn. He met the woman who became his first love from the moment he laid eyes on her. He had carried her vision in his memory, always believing she had died, never knowing that she had survived, until Dirk and Summer showed up on his doorstep.

The body had weathered time well, perhaps the muscles were not as hard as they once were, but his joints had yet to encounter the aches and pains that come with age. The black hair was still thick and wavy, with streaks of gray that was starting to spread on the temples. The mesmeric opaline green eyes still gleamed with intensity. His love of the sea and his work with NUMA still consumed his time. Memories of his exploits, some pleasant, some nightmarish, and more than a few physical scars, had yet to fade with the years.

His mind relived the many times he had cheated the old man with the scythe. The hazardous journey down the underground river in search of Inca Gold, the fight in the Sahara against overwhelming odds in the old French Foreign Legion fort, the battle in the Antarctic with the giant old snowmobile and the raising of the *Titanic*. The contentment and fulfillment that came with two decades of achievements gave him warm satisfaction, and made him feel his life had been worthwhile after all.

But it was the old drive, the lust of challenging the unknown, that had faded. He had a family now, and responsibility. The wild days were counting down. He turned and looked over at Giordino, who could enter a deep sleep in adverse conditions as easily as if he was in his own goose-down bed in his Washington condo. Their exploits together had become almost mythical, and although they were not particularly close in their personal lives, once they faced what seemed like overwhelming adversity and disaster, they came together as one, each playing off the physical and mental virtues of the other until they either won, or occasionally lost, which wasn't often.

He smiled to himself at remembering what a reporter wrote about him, in one of the few times his feats had gained distinction. "There is a touch of Dirk Pitt in every man whose soul yearns for adventure. And because he *is* Dirk Pitt, he yearns more than most."

THE LANDING GEAR dropped on the Cassa and pulled Pitt back from his reverie.

The landing lights were reflecting off the water of the rivers and lagoons surrounding the city's airport when he leaned toward the window and stared downward. A light rain was falling as the plane set down and taxied toward the main terminal. A fresh five-mile-an-hour wind blew the raindrops on an angle, giving the air a smell of humid freshness. Pitt followed Giordino down the boarding steps and was mildly surprised to find the temperature in the low seventies; he had expected it to be at least ten degrees higher.

They hurried across the tarmac and entered the terminal, where they waited twenty minutes for their luggage to appear on a cart. Their instructions from Sandecker only said that a car would be waiting at the terminal entrance. Pitt pulled two suitcases on wheels while Giordino shouldered a big duffel bag, heavy with diving gear. They walked fifty yards up a paved pathway to the road. Waiting for passengers were five cars and ten taxis, their drivers hustling for a fare. Waving away the cabbies, they stood expectantly for a minute, before the last car in line— a battered, scratched and dented old Ford Escort—blinked its lights.

Pitt walked up to the passenger's window, leaned in and started to ask, "Are you waiting for . . ."

That was as far as he got before going silent in surprise. Rudi Gunn exited the driver's side and came around the car to greet and shake hands. He grinned. "We can't go on meeting like this."

Pitt stared blankly. "The admiral never mentioned you'd be in on the project."

Giordino stared blankly. "Where did you come from and how did you get here before us?"

"I was bored sitting behind a desk so I sweet-talked Sandecker into letting me come along. I left for Nicaragua soon after our meeting. I guess he didn't bother to warn you."

"He must have forgot," Pitt said cynically. He put his arm around the shoulder of the little man. "We've had wild times together, Rudi. It's always a pleasure to work by your side."

"Like the time in Mali on the Niger River when you threw me off the boat?"

"As I recall, that was a necessity."

Both Pitt and Giordino respected NUMA's deputy director. He may have looked and acted like an academic schoolteacher, but Gunn wasn't afraid to get down and dirty if that's what it took to carry a NUMA project to a successful conclusion. The guys especially admired him because, no matter how much mischief they got into, Gunn never squealed on them to the admiral.

They threw their luggage in the trunk and climbed inside the tired Escort. Gunn snaked around the cars waiting outside the terminal and turned on the road leading from the airport to the main dock. They drove along the big bay of Bluefields that was surrounded by wide beaches. The Escondido River delta split off into several channels that ran around the city and then through the Straits of Bluffs to the sea. The lagoon, inlets and harbor were crowded with deserted and silent fishing boats.

"It looks as if the entire fishing fleet is in town," observed Pitt.

"Thanks to the brown crud, fishing has come to a standstill," replied Gunn. "The shrimp and lobster are dying off and the fish have migrated to safer waters. International fishing fleets like the commercial vessels from Texas have moved to more productive waters."

"The local economy must be down the sewer," said Giordino, slouched comfortably in the backseat.

"It's a disaster. Everyone living in the lowlands in some way depends on the sea for their livelihood. No fish, no money. And that's only half the misery. Like clockwork, Bluefields and the surrounding shoreline are struck by major hurricanes every ten years. Hurricane Joan destroyed the harbor in nineteen eighty-eight and what was rebuilt was wiped out by Hurricane Lizzie. But unless the brown crud dissipates or is neutralized, a lot of people are going to starve." He paused. "Things were bad enough before the storm. Unemployment was sixty percent. Now it's closer to ninety. Next to Haiti, the west coast of Nicaragua is the poorest stepchild of the Western Hemisphere. Before I forget, have you guys eaten?"

"We're good," answered Giordino. "We had a light dinner at the airport in Managua."

Pitt smiled. "You forgot the two rounds of tequila."

"I didn't forget."

The Escort rolled through the primitive city, bouncing in potholes that looked deep enough to strike water. The architecture on the crumbling buildings that seemed little more than derelicts was a style of mixed English and French. At one time they had been painted in bright colors, but none had seen a paintbrush in decades.

"You weren't kidding when you said the economy was a disaster," said Pitt.

"Much of the poverty is inspired by a complete lack of infrastructure, and local leaders who just don't get it," Gunn lectured. "Girls with no options go into prostitution as young as fourteen, while boys sell cocaine. None can afford electricity, so they hook wires from the hovels up to streetlights. There are no sewage facilities, and yet the governor took the entire yearly budget and used it to build a palace because she thought it was more important to put on a good face for visiting dignitaries. There is a big drug industry here, but none of the locals are getting rich off the smuggling that takes place mostly offshore or in secluded coves."

Gunn drove into the commercial dock area at El Bluff, the entrance of the lagoon and across the bay from Bluefields. The stench of the harbor was overpowering. Refuse, oil and sewage mingled together in the filthy water. They passed ships unloading at the docks that looked as though they might crumble and fall into the dirty water any minute. The roofs on most of the warehouses looked as if they had been torn away. Pitt noticed that one containership was unloading large crates with FARM MACHINERY stenciled on their wooden sides. The huge, immaculate, shiny semitrucks and -trailers being loaded with the cargo seemed out of place in such a sleazy background. The name of the ship, just visible under the ship's work lights, read: *Dong He*. The letters COSCO stretched along the center of the hull. Pitt knew it stood for the China Ocean Shipping Company.

He could only wonder what was inside the cases labeled FARM MACHINERY.

"This is their port facility?" asked Giordino incredulously.

"All that's left after Lizzie got through with it," answered Gunn.

Four hundred yards later the Escort rolled onto an old wooden wharf crowded with darkened and forlorn fishing boats. Gunn braked to a stop at the only one whose lights illuminated its decks. The boat appeared to have seen better days. Under the yellow glow, her black paint looked faded. Rust streaks ran from the deck and hull hardware. Fishing gear lay carelessly cluttered around the work deck. To a passerby on the dock, she looked uncompromisingly utilitarian, another fishing boat in a world full of fishing boats, with the same character as the vessels anchored and moored around her.

As Pitt's eyes swept the beamy vessel from stem to stern, where the

Nicaraguan flag hung limp with its twin horizontal blue stripes bordering one of white, he reached inside his shirt and felt the small folded silk bundle, reassuring himself it was still there.

He turned slightly and glanced briefly sideways at a lavender-colored pickup truck that was parked in the shadows of a nearby warehouse. It was not empty. He could see a dark shape behind the wheel and the red glow of a cigarette through the rain-streaked windshield.

Finally, he turned back to the boat. "So this is *Poco Bonito.*"

"Not much to look at, is she?" Gunn said, as he opened the trunk and helped retrieve the bags. "But she's powered by twin thousand-horsepower diesels and carries scientific gear most chemical labs would die for."

"There's a switch," said Pitt.

Gunn looked at him. "How so?"

"This has to be the only vessel in the NUMA fleet that isn't painted turquoise."

"I'm familiar with the smaller Neptune class of NUMA survey ships," said Giordino. "She's also built like an armored car and comfortably stable in heavy seas." He hesitated and looked up and down the wharf at the other fishing boats. "Nice job of disguise. Except for her larger deckhouse, which you can't reduce with a stage set, she fits right in."

"How old is she?" Pitt asked.

"Six months," answered Gunn.

"How did our engineers make her look so . . . so used?"

"Special effects," Gunn replied, laughing. "The shabby paint and rust are specially formulated to give that appearance."

Pitt leaped from the dock onto the deck and turned as Giordino passed over their luggage and duffel bag. The sound of feet thumping on the deck alerted a man and a woman, who appeared from the rear door of the deckhouse. The man, in his early fifties with a neatly trimmed gray beard and bushy eyebrows, stepped under the deck light. His head was shaven and gleamed with sweat. He wasn't much taller than Giordino and he stood with slightly hunched shoulders.

The other crew member was nearly six feet tall and willowy, with the anorexic figure of a fashion model. The blond hair, radiant and thick, splashed around her shoulders. Her face was tanned with high cheekbones and when she smiled a greeting she displayed a fine set of white teeth. Like most women who worked in the outdoors, she wore her hair tied back and little makeup, which did not distract from her overall attractiveness. At least not in Pitt's mind. He noted that she did adhere to certain feminine traits of beauty. She painted her toenails.

Both man and woman were dressed in native cotton shirts with vertical stripes over khaki shorts. The man wore sneakers that looked like they had been shot full of holes, while the woman's feet were slipped into wide-strapped sandals.

Gunn made the introductions. "Dr. Renee Ford, our resident fishery's biologist, and Dr. Patrick Dodge, NUMA's leading marine geochemist. I believe you know Dirk Pitt, special projects director, and Al Giordino, marine engineer."

"We've never worked on the same project together," said Renee in a husky voice only a few decibels above a whisper. "But we've sat together in conferences on several occasions."

"Likewise," said Dodge, as he shook hands.

Pitt was tempted to ask if Ford and Dodge shared a garage, but held back from making a bad joke. "Good to see you again."

"I trust we'll have a happy ship." Giordino flashed one of his congenial grins.

"Why wouldn't we?" Renee asked sweetly.

Giordino did not reply. It was another of the rare times he was at a loss for a comeback.

PITT STOOD for several moments, listening to the water slapping against the wharf pilings. Not a soul could be seen. The wharf looked deserted. Almost, but not quite.

He dropped down to his cabin in the stern, removed a small black case from his suitcase and eased back up the stairway onto the side of the deck opposite the wharf. Using the deckhouse as a cover, he opened the case and removed what looked like a video camera. He switched on its transformer and it gave off a muted high-pitched whine. Next, he draped a blanket over his head and slowly rose until his eyes could peer over a pile of rope coiled on the deckhouse roof. He pressed his face against the eyepiece of the night-vision monocular as the scope automatically adjusted the amplification, brightness control and infrared illuminator. Then he peered into the darkness across the wharf that was now illuminated in a greenish image that gave him the night vision of an owl.

The Chevrolet pickup truck he'd noticed when arriving at the *Poco Bonito* was still sitting in the dark. The ambient light from the stars and two dim lights a hundred yards down the wharf were now enhanced twenty thousand times, revealing the driver of the truck as if he were in a well-lit room. But as Pitt studied the driver, he saw that he was a she. Pitt could tell by the way the observer swept her scope back and forth across the lit portholes of the hull that she did not suspect that she had been detected. He could even tell that her hair was wet.

Pitt lowered the scope slightly until it was focused on the pickup truck's driver's door. The snoop was no professional, Pitt thought. Nor was she cautious. Probably a construction worker doing double duty as a spy, since the name of her employer was painted on the side of the door in gold letters:

ODYSSEY

The name stood alone, no "Limited," no "Corporation," no "Company" after it.

Below the name was the stylized image of a horse running with its legs outstretched. It looked vaguely familiar to Pitt, but he couldn't recall where he'd seen it.

Why was Odyssey interested in a NUMA research expedition?

Pitt wondered. What possible threat was a team of ocean scientists? He saw no sense to the stakeout by a giant organization with nothing to gain.

He could not refrain from standing up and walking to the wharf side of the boat and waving to the woman in the pickup, who immediately trained her nightscope on him. Pitt held up his scope to his eyes and stared back. Definitely not a professional snoop, the woman became so shaken that she dropped her scope on the seat, hurriedly kicked over the engine and roared across the wharf into the darkness, spinning her rear tires in a screech of protest.

Renee looked up in unison with Giordino and Dodge. "What was that all about?" asked Renee.

"Someone in a hurry," Pitt said in amusement.

Renee cast off the bow and stern lines while the men looked on. With Gunn manning the pilothouse, the powerful engines sputtered and rumbled into life with a mellow hum, as they gently shivered the deck. Then *Poco Bonito* slipped away from the wharf and churned into the channel that ran through the Straits of Bluffs to the sea. The course, programed into the computerized navigation equipment, set the bow on a heading toward the northeast. But Gunn—like most airline pilots, who would rather take off and land a commercial airliner than allow a computer to do it—took the wheel and steered the vessel seaward.

Pitt descended a ladder to his cabin, replaced the nightscope in his bag and retrieved a Globalstar tri-mode satellite phone. Then he returned to the deck and relaxed in a tattered lounge chair. He turned and smiled as Renee extended her hand through a porthole of the galley with a cup in her hand.

"Coffee?" she inquired from inside the galley.

"You're an angel," said Pitt. "Thank you."

He sipped at the coffee and then punched a number on the satellite phone. Sandecker answered on the fourth ring. "Sandecker," the admiral snapped briskly.

"Did you forget to tell me something, Admiral?"

"You're not clear."

"Odyssey."

There was a silence. Then, "Why do you ask?"

"One of their people was spying on us as we boarded the boat. I'm interested in knowing why."

"Better you learn later," Sandecker said cryptically.

"Has this to do with Odyssey's excavation project in Nicaragua?" Pitt asked innocently.

Another silence and an echo. "Why do you ask?"

"Just curious."

"Where did you obtain your information?"

Pitt couldn't resist. "Better you learn later."

Then he closed the connection.

19

Gunn guided *Poco Bonito* through the black water separating the high-bluffed straits. The water was deserted of all shipping as he kept the bow aimed straight down the middle of the channel. The lights on the top of the buoys that marked the entrance to the harbor swayed with the waves in the distance, one with a blinking green light, the opposite showing red.

As Pitt was sitting in the lounge chair enjoying the tropical evening at sea and watching the yellow glow of Bluefields fade into the darkness astern, the memory of the spy on the dock stayed in his mind and spread, like a plant with roots. There was an indefinite thought that seemed distant and unfocused. He was not concerned that they had been observed as they cast off their moorings. That part of the intrigue seemed inconsequential. The pickup truck with ODYSSEY painted on the door measured no more than two points on his trepidation scale. It was the haste of the driver when she shot off the dock that puzzled him. There had been no need for a quick getaway. So she was made by the NUMA crew? So what? They'd made no move to approach her. The answer had to lie somewhere else.

And then it all crystallized when he recalled the driver's wet hair.

Gunn's right hand was poised above the twin throttles leading to the big fuel-injected engines in readiness to ease them forward and send the boat whipping over the low swells rolling in from the Caribbean. Abruptly, Pitt sat up in his lounge chair and shouted.

"Rudi, stop the boat!"

Gunn half turned. "What?"

"Stop the boat! Stop it now!"

Pitt's voice was as sharp as a fencing saber, and Gunn quickly complied, pulling the throttles back to their stops. Then Pitt yelled at Giordino, who was down below in the galley with Ford and Dodge, savoring pie and coffee. "Al, bring up my dive gear!"

"What's this all about?" asked Gunn in confusion as he stepped from the side door of the pilothouse. Looking bewildered, Renee and Dodge also appeared on deck to see what all the fuss was about.

"I can't be certain," explained Pitt, "but I suspect we might have a bomb on board."

"What brought you to that conclusion?" asked Dodge skeptically.

"The driver of the truck couldn't wait to get away. Why the hurry? There must be a reason."

"If you're right," spoke up Dodge, seeing the light, "we'd better find it."

Pitt nodded decisively. "My thoughts exactly. Rudi, you, Renee and Patrick search every inch of the cabins. Al, you take the engine room. I'm going over the side on the possibility it was attached under the hull."

"Let's get a move on," said Al. "The explosives could be on a timer set to detonate as soon as we cleared the harbor and moved into deep water."

Pitt shook his head. "I don't think so. There was always the chance we might have hung around the dock until morning. Impossible for anyone to predict the precise time we'd cast off and reach the open sea. My guess is that when we pass the entrance, a transmitter attached to one of the channel buoys will activate a receiver connected to the explosives."

"I believe you have an overactive gray matter," Renee said dubiously. "I can't for the life of me imagine who has a motive to kill all of us and destroy the boat."

"Somebody is afraid of what we might find," Pitt continued. "And for now the Odyssey mob is our prime suspect. Their intelligence-gathering must be good if they saw through the admiral's scheme to smuggle the five of us and the boat into Bluefields."

Giordino appeared from below with Pitt's dive gear. He didn't require intuition to accept Pitt's theory. From their many years together since elementary school, he knew Pitt rarely if ever misinterpreted events. Their trust in each other's vision was more than a simple bond. Many times in the past their minds had acted as one.

"We better move quickly," Pitt advised strongly. "The longer we hang around, the sooner our friends know we're onto them. They'll be expecting to see a fireworks display in the next ten minutes."

The message came through. No one needed any urging. They quickly coordinated their efforts and assigned themselves sections of the boat to search while Pitt stripped to his shorts and strapped on his air tanks and regulator. He didn't bother, nor did he take the time, to slip into a wet suit. Without its buoyancy he felt no necessity to be hindered by a weight belt. Inserting the regulator's mouthpiece between his teeth, he strapped a small tool kit around his left leg, gripped a dive light in his right hand and stepped over the stern.

The water felt warmer than the air above. Visibility was almost diamond clear. Shining the light downward, he could make out a flat, sandy, nondescript bottom eighty feet below. Pitt felt remarkably comfortable as the tepid water pressed against his body. The hull below the waterline was free of growth, having been dry-docked and scraped clean before Sandecker ordered *Poco Bonito* south.

He moved from the rudder and propellers toward the bow, swinging the light from port to starboard and back. There was always the danger of a curious shark, nosing its way toward the light, but in all his years of diving Pitt had seldom crossed paths with the murder machines of the deep. He concentrated instead on the object caught in the beam of his dive light, protruding like a tumor from the keel amidships. His suspicions confirmed, he stroked his fins slowly until he was staring at what he knew without the slightest doubt was an explosive device no more than ten inches in front of his face mask.

Pitt was no bomb expert. All he could determine was that some kind of oval-shaped cannister about three feet in length and eight inches wide had been attached to the aluminum hull where it met the keel. Whoever had placed the cannister had anchored it with an adhesive tape impervious to liquid and strong enough to maintain a grip against the drag from the water as the boat cruised through the channel.

There was no way he could tell what type of explosive was being used, but it looked to him like a classic case of overkill. It seemed far more than enough to blast *Poco Bonito* into a thousand fragments and her crew into tiny shreds of flesh and bone. It was hardly a pretty thought.

He clamped the dive light under an armpit and gently placed both hands on the cannister. One deep breath and he attempted to pull the cannister away from the hull. Nothing happened. He increased his effort, but it was fruitless. Without a firm base to stand on, Pitt could exert too little force to overcome the adhesive. He backed off, reached into the tool kit strapped to his leg and pulled out a small fisherman's knife with a curved blade.

Under the light, he took a quick glance at the orange dial on his ancient Doxa dive watch. He had been down four minutes. He had to hurry before Specter's agent onshore got wise that something was up. Very cautiously slipping the edge of the knife under the cannister as far as he dared, Pitt sliced the blade through the tape as if he was sawing a piece of wood. Whoever had attached the bomb used enough tape to choke a whale. Though he had split the tape in four different areas, the cannister still remained stuck to the hull.

Putting the knife back in the kit, Pitt gripped both ends, curled his body until his finned feet were planted firmly against the keel and heaved, praying that only an electronic signal would set it off. The cannister abruptly came off the hull with such momentum that Pitt was hurled through the water nearly six feet before drifting to a stop. It was then, as he held the explosives in his hands, that he realized he was gasping air from his tank like a pump, while his heart felt like it was trying to beat through his rib cage.

Without waiting for his heart to slow and his breathing to return to normal, Pitt swam along the keel and surfaced beside the rudder at the stern. No one was visible. They were all busily searching the interior of the boat. He spit out his mouthpiece and shouted.

"I could use some help!" He wasn't surprised that Giordino was the first to respond.

The little Italian burst through the engine room hatch and leaned over the transom. "What have you got?"

"Enough explosives to disintegrate a battleship."

"You want me to lift it on board?"

"No." Pitt gasped, as a wave washed over his head. "Tie a long line to a life raft and throw it over the stern."

Giordino asked no questions as he hurried up a ladder to the roof of the deckhouse. There he feverishly yanked one of the two life rafts out of its cradle, where it was stowed untied so it could float free should the boat sink. Renee and Dodge appeared on the deck just in time to catch the raft as Giordino let it slide over the wheelhouse roof to the deck below.

"What's happening?" asked Renee.

Giordino nodded to Pitt's head bobbing in the water aft of the stern. "Dirk found an explosive device fastened to the hull."

Renee peered over the transom at the cannister revealed under the glow of Pitt's dive light. "Why doesn't he drop it on the bottom?" she murmured, her tone laced with fear.

"Because he has a plan," Giordino answered patiently. "Now give me a hand dropping the raft over the side."

Dodge said nothing, as the three of them manhandled the heavy raft over the railing into the water with a splash that covered Pitt's head. Kicking his fins furiously, he rose out of the water up to his chest, lifted the heavy cannister over his head and carefully lowered it onto the bottom of the raft, terribly aware that he could be overplaying his luck. His only consolation was that he would never realize he was sent to the great beyond until it was over.

Only after the cannister was safely secured inside the raft did Pitt utter a long sigh of relief.

Giordino dropped the boarding ladder and helped Pitt climb on board. As Giordino removed his air tanks, Pitt said, "Pour a few gallons of fuel into the raft, then pay out the line as far as it will go."

"You expect us to tow a raft full of explosives covered in gasoline?" Dodge asked hesitantly.

"That's the idea."

"What happens when it passes the buoy with the transmitter?"

Pitt looked at Dodge and flashed a crooked grin. "Then it will go bang."

20

WHEN ENTERING THE HARBOR from seaward, the port buoy marking the sides of the channel is usually painted green with a matching colored light on top, and is given an odd number. The starboard buoy directly opposite is red, mounts a red light and sports an even number. As *Poco Bonito* exited Bluefields Harbor, the channel buoys appeared reversed, red to port, green to starboard.

Except for Giordino, who took the helm, everyone huddled on the stern deck and stared expectantly over the top of the transom as the outer harbor buoys came even with *Poco Bonito*'s bow.

Secure in the knowledge that Pitt had discovered the explosives, and having witnessed him placing the cannister in the life raft before allowing it to fall astern, Ford and Dodge still half expected a fiery eruption that would destroy the boat. As they peered warily at the life raft, a small orange shape against the black water a hundred and fifty yards astern, you could have cut the cloud of apprehension with a chain saw until *Poco Bonito*'s hull safely passed the buoys without disintegrating.

Then the tension mounted again, this time even higher as the raft was towed closer and closer to the buoys. Fifty yards, then twenty-five.

Renee instinctively ducked and placed her hands over her ears. Dodge crouched and turned his back toward the stern while Pitt and Giordino calmly gazed aft, as if waiting for a shooting star to dart through the stars.

"Soon as she blows," Pitt said to Dodge, "switch off our running lights so they think we've evaporated."

He had no sooner finished giving the order than the life raft vaporized.

The sound of the explosion thundered and echoed through the straits between the bluffs as the concussion rolled across the water, slapped their faces and rocked the boat. The darkness became a nightmare of flame and fiery debris as a great boiling upthrust of white water twenty feet wide burst out of a crater in midchannel. The fuel that Pitt had used to fill the life raft burst into a column of flame. The crew of *Poco Bonito* stared as if hypnotized at the atomized wreckage of the raft raining down from the sky like streaking meteors. Tiny bits and pieces splattered down on the boat without injuring anyone or doing damage.

Then, just as suddenly, the night went silent and the water astern the boat closed over the crater and was empty again.

THE WOMAN sat in the pickup truck and checked her watch a dozen times from the time the boat pulled away from the dock, and exhaled a deep breath of satisfaction when at last she heard the distant rumble and saw the brief flash in the blackness nearly two miles away. It had taken longer than she estimated. Eight minutes late, by her calculation. Perhaps the helmsman was cautious and sent the boat slowly through the black waters of the narrow channel. Or, perhaps there was a mechanical problem and the crew stopped the boat for a quick fix. Whatever the reason, it no longer mattered. She could inform her colleagues that the job was accomplished successfully.

Rather than head directly for the airport and a waiting Odyssey corporate jet, she decided to go into the shabby downtown of Blue-fields and enjoy a glass of rum. For her work tonight, she felt entitled to a little rest and relaxation.

It had started to rain again, and she switched on the windshield wipers as she drove off the wharf and headed toward town.

THE CHANNEL was cleared and they were outward bound. A heading was set for Punta Perlas and the Cayos Perlas Islands beyond. The skies were clearing and the stars appeared through the clouds as they picked up a light southerly breeze. Pitt volunteered to take the midnight to three A.M. watch. He manned the pilothouse and let his thoughts wander while the computerized automated controls precisely followed the programmed course. For the first hour, it took all his willpower not to fall asleep.

His mind began to create a vision of Loren Smith. Theirs was an on-again, off-again relationship that had lasted almost twenty years. At least twice they had come within a shadow of marrying, but both were already wed to their jobs: Pitt to NUMA, Loren to Congress. But now that Loren expressed a desire not to run for a fifth term, perhaps it was time for him to retire to a less demanding job that didn't take him to the far reaches of the oceans. He had experienced too many brushes with death that had left scars both physical and mental. Chances were, he was now on borrowed time. His luck couldn't last forever. If he hadn't been suspicious of the woman in the Odyssey truck and struck by a sudden revelation about the explosives, he, his friend Giordino and the others would all be dead now. Maybe *it was* time to retire. After all, he was a family man now, with two grown children and responsibilities he'd never imagined two years earlier.

The only problem was that he loved the sea, above and below. There was no way he could simply turn his back and give it up. Somewhere there had to be a compromise.

He refocused on the current problem of the brown crud. Still only minor traces of it were on the chemical detection instruments, whose delicate sensors were mounted under the hull. Despite the fact that no ship's lights showed on the horizons, he picked up a pair of binoculars and idly scanned the darkness ahead.

At a comfortable cruising speed of twenty knots, *Poco Bonito* had left the Cayos Perlas Islands behind over an hour ago. Laying down the glasses and then studying a navigation chart, Pitt estimated that they were about thirty miles off the town of Tasbapauni on the Nicaraguan coast. He glanced at the instruments again. Their needles and digital numbers still stood unwavering on zero, and he began to wonder if they were on a wild-goose chase.

Giordino joined him with a cup of coffee. "Thought you might like a little something to keep you awake."

"Thank you. You're an hour early for your watch."

Giordino shrugged. "I woke up and couldn't get back to sleep."

Pitt gratefully sipped at the coffee. "Al, how come you never got married?"

The dark eyes squinted with curiosity. "Why ask me that now?"

"I've had nothing but time on my brain and it wanders to strange subjects."

"What's the old line?" Giordino said with a shrug. "I never found the right girl."

"You came close once."

He nodded. "Pat O'Connell. We both had our reservations at the last minute."

"What if I told you I'm thinking about retiring from NUMA and marrying Loren?"

Giordino turned and looked at Pitt as if he'd taken an arrow through one lung. "Say again?"

"I think you get the drift."

"I'll believe that when the morning sun rises in the west."

"Haven't you ever wondered about packing it in and taking it easy?"

"Not really," said Giordino thoughtfully. "I've never entertained any great ambitions. I'm happy at what I do. The husband and father routine never turned me on. Besides, I'm away from home eight months out of the year. What woman would put up with that? No, I guess I'll keep things just as they are until they wheel me into a nursing home."

"I can't picture you expiring in a nursing home."

"The gunslinger Doc Holliday did. His last words were 'I'll be damned' when he looked at his bare feet and realized he wasn't dying with his boots on."

"What do you want on your tombstone?" Pitt asked, not without humor.

"'It was a great party while it lasted. I trust it will continue elsewhere.'"

"I'll remember when your time comes—"

Suddenly, Pitt went silent as the instrument displays came to life and began detecting traces of chemical pollution in the water.

"Looks like we're picking up something."

Giordino turned for the stairway leading to the crew's cabins. "I'll wake Dodge."

A few minutes later, a yawning Dodge climbed to the pilothouse and began scanning the computer monitors and recordings. Finally, he stood back, seemingly perplexed. "This doesn't look like any man-made pollution I've ever seen."

"What do you make of it?" asked Pitt.

"I'm not sure yet till I run some tests, but it appears to be a veritable cocktail of minerals flowing from the chemical element chart."

Excitement began to mount as Gunn and Renee, aroused by the sudden activity in the pilothouse, joined them and offered to make breakfast. There was an underlying current of expectation and optimism as Dodge quietly began assembling the incoming data and analyzing the numbers.

The eastern sun was still three hours from sliding over the horizon when Pitt went out on deck and studied the black sea flowing past the hull. He lay on the deck, leaned through the railing and trailed his hand in the water. When he pulled it back and raised it before his eyes, the palm and fingers were covered with a brown slime. He reentered the pilothouse, held up his hand and announced, "We're in the crud now. The water has turned a dull brownish muck almost as if the bottom silt was stirred up."

"You're closer to the mark than you think," said Dodge, speaking for the first time in half an hour. "This is the wildest concoction I've ever seen."

"Any clues to its recipe?" asked Giordino, waiting patiently as Renee filled his plate with bacon and scrambled eggs.

"The ingredients are not what you might think."

Renee looked puzzled. "What type of chemical pollutants are we talking about?"

Dodge looked at her solemnly. "The crud is not derived from manufactured toxic chemicals."

"Are you saying man is not the culprit?" inquired Gunn, pushing the chemist into a corner.

"No," Dodge answered slowly. "The culprit in this case is Mother Nature."

"If not from chemicals, then what?" Renee insisted.

"A cocktail," replied Dodge, pouring himself a cup of coffee. "A cocktail containing some of the most toxic minerals found in the earth. Elements that include barium, antimony, cobalt, molybdenum and vanadium that are obtained from toxic minerals such as stibnite, barytine, patronite and mispickel."

Renee's finely defined eyebrows lifted. "Mispickel?"

"The mineral arsenic is obtained from."

Pitt looked at Dodge, soberly, speculatively. "How is it possible that such a heavily concentrated toxic mineral cocktail, as you call it, can multiply, since it's impossible for it to reproduce itself?"

"The accumulation comes from constantly being replenished," replied Dodge. "I might add that there are heavy traces of magnesium, an indication of dolomitic lime that has dissolved in unheard-of concentrations."

"What does that suggest?" queried Rudi Gunn.

"The presence of limestone, for one thing." Dodge answered directly. He paused a few moments to study a readout from a printer. "Another factor is the gravitational force that pulls minerals or chemicals in alkaline water toward true magnetic north. Minerals attract other minerals to form rust or oxidation. Chemicals in alkaline water pull other chemicals toward their surface to form toxic waste or gas. That is why most of the brown blob has moved north toward Key West."

Gunn shook his head. "That doesn't explain why Dirk and Summer were able to study sections of the blob on Navidad Bank on the other side of the Dominican Republic out in the Atlantic."

Dodge shrugged. "A portion must have been carried by wind and currents through the Mona Passage between Dominica and Puerto Rico before drifting onto Navidad Bank."

"Whatever the cocktail," said Renee, waving her environmentalist flag, "it's turned the water harmful and dangerous to all life that uses it—humans, animals, reptiles, fish, even the birds that land in it, not to mention the microbial world."

"What puzzles me," muttered Dodge, continuing as if he hadn't heard Renee, "is how something with the consistency of silt can bind together in a cohesive mass that floats over a great distance in a cloud no deeper than a hundred and twenty feet from the surface." As he spoke, he made notations in a notebook. "I suspect sea salinity plays a part in the spread, which might explain why the crud doesn't sink to the bottom."

"That's not the only odd part of the puzzle," said Giordino.

"Make your point?" Pitt softly probed.

"The water temperature is seventy-eight, a good five degrees below normal for this part of the Caribbean."

"Another problem to solve," muttered Dodge wearily. "A drop that low is a phenomenon that doesn't go by the book."

"You've accomplished a lot," Gunn complimented the chemist. "Rome wasn't built in a day. We'll collect specimens and let the NUMA lab in Washington find answers to the rest of the enigma. Our job now is to track down the source somehow."

"We can only do that by following a trail leading to the highest concentrations," said Renee.

Pitt smiled wearily. "That's why we came here—" He broke off suddenly, stiffened and gazed out through the windshield. "That," he continued quietly, "and our fun visit to Disneyland."

"You'd better get some sleep," said Giordino evenly. "You're beginning to babble."

"This is no Disneyland," said Renee, suppressing a yawn.

Pitt turned and nodded his head and pointed toward the sea beyond the bow. "Then why are we about to enter the Pirates of the Caribbean?"

All heads turned in unison, and all eyes stared into the dark water that ended where the stars began. They saw a faint yellow glow that slowly increased in brilliance as *Poco Bonito* moved steadily toward it. They stood there frozen in silence as the glow slowly materialized into a nebulous shape of an old sailing ship that became more defined with each passing minute.

For a moment, they thought they were losing touch with reality, until Pitt spoke in a quiet, matter-of-fact tone. "I wondered when old Leigh Hunt was going to show up."

21

THE MOOD ON BOARD the boat had suddenly changed. For nearly a minute, no one moved. No one spoke as they stared uneasily at the bizarre phenomenon. Finally, Gunn broke the silence.

"The same Hunt the pirate the admiral warned us about?"

"No, Hunt the buccaneer."

"It can't be real." Renee stared in awe, refusing to believe what her eyes relayed to her brain. "Are we really looking at a ghost ship?"

Pitt's lips curled in a vague smile. "Only in the eye of the beholder." Then he paraphrased from *The Rime of the Ancient Mariner.* "With never a whisper in the sea, oft darts the Odyssey ship."

"Who was Hunt?" asked Dodge, in a voice close to a quaver.

"A buccaneer who roamed the Caribbean from sixteen sixty-five until sixteen eighty, when he was captured by a British Royal Navy ship and fed to the sharks."

Not wanting to look at the phantom, Dodge turned away, his mind not functioning, and muttered, "What's the difference between a pirate and buccaneer?"

"Very little," answered Pitt. "*Pirate* is a general term that covers British, Dutch and French seafarers who captured merchant ships for prize money and treasure. The term *buccaneer* comes from the French for barbecue. The early buccaneers used to grill their meat and dry it. Unlike privateers, who had valid commissions from their government, buccaneers preyed on any ship, mostly Spanish, without papers. They were also known as freebooters."

The ghostly vessel was only a half a mile away now and closing fast. The eerie yellow glow gave the apparition a surrealistic image. As it neared and the details of the ship became more distinct, the sounds of men shouting across the water began to be heard aboard the phantom.

She was a square-rigged barque with three masts and a shallow draft, a favorite vessel of pirates before the seventeen hundreds. The foresails and topsails were billowing in a nonexistent breeze. She mounted ten guns, five run out on the main deck on both sides. Men with bandanas around their head were standing on the quarterdeck, waving swords. High on her mainmast, a huge black flag with a fiendishly grinning skull dripping blood stood straight out as if the ship was sailing against a headwind.

The expressions on the faces of those on the *Poco Bonito* varied from growing horror to foreboding to academic contemplation. Giordino looked as if he was staring at cold pizza, while Pitt peered through binoculars at the phantasm with the face of a man enjoying a science fiction movie. Then he lowered the glasses and began to laugh

"Are you mad?" Renee demanded.

He handed her the glasses. "Look at the man in the scarlet suit with the gold sash standing on the quarterdeck and tell me what you see."

She stared through the lenses. "A man with a feathered hat."

"What else sets him apart from the others."

"He has a peg leg and a hook on his right hand."

"Don't forget the eye patch."

"Yes. There's that too."

"All that's missing is a parrot on one shoulder."

She lowered the binoculars. "I don't understand."

"A bit stereotyped, don't you think?"

An old Navy man who had served fifteen years on the sea, Gunn read the ghost ship's change of course almost before it turned. "She's going to cross our bow."

"I hope she isn't planning on giving us a broadside," Giordino said half in jest, half seriously.

"Lay on the throttles and ram her amidships," Pitt instructed Gunn.

"No!" Renee gasped, staring at Pitt stupidly, stunned. "That's suicide!"

"I'm with Dirk," Giordino said loyally. "I say stick our bow in the sucker."

A smile began to creep across Gunn's face as he became aware of what Pitt was silently implying. He stood at the helm and punched the engines, laying on full power and lifting the bow three feet out of the water. The *Poco Bonito* leaped forward like a racehorse prodded in the rump with a pitchfork. Within a hundred yards, she was flying across the water at fifty knots straight toward the port side of the pirate ship. The cannon muzzles, already poking through the gun ports, opened fire, spouts of flames bursting from their muzzles, accompanied by the sound of a thunderous blast that echoed over the water.

One quick glance at the radar screen and Pitt dashed to his cabin to retrieve his nightscope. He returned to the open deck in less than a minute and motioned for Giordino to follow him up a ladder to the roof of the pilothouse. Without the slightest hesitation, Giordino climbed after him. They lay flat on the roof, elbows braced to steady the nightscope they passed back and forth. Oddly, they did not stare directly at the luminescent phantom, but eyed the darkness ahead and astern of it.

Wondering if the two NUMA men were losing touch with all reality, Dodge and Renee instinctively ducked down on the deck behind the pilothouse. Above them, Pitt and Giordino ignored the approaching disaster.

"I've got mine," declare Giordino. "Looks like a small barge to the west about three hundred yards."

"I have my target too," Pitt followed. "A yacht, a big one well over a hundred feet in length, the same distance to the east."

A hundred yards, fifty, on a collision course with the unknown. Then *Poco Bonito* lunged into and through the opaque shape of the ancient barque. For an instant the yellow glow burst like orange lasers at a rock concert and shrouded the little research boat. Renee and Dodge could see the pirates moving above them on the main deck, firing their guns with a vengeance. Oddly, none of them took the slightest notice of the vessel plunging through their ship.

Then *Poco Bonito* was speeding alone over a velvet black sea. In her wake, the yellow glow abruptly blinked out and was gone, and the sounds of the guns melted into the night. It was as if the ghostly vision had never been.

"Stay on the throttles," Pitt advised Gunn. "It's not healthy around here."

"Were we hallucinating?" Renee muttered, her face white as a paper towel. "Or did we really run through a ghost ship?"

Pitt put his arm around her. "What you saw, dear heart, was a four-dimensional image—height, depth, width and motion—all recorded and projected in a hologram."

Renee still seemed dazed as she stared into the night. "It looked so real, so convincing."

"About twice as real as its phony captain with his *Treasure Island* Long John Silver peg leg, *Peter Pan* hook and Horatio Nelson eye patch. And then there was the flag. Blood was dripping in all the wrong places."

"But why?" asked Renee to no one in particular. "Why such a production in the middle of the sea?"

Pitt's eyes were staring through the pilothouse doorway at the radar screen. "What we have here is a case of contemporary piracy."

"But who projected the holographic image?"

"I'm in the dark too," added Dodge. "I saw no other vessels."

"Your eyes and mind were focused on the apparition," said Giordino. "Dirk and I observed a large yacht to our port and a barge to the starboard, both three hundred yards away. Neither showing any lights."

A light went on in Renee's mind. "They projected the beam for the hologram?"

Pitt nodded. "They cast the illusion of a phantom ship and crew doomed to sail the sea forever. But their projection was one huge cliché. They must have created Hunt's ship and crew after watching too many old Errol Flynn movies."

"Judging from the radar, the yacht is giving chase," Giordino alerted them.

Standing at the helm, Gunn appraised the two blips on the screen. "One is stationary, which must be the barge. The yacht is following in our wake about half a mile astern, but is losing ground. They must be crazy mad at seeing an old fishing boat leave them in the foam."

Giordino threw a wet blanket over the relief and joy. "We'd better pray that they don't carry mortars or rockets."

"They'd have opened up on us by now—" Gunn's statement was punctuated by a missile that burst out of the early-morning night and whistled past *Poco Bonito,* grazing its radar dome, striking the water fifty yards ahead with a great thump.

Pitt looked at Giordino. "I wish you hadn't given them ideas."

Gunn didn't answer. He was too busy spinning the helm and heaving the research boat on a sharp bank to port and then to starboard, weaving unpredictably to avoid the rockets that began to come every thirty seconds.

"Douse our running lights!" Pitt shouted to Gunn.

His reply was instant darkness, as the little NUMA director flicked off the main lighting switch. The swells had risen to three feet and *Poco Bonito's* beamy hull was now splashing through the crests at almost forty-five knots.

"How are we fixed for weapons?" Giordino asked Gunn calmly.

"Two M4 carbines with attached forty-millimeter grenade launchers."

"Nothing heavier?"

"Easily hidden small arms is all the admiral would allow on board in case we were stopped and searched by a Nicaraguan patrol boat."

"Do we look like drug smugglers?" demanded Renee.

Dodge stared at her with a crooked smile. "What do drug smugglers look like?"

Pitt said, "I've got my old Colt forty-five. How about you, Al?"

"A fifty-caliber Desert Eagle automatic."

"We may not be able to sink them," said Pitt. "But at least we can repel boarders."

"If they don't blast us to smithereens first," grunted Giordino, as another missile landed in *Poco Bonito*'s wake no more than fifty feet astern.

"So long as their rockets aren't equipped with homing devices, they can't hit what they can't see."

Automatic weapons fire began to wink in the darkness behind them, as the modern pirates aimed by radar in their general direction. Tracers danced over the surface of the sea fifty yards to starboard in a spraying pattern. Gunn, playing the odds, turned the boat to port for a short distance before heading straight again. The tracers ever so slowly spiraled through the night, groping for their prey before falling away into the dark sea where *Poco Bonito* should have been but wasn't.

Two more rockets arced through the night. The pirates played the odds and fired them almost in parallel at the blip on their radar. They had the right idea, but they fired when Gunn was momentarily heading on a straight course before he feinted port before turning starboard. The rockets landed on opposite sides of the boat within fifty feet, showering the decks with twin cascades of water.

Then the firing stopped and it seemed as though a mantle of stillness had been drawn over the boat. Only the beat of the mighty engines straining in their mounts, the growl of the exhaust and the water sloshing past the bow broke the silence.

"Have they given up?" Renee murmured hopefully.

Staring at the radar, Gunn spoke happily through the pilothouse door, "They're turning away and reversing course."

"But who *are* they?"

"Local pirates don't use holograms or fire missiles from yachts," Giordino said flatly.

Pitt stared pensively out the back of the boat. "Our friends from Odyssey are the most likely suspects. No way they could have known our bodies weren't lying on the bottom of the sea. We simply walked into an ambush set for any boat or ship that wandered into this particular area."

"They won't be happy campers," said Dodge, "when they learn we're the ones who got away, not once but twice."

Renee felt even more lost. "But why us? What did we do to be murdered?"

"I suspect we're trespassing on their hunting grounds," Pitt said, taking a logical course. "There has to be *something* in this part of the Caribbean they don't want us or anyone else to see."

"A drug-smuggling operation, perhaps?" offered Dodge. "Could it be Specter is involved with the drug trade?"

"Maybe," said Pitt. "But from what little I know, his empire makes vast profits in excavation and construction projects. Drug running wouldn't be worth their time or effort, even as a side operation. No, what we have here goes far beyond drug smuggling or piracy."

Gunn set the helm on autopilot, stepped from the pilothouse and wearily dropped into the lounge chair. "So what heading do we program into the computer?"

There was a long silence.

Pitt was not happy about further endangering everyone's lives, but they were here and they had a mission. "Sandecker sent us to find the truth behind the brown blob. We'll continue searching for the highest concentration of its contamination in the hope it will lead us to the source."

"And if *they* chase after us again?" prompted Dodge.

Pitt grinned broadly. "We turn and run, now that we've gotten so good at it."

22

D AWN BROKE OVER an empty sea. The radar disclosed no vessels within thirty miles, and except for the lights of a hel-icopter that passed over an hour earlier, the search for the source of the brown crud went uninterrupted. Just to be on the safe side, they had run without lights the entire night.

Turning south soon after their confrontation with the bogus ghost ship, they were now sailing in Bahia Punta Gorda, where the trail of increasing toxicity in the seawater had led them. So far they had been blessed with good weather, with just the slightest hint of a breeze and low winds.

The Nicaraguan coastline was only two miles distant. The lowlands were a faint line across the horizon, as if some giant hand had drawn it using a T square and a pen with black ink. Mists covered the shore and drifted against the foothills in the low mountains to the west.

"Most strange," said Gunn, peering through binoculars.

Pitt looked up. "What?"

"According to the charts of the bay of Punta Gorda, the only habi-tation is a small fishing village called Barra del Rio Maiz."

"So?"

Gunn handed the glasses to Pitt. "Take a look and tell me what you see."

Pitt focused the lenses for his eyes and scanned the shoreline. "That's no isolated fishing village, it looks like a major deepwater container port. I count two containerships unloading at a huge dock with cranes, and another two ships anchored and waiting their turn."

"There is also an extensive area devoted to warehouses."

"It's a beehive of activity, all right."

"What's your take on the situation?" asked Gunn.

"My only guess is equipment and supplies are being stored to build the proposed high-speed railroad between the seas."

"They've been damned quiet about it," said Gunn. "I've read no reports that the project was actually funded and under way."

"Two of the ships are flying the Republic of China red flag," said Pitt. "That answers the question on funding."

The great bay of Punta Gorda that they were entering suddenly turned into a sea of ugly brown. Everyone's attention turned to the water. No one spoke. No one moved as the massive brown crud materialized out of the morning haze thick as a bowl of oatmeal.

They stood and watched silently as the bow plowed through water that looked as if it was suffering from a plague, its surface painted the burnt umber on a painter's palette. The effect was of skin invaded by leprosy.

Standing at the helm, chewing on an unlit cigar, Giordino slowed the engines while Dodge furiously recorded and analyzed the chemistry of the water.

During the long night, Pitt had become more familiar with Renee and Dodge. She had grown up in Florida and became a master diver at an early age. Falling in love with life underwater, she had achieved her master's degree in ocean biology. A few months before coming aboard *Poco Bonito,* she came off a divorce that left her with scars. Away from home during long projects at sea, Renee returned after a lengthy research program in the Solomon Islands to find the love of her life had moved out and was living with another woman. Men, she asserted, were no longer a priority.

Pitt launched a campaign to make her laugh at every chance he could think of something funny to say.

His wit fell on deaf ears when it came to Dodge. A taciturn man, somehow happily married for thirty years, he had five children and four grandchildren. He had worked for NUMA since its inception. With a Ph.D. in chemistry, he had specialized in water pollution, working in NUMA's laboratory. But with the death of his wife a year earlier, he had volunteered for fieldwork. He might have cracked a thin smile at Pitt's attempts at humor, but he never laughed.

Around them, the new sun revealed a sea surface thick with the notorious brown crud. It had the consistency of an oil slick, only much denser, and flattened the sea. No swells rolled through it, as Giordino held *Poco Bonito* at a reduced speed of ten knots.

After avoiding the explosion outside Bluefields and the narrow escape from the pirate yacht, the uneasy tension that had been building up in the ship all night seemed to become a mist so thick they could reach out and feel it. Pitt and Renee had pulled aboard several buckets of the crud and poured it into glass containers for future analysis in the NUMA labs in Washington. They also collected dead sea life they found floating in the contamination, for Renee to study.

And then, suddenly, Giordino shouted from the pilothouse, his hand motions animated by Italian breeding. "Off the port bow! Something is happening in the water!"

They all saw it then, a movement in the sea as though a giant whale was thrashing in its death throes. Everyone stood as still as a statue as Giordino turned the bow of the boat twelve degrees toward the turbulence.

Pitt stepped into the pilothouse and examined the readings on the depth finder. The bottom was coming up rapidly. It was almost as if they were crossing a steep slope rising from the bottom of the Grand Canyon. The naked ugliness of the crud gave the sea the look of a bubbling mud pot.

"Unbelievable," muttered Dodge, as if hypnotized. "According to the depth marked on the chart around our position, we should be recording six hundred feet."

Pitt didn't say anything. He was standing on the bow with the binoculars pressed to his eyes. "It looks as if the sea is boiling," he said to Giordino through the open window beside the helm. "Can't be from a volcanic source. There are no steam or heat waves."

"The bottom is coming up at an incredible rate," Dodge called out. "It's as though it was spewing out of a volcano but without molten lava."

The shore had drawn closer, less than two miles distant. The water was becoming more violent, with waves slashing in every direction. The boat was rocked violently, as if shook by a huge vibrator. The brown crud had thickened until it looked like pure, unadulterated mud.

Giordino stepped to the door of the pilothouse and hailed Pitt. "The water temperature has taken a jump. It returned to a normal eighty-three degrees in the last mile."

"How do you explain that?"

"No more than you can."

Dodge was having trouble accepting any of it. The water temperature's sudden increase, the unmarked rise on the seabed, the incredible amount of brown crud rising from nowhere. It was just inconceivable.

Pitt wasn't buying it either. Everything they'd discovered went against the known laws of the sea. Volcanoes were known to rise from the depths, but not an upheaval of mud and silt. This should have been a liquid, live environment where fish of every variety existed. Here there were no living creatures. They might have swum or crawled across the bottom once. Now they were either dead and buried under a mountain of crud or had migrated to clear water. Nothing grew, nothing lived. It was a world of the dead, covered over with toxic muck that seemed to have materialized from nowhere.

Giordino was having a difficult time keeping the boat on an even keel. The waves were not high, no more than five feet, but unlike waves generated in one direction by the winds of a storm, these whipped and buffeted the boat from every point of the compass. Another two hundred yards and the water went crazy with uncontrolled violence.

"A mass of mad mud," Renee spoke, as if gazing at a mirage. "Pretty soon it will become an island—"

"Sooner than you think," Giordino yelled, hauling the throttles into reverse. "Hang on. The bottom has come up beneath us." The boat yawed, but it was too late. The bow struck the rising muck, throwing everyone forward, and stuck fast. The bow wave died away and the propellers thrashed madly, chopping the mud into an ivory-brown froth as they tried to pull *Poco Bonito* off the mysterious rise. With the boat imprisoned in the mud, they felt like unproductive spectators.

"Cut the engines," Pitt ordered Giordino. "High tide is in another hour. Wait and try then. In the meantime, we'll carry all the heavy material and supplies to the stern of the boat."

"Do you really think that by moving a few hundred pounds, you can raise the bow enough to slip off the mud pile?" asked Renee doubtfully.

Pitt was already hauling a large coil of rope toward the transom. "Add another seven hundred pounds of bodies, and who knows? We just might get lucky."

Though every man and one woman worked as though their lives depended on it, it took the better part of the next hour to stack luggage, food supplies, nonessential equipment and furniture as far back on the stern deck as possible. The fishing nets and traps used to disguise the boat were thrown overboard, along with the bow anchors.

Pitt gazed at the hands on his Doxa watch. "High tide in thirteen minutes and then the moment of truth."

"The moment has come sooner than you thought," said Giordino. "We have a vessel approaching from the north on radar. And she's coming fast."

Pitt snatched up the binoculars and peered into the distance. "Appears to be a yacht."

Gunn shaded his eyes from the eastern sun and gazed out over the brown crud. "The same one that attacked us last night?"

"I didn't get a good look at her in the dark through the night glasses. But I think it's safe to say there is little doubt of it being the same vessel. Our friends have tracked us down."

"No time like the present," said Giordino, "to get a head start on the posse."

Pitt herded everyone to the very edge of the *Poco Bonito*'s transom. Giordino took the helm and looked astern. Making certain they all had a firm grip on the railing, Pitt nodded a signal for reverse full power. The mighty diesels reverberated as Giordino pushed the throttles as far as they could go. The boat slewed and fishtailed, but was stuck fast. The thickness of the brown crud acted as a glue, adhering to the keel of *Poco Bonito*. Even with the crew and a ton of solid substance crammed against the transom, the forward part of the boat had raised but two inches. Not enough to break loose.

Pitt hoped for a wave to lift the bow, but no waves came. The thick brown substance laid the sea flat as a newspaper. The engines strained and the propellers dug into the muck, but nothing happened. All eyes had turned to the yacht that was approaching at high speed directly toward them.

Now that he saw her clearly in the daylight, Pitt estimated her overall length at one hundred and fifty feet. Unlike the standard white, the mega-yacht was painted lavender, like he'd seen on the Odyssey pickup truck at the dock. A masterpiece of craftsmanship, she was the essence of oceangoing luxury. She carried a twenty-foot powerboat as a tender and a six-passenger helicopter.

She was near enough for him to make out her name in gold letters:

EPONA. Below the name, painted across the bulkhead of the second deck, was the same Odyssey logo of a running horse. A flag flying from the communications antenna also flaunted the golden horse on a lavender background.

Pitt observed two crewmen feverishly preparing to lower the tender while several others took up positions on the long forward deck, weapons in hand. None made any attempt at taking cover. They were lulled by the belief that a fishing boat had no bite and took no precautions. The hair on the nape of Pitt's neck rose a fraction as he spotted a pair of the men loading a rocket launcher.

"She's coming straight for us," muttered Dodge uneasily.

"They don't look like any pirates I ever read about," Giordino shouted from inside the pilothouse over the roar of the engines. "They never captured ships from an elegant yacht. Ten will get you twenty, it was stolen."

"Not stolen," Pitt retorted. "It belongs to Odyssey."

"Is it me, or are they everywhere?"

Pitt turned and called out, "Renee!"

She was sitting with her back against the transom. "What is it?"

"Go down in the galley, empty whatever bottles you can find, then fill them with fuel from the tank on the generator motor."

"Why not fuel from the engines?" asked Dodge.

"Because gas ignites more easily than diesel fuel," Pitt explained. "After the bottles are filled, insert a cloth and twist on the top."

"Molotov cocktails?"

"Precisely."

Renee no sooner disappeared below than the *Epona* swung in a wide arc toward them. Coming head-on, she was closing fast. From the new view, Pitt could see that she had the twin hulls of a catamaran. "If we don't get off this mud pile," he said irritably, "we'll have a most exasperating complication."

"Exasperating complication," Giordino shot back. "Is that the best you can do?"

Then to everyone's stunned amazement, Giordino suddenly ran from the pilothouse, scrambled up the ladder to the roof, stood poised for a moment like an Olympic diver and leaped onto the stern deck between Pitt and Gunn.

Call it luck, call it foresight or fate. Giordino's weight and momentum striking the stern deck was the extra inducement it took to jar the boat loose. Sluggishly, inch by inch, the boat slowly slithered off the unyielding muck. Finally, the keel slipped free and the boat leaped astern as if yanked on a big spring.

Creases of mirth crinkled the corner of Pitt's eyes. "Don't ever let me tell you to diet."

Giordino flashed a broad smile. "I won't."

"Now for our well-rehearsed getaway," said Pitt. "Rudi, take the helm and crouch down as far as you can go. Renee, you and Patrick lay low and take cover behind all this junk we've piled on the stern. Al and I will hide under a pile of nets."

The words were barely out of Pitt's mouth when one of the crewmen of the luxury yacht fired a handheld rocket launcher. The missile soared through the port door of the pilothouse and out the starboard window before impacting with the water fifty yards abeam and exploding.

"Good thing I wasn't in there yet," said Gunn, trying to act as if he was on a walk in the park.

"See what I mean about crouching down?"

Gunn jumped in the pilothouse and spun the wheel, sending the hull curling away from the muck rising from below the water. But before he could bring the boat up to speed, another rocket smashed through the side of the hull amidships and struck the starboard engine. Miraculously, it failed to explode, but it caused a fire by igniting oil spilling from the shattered engine. Almost as a reflex, Gunn immediately closed the throttle to prevent any broken lines from spraying fuel on the fire.

Dodge took the initiative, dove down the hatch into the engine room and snatched a fire extinguisher mounted on a bulkhead. Pulling the safety pin and squeezing the trigger, he smothered the flames until only a billow of black smoke spiraled through the open hatch.

"Are we taking on water?" Pitt shouted from under the fishnet.

"It's an ungodly mess down here, but the bilge is dry!" Dodge yelled back between coughing fits.

To those on board the pirate yacht, it looked as though the fishing boat was mortally hit, as they watched the column of smoke billowing from inside her hull. Believing her crew dead and too injured to resist, the yacht's captain backed off on his engines, slowed the vessel and drifted across *Poco Bonito*'s bow.

"Do we still have power, Rudi?"

"Our port engine is dead, but the starboard is still turning over."

"Then they just made a big mistake," Pitt said with a cold grin.

"And what was that?" Gunn replied.

"Remember the pirate ship?"

"I do indeed." Gunn cut back on the throttle to the good engine for the sucker play, allowing the little research boat to stop dead in the water. The ploy worked. Certain that his victim was about to sink, the yacht's captain swallowed the bait and idled closer.

Seconds crawled by, until the yacht was almost sitting on top of them at point-blank range. Seeing no movement on board and smoke still gushing from the hull, no small-arms fire was poured into the seemingly stricken vessel. Then a bearded man leaned out the window of the yacht's pilothouse, and with an American Deep South accent spoke through a bullhorn.

"Y'all who can hear me. If y'all do not abandon your boat, it will be blasted to kindlin'. Do not attempt to use any communication devices. Ah repeat, do not open communications. We'all have detection equipment on board and will know immediately if y'all transmit. Y'all have exactly sixty seconds to take to the water. Ah promise y'all safe passage to the nearest port."

"Shall we reply?" asked Gunn.

"Maybe we should do as he says," muttered Dodge. "I want to see my children and grandchildren again."

"If you trust a pirate's word," said Pitt coldly, "I've got a gold mine in Newark, New Jersey, I'll sell you cheap."

Seemingly ignoring the yacht, Pitt rose into view and climbed through the gear piled on the stern and approached the jackstaff on the transom that was flying the Nicaraguan flag. He lowered the flag, unclasped the fasteners and removed it. Then he retrieved the bundle he'd been carrying inside his shirt. In a few moments, a silk, three-by-five-foot emblem was raised.

"Now they know where we come from," Pitt said, as everyone stared reverently at the stars and stripes snapping defiantly in the breeze.

Renee returned on deck, carrying two glass jars and a wine bottle topped with gasoline. Quickly sizing up the situation, she suddenly had a revelation. "You're not going to ram him?" she cried.

"Say when," yelled Gunn, in a voice edged with anticipation and the stony face of a poker player bluffing to win a pot.

"No!" Renee moaned. "That isn't a hologram. It's a solid object. Ram that and we'll fold up like Lawrence Welk's accordion."

"I'm counting on it," Pitt snapped back. "You and Patrick light the wicks and get ready to toss the cocktails as soon as we collide."

There was no more hesitation. The yacht was creeping past *Poco Bonito*'s bow, now less than a hundred feet away.

Giordino threw Pitt one of the M4 carbines and they began blasting away at the yacht. Giordino fired full automatic, sending a spray of 5.56-millimeter NATO rounds into the pilothouse, while Pitt aimed and accurately fired single shots at the crewman holding the rocket launcher, taking him out with his second shot. Another man leaned down to pick up the weapon, but Pitt canceled him out too . . .

Stunned that *Poco Bonito* was unexpectedly fighting back, the crew of the yacht dashed for cover without returning fire. Giordino did not know it but he had put a bullet in the shoulder of the captain, who had fallen out of sight onto the deck of the pilothouse. At the same moment, the helmsman was dropped by the shower of shells, and the yacht began to lose steerage and angle away. With only just one engine providing power, *Poco Bonito* flattened out at less than half her top speed, but she still gamely thrust her bow through the water with more than enough power to do the job.

No one had to be told to sit against the bulkhead with their arms protecting their heads. Renee and Dodge shared apprehensive looks at the orange life jackets that Gunn had passed out. In the pilothouse, he stood firm, hands clutched on the wheel, knuckles turning ivory. The single screw chewed the water, driving the boat straight toward the big, opulent yacht. Its crew stared back, numbed with horror and disbelief, as they realized the innocent-looking fishing boat was not throwing in the towel but rather attacking them with the intention of ramming. A fox in sheep's clothing, surprise was total, no other boat or ship had offered resistance before being captured. They were also shaken by the unexpected show of the American flag.

Pitt and Giordino kept up their devastating fire, sweeping the decks and clearing them of the yacht's crew as *Poco Bonito* closed the gap. The *Epona* looked bigger than ever, as they surged toward her hull amidships just aft of the wheelhouse. The decks had been cleared. Like scared rabbits, the crew had concealed themselves belowdecks rather than risk the accurate fire pouring from the oncoming boat.

Poco Bonito looked like the boat from hell, with exhaust fumes issuing through the engine room hatch along with smoke, blown back on a ninety-degree trail astern by the wind over the bow. Gunn had served as executive officer of a missile destroyer that had rammed an Iraqi submarine in the Mediterranean during the conflict to rid the area of Saddam Hussein. But the conning tower of the sub was all that had been visible then. Now, he was looking at a big, solid ship that towered over him.

Ten seconds to impact.

23

PITT AND GIORDINO LAID aside their carbines and braced themselves for the collision. From her curled-up position against the deckhouse bulkhead, Renee could see that the two men's faces were impassive, with no indication of fear or stress. They seemed as indifferent as a pair of ducks sitting under pouring rain.

In the pilothouse, Gunn was planning his moves in sequence. He aimed the bow to strike into the yacht's engine room just aft of the main dining salon. After impact, the next trick was to reverse the engine and pray it could pull *Poco Bonito* out of the hole she just gouged and keep afloat while the enemy made a one-way trip to the seabed. The sleek hull of *Epona* looked so close now, Gunn felt as if he could reach through the shattered windshield and touch the elongated image of the horse.

The yacht loomed up and blocked out the sun. Then havoc piled on havoc and everything seemed to go into slow motion as the sound of a dull lingering crunch that never seemed to end broke the atmosphere. *Poco Bonito* sliced into her far larger antagonist, smashing a V-shaped slash, demolishing the engine room bulkheads on the starboard hull of the big catamaran and crushing anyone working inside.

Renee and Dodge stood and hurled their fuel-filled bottles, with soaked rags aflame. One bounced on the teak deck without breaking, but the other smashed and ignited a ball of fire that spread down the side of the yacht in a fiery waterfall. Without pause, they hurled the glass jars, then the wine bottle, and all burst into a holocaust that covered half the yacht. The once-beautiful vessel looked as though it was locked in a psychotic's nightmare.

Even before the research boat had lost her momentum, Gunn pulled the throttle into full reverse. For several tormented seconds, *Poco Bonito* just hung there, her shattered bow driven six feet into *Epona,* caught like a fist in a vise, propeller flogging the water convulsively. Ten seconds, fifteen seconds, then twenty. At last, with a great shriek of ripping debris, she began to pull free. As her crumpled bow unplugged the gash in the yacht's hull, the brown crud gushed into her like a raging river. The yacht immediately began to list sharply.

Two of *Epona*'s crewmen, protected on the opposite hull, recovered and began firing automatic weapons at *Poco Bonito.* Their aim was erratic and low because their eyes were influenced by the downward list of the starboard hull. Bullets splashed the water around the research boat's hull, some penetrating and leaving several small holes for water to spurt through.

Pitt and Giordino fired blindly into the smoke and fire until resistance aboard the yacht faded away. The superstructure was hidden by flame and smoke. Screams and shouts could be heard inside the conflagration. Fanned by a light breeze, flames flickered through the great hole driven in her starboard hull. The catamaran yacht was settling deeper in the water now, lifting the undamaged port hull free of the water surface.

Everyone on board *Poco Bonito* crowded the railing, staring in rapt fascination at the dying yacht. The *Epona*'s crew frantically scrambled aboard the helicopter, whose pilot started and revved the engine. Compensating for the angle of list, the pilot lifted the helicopter off the burning vessel and banked toward land, leaving any wounded behind to burn or drown.

"Pull alongside her," Pitt ordered Gunn.

"How close?" the little man inquired anxiously.

"Close enough for me to jump aboard."

Knowing it was senseless to argue with Pitt, Gunn shrugged and began easing the badly damaged boat toward the yacht that was aflame from bow to amidships. He kept the engine in reverse and moved astern to ease pressure from the water that was streaming into the smashed bow section.

Meanwhile, Giordino labored furiously in the mangled mess of the *Poco Bonito*'s engine room, making necessary repairs to keep the boat afloat and under power. Renee cleared the deck of any useless equipment and threw it over the side. Blackened and stained with smoke, Dodge went below and dragged a portable pump into the bow section and attacked the rising water that flowed in through the bow that had been smashed back to the forward bulkhead.

As Gunn carefully maneuvered *Poco Bonito* alongside *Epona,* Pitt waited until they nearly touched before he stood on the railing and leaped aboard, landing on the open teak deck behind the main dining salon. Thankfully, the breeze was blowing the fire forward and the aft section had not yet suffered the effects of the blaze. If he were to find anyone alive, he had to move fast before the once-sleek ship sank into the deep. The sound of a fire out of control was like a steam locomotive thundering down the track.

Pitt ran through the dining salon and found it empty. A fast search through the staterooms below failed to turn up any sign of crew member or officer. He tried to go up the plushly carpeted stairs to the pilothouse, but met a wall of fire that drove him back. The smoke seeped through his nose into his lungs. His eyes streamed tears from the acrid smoke and felt as though they were burning out of their sockets. With his hair and eyebrows singed, he was about to give up and abandon the search when he stumbled over a body in the galley.

He reached down and was stunned to feel that it was a woman wearing nothing but a brief bikini. Hoisting her over his shoulder, he stumbled out onto the stern deck, coughing and wiping the tears from his eyes onto one arm.

Gunn instantly appraised the situation and moved the boat ever closer to the yacht until their hulls bumped. Then he rushed from the pilothouse and took the limp shape of the woman that Pitt passed across the railing. The heat from the flames was beginning to blister the paint on the sides of the research boat, as Gunn laid the woman gently on the deck, noting only that she had long straight red hair before hurrying back to the helm and moving *Poco Bonito* away from the flames.

Pitt, barely able to see until his eyes cleared, felt her pulse and found it had a regular beat. Her breathing was also normal. He brushed back the flame-red hair from her forehead and found an egg-sized bump. He assumed that she had been knocked unconscious during the collision. The face, arms and long, shapely legs revealed an even tan. Her face was beautifully sculpted, with a flawless complexion and lips that were full and sensual. The upturned nose was a perfect complement to the face. Because her eyes were closed, he could not see their color. From what he could tell, she was a very attractive woman, with the lithe body of a dancer.

Renee finished throwing a box of net buoys over the side and rushed to the woman lying on the deck. "Help me get her down below," she said. "I'll take care of her."

Still partially blind, Pitt carried the woman from the yacht down the stairwell to his cabin and laid her out on his bunk. "She has a nasty bump on the head," he said, "but I think she'll come around. You might give her air from a dive tank to help clear the smoke from her lungs."

Pitt returned topside just in time to watch the end of the yacht.

It was slipping under the water, her once lavender-colored hull and superstructure now blackened by the fire and stained with the brown crud. A sad and pathetic ending for a beautiful ship. He regretted that he had been the cause of her demise. But then cold, hard logic took the place of sadness, as he envisioned *Poco Bonito* succumbing to the same fate, with all her crew dead. His regret was replaced with a euphoria that he and his friends were alive and unharmed.

The starboard hull of the catamaran had sunk completely under the brown water. The port hull hung briefly in the air as the superstructure slipped below the surface, leaving behind a swirling spiral of steam and smoke. Her polished bronze screws sparkled in the sun, and then they were gone. Except for the hiss of the water as it squelched the flames, she went down quietly, without protest, as if wanting to hide her disfigurement. The last sight of her was the pennant with the golden horse. Then it too was swallowed by the indifferent brown sea.

After she disappeared, fuel oil surfaced and spread across the muck, painting it black with rainbow-hued streaks reflecting under the sun. Bubbles came up and burst, along with distorted debris that popped to the surface and seemed to hang there, waiting to be carried to some distant shore by the currents and tides.

Turning from the tragedy, Pitt stepped into the pilothouse, his shoes crunching in the shattered glass scattered on the deck. "How's it look, Rudi? Can we make the coast or do we take to the rafts?"

"We might make it if Al can keep the engine running and Patrick slows the flooding in the bow, which isn't likely. It's gaining faster than the pumps can handle."

"We're also taking water from the bullet holes that penetrated below the waterline."

"There's a large canvas tarp in the storage locker below. If we could lower it over the bow like a mask, that might slow the water enough for the pumps to catch up."

Pitt could see the forward section of the boat was almost two feet down at the bow. "I'll work on it."

"Don't take too long," Gunn cautioned. "I'll keep us in reverse to slow the flooding."

Pitt leaned over the engine room hatch. "Al, how's the party down there?"

Giordino appeared and looked up. He was standing knee-deep in brown crud water, his clothes were soaked and his hands, arms and face were coated in oil. "Barely staying ahead of the game, and believe you me, it ain't no party."

"Can you give me a hand topside?"

"Give me five minutes to unclog the bilge pump. The crud plugs it if I don't clean out the filters every few minutes."

Pitt dropped down and made his way past the cabins to the storage locker, where he found a large folded canvas tarpaulin. It was heavy and bulky, but he managed to drag it up a ladder and through a hatch on the forward deck. Giordino soon joined him, looking like he'd fallen in a tar pit, and together they spread out the canvas and tied all four ends with a nylon line. Two of the ends they weighted with fractured parts from the engine struck by the rocket. When ready, Pitt turned and motioned for Gunn to reduce the speed astern.

Together, he and Pitt threw the canvas off the crunched bow into the water, holding on to all four ends of the line. They waited until the weighted side of the tarp sank slowly through the crud. Then Pitt called to Gunn.

"Okay, move ahead slowly!"

They stood on opposite sides of the bow and pulled in the lines until the weighted end hung beneath the remains of the bow. Next they tied off the lower lines and pulled on the upper ends until the tarp was spread over the damaged section, greatly reducing the flow of water inside. Soon as the lines were secured, Pitt pulled up the forward deck hatch and checked with Dodge.

"How's it look, Patrick?"

"That did the trick," Dodge replied, wearily but happy. "You've reduced the flooding by a good eighty percent. The pump should be able to hold its own now."

"I have to get back to the engine room," said Giordino. "It's not a pretty sight down there."

"Neither are you," Pitt said, smiling, as he put his arm around Giordino's shoulder. "Let me know if you need a hand."

"You'd only get in the way. I'll have things under control in another couple of hours."

Then Pitt entered the pilothouse. "We can get under way now, Rudi. Our patch seems to be working."

"Lucky for us the computerized navigation controls survived intact. I've programmed in a course for Barra del Colorado in Costa Rica. An old naval buddy of mine retired down there and lives next to a sport-fishing lodge. We can tie up at his dock and make the necessary repairs for the trip across the sea to the NUMA boatyard at Fort Lauderdale."

"A wise choice." Pitt gestured toward the huge and mysterious containership across the water. "We might find trouble if we run in there. Better safe than sorry."

"You're right. Once Nicaraguan authorities find out we sank a yacht in their backyard, we'd all be arrested." He dabbed a cloth at a trickle of blood that was oozing from a cut on one cheek. "What's the story on the woman you rescued?"

"Soon as she's conscious, I'll find out."

"Do you want to contact the admiral and give him a report, or should I?"

"I'll take care of it." Pitt entered the galley and sat down at a computer used by the crew mostly for entertainment, e-mail home and occasional research on the Internet via satellite. He typed in the name of the yacht, *Epona,* and waited. Within a minute, an image of a horse and a brief description came on the screen. Pitt absorbed it in his memory, shut down the terminal and left the galley.

He met Renee in the passageway separating the cabins. "How's she doing?"

"If it was up to me, I'd throw her arrogant ass into the sea."

"That bad?"

"Worse. Within seconds of coming awake, she began giving me a hard time. Not only is she demanding, but she only speaks in Spanish." Renee paused to smile smugly. "It's an act."

"How can you tell?"

"My mother was an Ybarra. I speak better Spanish than our guest."

"She won't reply in English?" asked Pitt.

Renee shook her head. "Like I said, it's an act. She wants us to believe she was only a poor Mexican who slaved in the galley. Her makeup and designer bikini are dead giveaways. This broad has class. She's no scullery maid."

Pitt pulled his old .45 Colt from a holster on his belt. "Let me play Let's Make a Deal with her." He stepped into the cabin with the mystery guest, approached her and gently pushed the muzzle against her nose. "I'm sorry to have to kill you, sweet stuff, but we can't leave any witnesses around. You understand."

The amber-brown eyes flew wide and crossed, staring at the gun. Her lips suddenly trembled as she felt the cold, hard barrel and looked into Pitt's inscrutable green eyes. "No, no, please!" she cried out in English. "Don't kill me! I have money. Let me live and I'll make you rich."

Pitt looked up at Renee, who was standing with her mouth open, not completely certain whether Pitt was not actually going to shoot the woman. "Do *you* want to be rich, Renee?"

Renee caught onto the game and came on stage. "We already have a ton of gold hidden aboard the boat."

"Don't forget the rubies, emeralds and diamonds," chided Pitt.

"We might find it in our hearts not to feed her to the sharks for a couple of days if she tells us about the fake pirate ship, and why the pirates chased us half the night so they could murder all of us and sink our boat."

"Yes. Yes, please!" the woman gasped. "I can only tell you what I know!"

Pitt saw a strange glint in her eyes that did not indicate trust. "We're listening."

"The yacht belonged to my husband and me," she began. "We were on a cruise from Savannah through the Panama Canal and up to San Diego, when we were approached by what we thought was an innocent fishing boat whose captain asked for medical supplies so they could treat an injured crewman. Unfortunately, my husband, David, fell for the ruse and before we could react, the pirates had boarded our boat."

"Before we continue," said Pitt, "my name is Dirk Pitt and this is Renee Ford."

"I'm rude for not thanking you for saving me. I'm Rita Anderson."

"What happened to your husband and crew?"

"They were murdered and their bodies thrown in the sea. I was spared because they thought I would be useful in luring passing boats."

"How was that?" asked Renee.

"They thought that seeing a woman on the deck in a bikini would attract them close enough to be attacked and captured."

"That was their only motive in keeping you alive?" asked Pitt doubtfully.

She nodded silently.

"Do have any idea of who they were or where they came from?"

"They were local Nicaraguan bandits turned pirates. My husband and I had been warned not to sail through this area, but the sea along the coast looked peaceful."

"Odd that local pirates knew how to fly a helicopter," Renee muttered under her breath.

"How many boats did they capture and destroy using your yacht?" Pitt pressed Rita.

"Three that I'm aware of. Once the crew was murdered and the boat ransacked for valuables, it was scuttled."

"Where were you when we collided with your yacht?" inquired Renee.

"So that's what happened?" she answered vaguely. "I was locked in my cabin. I heard sounds of explosions and gunfire. Then came a great shock and the boat shuddered, followed by fire. The last thing I remember before I blacked out was the wall of my cabin crashing in around me. When I woke up, I was here on your boat."

"Do you recall anything else leading up to the collision and fire?"

Rita shook her head slowly back and forth. "Nothing. They held me prisoner in my cabin and only let me out when they were preparing to capture another vessel."

"Why the hologram of the pirate ship?" asked Renee. "That seemed more like a gimmick to keep boats out of the area than an act of piracy."

Rita looked uncomprehending. "Hologram? I'm not even sure what one is."

Pitt smiled inwardly. He saw little cause not to believe that Rita Anderson was fabricating a wild story. Renee was right. Rita's makeup hardly looked like it belonged on a woman who had seen her husband murdered and had been cruelly dealt with by pirates. The beige-rose lipstick with lip gloss was too precisely applied, the eyes defined with a deep chestnut liner and a shimmer highlighter on the brow—all spelled a life of elegance. He decided to go for the jugular, watching closely for a reaction.

"What is your connection with Odyssey?" he said suddenly.

At first, she didn't get it. Then it began to dawn on her that these people were no innocent fishermen. "I don't know what you're talking about," she hedged.

"Wasn't your husband an employee of the Odyssey conglomerate?"

"Why do you ask?" she threw out, stalling while she came back on keel.

"Your boat bore the same image of a horse as the Odyssey logo."

The immaculately plucked and penciled eyebrows pinched fractionally. She was good, Pitt thought, very good. She didn't faze easily.

He began to realize that Rita was no mundane wife of a rich man. She was comfortable being in command, with power to wield. He was amused as she made a flank attack and tried to turn the tables.

"Who are you people?" Rita suddenly demanded. "You're not fishermen."

"No," Pitt said slowly, with effect. "We're with the United States National Underwater and Marine Agency on a scientific expedition to find the source of the brown crud."

He might as well have slapped her in the face. The calm composure abruptly fell away. Before she could stop herself, she blurted, "Not possible. You're—" She caught herself and her voice trailed off.

"Supposed to be dead from the explosion in Bluefields Channel," Pitt finished for her.

"You knew?" Renee gasped, moving toward the bed as if to strangle Rita.

"She knew," Pitt agreed, gently taking Renee by the arm and restraining her.

"But why?" Renee demanded. "What did we do to deserve a horrible death?"

Rita would say no more. The expression on her face altered from surprise to anger mixed with hatred. Renee would have loved to have rammed her fist into Rita's face. "What will we do with her?"

"Nothing," Pitt replied with a slight shrug. He knew he could no longer bluff Rita. She had said all she was going to say. "Keep her locked in the cabin until we reach Costa Rica. I'll have Rudi call ahead and have the local law authorities waiting on the dock to take her into custody."

E XHAUSTION CREPT up on Pitt. He was dead tired, but so were the others. He had one more chore to perform before he could catch a short catnap. He looked around for the lounge chair, but remembered Renee had thrown it overboard. He stretched out on the deck that had been cleared of the phony fishing gear, leaned his back against a bulwark and dialed his Globalstar tri-mode satellite phone.

Sandecker sounded angered. "Why haven't I heard from you people before now?"

"We've been busy," Pitt muttered. Then he spent the next twenty minutes bringing the admiral up to speed. Sandecker patiently listened without interruption until Pitt ended by relating his conversation with Rita Anderson.

"What could Specter possibly have to do with any of this?" Sandecker's voice sounded confused.

"At the moment, my best guess is that he has a secret he wants to keep and will murder the crew of any boat that stumbles into his realm."

"I've heard they have construction contracts with the Red Chinese throughout Nicaragua and Panama."

"Loren mentioned the same connection over dinner the other night."

"I'll order an investigation into Odyssey's activities," said Sandecker.

"You might also check out Rita and David Anderson and a yacht named *Epona*."

"I'll put Yaeger on it first thing."

"It will be interesting to see how this woman ties in to this thing."

"Did you discover a source of the brown crud?"

"We homed in on the position where it's rising from the seafloor."

"Then it looks like a natural phenomenon?"

"Patrick Dodge doesn't think so." Pitt stifled a yawn. "He claims there is no way the mineral ingredients that make up the crud can rise up from the bottom like it was shot out of a cannon. He says it has to be an artificial upwelling. There must be something nasty going on here that borders on *The Twilight Zone*."

"Then we're back to square one," said Sandecker.

"Not quite," Pitt said quietly. "I have a little expedition of my own I'd like to carry out."

"I've sent a NUMA jet transport to the airport near the Rio Colorado Lodge with a crew to patch up *Poco Bonito* before they sail it north. Gunn, Dodge and Ford will be transported back to Washington. I'd like you and Al to join them."

"The job isn't finished."

Sandecker didn't argue. He'd learned long ago that Pitt's judgment was generally on the money. "What is your plan?"

Pitt stared across the sea toward the green forested coastal mountain ranges rising beyond white sandy beaches. "I think a cruise up the San Juan River to Lake Nicaragua might be in order."

"What do you expect to find so far from the sea and the brown crud?"

"Answers," Pitt answered, his mind already traveling upriver. "Answers to this whole mess."

PART THREE

From Odyssey
to Odyssey

EL CASTILLO

24

I F THERE WAS ONE SMALL BENEFIT to Hurricane Lizzie, it
was that she had swept the brown crud away from Navidad Bank.
The water over the coral was blue-green again, with visibility at nearly
two hundred feet. Along with the clean water, the fish had returned
to their habitat and took up residence again as if no tempest had cast
them out.

Another research vessel replaced *Sea Sprite* for the investigation of
the sunken structure. Built and designed specifically as a dive support
vessel for archaeological exploration in shallow water, *Sea Yesteryear*
rarely worked out of sight of the shore. Her projects had included the
underwater ruins of the Alexandria Library in Egypt, the Chinese
fleet sunk by kamikaze winds off Japan, early Swedish and Russian
trade ships in the Baltic and a host of other historical events her team
of scientists had surveyed.

She featured four-point mooring capabilities and both saturation
and surface gas/air diving system configurations. A moon pool in the

center of her hull was fully equipped for diving operations and robotic vehicle launch and recovery, and included machinery for retrieving artifacts from the seafloor. A spacious laboratory occupied the entire bow section of the boat and incorporated the most up-to-date scientific equipment for the analysis and conservation of recovered ancient artifacts.

Short by most research ship standards at one hundred and fifty-one feet in length, she was broad and roomy with an overall breadth of forty-five feet. Two big diesel engines moved her through the water at twenty knots, and she carried a crew of four and a team of ten scientists. Those who had served aboard *Sea Yesteryear* were proud of the times they had rewritten maritime history. And, as the Navidad Bank exploration proceeded, they were certain they were on the verge of the greatest discovery yet.

At first, the marine archaeologists who examined the rooms of stone were not even certain the structures were man-made. Nor did the area produce an abundance of artifacts. Except for the contents of the stone bed and the cauldron, the only others found came from the kitchen. But as the investigation continued, more and more incredible archaeological treasures were recorded. One revelation that the geologists on the team discovered was that the structure once sat in the open above a small hill. This came to light when the encrustation on one six-inch-square piece of wall in the bedroom was delicately brushed away and it became obvious the rooms were not carved from the rock but constructed of stone fitted on stone when Navidad Bank was an island rising above the water.

Dirk stood in the laboratory with his sister at his side, examining the artifacts that had been carefully transported to the ship's laboratory and immersed in trays of seawater in preparation for the lengthy conservation process. He very gently held up an exquisite gold torque, the neck chain that had been found on the stone bed.

"Every relic we've removed from the bed and the cauldron has belonged to a woman."

"It's even more intricate than much of the jewelry produced today," said Summer, admiring the chain as the gold reflected the sun coming through the ship's ports.

"Until I can make a comparison with archaeological records in European archives, I'd have to date it as Middle Bronze Age." The voice was soft and punctuated, like a mild summer shower on a metal roof. It belonged to Dr. Jeffrey Parks, who carried himself like a wary wolf, with his face low and thrust out. He was six feet eight inches in height and constantly bent over from the stratosphere. A collegiate all-star basketball player, he was sidelined because of a serious knee injury and never played again. Instead, he studied marine archaeology, eventually gaining a doctorate with his thesis on ancient underwater cities. He had been invited on the expedition by Admiral Sandecker because of his specialized expertise.

Parks walked past the long table fitted with open tanks that held the ancient relics and stopped at a large board mounted on a bulkhead that displayed more than fifty photos taken of the interior of the underwater edifice. He paused and with the eraser end of a pencil tapped a montage of photos showing the floor plan. "What we have is not a city or a fortress. No structures that extend beyond the rooms of your original discovery are apparent. Call it a mansion for its time or a small palace that became the tomb of an elite woman. Perhaps a queen or a high priestess who was rich enough to commission her own jewelry."

"Pity there is nothing left of her," said Summer. "Not even an indication of her skull. Even her teeth are gone."

Parks gave a slight twist of his mouth. "Her bones disappeared centuries ago, along with all her garments, soon after the structure was inundated by the sea." He moved to a large photograph taken before the artifacts were removed from the stone bed and tapped the pencil again on a close-up picture of the bronze body armor. "She must have been a warrior who led men into battle. The cuirass in the photo looks made of one piece and had to be put on over the head like a metal sweater."

Summer tried to imagine how the cuirass would fit on her. She had read that the Celts were large people for their time, but the armor looked far too small for her torso. "How in the world did she come to be here?"

"I haven't a clue," said Parks. "As a traditional archaeologist who isn't supposed to believe in diffusion, the contact between the Americas and other parts of the world before Columbus, I'm required to say that this is an elaborate hoax perpetrated by the Spanish sometime after fifteen hundred."

Summer frowned. "You can't really believe that?"

Parks gave a tiny smile. "Not really. Not after what we've seen here. But until we can prove without doubt how these artifacts came to be on Navidad Bank, the controversy will shake the world of ancient history."

Summer made her case. "But it *was* possible for ancient seafarers to cross the sea."

"No one says it was impossible. People have crossed the Atlantic and Pacific in everything from boats made out of cowhides to six-foot sailboats. It's entirely conceivable that fishermen from Japan or Ireland were blown by storms to the Americas. Archaeologists admit there are many curious bits and pieces of evidence that suggest European and Asian influence throughout Central and South American art and architecture. But no legitimate object from this side of the pond has been found over there."

"Our father found proof of the Vikings' presence in the United States," argued Summer.

"And he and Al Giordino discovered artifacts from the Alexandria Library in Texas," added Dirk.

Parks shrugged. "The fact still remains that artifacts proven to have come from the Americas have yet to turn up from excavations in Europe or Africa."

"Ah," said Summer, shooting her arrow, "what about the traces of nicotine and cocaine that have been found in Egyptian mummies? Tobacco and cocoa leaves came only from the Americas."

"I thought you'd bring that up," Parks said, with a sigh. "Egyptologists are still fighting over that one."

Summer frowned thoughtfully. "Could the answers still be down in the rooms?"

"Maybe," Parks admitted. "Our marine biologists are running tests on the encrustation found on the walls, while our phytochemist examines studies about the remains of plant life in an effort to determine a time line for how long the building was covered by the sea."

Summer looked lost in thought. "Could there be any inscriptions under the encrustation, something the archaeologists might have missed?"

Parks laughed. "The early Celts left behind no art or written records depicting their culture. Finding carved inscriptions would be implausible, unless, of course, we're wrong in our dating of Navinia."

"Navinia?"

Parks stared at a computer printout of the architecture of the sunken structure as it might have looked when built. "It's as good a name as any, don't you think?"

"As good as any," Dirk echoed. He looked at Summer. "Why don't you and I dive first thing tomorrow morning and search the walls for inscriptions? Besides, I think it only fitting that we pay our respects to our high priestess for the last time."

"Don't linger too long," said Parks. "The captain has given notice that the anchors come up at noon. He wants to transport the artifacts to Fort Lauderdale as soon as possible."

As they exited the laboratory, Summer looked at Dirk with a curious gleam in her eye. "Since when are you overcome with nostalgia?"

"There is a practical method to my madness."

"Oh, and what is that?" she asked dryly.

He stared back at her with a crooked little grin. "I have an idea something important was missed."

Now that they knew where to continue the search, they swam straight to the anteroom. The ancient compartments were empty now. Only yesterday it had looked like an airport waiting room. The ship's scientists were probing every nook and cranny. Now, with all the artifacts removed and under preservation aboard *Sea Yesteryear,* and their investigation all but finished, they were back on board, compiling and evaluating their findings. Dirk and Summer had the submerged rooms all to themselves. Now that there were no archaeologists looking over their shoulders, they saw little reason to treat the walls with gloves of velvet.

As planned, they began their search in the entry chamber, Summer examining one wall while Dirk took the other, scraping away any sea growth or encrustation with putty knives until they reached bare stone, knowing they were committing sacrilege in the eyes of a conscientious archaeologist. They worked the walls, scraping in long horizontal bands, concentrating from four to five feet from the floor. Because the average height of people three thousand years ago was several inches shorter than in the present, their eye level would have been lower. Using this historical fact, Dirk and Summer decided to compress their search area.

It was slow going. After an hour of fruitless inspection, they returned to *Sea Yesteryear* to replace their nearly empty air tanks. Although all NUMA dive support vessels carried hyperbaric chambers, Dirk meticulously checked the repetitive dive tables with his computer to avoid decompression sickness.

Twenty minutes into their second dive, after they moved from the antechamber deeper into a long hallway, Summer suddenly tapped the handle of her putty knife on the wall to attract Dirk's attention. He im-

mediately swam to her side and stared at the section on the wall she
had scraped and was excitedly pointing at.

She had scraped the letters PICTOGRAPHS in the growth.

Dirk nodded and gave a thumbs-up in elation. Together, they began
feverishly cleaning the encrusted stones with their gloved hands and
fingers, working cautiously so they did not damage the precious relic
that slowly materialized in the gloom. Finally, the carved images in the
stone were exposed. Brother and sister felt a sense of triumph in
knowing they had outfoxed the professionals and were looking at
something no other human had laid eyes on in three thousand years.

The pictographs offered a much-sought-after clue to the mystery
of the sunken house. Dirk turned his dive light on the stone depictions
to highlight their details. Further investigation revealed that the images
traveled down both sides of the hallway in two bands two feet wide
and about five feet off the floor. The pattern was similar in design to
the Bayeux Tapestry that illustrated the Battle of Hastings in 1066.

Dirk and Summer hung in the water and stared in almost religious
awe at the sculpted carvings that depicted men sailing in ships. They
were strange-looking men, with large round eyes and thick beards.
Their weapons consisted of long daggers, short swords with an angle
and battle-axes with curved edges. Several of the soldiers rode in chariots alone, but most fought on foot.

Battle scenes with much carnage were rendered. The scenes seemed
to portray several battles in a protracted war. There were also images
of women with bared breasts throwing spears into their enemy.

Summer lightly ran one gloved hand over the female figures. She
turned to Dirk and smiled a superior feminine smile.

The ornamental scenes began with ships leaving a burning city.
Farther along, the ships were tossed about by storms, followed by
land battles with odd-looking creatures. Near the bottom, there was
only one ship left of the fleet, the rest having been destroyed. Then
it too was depicted sinking in a storm. Near the end, an image showed

a man and woman embracing before he sailed away on what looked like a raft with a sail.

They had found a classic chronicle carved in stone by an ancient artisan that had stood unseen by human eyes under the sea for thousands of years. Dirk and Summer gazed at each other through their face masks in exhilaration, never imagining that they would find anything so incredible and so extraordinary.

Dirk motioned toward the doorway leading out into the reef. The dive light blinked out, and they turned and swam toward the surface, leaving the precious treasure exposed for those who would soon follow and photograph and reveal the pictographs in their full glory.

25

Poco Bonito passed through the mouth of the Rio Colorado in the early afternoon in water that changed from the traces of the brown crud to the algae green of the river. Burly white clouds splashed the blue sky, some dropping light showers as they blocked out the sun. The NUMA crew stood on the deck and waved to the fleet of small fishing boats that darted past, outboard motors buzzing like a swarm of hornets, fishermen proudly displaying their catch of tarpon, snook and barracuda. One boat celebrated with raised bottles of beer as they passed the crippled research boat. Two of the anglers held up a tarpon that looked as if it weighed more than a hundred pounds.

Gunn ran *Bonito* in slowly, keeping to one side of the river out of the way of the little fiberglass fishing boats, skirting the buoys and angling around a slight bend. He made a half turn on the wheel, setting the bow on a heading past the Rio Colorado Lodge and beyond, to a dock that led to a covered walkway bordered by flowers that trailed up to a large house set under a grove of palm trees.

"It looks heavenly," said Renee, admiring the lush beauty of the tropical forest surrounding the house that was built from lava rock with a large thatched palm frond roof.

"A fisherman's paradise," Gunn said from the pilothouse. "Built by an old friend from my academy days, Jack McGee. If you enjoy seafood, you'll get your fill of exotically prepared fish here. He's accumulated thousands of recipes from around the world and has written several books on the subject."

Pitt jumped to the dock and took the lines thrown by Giordino and tied them to the cleats. By law, they stayed close to the boat until their papers were checked by the local border guards, who were surprised at the damage suffered by *Poco Bonito.* Renee used her Spanish to spin a wild story of how they escaped a fleet of drug-smuggling pirates, as cutthroat as any of their ancestors who pillaged the Spanish Main.

Since the incident happened in Nicaraguan waters, the guards didn't request a report. Rita Anderson, on the other hand, would have created a sticky problem. She had no papers, and since Pitt and Gunn had no wish to explain her presence on board their boat, Renee bound and gagged her before she and Giordino crammed Rita into a storage closet in the engine room. The guards made a cursory inspection of the boat, and had no desire to stain their starched and neatly pressed uniforms in the engine room after seeing Giordino looking like James Dean after the oil well came in in *Giant.*

After the guards had walked up the dock out of earshot, Dodge turned to Pitt. "Why are we treating Mrs. Anderson like a criminal and keeping her as a prisoner? Her husband was murdered and her yacht seized by pirates."

"She's not what you think," said Renee curtly.

Pitt kept his eyes trained on the guards as they climbed into a Land Rover and drove from the dock over a dirt road muddied from rain. "Renee is right. Mrs. Anderson is no pawn. She's mixed up to her ears in shady business. Admiral Sandecker has contacted Costa Rican law authorities, who agreed to take her into custody and launch an investigation. They should be along any time."

Renee stepped down the ladder to the cabin. "I'd better get our princess ready for her incarceration."

She had no sooner dropped out of sight than a man strode briskly down the walkway and onto the dock. Jack McGee was a ruddy-faced man in his late forties. His hair was blond without a trace of gray, as was his Wyatt Earp mustache. The adobe brown eyes set far apart gave him the look of an animal on constant lookout for a predator. He wore navy blue shorts with a flowered shirt and a tired old Navy officer's cap that looked like it had seen action in World War II.

Gunn stepped forward and they shook hands before embracing. "Jack, you age ten years every time we meet."

"That's because we only meet every ten years." McGee greeted Gunn in a voice that sounded like he sang bass in a choir.

Gunn made the introductions. Giordino merely waved from the engine room hatch. "We have one more of our crew for you to meet, Renee Ford. She's handling a little matter below."

McGee smiled knowingly. "Your unexpected guest?"

Gunn nodded. "Rita Anderson, the lady I mentioned over the satellite phone when I announced our dropping in."

"Police Inspector Gabriel Ortega is an old friend," said McGee. "He'll require you to come down to the station and fill out a report, but I think you'll find him most courteous and considerate."

"Are you plagued by piracy in these waters?" asked Pitt.

McGee laughed and shook his head vigorously. "Not in Costa Rica. But they sprout like weeds to the north in Nicaragua."

"Why there and not here?"

"Costa Rica is the success story of Central America. The standard of living is higher than in most other Latin nations. Although largely agricultural, tourism is booming and, surprisingly, they're a big exporter of electronics and microprocessors. In contrast, Nicaragua has gone through thirty years of revolution that's left the infrastructure in ruins. After the government finally stabilized, most of the rebels, who possessed no job skills other than fighting guerrilla warfare, refused to take up farming or menial labor jobs. They found drug smuggling more profitable. This led to piracy, since they had to build a fleet of cocaine runners."

"Have you heard any rumors about the brown crud?"

McGee gave a little shake of his head. "Only that it exists north and east out in the Caribbean. Between the bandits, the missing ships and the contamination, the fishing industry off Nicaragua has died an unnatural death." McGee turned and doffed his hat as a uniformed police official came down from the house and stepped onto the dock. "Ah, Gabriel, there you are."

"Jack, old friend," said Ortega. "What mischief have you gotten yourself into now?"

"Not me," McGee laughed. "My friends from the States here."

Though decidedly Latin, Ortega looked like Agatha Christie's Hercule Poirot—the same black, slicked-back straight hair and thin, immaculately trimmed black mustache, the soft dark eyes that missed nothing. He spoke in English, with just a bare trace of Spanish. He revealed perfectly capped teeth when he smiled during the introductions.

"Your Admiral Sandecker alerted me of your situation," he said. "I hope you will accommodate me with a detailed report of your adventures with the pirates."

Pitt nodded. "Count on it, Inspector."

"Where is this woman you saved from the pirate ship?"

"Down below." A concerned frown crossed Pitt's forehead. He turned to Giordino. "Al, why don't you drop below and see what's keeping Renee and our guest?"

Giordino wiped his hands on an oily rag without comment and disappeared below. He was back in less than a minute, his face a mask of wrath, his dark eyes bleak. "Rita is gone and Renee is dead," he said, his face a mask of anger. "Murdered."

26

DURING THOSE INITIAL MOMENTS of shock, everyone stood there stunned with disbelief. They stared at Giordino stupidly, not understanding what he'd said. It took another five seconds for the implication to sink in.

Then Dodge blurted, "What are you saying?"

"Renee is dead," Giordino repeated simply. "Rita murdered her."

Pure rage flooded Pitt. "Where is she?" he demanded.

"Rita?" Giordino's face had the look of someone who had woken up from a nightmare. "She's gone."

"Impossible. How could she leave the boat without being seen?"

"She's not to be found," Giordino said.

"May I see the body?" Ortega asked, with official dispassion.

Pitt was already dropping down the ladder, almost falling on Giordino, who leaped off to one side. "This way, Inspector. The women were in my cabin below."

Inwardly, Pitt felt a flood of guilt at not recognizing Rita as a woman who was capable of murder. He cursed himself for not accompanying Renee, for sending her alone to release her killer.

He muttered, "Oh God, no!" under his breath at the sight of Renee,

stripped nude, lying on the bed with her legs together, arms outstretched in the position of a cross. The image of the Odyssey logo, the
Celtic White Horse of Uffington, had been carved into her stomach.

R ITA HAD acted compliant and docile when Renee removed the
   duct tape from around her arms. But when Renee, innocently unaware that her life was in jeopardy with five men less than ten feet
away, knelt to remove the duct tape from Rita's legs and ankles, the
witch clenched her hands and brought them down in a vicious chop
to the nape of the neck. Renee dropped without uttering a sound.

Rita quickly removed Renee's clothes, laid her out on the bed and
pressed a pillow over her face. There was no struggle. Already unconscious, Renee was never aware of being smothered to death. Then
Rita took a pair of hair scissors from Pitt's shaving kit in the bathroom
and carved the image of the Celtic horse on Renee's stomach. From
start to finish, the hideous act took less than four minutes.

Moving quickly toward the forward section of the boat, Rita came
up through the bow hatch, shielded by the pilothouse. Out of sight
of the men conversing on the stern deck, she climbed over the side
and slipped into the water without making a splash. Then she swam
underwater to the opposite side of the dock, reached the shore and
crawled through the thick vegetation that covered the bank. In the
exact moment Giordino discovered Renee's body, Rita disappeared
into the jungle.

T HE WOMAN cannot get far," said Ortega. "There are no roads
   leading in and out of Rio Colorado. She cannot flee into the jungle and live. My men will apprehend her before she can obtain air
transportation or a boat."

"All she has is the bikini she's wearing," Pitt informed him.

"She took no clothes?"

"Renee's closet is still closed and her clothes are scattered on the deck," said Gunn, pointing to where Rita had thrown them.

"Does she have money?" Ortega asked.

Pitt shook his head. "Not unless Renee had some on her person, which I doubt."

"Without money or a passport, she has no place to run except the jungle."

"Hardly a place a woman could survive in only a bikini," said McGee, who stood in the doorway.

"Please secure the cabin," instructed Ortega. "And do not touch anything."

"Can't we at least dress her?" Pitt requested.

"Not until my forensic staff arrives and conducts a formal examination."

"When can we remove her for a flight to the States?"

"Two days," Ortega replied politely. "In the meantime, please remain here and enjoy Mr. McGee's hospitality until you can all be questioned and reports filled out." He paused to look down at Renee indifferently. "She is from your country?"

Dodge could not bear to look at Renee and turned away. "She lives in Richmond, Virginia," he whispered in a voice that choked.

Pitt looked at Gunn. "We'd better inform the admiral."

"He won't take this sitting down. If I know him, he'll demand Congress declare war and send in the Marines."

For the first time, Ortega's eyes widened. "He would do what, *senor*?"

"A play on words," said Pitt, ignoring the police inspector and drawing a blanket over Renee.

R ITA HURRIEDLY made her way through the jungle, staying close to the riverbank until she reached the Rio Colorado Sport Fishing Lodge. She followed the signs on the walkway to the swimming pool. Wearing her bikini, she fit right in with the other fishing widows lying around the pool while their husbands indulged themselves trolling for tarpon and snook in the river.

Ignoring the stares from the pool attendants and waiters, she snatched up a towel from an empty lounge chair and draped it over one shoulder. Then she stepped along the walkway between the lodge's rooms. Finding one where the maid was cleaning the room, she stepped inside.

"Tome su tiempo." She told the maid to take her time, acting as if it were her room.

"Me casi acaban," the maid replied, as she carried the dirty towels to her cart on the walkway and closed the door.

Rita sat at the desk, picked up a phone and requested an open line. When a voice answered, she said, "This is Flidais."

"One moment."

Then came another voice. "The line is clear. Please go ahead."

"Flidais?"

"Yes, Epona, I'm here."

"Why are you calling on an open line from a hotel?"

"We have an unexpected problem."

"Yes?"

"A NUMA research boat looking for the source of the brown crud was not deceived by the hologram and destroyed our yacht."

"Understood," said the woman called Epona, without the slightest trace of emotion. "Where are you?"

"After our yacht sank, I was captured by the NUMA people, who held me prisoner. I escaped and am now sitting in a room at the Rio Colorado Lodge. It's only matter of minutes before the local police trail me here."

"Our crew?"

"Some were killed. The rest escaped in the helicopter and abandoned me."

"They will be dealt with." The voice paused. "Did they interrogate you?"

"They tried, but I gave them a phony story and told them my name was Rita Anderson."

"Keep the line open and wait."

Flidais, alias Rita, went to the closet and found a flowered-print summer dress that was a size ten to her size eight. Close enough, she thought. Better large than too small. She pulled it on over her bikini and found a scarf, which she tied around her head to hide her red hair. It didn't bother her in the least that she was stealing another woman's clothes and running up a large phone bill, certainly not after having killed Renee. Next she pulled on open sandals that were a close fit. A pair of sunglasses were sitting on a bed stand, so she slipped them on.

She smiled to herself as she searched the drawers of the dresser and found the room occupant's purse. Why women never used any creativity in hiding their valuables was a mystery to Flidais. It was well known among hotel thieves that women invariably hid their purses, including their wallets, under their clothes in a drawer. She found eight hundred dollars American and a few Costa Rican colones. With an exchange rate of 369,000 colones to the dollar, most monetary transactions in Costa Rica were handled in foreign currency.

Barbara Hacken was the name below the picture of the face on the driver's license and the photo inside the passport. Except for a different hair color and a few years' difference in age, they might have passed for sisters. Flidais cracked the door to see if the room's occupant was coming up the walkway, when Epona came back on the line. "All is arranged, sister. I'm sending my private plane to pick you up at the airport. It will be waiting on the tarmac when you arrive. Do you have transportation?"

"The hotel should have a car to carry guests to and from the airport."

"You may have to show identification to get past airport security."

"All is established on that score," answered Flidais, slinging the purse strap over her shoulder. "I'll see you and our sisters at the ritual in three days."

Then she hung up and walked to the hotel lobby past two local uniformed policemen who were checking the grounds. Looking for a woman last seen in a bikini, they gave her a quick glance, thinking she was a guest of the lodge, and passed on. She spotted Barbara Hacken sunning at the pool. She looked to be dozing. When Flidais reached the lobby, the owner of the lodge was standing behind the desk and smiled when she asked for a car.

"You and your husband are not leaving us, I hope."

"No," she said vaguely, scratching her nose to cover her face. "He's still out on the river after the big ones. I'm meeting some friends who are dropping in at the airport to refuel before continuing on to Panama City."

"We'll see you for dinner?"

"Of course," Flidais said, turning away. "Where else would I eat?"

When her car reached the airport gate to the tarmac, the driver stopped, as the security guard stepped from a small office.

"Are you leaving Rio Colorado?" he asked Flidais through the open window.

"Yes, I'm flying to Managua."

"Passport, please?"

She handed him Barbara Hacken's passport and sat back looking out the opposite window.

The guard went by the book. He took a long moment comparing the passport photo with Flidais's facial features. The hair was covered by a scarf, but a few red strands seeped from under the silk. He was not concerned. Women seldom tinted their hair the same color they wore the month before. The face seemed similar, but he could not see the eyes behind the sunglasses.

"Please open your luggage."

"Sorry, I don't have luggage. Tomorrow is my husband's birthday.

I forgot to buy him a gift, so I'm on a shopping trip to Managua. I intend to return in the morning."

Satisfied, the guard handed back the passport and waved the car through.

Five minutes later, everyone within a mile of the airport stared in awe as a lavender-colored aircraft that looked too large to land on the airstrip came in low over the trees and set down smoothly. Reversing engines and braking, it stopped a hundred yards short of the runway's north end. Then it turned and taxied to where Flidais was waiting in the car. Five minutes later, she was aloft on the Beriev Be-210 bound for Panama City.

27

THE TWO MEN CASUALLY lolling in what the native villagers called a *panga* looked like any of the local men who fished the Rio San Juan. They wore baggy white shorts and T-shirts with soft white baseball-style caps. Two outriggers hung over the *panga*'s stern on an angle, their lines trolling for the fishermen's next dinner.

Except for a passing experienced fisherman who bothered to notice, no one on shore would have guessed the lines carried no hooks. In a waterway teeming with fish, no hook went without a bite more than a few seconds after it dropped under the surface.

The skiff was propelled by a thirty-horsepower Mariner outboard steered by cables running to a center console-column surmounted by an automobile steering wheel. The flat-bottomed, twenty-foot *panga* moved smartly up the calm river through the tropical rain forest under a light shower. They were traveling in the middle of the long rainy season that began in May and lasted through January. The jungle vegetation was so thick along the shore it seemed that every plant was in constant battle against its neighbor for a glimpse of the sun that beamed down infrequently through the never-ending mass of clouds.

Pitt and Giordino had purchased the *panga*, whose bow was painted with the name *Greek Angel,* along with fuel and supplies, within hours after the NUMA jet had taken off for Washington with Rudi Gunn, Patrick Dodge and Renee Ford's body. The repair crew that was flown into Barra Colorado had beached *Poco Bonito* at low tide and were working efficiently to make her seaworthy for the voyage north.

Jack McGee threw them a going-away party and insisted on stocking their boat with enough beer and wine to start a saloon. Inspector Ortega was on hand, graciously expressing his appreciation for their cooperation in his investigation, and his sorrow for Renee's senseless murder. He was also irritated and regretful that the woman they knew as Rita Anderson had eluded his dragnet. Once Ortega's team learned of Barbara Hacken's missing passport, and they interrogated the owner of the lodge and the security guard at the airport gate, they were certain Rita had fled Costa Rica to the United States. Pitt added a piece to the puzzle when he heard the aircraft was painted lavender. This fact placed Rita squarely in the Odyssey camp. Now Ortega vowed to pursue Renee's murder internationally and to seek the cooperation of American law enforcement.

Pitt sat relaxed, leaned back in a raised chair in front of the wheel column, and steered the boat with one foot as they passed quiet picturesque lagoons that opened onto the river. Giordino had borrowed a lounge chair and pad from McGee, and reclined with his feet hanging over the bow, warily eyeing the occasional eighteen-foot crocodile that he spotted sunning itself on the bank.

Wise to the ways of a rain forest, Giordino shrouded himself with mosquito netting. Not usually mentioned in the travel brochures, in this part of the world the little bloodsuckers were nearly as prolific as raindrops. Not wanting to hinder his movements, Pitt soaked his exposed skin with repellent.

The first twenty miles took them northwesterly along the Rio Colorado until it eventually met the muddy waters of the Rio San Juan that served as the meandering borderline between Nicaragua and Costa Rica. From here, it was another eighty kilometers up the river until they reached the town of San Carlos on Lake Cocibolca, better known simply as Lake Nicaragua.

"I've yet to see any signs of construction," said Giordino, studying the shoreline through a pair of binoculars.

"You've already seen it," said Pitt, watching the multicolored birds nesting in the trees whose branches reached over the flowing water.

Giordino twisted in his lounge chair, pulled down his sunglasses and stared at Pitt over the rims as if he were looking at a bookie giving hundred-to-one odds on a favorite to win the next race. "Run that by me again."

"Your friend Micky Levy. Remember her?"

"The name rings a bell," muttered Giordino, still trying to follow Pitt's tack.

"Over dinner she talked about plans to build an 'underground bridge,' a railroad tunnel system that was designed to travel through Nicaragua between the oceans."

"She also said the project was never launched because Specter pulled out."

"A deception."

"A deception," Giordino parroted.

"After the engineers and geologists, like your friend, Micky, finished their survey, Odyssey officials insisted they sign confidentiality agreements never to reveal any information about the proposed project. Specter threatened to withhold any payment until they agreed. Then they announced that after studying the reports, they decided the project was not practical, and cost-prohibitive."

"How do you know all this?"

"I called your friend Micky just before we left Washington and after she faxed me the site plans," Pitt said casually.

"Go on."

"I asked her a few more questions regarding Specter and the underground bridge. Didn't she tell you?"

"I guess she forgot," said Giordino pensively.

"Anyway, as it turns out, Specter never had any intention of dumping the project. His Odyssey engineers have been digging furiously for more than two years. This is borne out by the port we passed, with containerships unloading what was probably mining equipment."

"Wasn't it I who said, 'A neat trick if he could hide millions of tons of excavated rock and muck'?"

"And you were right, it is a neat trick."

A light suddenly flashed on in Giordino's head. "The brown crud?"

"The million-dollar answer," Pitt acknowledged. "Satellite photos never showed construction activity because there was none to be seen. The only way to hide millions of tons of dirt and rock was to build a large tube, mix the muck with water and pump it a couple of miles offshore into the sea."

Giordino opened a Costa Rican beer and wiped the humidity-induced sweat with a towel across his face under the mosquito net. He rolled the cold can across his forehead. "Okay, mister smart guy, why the secrecy? Why would Specter go to such great lengths to cover up the project? Where is the gain if it was created and built to transport goods and materials from sea to shining sea and no one knows it's there?"

Pitt took a beer thrown by Giordino and pulled the tab. "If I knew that, we wouldn't be swimming in our own sweat cruising up the river admiring the wildlife."

"What do we hope to find?"

"An entrance, for one thing. They can't completely hide men and equipment going in and out of the tunnels."

"You think we'll find it on the jungle ride through hell on the *African Queen*?"

Pitt laughed. "Not on, but under. According to Micky's site plan, the excavation would have run under a town called El Castillo halfway up the river."

"So what's the attraction in El Castillo?"

"Tunnels of extreme length require ventilation shafts to supply air to the workers, cool or heat the air as required and bleed off exhaust fumes from the excavation equipment and smoke in the event of a fire."

Giordino stared uneasily at a huge crocodile swiveling off the bank into the water. Then his gaze turned to the impenetrable jungle along the north bank. "I hope you don't have any plans to hike in there. Mama Giordino's sonny boy would never be seen again."

"El Castillo is an isolated community on the river with no roads in or out. The main attraction is an old Spanish fortress."

"And you think a ventilation shaft pops up where everybody in town can see it," Giordino said dubiously. "Seems to me the jungle is a more ideal hiding place for ventilator shafts. It's so thick no aircraft or satellite photo could spot a shaft from above."

"No doubt most are hidden in the jungle, but I'm counting on them constructing one that comes up near civilization in case they have to use it for an emergency evacuation."

The scenery along the river was so spectacular, the two men drifted off into silence as they absorbed the beauty of the vegetation and the varied species of wildlife. It was like a boating wildlife safari through untouched tropical splendor. They spotted white-faced spider monkeys jabbering at jaguars which lurked under the trees. Anteaters as large as blue-ribbon state fair sows ambled through the brush, keeping a safe distance inshore from the caimans and crocodiles. Colorfully beaked toucans and multihued feathered parrots flew amid rainbows of butterflies and orchids. The jungles around the Rio San Juan had been described by Mark Twain when he journeyed down the river as an earthly paradise, the most enchanted land to be experienced anywhere.

Pitt kept the *Greek Angel* at a steady and smooth five knots. This was not water to speed through and cause waves from your wake to wash over the environmentally perfect shoreline. The fabulous three thousand acres of virgin rain forest was preserved as the Indio Maiz Biological Reserve. Three hundred species of reptiles, two hundred species of mammals and over six hundred species of birds called it home.

It was four o'clock in the afternoon when they turned off the Rio San Juan onto the Rio Bartola and cruised a short distance before docking at the Refugio Bartola Lodge and Research Center. Nestled in the rain forest, the compound had eleven rooms with private baths and mosquito nets. Pitt and Giordino each registered for a room.

After cleaning up, they headed for the bar and restaurant. Pitt had a tequila on the rocks whose brand was unknown to him. Giordino, claiming he had seen over a dozen Tarzan movies crawling with Englishmen on safari, opted for gin. Pitt noticed a fat man in a white suit sitting by himself at a table near the bar. There was an air about the man that suggested he was a respected local resident of the river, someone who might be a wealth of information.

Pitt approached the man. "Pardon me, sir, but I wondered if you might like to join my friend and me."

The man looked up and Pitt could see he was quite elderly, approaching his eighties. His face was flushed and he sweated freely, but miraculously managed not to stain his white suit. He wiped a handkerchief over his bald head and nodded. "Of course, of course, I'm Percy Rathbone. Please, it might be easier if you joined me," he said, pointing at his girth that amply filled his wicker chair.

"My name is Dirk Pitt and my friend here is Al Giordino."

The handshake was firm but sweaty. "Pleased to meet you. Sit down, sit down."

Pitt was amused that Rathbone had a habit of repeating his words. "You have the look of a man who knows and enjoys the jungle."

"It shows, it shows, does it?" said Rathbone, with a short laugh. "Lived along the river in Nicaragua and Costa Rica most all my life. My family came here during World War Two. My father was an agent for the British, keeping an eye on Germans who tried to operate hidden facilities in the lagoons to service and refuel their U-boats."

"If I may ask, how does someone earn a living on a river in the middle of nowhere?"

Rathbone looked at Pitt slyly. "Would you, would you believe I rely on tourism?"

Pitt wasn't sure he believed him, but played along. "Then you own a local business."

"Right on, right on. I make a tidy income off fishermen and nature lovers who come to visit the refuge. I have a small chain of resorts between Managua and San Juan del Norte. You gentlemen should look me up on my website when you get home."

"But this refuge is owned and run by the wildlife refuge."

Rathbone seemed to stiffen slightly at Pitt's perception. "True, true. I'm on holiday. I like to get away from my own ventures and relax here where I'm not bothered by guests. How about you fellows? Come for the fishing?"

"That, and the wildlife. We began our cruise at Barra Colorado and intend to reach Managua eventually."

"A marvelous tour, a marvelous tour," said Rathbone. "You'll enjoy every minute of it. There's nothing like it in the hemisphere."

A round of drinks came and Giordino signed for them on his room. "Tell me, Mr. Rathbone, why is a river that runs almost from the Pacific to the Atlantic known to so few outsiders?"

"The river *was* world-famous until the Panama Canal was built. Then the Rio San Juan fell into the dustbin of history. A Spanish conquistador named Hernandez de Cordoba sailed up the San Juan in 1524. He made it all the way into Lake Nicaragua and established the colonial city of Granada on the opposite end. The Spanish who followed Cordoba built forts bristling with guns throughout Central America to keep the French and English out. One was El Castillo a few miles up the river from here."

"Were the Spanish successful?" asked Pitt.

"Indeed yes, indeed yes," Rathbone said, waving his hands. "But not entirely. Henry Morgan and Sir Francis Drake sailed up the river, but never made it past El Castillo into the lake. A hundred or more years later, they were followed by Horatio Nelson when he was a mere captain. He sailed a small fleet of ships up the San Juan and attacked El Castillo, which still stands. His assault failed. The only time in his career he lost a battle. He was reminded of the embarrassment the rest of his life."

"Why is that?" asked Giordino.

"Because he lost an eye during the attack."

"Right or left?"

Rathbone thought a moment, not getting the joke, then shrugged. "I don't remember."

Pitt savored a sip of the tequila. "How long did the Spanish control the river?"

"Until the early eighteen fifties and the California gold rush. Commodore Vanderbilt, the railroad and shipping tycoon, saw a golden opportunity. He made a deal with the Spanish for his ships to provide ferry service for eager prospectors who had booked his steamers in New York and Boston for the long voyage to California. His passengers changed from oceangoing ships to river steamers at San Juan del Norte. Then they steamed up the San Juan and across the lake to La Virgen. From there, it was only a short twelve-mile wagon ride to the little Pacific port of San Juan del Sur, actually only a couple of docks, where they reboarded Vanderbilt steamers that carried the gold-hungry miners onto San Francisco. Not only did they cut off hundreds of miles by not sailing around Cape Horn, but they saved another thousand miles bypassing the isthmus at Panama to the south."

"When did river traffic die?" asked Pitt.

"The Accessory Transit Company, as Vanderbilt called it, faded away with the construction of the Panama Canal. The Commodore built a huge mansion in San Juan del Norte, which still stands, although it is abandoned and overgrown with weeds. For eighty years the river lay forgotten, until the nineteen nineties when it emerged as a tourist attraction."

"Seems like it was a more logical route for a canal than Panama."

Rathbone shook his head sadly. "By far, by far, but a complicated game of politics played by your President Teddy Roosevelt put it in hundreds of miles out of the way to the south."

"They could still dig a canal through here," said Giordino thoughtfully.

"Too late. Big business interests in the Panama Canal, environmentalists and ecologists would all fight the project tooth and nail. Even if the Nicaraguan government gave its blessing, no one would put up the money."

"I heard there were plans afoot to build a railroad tunnel through Nicaragua between the oceans."

Rathbone stared out over the river. "There were rumors circulating up and down the river for months, but nothing ever came of it. Surveyors came with transits and tramped through the jungles. Helicopters were buzzing all over the place. Geologists and engineers filled my lodges and drank my whiskey, but after nearly a year they packed up their equipment, went home and that was the end of that."

Giordino finished off his scotch and ordered another. "None ever came back?"

Rathbone shook his head. "Not that I'm aware of."

"Did they give a reason for not pursuing the project?" Pitt queried.

Again, a shake of the head. "None seemed to know more than I did. Their contracts were finished and they were paid off. It all seemed very cloak-and-dagger. I got one of the engineers drunk the night before he was to depart, but all I got out of him was that he and his fellow engineers were all sworn to secrecy."

"Was the general contractor called Odyssey?"

Rathbone stiffened slightly. "Yes, that was it, that was it, Odyssey. The head man even came and stayed at my lodge in El Castillo. A huge fellow. Must have weighed four hundred pounds. Called himself Specter. Very strange. Never did get a good look at his face. He was always surrounded by an entourage, mostly women."

"Women?" Giordino perked up.

"Most attractive, but business executive types. Very aloof, very efficient. Never talked or offered to be friendly with any of the local people."

"How did they arrive?" Pitt put to Rathbone.

"Landed and took off on the river in a big amphibian airplane painted like an orchid."

"Lavender?"

"I guess you could call it that."

Giordino swirled his scotch around the ice cubes. "Did you ever get a hint about why the project never got off the ground?"

"Rumor, gossip and hearsay came up with at least fifty reasons, but none made any sense. My friends in the government at Managua acted as amazed as everyone along the river. They claimed the fault was not theirs. They offered Odyssey every benefit, every advantage, since the project would have greatly enhanced Nicaragua's economy. My own opinion is that Specter found other more profitable projects for the Odyssey Corporation and simply moved on."

At that moment, it felt as if the earth was twitching and the ice in their glasses tinkled, and the contents quivered as if invisible raindrops were falling on it. The tops of the trees in the jungle swayed in unison with the birds squawking and the moan of unseen animals.

"Earthquake," Giordino said indifferently.

"More like a slight earth tremor," Pitt agreed, taking another sip from his drink.

"You fellows don't seem upset at our local ground movement," said Rathbone in mild surprise.

"We grew up in California," Giordino explained.

Pitt exchanged glances with Giordino. Then he said, "I wonder if we'll experience any tremors on the rest of our voyage up the river."

Rathbone looked uneasy. "I doubt it. They come and go like thunder, but very infrequently and have yet to cause any damage. The natives are a superstitious lot. They believe the ancient gods of their ancestors have returned and are living in the jungle."

He slowly, with some effort, rose from his chair and stood unsteadily. "Gentlemen, thank you for the drinks. It was indeed, indeed, most delightful talking with you. But with age comes an urge to go to bed early. Will I see you again tomorrow?"

Pitt came to his feet and shook Rathbone's hand. "Perhaps. We'll probably take a nature hike in the morning and continue our journey later in the afternoon."

"We'd like to spend a day in El Castillo and see the ruins of the fortress before we head upriver into Lake Nicaragua," added Giordino.

"I'm afraid you can only see the fortress from a distance," said Rathbone. "Government police have put it off-limits to all locals and visiting tourists. They claimed it was deteriorating under the crowds wandering the ruins. So much humbug in my book. The rain does far more damage than the feet of a few tourists."

"Are Nicaraguan police guarding the walls?"

"More security than a nuclear bomb factory. Security cameras, guard dogs and a ten-foot fence around the fort, with barbwire running along the top. One resident of El Castillo, a fellow by the name of Jesus Diego, became curious and tried to penetrate the security. Poor fellow was found hanging in a tree on the riverbank."

"Dead?"

"Very dead." Rathbone quickly changed the subject. "If I were you, I wouldn't go near the place."

"We shall take your advice," said Pitt.

"Well, gentlemen, it was a pleasure. Good evening."

As they watched the old man shuffle away, Giordino said to Pitt, "What do you think?"

"Not what he appeared," Pitt said briefly. "He made no mention of the container port."

"You caught the dainty hands too."

"The skin was too smooth and free of blemishes for a man over seventy."

Giordino motioned to a waiter. "Did you pick up on the voice? It sounded unnatural, as if it was a recording."

"Apparently, Mr. Rathbone was handing us a bill of goods."

"It would be nice to know what game he's playing."

When the waiter brought over another round of drinks and asked them if they were ready to be seated for dinner, they both nodded and followed him into the dining room. As they were seated, Pitt asked the waiter, "What is your name?"

"Marcus."

"Marcus, do you often experience earth tremors here in the jungle?"

"Oh, *sí, senor.* But not until three, maybe four, years ago when they began moving up the river."

"The tremors move?" asked Giordino, puzzled.

"*Sí,* very slowly.

"In what direction?"

"They started at the mouth of the river at San Juan del Norte. Now they shake the earth in the jungle above El Castillo."

"Definitely not an eerie phenomenon caused by Mother Nature."

Giordino sighed. "Where is Sheena the Jungle Queen when you need her?"

"The gods will never let man find their secret, not in the jungle," said Marcus, looking around him as if expecting an assassin to creep up on him. "No man who goes in, comes out alive."

"When did men start disappearing in the jungle?" asked Pitt.

"About a year ago, a university expedition went in to study the wildlife, and vanished. No trace of them was ever found. The jungle guards its secrets well."

For the second time that evening, Pitt looked at Giordino and they both cracked tight smiles. "Oh, I don't know," Pitt said slowly. "Secrets have an intriguing habit of becoming revealed."

28

THE FORTRESS COMMANDED the top of an isolated hill that looked more like a huge grassy mound surrounded by several different varieties of trees. El Castillo de la Inmaculada Concepcion, castle of the immaculate conception, was designed along the lines of a Vauban fortification, with bastions on each of its four corners. It was in amazingly good shape after withstanding the onslaught of torrential rains for four hundred years.

"I guess you know," said Giordino as he lay on his back and stared up at the carpet of stars, "that breaking and entering are not in our line of work."

Pitt was stretched out beside him, peering through a nightscope at the fence surrounding the fortress of El Castillo. "Not only that, but NUMA doesn't give us hazard pay."

"We had better call the admiral and Rudi Gunn and give them an update on our adventures. Once we go underground, the phone will be useless."

Pitt took the satellite phone from his knapsack and began dialing a number. "Sandecker is an early riser, so he hits the bed early. Rudi should be handy, since we're only an hour behind Washington."

Five minutes later, Pitt closed the connection. "Rudi is going to have a helicopter standing by at San Carlos if we have to beat a hasty exit."

Giordino returned his attention to the fortress. "I don't see any stairways, only ramps."

"Stone slopes were more efficient for hauling cannons up and down from the ramparts," said Pitt. "Builders in those days knew as much about building strongholds as contractors today know about constructing skyscapers."

"See anything that resembles an air vent to a tunnel?"

"It must come up through the central battlement."

Giordino was glad there was no moon. "So how do we get over the fence, past the security cameras, security alarms, security guards and the dogs?"

"First things first. We can't deal with the security until we penetrate the fence," Pitt replied, quietly absorbed in studying the fortress grounds.

"And how do we do that? It must be ten feet high."

"We could try pole-vaulting over it."

Giordino looked at Pitt queerly. "You must be kidding."

"I am." Pitt pulled a coil of rope from his knapsack. "Can you still climb a tree or does your arthritis limit any physical activity?"

"My aging joints aren't half as stiff as yours."

Pitt slapped his old friend on the shoulder. "Then let's see if two old fogeys can still perform daring feats of agility."

AFTER BREAKFAST at the lodge, and true to their word with Rathbone, Pitt and Giordino had latched on to a tour guide who was leading a dozen tourists through the wildlife reserve, and took a nature hike. They hung in the back of the group, talking between themselves as the tour progressed, hardly noticing the abundance of wildly colored birds and strange animals.

When they returned to the lodge, Pitt made some discreet inquiries about the old man and, as he suspected, the employees of the lodge said that as far as they knew, Rathbone was simply a guest who had showed a Panamanian passport when he registered. If he owned a chain of lodges up and down the river, it was news to them.

At noon, they loaded up the *Greek Angel* with their gear and a few sandwiches from the kitchen and shoved off into the river. The engine caught on the first flick of the starter and they headed out of the lagoon into the main current of the San Juan. The virgin jungle gave way to more open land enhanced by green rolling hills, with trees neatly spaced as if planted by a landscaper in a vast park.

El Castillo was only six kilometers upriver and they had crawled along at a pace just slightly above idle, rounding the final bend an hour later before passing under the colonial fortress that loomed above the town. Moss spread over the ancient lava rock ruins, giving it the appearance of an ugly blot on an otherwise gorgeous landscape, while the picturesque little town below, with its roofs of red tin and colorfully painted *pangas* littering the riverbank, seemed an inviting oasis.

Except for river traffic, the village of El Castillo was completely detached from the rest of the world. There were no roads in or out, no cars and no airport. The residents subsisted by farming the encircling hills, fishing and working in the sawmill or palm oil factory twenty kilometers up the river.

Pitt and Giordino wanted to be seen coming and departing from the little fishing community as they continued their cruise up the river toward Lake Nicaragua, so they tied up the *panga* at a small dock and walked about fifty yards up a dirt road toward a little hotel with a bar and restaurant. They passed several gaily painted wooden houses and waved to three freshly scrubbed little girls in yellow dresses who were playing barefoot on a porch.

They saved their sandwiches from the kitchen of the Refugio Bartola for the coming night excursion and ordered a lunch of fresh fish from the river, downed by the local beer.

The owner, whose name was Aragon, waited on their table. "May I recommend the gaspar. It's not often caught, and when prepared with my special sauce, it is a great delicacy."

"Gaspar," repeated Giordino. "Never heard of that one."

"A living relic millions of years old with armored scales, a snout and fangs. I promise you'll never be able to enjoy it anyplace but here."

"I'm always game for an adventure in gourmet dining," said Pitt. "Bring on the gaspar."

"I'm only going along with great trepidation," Giordino muttered.

"Too bad about the fortress being off-limits," said Pitt conversationally. "I hear the museum was worth a visit."

Aragon stiffened slightly and looked furtively through a window at El Castillo. "*Sí, senor,* it is a pity you must miss it. But the government closed it down as too dangerous for tourists."

"Looks pretty sturdy to me," said Giordino.

Aragon shrugged. "All I know is what the police from Managua told me."

"Do its guards stay in town?" asked Pitt.

Aragon shook his head. "They set up a barracks inside the fortress and are rarely seen except when they are relieved by helicopter from Managua."

"None leave the fort, even for food, drink or pleasure?"

"No, *senor.* They do not socialize with us. Nor do they allow anyone within ten meters of the fence."

Giordino poured his bottle of beer into a glass. "First time I ever heard of a government keeping tourists out of a museum because it might fall down."

"Do you gentlemen wish to stay at the hotel tonight?" asked Aragon.

"No, thank you," answered Pitt. "I'm told there are rapids upriver and we'd like to pass through while it's still light."

"You shouldn't have a problem if you stay inside the channel. Boats rarely overturn in the rapids if people are careful. It's the crocodiles in calm water that present a problem to anyone who falls over the side."

"Does your restaurant serve steak?" Pitt inquired.

"*Sí, senor.* Do you wish more to eat?"

"No, we'd like to take the meat with us for later. Once we pass through the rapids, my friend and I will camp onshore and cook dinner over a fire."

Aragon nodded. "Be sure and camp inland from the banks of the river or you might become food for a hungry crocodile."

"Feeding a croc wasn't exactly what I had in mind," Pitt said, with a broad smile.

D EPARTING LATE in the afternoon, they cruised through the rapids above El Castillo without mishap until they were out of sight of the town. Seeing no other *pangas* but their own between bends in the river, they drove the *Greek Angel* onto the bank, raised the outboard motor and pulled it into the lush underbrush until it was completely hidden from all water traffic.

While it was still light, they found a narrow path that headed toward the town. Then they ate their sandwiches and relaxed and slept till after midnight. Moving cautiously along the path while using their nightscope to penetrate the night, they skirted the little houses and made their way into a thicket of bushes, where they lay now and studied the security surrounding the fortress, spotting and marking the TV security cameras in their minds.

A light drizzle began to fall and soon their thin clothes were soaked through. Standing in a rain in the tropics was like standing in a shower at home. The water temperature was as comfortable to the skin as if it had been preset on a faucet.

When ready, Pitt, followed by Giordino, climbed into a high jatoba tree that towered more than a hundred feet high with a trunk diameter of four feet. The tree stood within several feet of the fence around the fortress, and its lower limbs stretched far over the fence top that was circled with a razor-sharp spiral of steel. Throwing a looped rope around a thick branch ten feet above, Giordino climbed up onto a higher limb before crawling through the smaller branches until he was beyond the fence and twelve feet above the ground. There he paused and swept the ground below with the nightscope.

Using the rope, Pitt hauled his body upward with his hands while his feet walked the tree trunk. Reaching the limb, he crept through the branches until he was even with Giordino's booted feet. "Any sign of the guards and their dogs?" he whispered.

"The guards are lazy," Giordino replied. "They loosed the dogs to run by themselves."

"A wonder they haven't scented us by now."

"You spoke too soon. I see three of them staring in our direction. Oh, oh, here they come on the run."

Before the dogs began barking, Pitt reached into the knapsack on his back, grabbed the steaks from the restaurant and heaved them onto a ramp leading to the nearest bastion. They landed with a distinct plop sound that the dogs heard and homed in on.

"Are you sure this will work?" Giordino murmured.

"It always does in the movies."

"Now there's cheery assurance," Giordino groaned.

Pitt dropped down off the tree limb to the ground and stayed on his feet. Giordino followed, casting a wary eye on the dogs, who chewed their raw meat in happy delirium without paying the least attention to the two intruders.

"I may never doubt you again," Giordino said under his breath.

"I won't forget you said that."

Pitt led the way toward one of the stone ramps, using the night-scope to see when the nearest TV camera swung to its widest arc. When he signaled with a whistle, Giordino ran under the camera's blind side and sprayed the lens with black paint. Moving on, they paused outside the closed and darkened museum, listening for suspicious sounds. Muted voices could be heard over the ramparts inside the main courtyard, where the guards' temporary barracks had been constructed. They entered what was once a storeroom. The stone walls were still solid, but the wooden beams and roof were long gone.

Pitt motioned toward a central turret that rose above the rest of the fort. It was built like a pyramid with the upper half sliced off at the middle. "If there is a vertical ventilator shaft from below, it has to come out there," he said softly.

"The only logical place," Giordino agreed. Then he cocked an ear. "What's that racket?"

Pitt paused, listening, his senses alert, his ears piercing the night. Then he nodded in the darkness. "That whirring sound must be coming from the ventilator fans."

Keeping in the darkened shadows, they climbed a narrow ramp of stones that protruded from the walls of the turret and ended at a small access door. A rush of cool air through the narrow opening struck them with nearly the force of a wind tunnel. Bending low against the draft, Pitt entered and found himself standing at the base of a large wire-mesh cage. The whirring noise from the fan blades beating the air below the mesh opening magnified and tore at their eardrums.

"Noisy devil," yelled Giordino.

"That's because we're right on top of it. Be a lot worse if it didn't have silencers installed. As it is, the noise is pretty well muted outside the turret."

"I didn't bargain for a gale-force wind," said Giordino, as he examined the thickness of the wire-mesh cover.

"The fans are designed to produce a computer-calculated volume of air at an efficient pressure."

"There you go again with the lecture. Don't tell me you took a basic course in tunnel construction."

"Have you forgotten the summer between semesters at the Air

Force Academy when I worked in a silver mine in Leadville, Colorado?" retorted Pitt.

"I remember," said Giordino, smiling. "I spent my summer as a lifeguard in Malibu." Giordino peered through the wire mesh. A glow of light rose from the opening. He walked around the mesh until he found a bolt holding it to a latch. "Locked from the inside," he observed. "We'll need to cut through the mesh."

Pitt produced a small pair of wire cutters from his backpack. "I thought we might need these if we ran into barbwire."

Giordino held them up to the light from below. "They should do nicely. Now please stand back while the master creates an entrance."

It looked easy, but wasn't. Giordino was sweating rivers twenty-five minutes later when he finally cut a hole high and wide enough for them to crawl through. He handed the cutters back to Pitt, pulled the mesh apart and peered into the shaft. The square-cut ventilator shaft, acting as the passage for the expelled air from the tunnel far below, was fifteen feet wide. A circular metal tube filled one corner. This was the access shaft, with a ladder that seemed to vanish into a bottomless pit.

"For maintenance in case the ventilator system needs repair," Pitt volunteered loudly over the fan noise. "It also serves as an emergency exit for the mine workers should there be a fire or a roof collapse in the main tunnel."

Giordino entered the shaft feet first onto the lower rungs of the ladder. He paused and looked up at Pitt sourly. "I hope I won't regret this!" he shouted over the roar of the fans, as he began his descent.

Pitt was thankful the shaft was lit. After dropping down the ladder fifty feet, he paused and looked below. All he could see was the ladder stretching into infinity, like the tracks of a railroad. No sign of the bottom was visible.

He pulled out a paper towel from a pocket, tore it into two small pieces, wadded them up and stuffed them in his ears as plugs against the irritating noise level of the fans. Besides the main fan system,

booster fans had been installed every hundred feet to maintain the required pressure to vent the tunnel to the surface.

After what seemed half a lifetime, and what Giordino estimated was
a drop of five hundred feet, he stopped his descent and waved a hand.
The bottom of the ladder was in view. Slowly, cautiously, he turned
until he was upside-down. Then he crawled downward until his eyes
could see under what was now the roof of a small control center that
monitored and detected the gasses, carbon monoxide, temperature
and fan system operations.

Pitt and Giordino had passed far below the main fan system and
could now converse in low tones. Giordino raised up until he was on
his feet again and spoke to Pitt, who had slid down the ladder beside him.

"What's the status?" Pitt asked softly.

"The ladder runs through a ventilator systems control center that
sits about fifteen feet above the floor of the tunnel. A man and a
woman are sitting at computer consoles. Luckily, they're facing away,
with their backs to the ladder. We should be able to take them out before they know what hit them."

Pitt looked into Giordino's dark eyes, only inches away. "How do
you want it?"

Giordino's lips parted in a conniving grin. "I'll take the man. You're
better at incapacitating women than I am."

Pitt glared at him. "You big chicken."

They wasted no more time and dropped down the ladder into the
control booth silently without being detected. The system operators—
the man wearing black coveralls, the woman in white—were intent on
monitoring their computers and did not see the reflection of their as-
sailants in their screens until it was too late. Giordino came in from
the side and slugged the man with a right hook to the jaw. Pitt opted
for striking the back of the woman's neck just below her skull. Both
went out with no more than slight moans.

Keeping unseen below the windows, Pitt pulled a roll of duct tape from his knapsack and tossed it to Giordino. "Bind them up while I remove their coveralls."

In less than three minutes the unconscious ventilation systems operators were bound and gagged in their underwear and rolled under counters out of sight from anyone passing by below. Pitt slipped on the black coveralls, which were a loose fit, while Giordino burst the seams of the white coveralls that came off the woman. They found matching hard hats on a shelf and put them on. Pitt casually carried his knapsack over one shoulder, while Giordino looked official with a clipboard and pencil. One after the other, they dropped down the ladder to the tunnel floor.

When they got their bearings and stared around their surroundings, Pitt and Giordino stood spellbound in awe, as they stared at the immense spectacle, their eyes narrowing under the glare of an unending array of lights.

This was no ordinary railroad tunnel. It was no railroad tunnel at all.

29

THE HORSESHOE-SHAPED TUNNEL was far more immense than either he or Giordino had imagined. Pitt felt as though he was standing in a Jules Verne fantasy. He estimated the bore at fifty feet in diameter; far wider than any tunnel ever constructed. The diameter of the Chunnel that ran between France and England was twenty-four feet and the Seikan Tunnel that connected Honshu with Hokkaido was thirty-two.

The whirr of the ventilator fans was replaced with a buzzing sound that echoed up and down the tunnel. Above them, mounted on a series of steel beams, a huge conveyor belt traveled continuously toward the eastern end of the tunnel. Instead of rocks twelve to eighteen inches in size, the muck had been crushed almost to sand.

"There's the source of your brown crud," said Pitt. "They grind down the rock until it has the consistency of silt so it can be pumped through a pipe into the Caribbean."

A railroad track and a parallel concrete roadway ran beneath the conveyor belt. Pitt knelt and studied the rails and ties. "Electric-powered, like the subways of New York."

"Mind the third rail," warned Giordino. "No telling how much voltage is running through it."

"They must have generator substations every few miles to provide power."

"You going to put a penny on the track?" Giordino asked in jest.

Pitt stood and stared into the distance. "No way these tracks could handle high-speed two-hundred-and-forty-mile-an-hour trains carrying cargo containers. The rails are not of superior quality and the metal ties are laid too far apart. On top of all that, standard railroad gauge between rails is four feet eight and a half inches. These measure about three feet, which makes it a narrow-gauge railroad."

"Laid as equipment support and supply transport for a tunnel-boring machine."

Pitt's eyebrows rose. "Where did you come up with that?"

"I read about TBMs in a book somewhere."

"You move to the head of the class. This tunnel *was* excavated by a boring machine, a big one."

"Maybe they intend to replace the tracks later," Giordino speculated.

"Why wait until the entire tunnel is dug? Tracklaying men and equipment should follow in the wake of the boring machine to save time." Pitt slowly shook his head pensively. "A tunnel this size wasn't built for train traffic. It must serve another purpose."

They turned as a large double-decker bus painted lavender silently passed, its driver waving. They turned away and acted as if they were discussing something on Giordino's clipboard as workers sitting inside, wearing different-colored jumpsuits and hard hats, passed by. All were wearing sunglasses. Pitt and Giordino also noted the Odyssey name and horse logo on the side of the bus. The driver slowed, not sure if they wanted a ride, but Pitt waved him on.

"Electric-powered," said Giordino.

"Eliminates carbon monoxide exhaust pollution."

Giordino walked over to a pair of empty battery-powered golf carts that looked like miniature sports cars. "Nice of them to provide us with transportation." He climbed behind the wheel. "Which way?"

Pitt thought a moment. "Let's follow the excavated muck on the conveyor belt. This may well be our only chance to confirm if that's the source of the brown crud."

The cavernous tunnel seemed to trail off forever. The road traffic looked to be restricted to transporting mine workers, while the narrow-gauged railroad carried only muck and cargo. The golf cart's panel held a speedometer, and Pitt clocked the speed of the conveyor belt. It was traveling at the rapid clip of twelve miles an hour.

Pitt turned his attention to the upper works of the tunnel. After the boring machine had passed, the miners had installed rock bolt support systems to strengthen the rock's natural tendency to reinforce itself. Then a thick lining of shotcrete or gunite was sprayed on the tunnel pneumatically at high velocity. Conveying the concrete for long distances would have been accomplished by booster pumps spaced from the entrance source to the recently excavated area behind the boring machine. This would have been followed by an injection of fluid grout under pressure to seal off leaks from groundwater. Besides ensuring water tightness from without, the shotcrete and grout would also improve the flow of fluid through the tunnel, a phenomenon that Pitt began to believe was a distinct possibility.

The overhead lights illuminated the tunnel so brilliantly it almost hurt the eyes. Both men could now understand why the workers in the bus had worn sunglasses against the glare. Almost as if they timed their actions, Pitt and Giordino put on their own sunglasses.

An electric locomotive pulling several flatbed cars and carrying open crates of rock bolts passed, headed in the opposite direction toward the ongoing excavation. The train crew all waved at the two men in the golf cart, who responded by waving back.

"Everyone is real down-home friendly in these parts," remarked Giordino.

"Did you notice the men wear black jumpsuits and the women either white or green?"

"Specter must have lived a former life as an interior decorator."

"More like some sort of caste identification system," said Pitt.

"I'd cut off an ear before I wore lavender," muttered Giordino, suddenly becoming aware that he was covered in white. "I think I'm out of uniform."

"Stuff something in your chest."

Giordino said nothing, but his bitter stare at Pitt said it all.

A sober look crossed Pitt's face. "I wonder if those miners have any idea of the toxic mineral content of the muck they're pouring into the sea."

"They will," added Giordino, "when their hair starts falling out and their internal organs dissolve."

They continued on, conscious of an unnatural atmosphere deep below the earth and sea. They passed several smaller crosscut tunnels leading off to their left that aroused their curiosity. Another parallel tunnel appeared to be linked by the crosscuts every thousand yards. Pitt assumed it was a service tunnel for electrical conduits.

"There's the explanation for the earth tremors on the surface," said Pitt. "They didn't use a big tunnel-boring machine for these small tunnels. They were excavated by drilling and blasting."

"Shall we turn in?"

"Later," replied Pitt. "Let's push ahead and follow the muck on the conveyor belt."

Giordino was stunned at the power of the golf cart. He got it up to fifty miles an hour and he soon began overhauling other vehicles on the concrete road.

"Better slow down," cautioned Pitt. "We don't want to arouse suspicion."

"You think they got traffic cops down here?"

"No, but big brother is watching," Pitt countered, discreetly nodding at a camera mounted above on the overhead lighting system.

Giordino reluctantly slowed and settled behind a bus traveling in the same direction. Pitt began timing the bus schedule and quickly calculated that the buses ran twenty minutes apart and stopped at work sites when and wherever miners waited to board or requested to get off. He glanced at the hands on his watch. It was only a question of time before the technicians on the replacement shift entered the ventilator control room and found their coworkers duct-taped to the floor. So far, no alarms had been sounded, nor had they seen security guards cruising up and down the tunnel as if searching for someone.

"We're coming up on something," Giordino alerted Pitt.

A thumping sound became stronger as they moved closer to what Pitt quickly identified as a giant pumping station. The rock that had been crushed to sand was sent from the conveyor belt into a monstrous bin. From there, pumps the size of a three-story building thrust it into huge pipes. As Pitt had concluded, the contaminated muck was then propelled into the sea where *Poco Bonito* had run aground on the accumulation. Beyond the pumping stations were giant steel doors.

"The enigma goes deeper," said Pitt thoughtfully. "Those pumps are monumental, far more capable of pumping ten times the excavated muck. They must serve another purpose."

"They'll probably dismantle them when the tunnel is finished."

"I don't think so. They look permanent."

"I wonder what's on the other side of those doors," said Giordino.

"The Caribbean," answered Pitt. "We must be miles from shore and deep beneath the surface of the sea."

Giordino's eyes never left the doors. "How in the world did they dig this thing?"

"They began with an open excavation onshore by digging a portal. First, a starter tunnel was launched with a different type of machine called a roadheader excavator. When it reached a calculated depth, the big boring machine was brought in and assembled in the excavated tunnel. It worked east under the sea, then it must have been disas-

sembled and reassembled so it could begin excavating in the opposite
direction toward the west."

"How could an operation this size be kept secret?"

"By paying the miners and engineers big bucks to keep their mouths
shut, or perhaps by threats and blackmail."

"According to Rathbone, they don't hesitate to kill intruders. Why
not workmen with loose tongues?"

"Don't remind me about intruders. Anyway, suspicions confirmed,"
Pitt said slowly. "The brown crud is spread into the sea by man without the slightest consideration for the terrible consequences."

Giordino shook his head slowly. "A contaminated dump operation
that puts all others to shame."

Pitt reached into his knapsack again and lifted out a small digital
camera and began taking pictures of the giant pumping operation.

"I don't suppose your magical kit can produce any food and drink?"
probed Giordino.

Pitt reached inside and produced a pair of granola bars. "Sorry,
that's the best I can do."

"What else is in there?"

"My trusty old Colt forty-five."

"I guess we can always shoot ourselves before they hang us,"
Giordino said glumly.

"We've seen what we came for," said Pitt. "Time to go home."

Giordino was pressing his foot on the accelerator before Pitt finished his sentence. "The sooner we're out of here, the better. We're
on borrowed time as it is."

Pitt continued snapping pictures as they drove. "One more detour,
I want to see what's inside those crosscut tunnels."

As he accelerated, Giordino sensed that heading off into a side
tunnel was only part of Pitt's plan. He was dead certain that Pitt
wanted to check out the other end of the tunnel and observe the big
boring machine in action. Pictures were taken of every piece of equip-

ment they passed. No small detail of the tunnel's construction went unrecorded.

Giordino swung right into the first crosscut he reached without slowing down, taking the turn on two wheels. Pitt hung on and gave him a waspish look, but said nothing. They had traveled less than two hundred feet when abruptly the golf cart shot into another tunnel. They came to a fast stop and stared in total astonishment.

"Mind-boggling," Giordino muttered under his breath in awe.

"Don't stop," ordered Pitt. "Keep going."

Giordino acquiesced and drove the golf cart at top speed into another tunnel. He didn't hesitate or wait for Pitt to urge him forward. His foot never came off the pedal as they charged through the crosscut into a fourth tunnel. At last they could go no farther, and Giordino braked the cart before they struck the far wall. They sat there for several moments, staring left and right into eternity, taking in the immensity of what they were seeing.

The gargantuan proportions of the tunnel network became even more spectacular when Pitt and Giordino in stunned disbelief forced themselves to accept the fact that there was not one but four immense interconnected tunnels of equal size.

Giordino didn't astound easily, but he was shamelessly overwhelmed. "This can't be real," he said, in a voice barely above a whisper.

Carefully, Pitt steeled himself, shutting out all inclinations to fog his mind from the impact and blind his concentration. There had to be an explanation for the Herculean undertaking. How was it possible that Specter had built four massive tunnels under the mountains of Nicaragua without exposure by international intelligence or the media? How could such a vast project have gone unnoticed for more than four years?

"How many railroads does Specter intend to operate?" Giordino muttered dazedly.

"These tunnels weren't built to run cargo across the land by rail," Pitt mused.

"Barge transportation, maybe?"

"Not cost-efficient. There has to be another objective behind it all."

"There has to be a colossal bonanza at the end of the rainbow for such an expensive undertaking."

"The cost must have easily run more than the estimated seven billion."

Their voices reverberated up and down the cavernous tunnel that was completely empty of men and vehicles. If not for the perfectly arched walls and roof and the smooth concrete surface, they could have imagined themselves in an immense natural grotto.

Pitt tilted his head down at the floor of the tunnel. "So much for a rapid transit cargo system. They removed the railroad tracks."

Giordino nodded discreetly at a security camera mounted on a post that was aimed directly at them. "We'd better beat a hasty retreat back to the main tunnel and find another means of transportation. This cart is too conspicuous."

"Good thinking," said Pitt. "If they haven't figured out that they have unwelcome intruders by now, they must be brain-dead."

They retraced their journey through the three empty tunnels, stopping just short of the fourth, where they had started. They parked the golf cart in the crosscut tunnel beyond a security camera and nonchalantly walked down the roadway until they reached a stop where eight other miners were standing around waiting for the bus. Close up and through their sunglasses, Pitt could see their eyes. They were all Asian.

Pitt nudged Giordino, who got the message.

"Ten will get you twenty, they're Red Chinese," whispered Pitt.

"I won't take the bet."

No sooner had the double-decker bus arrived than a fleet of carts with red and yellow lights flashing sped past and into the crosscut tunnel they'd just deserted.

"Once they find the cart, it will take them all of ten seconds to know we're on this bus," said Giordino.

Pitt's eyes were on a train that was approaching from the east sector of the tunnel. "My thoughts exactly." He held up a hand and motioned for the bus driver to continue after the waiting miners had boarded. The door closed with a hiss and the bus moved on.

"When was the last time you chased a freight train?" Pitt asked Giordino, as they hurried across the road and stood talking in detachment as the locomotive passed by, the engineer inside the cab reading a magazine.

"Several years ago in the Sahara Desert, the train carrying toxic chemicals to Fort Foureau."

"As I remember, you almost fell off."

"I hate it when you make sport of me," said Giordino, with a downward twist of his lips.

The instant the locomotive passed by, they sprinted along the track. Pitt had already clocked the train's speed at twenty miles an hour, and they judged their running speed accordingly. Giordino was fast for his size. He put his head down and charged after a flatbed car as if he was carrying a football toward the end zone. He grabbed the hand ladder as it passed, held on and was literally swept onto the car. Pitt also used the momentum of the train to swing himself aboard.

The flatbed car was loaded with two pickup trucks of unknown origin powered by an electrical motor. Shiny new, they looked to be fresh off the boat. Without a word between them, Pitt and Giordino threw open a door and slipped into one of the truck's cabs, crouching down below the windows and the dashboard. Their timing couldn't have been more perfect, as two security patrol cars came screaming past the train, lights flashing as they raced after the bus.

Pitt looked pleased. "Our little maneuver was missed by the cameras or they'd have come after us instead of the bus."

"About time we had some luck."

"Stay put," instructed Pitt. "I'll be right back."

He opened the door on the side of the train away from the road and lowered himself to his hands and knees. Crawling from front to back, he removed the chocks and tie-down chains that held the pickup truck to the rail car. Then he scrambled back inside.

Giordino looked at him strangely. "I can read your mind, and I can't see how we're going to drive off a moving train into a tunnel that's blocked on both ends."

"We'll worry about it when the time comes," Pitt tossed off placidly.

THERE IS nothing on earth that remotely resembles a big tunnel-boring machine.

The TBM that dug the tunnels under Nicaragua from the Atlantic coast to the Pacific shore stretched over one hundred and twenty yards in length, followed by another hundred yards of its equipment train.

An incredibly complicated monster that looked like the first stage of a Saturn rocket, it was driven by an electric variable-speed drive that eliminated any hydraulic oil leakage and pollution. The Specter TBM fractured flakes of bedrock by the continuous rotation of a series of carbide cutters mounted on a massive steel cutter head that could cut a circular tube through hard rock fifty-two feet in diameter at the rate of one hundred and fifty feet a day. The body that enclosed the cutter head also contained the drive motors that provided the enormous power it took to thrust the cutter's teeth into the rock, and the hydraulic presses that exerted the immense pressure it took to force the TBM into solid wall and grind away the rock.

The giant machine was articulated, and its operator, who was positioned at the front of the machine, could automatically steer it with the use of a laser while he monitored the operation. The excavated muck was transported to the rear section of the TBM and passed through a rock crusher that mashed the rock into fine sand. From there, the conveyor belt carried it back toward the opposite end of the tunnel, where it was pumped out into the sea.

. . .

THE TRAIN stopped two hundred yards behind the TBM and beneath the overhead conveyor to unload at a supply depot and terminal. A series of large freight elevators ran out of sight through the roof of the tunnel. A group of women in white jumpsuits exited one of the elevators and climbed into a bus. Pitt angled close to them and overheard one woman say the inspection had to be finished in eight hours so a report could be sent to company headquarters above.

It made no sense to Pitt. Headquarters? Where above?

No one seemed to mind as he casually drove the truck from the flatbed onto the loading dock and down a ramp to the concrete road. Then he pulled over and stopped behind a row of three other electric trucks.

Giordino looked around the busy area, where at least thirty miners were engaged in operating the mass of machinery. "That was too easy."

"We're not home yet," said Pitt. "We've got to find a way out of here."

"We could always climb out through another ventilator."

"Not if we're under Lake Nicaragua."

"How about the one we came from?"

"I think we can safely forget that plan."

Giordino was absorbed, watching the operation of the big TBM. "Okay, mastermind, what's your next scenario?"

"We can't escape from this tunnel, because it isn't completed yet. Our only hope is to sneak out the Pacific side from one of the other three tunnels' ventilators."

"And if it proves impossible?"

"Then I'll have to come up with another plan."

Giordino pointed down the loading dock, where security guards were checking the ID passes of the miners. "Time to shove off. We don't exactly fit our descriptions."

Pitt held up the ID clamped to the breast pocket of his jumpsuit and stared at it with amusement. "I'm in trouble. This guy is five foot two. I'm six-three."

"What about me?" Giordino said with a sly smile. "How will I ever produce a head of long hair and a set of boobs?"

Pitt cracked the door and looked up and down the far side of the loading dock and found it deserted. "Out this way."

Giordino followed Pitt and slid across the front seat of the pickup. They hit the loading dock crouched and running before cutting into an open door of a warehouse. Sneaking around unopened crates containing replacement parts for the various equipment and TBM, they found a rear passage that took them out of the warehouse and back along the railroad track. They paused behind a row of Porta Pottis and took stock.

"It'd help if we had transportation," said Giordino, wrinkling his nose distastefully.

"Wishing will make it so," Pitt said with a big grin.

Without waiting for Giordino, he stood up, walked from behind the Porta Pottis and casually approached one of the security guards' vehicles that was parked unattended. He settled behind the wheel, turned the ignition to the electric motor and pressed his foot on the accelerator, as Giordino leaped through the opposite door. The electrical power from the batteries flowed through the front-wheel-drive, direct-coupled differential and the car silently moved away.

The Pitt luck still held. The security guards were so busy examining the miners' IDs that they did not notice their patrol car being stolen. Not only was the electric car whisper quiet, but the noise and clatter of the TBM made it impossible for them to hear the workers trying to call their attention to the car theft.

To make it look official, Giordino reached toward the dashboard and flicked the switch to the revolving lights on the forward edge of the roof. As soon as they came to the first crosscut tunnel, Pitt hung a hard left and repeated the maneuver, swinging into the main tunnel and heading toward its western portal.

Pitt assumed that the four tunnels had been excavated under Lake Nicaragua to come up beyond the narrow stretch of land separating the lake from the ocean at the old port of San Juan del Sur. Here the ventilators had to be placed before the tunnels continued out from shore.

But Pitt was wrong.

After driving several miles, they came to a massive set of pumps like the ones they had encountered on the eastern end of the tunnel network. Then the tunnel abruptly ended at another pair of gigantic doors. The trickles of water that seeped around their edges and down the tunnel gave proof that they were not surfacing near San Juan del Sur but had come to a dead end far out under the Pacific Ocean.

30

A FTER ADMIRAL SANDECKER'S morning run from his Watergate condominium to NUMA headquarters, he went directly to his office without stopping off at the agency gym to shower and change into a business suit. Rudi Gunn was waiting for him, a grim expression on his hawklike face. He stared over his horn-rim glasses as Sandecker sat down at his desk, wiping the sweat from his face and neck with a towel.

"What's the latest word from Pitt and Giordino?"

"Nothing in the last eight hours." Gunn was uneasy. "Not since they entered what they described as a ventilator shaft leading to a deep underground tunnel that Pitt reckoned ran through the jungle of Nicaragua from the Pacific to the Caribbean."

"No contact at all?"

"Only silence," answered Gunn. "Impossible to communicate by phone when they're deep underground."

"A tunnel running from sea to sea," murmured Sandecker, his voice dubious.

Gunn nodded slightly. "Pitt was certain of it. He also reported that the builder was the Odyssey conglomeration."

"Odyssey?" Sandecker looked at Gunn in confusion. "Again?"

Gunn nodded again.

"They seem to crop up everywhere." Sandecker rose from his desk and gazed out the window overlooking the Potomac River. He could just see the furled red sails of his little schooner docked at a marina downriver. "I'm not aware of any tunnel being dug through Nicaragua. There was talk about building an underground railroad to transport cargo on high-speed trains. But that was several years ago, and as far as I know nothing ever came of it."

Gunn opened a file, pulled out several photos and spread them on the admiral's desk. "Here are satellite photos taken over a period of several years of a sleepy little port called San Juan del Norte."

"Where did these come from?" asked Sandecker with interest.

Gunn smiled. "Hiram Yaeger tapped his library of satellite photos from the various intelligence services and programmed them into NUMA's data files."

Sandecker adjusted his glasses and began examining the photos, his eyes touching on the dates they were taken, printed on the bottom borders. After a few minutes, he looked up. "Five years ago, the port looked deserted. Then it looks like heavy equipment was barged in and dock facilities built for cargo containerships."

"You'll notice that any and all supply and equipment containers were immediately moved into prefabricated warehouses, and never came out."

"Incredible that such a vast undertaking has gone unnoticed for so long."

Gunn laid a file on the desk beside the photos. "Yaeger also obtained a report on the Odyssey's programs and operations. Their financial dealings are sketchy. Because they're headquartered in Brazil, they are not required to release profit-and-loss statements."

"What about their stockholders? Surely they must receive annual reports."

"They're not listed on any of the international stock markets because the company's wholly owned by Specter."

"Could they have funded such a project on their own?" asked Sandecker.

"As far as we can tell, they have the resources. But Yaeger believes that on a project of this magnitude, they were likely funded by the People's Republic of China, which has bankrolled Specter's Central American developments in the past."

"Sounds logical. The Chinese are investing heavily in the area and are building a sphere of influence."

"Another factor in the secrecy," explained Gunn, "is the opportunity to sidestep all environmental, social and economic impacts. Opposition by Nicaraguan activists and any problems dealing with right-of-way would simply be ignored by their government while the work progressed covertly."

"What other projects are Specter and the Red Chinese working on together?"

"Port facilities on both sides of the Panama Canal and a bridge that will cross it, scheduled to open early next year."

"But why all the secrecy?" muttered Sandecker, as he returned to his chair. "What is to be gained from it?"

Gunn threw up his hands helplessly. "Without more intelligence, we're in the dark on that score."

"We can't just sit on this thing."

"Shall we contact Central Intelligence and the Pentagon about our suspicions?" asked Gunn.

Sandecker looked pensive for a moment. Then he said, "No, we'll go direct to the president's national security advisor."

"I agree," said Gunn. "This could prove to be a very serious situation."

"Damn!" Sandecker blurted in frustration. "If only we'd hear from Pitt and Giordino. Then we might have a clue as to what's going on down there."

. . .

Having reached the dead end, Pitt and Giordino had no option but to turn around and speed back in the direction they'd come. The fourth of the four tunnels appeared deserted and devoid of all equipment. It was as empty as though men had never created it. Only the pumps on both ends, standing eerily silent, revealed a veiled purpose that Pitt was at a loss to explain.

What was also strange was that no fleet of security guard cars, lights flashing, came hurtling though the empty and darkened tunnel after them. Nor were there any security cameras. They had all been removed when the tunnel was completed.

The answer quickly became obvious.

"I can see now," said Giordino calmly, "why the security guards are in no hurry to grab us."

"We have no place to go," Pitt finished answering the puzzle. "Our little venture into the bizarre is over. All Specter's security people have to do is wait until we get hungry and thirsty, then welcome us back into the main tunnel when we give ourselves up in hope of a last meal before we're hung."

"They would probably prefer to let us rot in here."

"There is that."

Pitt wiped a sleeve across his forehead to blot the sweat that suddenly began streaming into his eyes. "Have you noticed the temperature in this tunnel is much higher than the others?"

"It's beginning to feel like a steam bath in here," said Giordino, his face glistening.

"The air like sulfur."

"Speaking of hunger. How's your supply of granola bars?"

"Fresh out."

Abruptly, the thought crossed their minds at the same time, and they turned to each other and uttered two words in unison.

"Ventilator shaft."

Giordino suddenly became sober. "Maybe not. I didn't see any raised control booths in the outer tunnels."

"They would have been removed along with the railroad tracks and the overhead lighting and sealed, since they were no longer essential to remove pollution from the excavation."

"Yes, but the ladder rungs were embedded in the tunnel walls. I'll bet next month's pay, if I live to spend it, that they didn't bother to remove them."

"We'll know soon enough," said Pitt, as Giordino hit the accelerator and the cart leaped forward, its headlights probing the darkness ahead.

After covering nearly twenty miles, Giordino spotted the rungs of a ladder crawling up one wall. He parked about thirty feet away so the headlights would illuminate a wider area of the tunnel wall. "The rungs go up to where a ventilator shaft control booth once hung," he said, rubbing the stubble that had sprouted on his cheeks and chin.

Pitt stepped from the cart and began climbing the rungs. It had been a year or more since the tunnel was completed and stripped down. The rungs were slimy with dampness and flaked with rust. He reached the top and found a round manholelike iron cover sealing the entrance to the ventilator shaft above. There was a sliding bolt holding it against bottom stops.

Wrapping one hand through a rung for balance, he used both hands to grip the bolt and pull. It slid out of its clamp with little resistance. Then Pitt leaned to the side until his shoulder was pressed against the cover, and heaved.

It moved a millimeter at most.

"It's going to take the two of us," he called down.

Giordino came up the ladder until he was standing one rung up from Pitt to compensate for the difference in their heights. It was the wolf matching strength with the bear. With two shoulders against the heavy iron cover, they both put their strength into the effort.

The cover fought back, budged less than an inch and froze in place.

"Stubborn devil," grunted Giordino.

"At least it moved and isn't welded," Pitt replied.

Giordino grinned. "Once more with feeling."

"On three."

They stared at each other briefly and nodded.

"One," said Pitt, "two and threeeee."

They both thrust upward with every ounce of strength they possessed. For an instant, the cover resisted. Then it slowly gave, and with a loud screech it abruptly swung open and clanged against one wall of the ventilator shaft. They stared upward into the ominous black cavity as if it was a stairway to paradise.

"I wonder where it comes out," murmured Giordino between breaths.

"I have no idea, but we're going to find out."

Giordino gave Pitt's arm a light squeeze. "Hold on. In case the Specter goons come looking for us, let's give them something to chase."

He dropped down the ladder and climbed in the electric security guard car. He removed the belt off his shorts and tied the steering wheel so the front tires were positioned straight ahead. Then he pulled the front seat out of the car and stood it on end, using it to press the accelerator against the floorboard. Finally, he turned on the ignition and stepped back.

The car shot down the tunnel, its headlights carving weird patterns through the darkness. Within a hundred yards, it yawed against one wall of the tunnel, then careened against the other side in its wild ride, bouncing back and forth with a rending screech of tortured metal far into the distance.

"I wonder how Specter will explain that to his insurance adjuster," said Giordino. He turned, but Pitt was already scaling the ladder.

In the tension and stress of the past several hours, Pitt was surprised at how stiff and cramped his muscles had become. He climbed slowly, conserving his strength. With no lights, he felt a touch of claustrophobia as he ascended in the pitch-blackness. He began counting the rungs and paused whenever he reached the fiftieth to catch his breath. They were spaced twelve inches apart, so it was a matter of simple arithmetic to calculate the distance they had climbed. Climbing down the ventilator shaft into the control booth from El Castillo, assisted by gravity, seemed like a swim in the bathtub in comparison. At rung three hundred and fifty, Pitt stopped and waited for Giordino to catch up. "Does this never end?" Giordino gasped.

"Pardon the pun," Pitt muttered between heavy breaths, "but there is light at the end of the tunnel."

Giordino looked upward and saw a tiny glow in the distance. It looked ten miles away to him. "Is there any way it could come to us?"

"Just hope it doesn't move farther away."

They continued on, increasingly conscious of the eeriness of the shaft. The glow above grew larger and magnified with agonizing slowness. Water dripped down the walls and onto the rungs. Their hands pulling and scraping against the rust on the rungs as they struggled upward soon became red and raw, the skin scoured as if by sandpaper.

At long last, the glow became a bright light and the nearness renewed their strength. Pitt began climbing two rungs at a time, using up his failing strength at an increased rate. But the end was only a few short feet away now.

With a final effort that cast him over the edge of exhaustion, he came to the wire mesh that covered the top of the shaft, hanging there with breaths coming in great heaves, blood trickling from his palms and fingers. "Made it," he gasped.

Giordino soon joined him. "I'm not up to cutting through that stuff again," he panted.

As soon as the numbness and aches subsided, Pitt reached into the knapsack, retrieved the wire cutters and wearily began snipping at the wire mesh. "We'll take turns and spell each other as we tire."

Pitt cut only a few inches in as many minutes before he could no longer squeeze the handles of the wire cutters. He moved aside and handed the cutters to Giordino. Because of the blood on his hands, they nearly slipped from his fingers. Pitt held his breath, but Giordino barely caught them before they fell out of sight into the darkness below.

"Keep a tight grip," Pitt said, with a grim smile. "You wouldn't want to make the climb all over again."

"I'd die first," Giordino muttered bravely. He cut almost ten minutes before he let Pitt relieve him.

It took the two of them almost an hour before they cut an opening large enough to crawl through. Once past the mesh that had shaded the exterior light, Pitt's eyes were blinded by the sunlight that streamed all around him. Putting on his sunglasses to relieve the glare from eyes accustomed to darkness, he found himself in a round room whose walls were glass from floor to ceiling.

While Giordino squirmed through the opening, Pitt walked around the glass-enclosed room and gazed down at a spectacular three-hundred-and-sixty-degree view of a huge lake and surrounding islands.

"Where did we come up?" asked Giordino.

Pitt turned and looked at him with a bemused expression. "You're not going to believe this, but we're at the top of a lighthouse."

A LIGHTHOUSE!" burst Sandecker at Pitt's description over his speakerphone. His voice betrayed his elation at hearing Pitt and Giordino were alive and safe.

"Yes, sir," Pitt's voice came back over his satellite phone. "Specter built it as a folly."

"A folly?"

"A structure built to look like the ruins of an ancient castle or historic structure," Gunn explained. He leaned over the speakerphone. "You're saying the lighthouse was built to hide a ventilator shaft rising from the tunnel."

"Exactly," answered Pitt.

Sandecker twisted one of his cigars. "Your story sounds fantastic."

"All true down to the last item," said Pitt.

"A tunnel-boring machine that can cut through a mile of rock a day?"

"Which explains how Specter was able to excavate four tunnels, each nearly a hundred and fifty miles in length, in four years."

"If not for railroads," said Gunn, "for what purpose?"

"Al and I can't even make a good guess. The pumps on each end of the tunnels suggest they'll be used to drive water through them, but that doesn't make a lot of sense."

"I've taped your brief report," acknowledged Sandecker, "and will give it to Yaeger to come up with possible concepts until you can arrive and make a more comprehensive report."

"I also have photos taken with a digital camera."

"Good, we'll need every piece of evidence you collected."

"Dirk?" probed Gunn.

"Yes, Rudi."

"I plot your location as only thirty miles from San Carlos. I'll charter a helicopter. They should be in the air and over your lighthouse in another two hours."

"Al and I can't wait to clean up and eat a decent meal."

"No time for luxuries," snapped Sandecker. "The copter will take you direct to the airport in Managua, where a NUMA jet will be waiting. You can wash and eat after you arrive."

"You're a hard man, Admiral."

"Learn from it," Sandecker said, with a canny grin. "You might be sitting in my chair someday."

As Pitt closed the connection, he was totally in the dark concerning Sandecker's insinuation. He sat down next to Giordino, who was dozing, not happy about telling his friend he wasn't going to eat anytime soon.

31

AFTER COMMUNICATIONS with Pitt ended, Sandecker waited patiently while Gunn arranged for a helicopter to pick up his special projects director at the phony lighthouse. Then they exited the admiral's office and dropped down a floor to the conference room, where Sandecker had arranged a meeting to discuss the Celtic discoveries on Navidad Bank.

Sitting around a huge oval table built of teak and resembling the deck of a ship was Hiram Yaeger, Dirk and Summer Pitt and St. Julien Perlmutter. Seated next to Summer was historian Dr. John Wesley Chisholm, professor of ancient history at the University of Pennsylvania. Everything about Chisholm's appearance was average. The height and weight were average. The hair a medium average brown that matched the eyes. But there was nothing average about his personality. He smiled constantly and was extremely warm and courteous. His mind went far above the level of ordinary.

Everyone was paying rapt attention to Dr. Elsworth Boyd, who stood in front of a large monitor displaying a montage of photos and lectured on the artifacts and images of the stone carvings recovered and recorded at Navidad Bank. The story that was coming together was so startling, so fabulous, that everyone seated around the spacious table sat in awed silence as Boyd described the artifacts, their approximate dates and original source. All this before shifting to the stone carvings.

Boyd, a limber man with the body of an acrobat, sinewy and nimble in the full vigor of his early forties, stood erect, occasionally brushing back a forelock of yellow-red hair, and gazed at his rapt audience through eyes as gray as a pigeon wing. A professor emeritus of classics at Trinity College, Dublin, he devoted his energies to researching the early history of the Celts. He had published numerous books on every aspect of the complex Celtic society. When invited by Admiral Sandecker to fly to Washington and study the artifacts under conservation, he was on the next plane from Dublin. When he saw the relics firsthand and a photo montage of the wall sculptures, he came within an inch of going into complete shock.

At first, Boyd refused to believe what he was seeing were not forgeries from an elaborate hoax, but after twenty hours straight of examining the artifacts, he became convinced of their authenticity.

Summer experienced a tingling of excitement as she took in every word of Boyd's lecture, transcribing it with a lightning display of the lost art of shorthand on a legal-sized tablet.

"Unlike the Egyptians, Greeks and Romans," explained Boyd, "the Celts have been sidetracked by most historians, despite the fact that they were the keystone of Western civilization. Much of our heritage—religious, political, social and literary traditions—was born within Celtic culture. Industry too, since they were the first to produce bronze and then iron."

"So why aren't we more aware of Celtic influence?" asked Sandecker.

Boyd laughed. "There lies the rub. Three thousand years ago, the Celts transmitted all their information, gossip and knowledge orally. Their rituals, customs and ethics were passed down through succeeding generations by word of mouth. Not until the eighth century B.C.

did they begin to write anything down. Much later, when Rome swept over Europe, they considered the Celts little more than uncouth barbarians. And what little the Romans wrote about them was anything but flattering."

"And yet they were inventive," added Perlmutter.

"Contrary to what many people think, the Celts were advanced in more ways than the early Greeks. They only lagged in a written language and elaborate architecture. Actually, their culture and civilization predates the Greeks by several hundred years."

Yaeger leaned forward in his chair. "Does your dating of the artifacts agree with my computer calculations?"

"In the ballpark, I'd say," Boyd replied, "if you consider plus or minus a hundred years a chronologically tight case. I also believe the pictographs give us an excellent time frame for Navinia."

Summer smiled. "I love that name."

Boyd held a remote and flashed an image on a huge monitor covering one wall of the conference room. A three-dimensional perspective of the underwater structure as it might have looked when built filled the screen. "What is interesting," Boyd continued, "is that the structure was not only the dwelling of a very important woman, comparable to a tribal queen or high priestess, but it also became her tomb."

"When you say 'high priestess,' " said Summer, "like in Druid?"

"A Druidess," Boyd answered, nodding. "The intricate carvings and the gold of her ornaments indicate that she very likely held a high position in the sacred world of Celtic Druidism. Her bronze cuirass body armor is especially revealing. There is only one other known to have come from a woman, which is dated between the eighth and eleventh century B.C. At one time or another, she must have fought in battle. When she was alive, she was probably revered as a goddess."

"A living goddess," Summer said softly. "She must have led an interesting life."

"I also found this interesting." Boyd pulled up a photo taken of the foot of the stone funeral bed, with the carved image of a stylistic horse. "Here you see a sophisticated and modern-looking pictograph of a galloping horse. Called the White Horse of Uffington, it was carved into a chalk hillside in Berkshire, England, in the first century A.D. It represents the Celtic horse goddess, Epona. She was worshiped throughout the Celtic world and what would later become Gaul."

Summer studied the horse. "You think our goddess was Epona?"

Boyd shook his head. "No, I don't think so. Epona was worshiped as the goddess of horses, mules and oxen during the Roman era. It's thought that a thousand years earlier she may have been a goddess of beauty and fertility, with the power to throw a spell over men."

"I wish I had her clout," Summer said, laughing.

"What brought down the Druids?" asked Dirk.

"As Christianity gradually took hold and spread throughout Europe, it ridiculed Celtic religion as paganism. Women especially were not accorded the respect they had under the Druids. The heads of the church could not allow any irreverence or opposition to masculine authority. The Romans particularly made a crusade of stamping out the Druid religion. Druidesses were reduced to the category of witches. Women of power were recast as creatures of evil who took up with the devil. Women rulers were especially targeted for exclusion, and were cast from mother goddess to male-oriented domination."

Gunn's academic mind was soaking up every word of Boyd's discourse. "The Romans themselves worshiped pagan gods and goddesses. Why were they driven to erase the Druids?"

"Because the Romans saw the Druids as a source of rebellion against Rome. They were also disgusted by Druid ritual savagery."

"What form of savagery?" asked Sandecker.

"Early Druids conducted human sacrifice. It's claimed that their pagan cult knew no barbaric bounds. Sacrificial blood rites were not uncommon. Another infamous legend concerns 'The Wicker Man.' The Romans recounted events where condemned men and women were placed in huge cane effigies and burned to death."

Summer looked unconvinced. "Were Druidesses known to have participated in these barbaric rituals?"

Boyd made a noncommittal shrug. "It can only be assumed they were as responsible as the Druid priests."

"Which brings us back to the question we've asked ourselves a hundred times," said Dirk. "How did a high-ranking Celtic Druidess come to be entombed on what was once an island in the Caribbean five thousand miles from her homeland in Europe?"

Boyd turned and nodded at Chisholm. "I believe my colleague John Wesley may have some extraordinary answers to your question."

"But first," interrupted Sandecker—he turned to Yaeger—"have you and Max been able to discover how the structure came to be standing under fifty feet of water?"

"Early geological records for the Caribbean are all but nonexistent," replied Yaeger, fanning out a file of loose papers on the table in front of him. "We know more about prehistoric meteor strikes and land movement millions of years ago than we know about geological upheavals three thousand years ago. The best projections from leading geologists whom we've questioned is that Navidad Bank, once an island, sank during an underwater earthquake somewhere between eleven hundred and one thousand B.C."

"How did you arrive at that date?" asked Perlmutter, shifting his huge bulk in a chair too small for him.

"Through various chemical and biological studies, scientists can read how old the encrustations are and how long they took to form on the rock walls, the amount of corrosion and deterioration of the artifacts and the age of the coral surrounding the structure."

Sandecker, reaching in his breast pocket for a cigar and not finding one, began tapping a pen on the table. "The hype-mongers will have a field day claiming Atlantis has been found."

"Not Atlantis." Chisholm shook his head and smiled. "I tossed that one in the air for years. My own opinion is that Plato wrote a fictitious account of the disaster using the eruption of Santorini in sixteen fifty B.C. as background material."

"You don't think Atlantis was in the Caribbean?" said Summer somewhat facetiously. "People claim to have found sunken roads and cities deep under the water."

Chisholm did not look amused. "Geological formations, nothing more. If Atlantis had existed somewhere in the Caribbean, why hasn't *one*"—he paused for effect—"just *one* potsherd or artifact of ancient origin been discovered? Sorry, Atlantis did not exist on this side of the ocean."

"According to paleontology records in my library," offered Yaeger, "the Arawak Indians found by the Spanish when they arrived in the New World were the first humans into the West Indies. They had migrated from South America around twenty-five hundred B.C., or fourteen hundred years before the lady was laid to rest in her tomb."

"Somebody always gets there first," said Perlmutter. "Columbus reported seeing the hulks of large European-built ships abandoned on an island beach."

"I can't tell you how she got there," said Chisholm. "But I might shed some light on who she was."

He pressed a button on the remote and the first image on the stone-carved montage found by Dirk and Summer appeared on the monitor. The scene showed what appeared to be a fleet of ships in procession landing on a shoreline. They looked similar to the Viking longboats, but much stubbier, with flat bottoms that enabled them to travel in shallow coastal waters and rivers. Single masts supported square sails that appeared to be made of hides so they wouldn't shred under the onslaught of Atlantic gales. The hulls had high bows and sterns for sailing through rough seas. Banks of oars extended through locks on the top rails of the hulls.

"The first scene from the stone panel shows a fleet of ships unloading fighting men, horses and chariots." He pressed another button on the remote, creating a montage. "Scene Two, the opposing army is seen rising from a huge ditch surrounding a citadel on a steep hill. The next panel has them charging across a flat plain and attacking the enemy before they can unload their ships. Scene Four is the battle to repel the fleet."

"If it wasn't for all the earthen works and the citadel looking as if it was built of wood," said Perlmutter, "I'd say we were looking at the Trojan War."

Chisholm had the look of a wolf watching a herd of sheep approach his den. "You *are* looking at the Trojan War."

Sandecker fell into the trap. "Strange-looking Greeks and Trojans. I always thought they grew beards, not bushy mustaches."

"That's because they were not Greeks or Trojans."

"Who, then?"

"Celts."

Perlmutter's face wore an expression of genuine satisfaction. "I've also read Iman Wilkens."

Chisholm nodded. "Then you know his remarkable revelations about ancient history's greatest misconception."

"Could you please enlighten the rest of us?" Sandecker asked impatiently.

"I'll be happy to oblige," Chisholm replied. "The battle for Troy . . ."

"Yes?"

"Did not take place on the west coast of Turkey on the Mediterranean Sea."

Yaeger stared at him, looking puzzled. "If not Turkey, then where?"

"Cambridge, England," Chisholm answered simply, "near the North Sea."

32

E VERYONE, with the exception of Perlmutter, gave Chisholm a look of pure disbelief.

"The skepticism in your eyes is obvious," Chisholm challenged. "The world has been misled for a hundred and twenty-six years, when a German merchant named Heinrich Schliemann declared emphatically that he had found Troy by using Homer's *Iliad* as his guide. He claimed that the ancient mound called Hisarlik was the perfect location for the fortified city of Troy."

"Don't most archaeologists and historians back Schliemann's case?" Gunn queried.

"It's still a hotly debated subject," said Boyd. "Homer was a man of great mystery. There is no proof that he actually existed. All legend tells us is that a man called Homer took epic poems of a great war that had been passed down orally for hundreds of years, and recorded them in a series of adventure tales in what became the world's earliest written literature. Was he one man or a group, who over the centuries refined the poems until the *Iliad* and the *Odyssey* became history's greatest classics? The truth will never be known. Besides the enigma of his identity, the great puzzle he left behind is whether the Trojan

War was fable or fact. And if it really occurred in the Early Bronze Age, were the Greeks the true enemies of the Trojans, *or* did Homer write about an event that took place more than a thousand miles away?"

Perlmutter grinned broadly. Boyd and Chisholm were affirming what he had always believed. "What no one considered until Wilkens was that, instead of being Greek, Homer was a Celtic poet who wrote about a legendary battle that occurred four hundred years earlier, not in the Mediterranean but in the North Sea."

Gunn looked adrift. "Then the epic voyage of Odysseus . . ."

"Took place in the Atlantic Ocean."

Summer's mind was spinning. "Are you implying that Helen's face didn't launch a thousand ships?"

"What I was about to suggest," Boyd countered with a tired smile, "is that the truth behind the myth was not about a conflict fought because of a king's rage for revenge over the abduction of his wife by her lover. Hardly an excuse for thousands of men to fight and die for a promiscuous woman, is it? Wise old Priam, the king of Troy, would never have risked his kingdom nor the lives of his people merely to allow a wayward son to live with a woman, who, if the truth were known, willingly left her husband for another man. Nor was it a quest for the treasures of Troy. Rather, realistically, the conflict was fought over a soft crystalline metallic element called tin."

"St. Julien gave Summer and me a lecture about how the Celts ushered in the Bronze and Iron Ages," said Dirk, looking up from diligently taking notes.

Chisholm nodded in agreement. "To be sure, they launched the industry, but no one can say with any degree of certainty who actually discovered that mixing ten percent tin with ninety percent copper forged a metal twice as hard as anything known before. Even the exact dating is hazy. The best guess is that it appeared around two thousand B.C."

"Smelting copper was known as far back as five thousand B.C. in central Turkey," said Boyd. "Copper was in abundance throughout the ancient world. Mining took place on a grand scale in Europe and the Middle East. But when bronze came along, there was a problem. Tin ore is rare in nature. Like later gold rushes, prospectors and traders spread throughout the ancient world in search of the ore. They eventually found the largest deposits in Southwest England. The British Celtic tribes quickly cashed in and built an international marketplace for dealing in tin that they mined, smelted into bars and traded throughout the ancient world."

"Due to the high demand, the ancient Brits quickly developed a monopoly and commanded high prices from foreign traders," added Chisholm. "Though traders from rich empires such as Egypt could afford to trade in expensive goods, the Celts of Central Europe had only handmade objects and an abundant supply of amber to offer. Without a bronze industry, they had little hope of going beyond an agricultural society."

"So they decided to band together and seize the tin mines from the Brits," Yaeger anticipated.

"Precisely," Boyd replied. "The Celtic tribes on the continent formed an alliance to invade southern England and seize the mines in a territory then known as the Troad, or later Troy. The capital city was called Ilium."

"So the Achaeans were not Greeks," said Perlmutter.

Boyd gave a slight nod of his head. "*Achaean* was a loose term for allies. The Trojans generally referred to themselves as Dardanians. Just as Egypt was not the title for the Land of the Pharaohs."

"Hold on," said Gunn. "Then where did the name Egypt come from?"

"Before Homer, it was known as Al-Khem, Misr or Kemi. Not until hundreds of years later, when the Greek historian Herodotus gazed upon the pyramids and the temple of Luxor, did he call the fading empire Egypt, from a land described in Homer's *Iliad*. From then on, the name stuck."

"What evidence does Wilkens give for his theory?" asked Sandecker.

Boyd looked expectantly at Chisholm. "Do you want to take the ball, Doctor?"

"You probably know as much about it as I do," Chisholm said, with a pleased smile.

"May I jump in?" asked Perlmutter. "I've studied Wilkens's book *Where Troy Once Stood.*"

"Be our guest," Boyd acquiesced.

"There is a mountain of evidence," Perlmutter began. "For one thing, almost nothing that Homer described in his epic works stands up to scrutiny. Nowhere does he call the invading fleet 'Greeks.' During eleven hundred B.C., when the war supposedly took place, Greece was sparsely populated. There were no major cities that could support a large fleet of fighting ships and crews. The early Greeks were not considered seafaring people. Homer's reports of the ships and the men who rowed them across the sea seems better suited to the Vikings two thousand years later. Also, his descriptions of the sea more closely match the Atlantic European coastline than the Mediterranean.

"Nor do his climate narratives jibe. Homer recounts heavy, constant rain, thick mists or fog and sleet. Weather conditions more common for England than southern Turkey, which is just across the Med from the Sahara Desert."

"And there is the vegetation," Boyd prompted.

"To be sure," Perlmutter said with a modest nod. "Most all the trees Homer details are better suited to the damper atmospheres of Europe than the more arid land of Greece and Turkey. He talks mostly of deciduous green-leafed trees, while Greeks would be more familiar with evergreen conifers. And then we have horses. The Celts were a horse-loving people. The use of horses by ancient Greeks in battle was unheard of. The Egyptians and the Celts used chariots as fighting platforms, but not the Greeks or Romans. They preferred to fight on foot, using chariots only for transport and races."

"Any differences on the subject of food?" inquired Gunn.

"Homer mentions eels and oysters. Eels start from their breeding ground in the Sargasso Sea and migrate to the cold waters around Europe. He used the term *diving for oysters,* which are far more prevalent in the oceans outside the Mediterranean. If a Greek dove, it would have been for sponges, which were common in Greece at the time."

"What about the gods?" Sandecker put forth. "The *Iliad* and *Odyssey* are filled with the interference of the gods on both the Trojan and Greek armies."

"The Celts were there first. Classical scholars have concluded that the gods Homer portrayed were originally Celtic and inherited from Homer's works by later Greeks." Perlmutter paused and then added: "Another interesting point. Homer stated the Greeks and Trojans cremated their dead. This was a custom of the Celts. People around the Mediterranean generally interred their deceased."

"Intriguing hypothesis," said an unconvinced Sandecker. "But conjecture just the same."

"I was coming to the best part." Perlmutter showed his teeth in a wide smile. "Wilkens's most extraordinary revelations prove convincingly that the cities, islands and nations that Homer wrote about in his epic poems either did not exist or were called something completely different. The geography and the topography in the *Iliad* simply do not match with the existing land and seascapes around the Mediterranean. Wilkens discovered that Homer's names for towns, regions and rivers have their source in continental Europe and England. The Greek names do not fit the neighborhood of both Troy and the kingdoms of the Greek heroes, nor do the descriptions of settings match geophysical reality."

"The list goes on," said Chisholm. "Homer describes Menelaus with red hair, Odysseus with reddish brown and Achilles as blond. Also, some warriors were depicted with fair skin. None of these are characteristic of Mediterranean people. It's almost as if they came from another time and dimension."

"The invading Achaean tribes came from the bronze-making regions of France, Sweden, Denmark, Spain, Norway, Holland, Germany and Austria. Their fleet probably assembled at what is now Cherbourg and sailed across the Sea of Helle, which gave its name to the Hellespont in Turkey and is now known as the North Sea. They landed in a large bay once called the Thracian Sea, which is now labeled on present-day maps simply as the Wash in Cambridgeshire. The waters touched the shores of the East Anglian plain."

Boyd added another plus to Perlmutter's report. "Homer mentioned fourteen rivers in and around Troy. There is an amazing correlation with the fourteen rivers near the East Anglian plain. Wilkens discovered that even after thirty centuries their names remained very similar in spelling and could easily be compared. In Greek, for example, Homer alludes to the Temese River. This translates to the Thames."

"And the Trojans?" queried Sandecker, still not totally convinced.

"Their army came from all over England, Scotland and Wales," Perlmutter moved on. "They were also aided by allies from Brittany and Belgium on the continent. And now that we have the bay and the plain we can begin zeroing in on the battleground and defenses. Two immense parallel ditches still exist northeast of Cambridge. Wilkens believes they were built by the invaders, much like the trenches of World War One, to keep the defenders from attacking the camp and ships."

"Then where was the citadel of Troy?" Sandecker persisted.

Perlmutter took up the challenge. "The best bet goes to the Gog Magog Hills, where large earthworks of round fortifications with deep defensive ditches have been discovered and excavated, which revealed evidence of wooden palisades and many bronze artifacts. Funeral urns and vast numbers of skeletons that showed signs of mutilation have also been uncovered."

"Where did the odd name of Gog Magog come from?" asked Summer.

"Many years ago, as residents began accidentally uncovering an army of bones, they referred to it as the site of a great battle or war with immense slaughter. They were reminded of Ezekiel's biblical conjuring up of evil spirits in a war launched by King Gog of Magog."

Sandecker looked from Boyd to Chisholm. "All right, now that we've heard how the Trojan War was fought in southern England over tin mines, what has it got to do with the Celtic discoveries by Dirk and Summer on Navidad Reef?"

The two scholars exchanged amused looks. Then Boyd said, "Why, everything, Admiral. Now that we're reasonably sure the true battle site of the Trojan War was in England, we can begin to tie Odysseus' great voyage of adventure to Navidad Bank."

You could have heard the proverbial pin drop in the conference room. The bombshell was so unexpected that it was nearly half a minute before anyone could bring themselves to respond.

"What are you saying?" asked Gunn, trying to digest what he had just heard.

Sandecker turned slowly to Perlmutter. "St. Julien, do you go along with this craziness?"

"Not crazy at all," said Perlmutter, with a broad grin. "It was written in Homer's epics that Odysseus was king of the island of Ithaca. But the Greek island never had a kingdom nor does it have any significant ruins. Wilkens shows, to my satisfaction, at least, that Odysseus' kingdom was not in Greece. A Belgian attorney from Calais, France, Theophile Cailleux, after much research, claimed that Cadiz, Spain, was the site of Homer's Ithaca. And although the land has filled in over the past three thousand years, geologists can show the outline of several islands that are now part of the mainland. Cailleux and Wilkens have identified most of Odysseus' ports of call, none of which are in the Mediterranean."

"I have to agree," said Yaeger. "By using all the known information on Odysseus' itinerant voyage, Homer's descriptions, Cailleux and Wilkens's theories, Bronze Age navigation methods, tides and currents, Max and I have arrived at a travel plan for his ports of call."

Yaeger picked up the remote and pressed a numbered code. A chart of the north Atlantic Ocean filled the screen. A red line traveled down the coast of Africa from southern England before it crossed over the water past the Cape Verde Islands into the isles of the Caribbean. He used a laser beam as a pointer and began to trace Odysseus' journey from England.

"Odysseus' first landfall after being swept out to sea was what he described as the Land of the Lotus Eaters. According to Wilkens, this was probably the West Coast of Africa at Senegal. Lotus here is a genus of the pea family and readily consumed by the natives for thousands of years, since it has a narcotic effect. From there, the winds took him west to the Cape Verde Islands, which is the logical choice for the island of the Cyclops, because Odysseus' description matches them almost perfectly."

"That land of one-eyed people," Sandecker said with a tight smile.

"Nowhere does Homer suggest all of the people had one eye," Yaeger explained. "They had two, only Polyphemus had one, and it wasn't in the middle of his forehead."

"If I recall my *Odyssey*," said Gunn, "after escaping the Cyclops, Odysseus was then blown west across the sea to the Aeolian Isle."

Yaeger merely nodded. "By computing the prevailing winds and currents, I put Odysseus' next landfall somewhere on one of the many islands south of Martinique and north of Trinidad. From there, he and his fleet were driven by a storm to the Land of the Laestrygonians. Here, one of the small islands called Branwyn, off Guadeloupe, fits the bill. The high cliffs on each side of the narrow channel he described his ship entering matches the island geography to a T."

"This is where the Laestrygonians destroyed Odysseus' fleet," added Perlmutter.

"If that were true," said Yaeger, "the ships loaded with treasure would still lie in the silt of the harbor."

"What is the name of the island?"

"Branwyn," responded Yaeger, "was a Celtic goddess and one of the three matriarchs of Britain."

"What country owns the island?" asked Dirk.

"It's privately owned."

"Do you know by whom?" asked Summer. "A rock star, an actor, maybe some wealthy businessmen?"

"No, Branwyn is owned by a wealthy woman." He paused to check his notes. "Her name is Epona Eliade."

"Epona is the name of the Celtic goddess," said Summer. "Now there's a coincidence."

"Maybe more than mere serendipity," said Yaeger. "I'll check it out."

"Where was Odysseus' next port?" asked Sandecker.

"Now with only one ship out of twelve," Yaeger continued, "he sailed to the island of Circe, called Aeaea, which computes as Navidad Bank, a spot Homer placed on the edge of the world."

"Circe!" Summer gasped. "Circe was the woman who lived and died in the structure we found?"

Yaeger shrugged. "What can I say? This is all conjecture, which is next to impossible to prove."

"But what brought her across the ocean so many centuries ago?" Gunn wondered aloud.

Perlmutter placed his folded hands on his ample stomach. "There was more travel back and forth between the continents than anyone has envisioned."

"I'd be interested in learning where you place Hades," said Sandecker to Yaeger.

"The best guess is the Santo Tomás caverns on Cuba."

Perlmutter daintily blew his nose, then asked, "After he left Hades, where did he meet with the Sirens, Scylla the monster and Charybdis the whirlpool?"

Yaeger threw up his hands. "I have to write those events off to Homer's wild imagination. No geographical location works for any of them this side of the Atlantic." He paused a moment before picking up Odysseus' journey on the chart again. "Next, Odysseus sails eastward until he reaches Calypso's island of Ogygia, which Wilkens and I agree is St. Miguel in the Azores."

"Calypso was the beautiful sister goddess of Circe," said Summer.

"They were women of the very highest rank. Didn't Odysseus and Calypso spend a romantic interlude together in a virtual garden paradise
after his affair with Circe on her island?"

"He did," Yaeger replied. "After Odysseus leaves a tearful Calypso
on the shore, his final stop is a detour by adverse winds to the palace
of King Alcinous, which works out to be Lanzarote Island in the Ca-
naries. After relating his adventures to the king and his family, he is
given a ship and finally makes his way home to Ithaca."

"Where do you put Ithaca?" inquired Gunn.

"As Cailleux said, the port of Cadiz in southwestern Spain."

There came a few moments of silence around the table as everyone assimilated the classic tale and the multitude of theories. How
much was remotely close to the truth? Only Homer knew, and he
hadn't spoken for three thousand years.

Dirk smiled at Summer. "You have to give Odysseus credit for masculine charisma, having affairs with the two most beautiful and influ-
ential women of his time. Before he came along and seduced them,
both ladies were chaste and inaccessible."

"If the truth be known," said Chisholm, "neither lady was a goddess nor pure as the driven snow. They were both described as incredibly beautiful women with magical personalities. Circe was a
sorceress, Calypso an enchantress. As a mere mortal, Odysseus could
have never satisfied either one. Chances are they were Druidesses who
took part in all manner of wild and perverse rituals. And as such, they
intimately conducted human sacrifice, which they considered necessary for eternal life."

Summer shook her head. "It's still hard to believe."

"But true," replied Chisholm. "Druidesses were known to have
drawn men into sacrificial rites and orgies. And as leaders of their
feminine cult, they had the power to control their worshipers into
waging whatever acts they desired."

Yaeger nodded. "Lucky for us, Druidism died out a thousand
years ago."

"There lies the catch," said Chisholm. "Druidism is still very much with us in the present. There are cults throughout Europe that follow the ancient rituals."

"Except for the human sacrifice," Yaeger said with a grim smile.

"No," Boyd said seriously. "Despite it being a crime of murder, human sacrifice among the underground Druid cults still takes place."

After the others had left, Sandecker called Dirk and Summer into his office. As soon as they were all seated, he came quickly to the point.

"I'd like you two to conduct an archaeology project."

Summer and Dirk swapped confused looks. They had no idea where the admiral was leading them.

"You want us to go back to Navidad Bank?" asked Dirk.

"No, I want you to fly down to Guadeloupe and survey the harbor on the island of Branwyn."

"Since it's privately owned, won't we need permission?" asked Summer.

"As long as you don't step ashore, you won't be trespassing."

Dirk looked at Sandecker skeptically. "You want us to search for the treasure lost in the land of the Laestrygonians by Odysseus' fleet?"

"No, I want you to find the ships and their artifacts. If successful, they would be by far the oldest shipwrecks found in the Western Hemisphere and alter recorded ancient history. If it can be done, I want it done by NUMA."

Summer folded her hands on the table nervously. "You must realize, Admiral, the odds of making such an incredible find are a million to one."

"The one chance is worth the effort. Better to have tried than sit on our hands and never know."

"Do you have a timetable?"

"Rudi Gunn will arrange a NUMA plane. You'll leave tomorrow

morning. After your plane lands at the airport near the town of Pointe-a-Pitre in Gaudeloupe, you'll be met by a NUMA representative by the name of Charles Moreau. He has charted a boat for you to sail to Branwyn Island, which lies to the south. You'll have to carry your own dive equipment. Rudi will arrange to airfreight a subbottom profiler to read any anomalies you might find under the silt and sand."

"Why the rush?" demanded Dirk.

"If word gets out about this, and it will, every treasure hunter in the world will swarm over the island. I want NUMA to get in quick, survey the seabed and get out. If you're successful, we can work with the French who own Guadeloupe to secure the area. Any questions?"

Dirk took Summer's hand. "What do you think?"

"Sounds exciting."

"Somehow I knew you'd say that," Dirk said wearily. "What time do you want us at the NUMA terminal, Admiral?"

"Better you get an early start. Your plane will take off at six."

"In the morning?" asked Summer, losing some of her enthusiasm.

Sandecker grinned jovially. "With luck, you might even hear a rooster crowing on the way to the airport."

33

AFTER THE MEETING, Yaeger took the elevator down to his domain on the tenth floor. Never one for power lunches in Washington's established restaurants, he carried an old-fashioned lunch pail that contained fruit and vegetables and a thermos filled with carrot juice.

He was a slow starter in the morning and didn't have the momentum to jump into work with both feet. Yaeger sat and slowly sipped from a cup of herbal tea he brewed in a cabinet beside his desk, before leaning back and reading the *Wall Street Journal* to check on the status of his investments. Finally, he laid the paper aside and read the transcribed report from Sandecker's office regarding Pitt and Giordino's discovery of huge underground tunnels crossing Nicaragua. Then he ran a program that copied the typed report onto a computer disc. One more sip of his tea and he punched up Max.

She slowly materialized wearing a brief blue silk robe with a yellow sash, blue stars and an emblem across the back that read WONDER WOMAN. "How do you like my threads?" she asked in a syrupy voice.

"Where did you find that?" Yaeger demanded. "In a Goodwill reject box?"

"I surf Internet catalogs in my spare time. I charged it to your wife's Neiman Marcus account."

"You wish." Yaeger smiled. Max was a hologram. There was no way she could order, wear or pay for material objects. He shook his head in amazement at Max's nebulous yet vivacious temperament. There were times when he thought that programming Max with his wife's appearance and personality might have been a mistake. "If you're through showing off, Wonder Woman, I have a little job for you."

"I'm ready, master," she replied, mimicking Barbara Eden in the old *I Dream of Jeannie* TV show.

Yaeger programmed the disc contents into Max's memory. "Take your time and see what you make of this."

Max stood unblinking for a few moments and then asked, "What do you wish to know?"

"The question is, what possible motive do Odyssey and the Red Chinese have for digging four massive tunnels across Nicaragua from the Atlantic to the Pacific?"

"That's easy. The conundrum doesn't even warm my circuits."

Yaeger looked at her apparition. "How can you have an answer? You haven't analyzed the problem yet."

Max patted her mouth in a yawn. "This is so elementary. I'm constantly astounded that humans can't think beyond their noses."

Yaeger was certain he had made a mistake in the program. Her response was far too quick. "All right, I'm eager to hear your solution."

"The tunnels were built to transfer a vast amount of water."

"I don't count that as a dazzling revelation." He began to feel she had gotten off track. "A series of tunnels leading into the oceans, and mounting huge pumps, makes that an obvious conclusion."

"Ah," Max said, holding up one hand with the index finger raised. "But do you know why they want to pump massive amounts of water through the tunnels?"

"For a huge desalinization program, an irrigation project? Hell, I don't know."

"How can humans be so dense?" Max said in frustration. "Are you ready, master?"

"If you would be so kind."

"The tunnels were created to divert the South Equatorial Current that flows from Africa into the Caribbean Sea."

Yaeger was confused. "What kind of environmental threat would that provoke?"

"Don't you see it?"

"There's more than enough water in the Atlantic Ocean to make up for the loss of a few million gallons."

"Not funny."

"What, then?"

Max threw up her hands. "By diverting the South Equatorial Current, the temperature of the Gulf Stream would drop almost eight degrees by the time its flow reached Europe."

"And?" Yaeger probed.

"An eight-degree drop in the water that warms Europe would send the continent into a weather pattern equal to northern Siberia's."

Yaeger could not immediately grasp the enormity of Max's words, nor the unthinkable consequences. "Are you sure about this?"

"Have I ever been wrong?" Max pouted.

"Eight degrees seems like an excessive decrease," Yaeger persisted, doubtfully.

"We're only talking maybe a three-degree drop in the water temperature as the Gulf Stream cuts past Florida. But when the icy Labrador Current moves down from the Arctic and meets it after the Stream arcs past the Canadian Maritime Provinces, the temperature drop is magnified. This in turn greatly influences a further temperature decrease across Europe, altering the weather patterns and causing a disruption in the atmosphere from Scandinavia to the Mediterranean."

The horrendous scheme suddenly became crystal clear to Yaeger. Very slowly, he picked up the phone and dialed Sandecker's office. The admiral's secretary put Yaeger right through.

"Did Max come up with any answers?" asked Sandecker.

"She did."

"And?"

"Admiral," Yaeger began in a hoarse voice, "I'm afraid we have a catastrophe in the making."

34

WAITING FOR THE HELICOPTER that was over an hour late, Giordino happily slipped into dreamland while Pitt peered over the waters of Lake Nicaragua surrounding the lighthouse through his binoculars. The shoreline to the west was less than three miles away and he could make out a small village. He checked his map and determined that it was the town of Rivas. He then turned his attention to a large majestic island in the shape of a figure eight, no more than five miles to the west, that looked to be quite fertile and thickly forested. Pitt estimated the total area of land to be roughly one hundred and fifty square miles.

According to his map, it was called Isle de Ometepe. Pitt focused in on two volcanic mountains tied together by a narrow isthmus a couple of miles in length. The volcano on the northern end of the island rose over five thousand feet and appeared to be active by the wisp of steam that issued through the cone on top of the crater and touched the billowy clouds passing over the summit.

The southern volcano formed a perfect cone and sat dormant. Pitt judged it to be a good thousand feet lower than its mate to the north. He also estimated that the four underground tunnels ran directly under the isthmus of the island near the base of the northern volcano. That would explain, he thought, the unusual rise in temperature that he and Giordino had experienced inside the fourth tunnel.

A quick glance at the map revealed that the active volcano was named Concepcion, while its mate was labeled Madera. He swung the glasses and totally unexpectedly found himself staring at what looked to be a vast industrial enterprise spreading over the southern slopes of Concepcion just above the isthmus. He guessed that it covered over five or six hundred acres. It struck him as being in an out-of-the-way location. It hardly seemed a practical place for a business to pour millions of dollars into an industrial complex nowhere near major transportation facilities. Unless, he mused, it was cloaked in secrecy.

Then he observed an aircraft appear from the north and line up on a runway that ran across the isthmus to the entrance of the complex. It banked around the peak of the Madera volcano and landed, taxiing to a large terminal at the end of the runway.

Pitt lowered the glasses, an expression on his face as if he was seeing something he didn't want to see. A look of deep concentration clouded his green eyes. He cleaned the lenses of the binoculars with a few drops of water from his canteen and wiped them with the tail of his shirt from under the Odyssey jumpsuit. Then he raised the glasses again, and as if to reassure himself, refocused on the aircraft.

The sun shone between a pair of clouds, bathing Isle de Ometepe in bright light. Though the aircraft seemed no larger than an ant through the glasses, there was no mistaking the lavender color reflected by the sunlight on the fuselage and wings.

"Odyssey," he muttered to himself, his mind in turmoil. Only then did he realize the facility sat directly above the tunnels. That explained the freight elevators he and Giordino saw at the rail supply terminal. Whatever its purpose, the facility may have been connected to the tunnels, but its size dictated that it had to be a separate operation.

As he swept his gaze past the buildings rising around the base of the volcano, he paused, spotting what looked like an extensive dock area behind a row of warehouses. The warehouse roofs shielded the docks, but he could discern four cargo-loading cranes against the blue sky and realized that the complex didn't require an outside transportation system. It was totally self-sufficient.

Then three things happened almost simultaneously that alerted him to trouble.

The lighthouse began inexplicably to sway like a hula dancer. As he'd told Percy Rathbone, having grown up in California, he was familiar with earthquakes. He'd once been in a thirty-story office building on Wilshire Boulevard when a quake hit and the building began to rock and oscillate. Fortunately, the base of the building rested on giant concrete roller bearings deep underground for just such an event. This felt much the same, except the lighthouse trembled and reeled like a palm tree caught in opposing winds.

Pitt immediately turned and gazed at the Concepcion volcano, thinking that it might have erupted, but the peak appeared peaceful, with no sign of smoke or ash. He glanced down at the water and saw the surface ripple as if being shook from below by some unseen giant vibrator. One minute and what seemed an eternity later, the quake faded. Not surprisingly, it did not wake up Giordino.

The second danger came from a small lavender patrol boat that was coming from the island and headed directly toward the lighthouse. The security guards on board must have been confident of their trapped quarry. They were traveling over the water at a leisurely pace.

The third and final danger came from below their feet. What probably saved their lives in the next few seconds was an almost scarcely heard sound: a slight clink of metal against metal coming from the shaft leading to the tunnel deep below.

Pitt kicked Giordino. "We have callers. It seems they picked up our trail."

Giordino came instantly awake and pulled the .50 caliber Desert Eagle automatic from inside his belt under the white jumpsuit, as Pitt retrieved the ancient Colt .45 from his carry bag.

Crouched beside the shaft, Pitt shouted down without looking over the edge. "Stay where you are . . . !"

What happened next was not totally unexpected. His reply was a hail of automatic fire that burst from the shaft and peppered the metal roof of the lighthouse with enough holes to turn it into a colander. The blast was so intense that Pitt and Giordino withheld their fire so as not to risk poking a hand over the edge and having their fingers shot off.

Pitt crawled over to one of the lighthouse windows and pounded on the glass with the butt of the Colt. The panes were thick and it took several hammerlike blows to shatter the glass. Most of the shards fell to the sea below, but Pitt quickly extended his arm outside and smashed the remaining fragments onto the floor inside. Pushing them into piles with his feet, he kicked them over the edge of the shaft, where they fell like a deluge of razor-edged knives. Shouts and cries of pain erupted from the shaft, as the fire fell off.

Taking advantage of the lull, Pitt and Giordino blindly fired their automatics down the shaft, their bullets ricocheting against the concrete walls and causing havoc among the Odyssey security guards climbing the ladder. Their cries of pain ended and were replaced by the sickening thud of bodies hurtling down the shaft to the tunnel far below.

"That should put a crimp in their plans," said Giordino, in a voice devoid of remorse while he inserted a full clip.

"We still have unwanted guests to deal with," said Pitt, pointing at the patrol boat speeding toward the lighthouse, its bow lifted above the water, a rooster tail rising in its wake.

"It's going to be close." Giordino nodded out the shattered glass toward a blue helicopter that was skimming over the lake from the north.

Swiftly figuring the distance the boat and helicopter had to travel, Pitt allowed himself a tight grin. "The bird is faster. It should arrive a good mile ahead of the boat."

"Pray they don't mount rocket launchers," Giordino said, throwing cold water on Pitt's confidence.

"We'll know shortly. Get ready to grab the harness when it's dropped."

"Take too long for it to haul us up one at a time," said Giordino. "I strongly suggest we bid a tearful goodbye to the lighthouse together."

Pitt nodded. "I'm with you."

They stepped out onto a narrow balcony that ran around the top of the lighthouse. Pitt recognized the helicopter as a Bell 430 with twin Rolls-Royce engines. It was painted yellow and red, with MANAGUA AIRWAYS lettered across the sides. He watched intently as the pilot took a no-nonsense approach once around the lighthouse, while a crewman began lowering a harness attached by a cable to a winch out the open side door.

Taller by almost a foot than Giordino, Pitt leaped up and snagged the harness on the first pass as it swung in circles under the rotor wash. He looped it around Giordino's shoulders.

"You're built tougher than I am. You take the strain and I'll hold on to you."

Giordino looped his hands through the opening and clutched them around the cable as Pitt gripped him tightly around the waist. The crewman, unable to be heard above the exhaust whine of the turbines, waved frantically, trying to signal them that he could lift only one man at a time.

His warning came too late. Pitt and Giordino were dragged off the balcony of the lighthouse and dangled a hundred feet above the water as a gust of wind struck the copter. The pilot was surprised as the aircraft suddenly tilted to starboard from the combined weight of both men. He quickly corrected and hovered on an even keel as his crewman watched the overloaded winch strain to pull both men aboard.

Fortune prevailed and the pursuing boat did not fire missiles. However, a pair of heavy-caliber guns mounted on the bow began a staccato burst. Fortunately, the boat was still too far away, and with the keel bouncing over the water, the gunner's aim was fifty yards wide.

The pilot, horrified at seeing himself shot at, forgot about the men he had come to rescue and threw the helicopter on its side away from the boat and beat a hasty retreat toward the safety of the shore. With twenty feet to go, Pitt and Giordino were crazily windmilling beneath the craft. Giordino felt as if his arms were coming out of their shoulder sockets. Pitt, suffering no pain, could do little but clutch Giordino in a death grip and shout at the crewman to speed up the lift.

Pitt could see the strain of the agony on Giordino's face. For perhaps two minutes that were the longest minutes he had ever experienced, he was almost tempted to let go and fall, but one look at the water now nearly five hundred feet below his dangling feet quickly changed his mind.

Then he was looking into the dazed eyes of the crewman only five feet away. The crewman turned and shouted to the pilot, who deftly banked the copter just enough for Pitt and Giordino to fall inside the cargo section. The side door was rapidly slammed closed and locked.

The still-shocked crewman stared at the two men sprawled on the floor. "You hombres are loco," he grunted with a heavy Spanish accent. "Lift only for mail sacks weighing one hundred pounds."

"He speaks English," Giordino observed.

"Not very well," added Pitt. "Remind me to write a letter of recommendation to the company who manufactured the winch." He came to his feet and hurried into the cockpit, where he stared out a side window until he spotted the patrol boat. It had cut the chase and was circling back to the island.

"What in hell was that all about?" demanded the pilot. He was genuinely angry. "Those clowns were actually shooting at us."

"We're lucky they're bad shots."

"I didn't count on trouble when I took this charter," said the pilot, still keeping a wary eye on the boat. "Who are you guys and why was that patrol boat after you?"

"Like your charter says," Pitt answered. "My friend and I are with the National Underwater and Marine Agency. My name is Dirk Pitt."

The pilot removed one hand from the controls and extended it over his shoulder. "Marvin Huey."

"You're American. Montana, judging from your accent."

"Close. I grew up on a ranch in Wyoming. After twenty years flying these things in the Air Force, and after my wife left me for an oilman, I retired down here and started a small charter company."

Pitt shook the hand and gave the pilot a cursory look. He looked short behind the controls, with thinning red hair leaving a widow's peak. He was wearing faded Levi's with a flowered shirt and cowboy boots. The eyes were pale blue and looked like they had seen too much. He looked to be slightly on the downside of fifty.

Huey looked up at Pitt curiously. "You haven't told me why the big getaway."

"We saw something we shouldn't," Pitt answered, without elaborating.

"What's to see in an abandoned lighthouse?"

"It isn't what it seems."

Huey wasn't buying, but he didn't pursue the issue. "We'll be on the ground at our field in Managua in another twenty-five minutes."

"The sooner the better." Pitt motioned to the empty copilot's seat. "Do you mind?"

Huey gave a slight nod. "Not at all."

"I don't suppose you could make a pass over the Odyssey facility on the island?"

Huey turned fractionally and shot Pitt a look usually reserved for the insane. "You're joking. That place is guarded tighter than Area 51 at Groom Lake, Nevada. I couldn't fly within five miles without a security aircraft chasing me away."

"What goes on down there?"

"Nobody knows. The installation is so secret, the Nicaraguans deny it exists. What began as a small facility underwent vast expansion in the past five years. The security measures go beyond extreme. Huge warehouses, and what some people think are assembly areas, were constructed. Rumor has it there is a housing section accommodating three thousand people. The native Nicaraguans used to grow coffee and tobacco on the islands. Alta Garcia and Moyogalpa, the main towns, were torn down and burned after the Nicaraguan government forced the people off their land and relocated them in the mountains to the east."

"The government must have a heavy investment in the facility."

"I don't know about that, but they've been extremely cooperative in allowing Odyssey to operate without interference."

"No one has ever sneaked through Odyssey security?" asked Pitt.

Huey smiled tautly. "Nobody who lived."

"It's that tough to penetrate?"

"The entire island's beaches are patrolled by vehicles equipped with high-tech surveillance gear. Patrol boats circle the island, assisted by helicopters. Remote sensors detect movement along every path and road leading to the complex. It's said Odyssey engineers perfected sensory equipment with the ability to smell a human approaching the buildings, and distinguish them from animals."

"There must be satellite photos?" Pitt persisted.

"You can buy them from the Russians, but they won't tell you what goes on inside the maze of buildings."

"There must be rumors."

"Sure, lots of them. The only one that has any substance is that it's a research and development installation. What they research is anybody's guess."

"It must have a name."

"Only what the locals call it."

"Which is?" Pitt had to prompt.

"In English," Huey finally replied, "house of the invisible ones."

"Any reason?"

"They say it's because everybody who goes in is never seen again."

"The local officials never investigate?" asked Pitt.

Huey shook his head. "Nicaraguan bureaucrats keep a hands-off policy. The word is that Odyssey management has bought off every politician, judge and police chief in the country."

"How about the Red Chinese? Are they involved?"

"They're everywhere in Central America these days. They contracted with Odyssey about three years ago to build a short canal through Lake Nicaragua's western shoreline at Pena Blanca, so deepwater cargo ships can enter and exit."

"The nation's economy should have profited."

"Not really. Most all of the ships that use the canal are from a Chinese cargo fleet."

"COSCO?"

Huey nodded. "Yeah, that's the one. They always dock at the Odyssey facility."

Pitt spent the rest of the trip in silence, his mind sifting through the myriad of contradictions and unknowns of Odyssey, its strange founder and even stranger operations. As soon as Huey set the helicopter down at his company hangar two miles outside Managua, Pitt walked off by himself and called Admiral Sandecker.

As was his style, Sandecker minced no words. "Haven't you taken off for Washington yet?"

"No," Pitt replied smartly. "And we're not going to."

Sandecker knew something was on Pitt's mind and he went into neutral. "I assume you have a good reason."

"Are you aware of a huge secret facility built and owned by Odyssey on an island in Lake Nicaragua that sits directly over the tunnels?"

"The closest I can come is a report I read on Odyssey expanding a canal from the ocean into the lake to allow entry for cargo ships." Sandecker paused. "Come to think of it, the report was vague on the dock facilities the Nicaraguans were building at the port city of Granada a few miles east of Managua."

"The report was vague because the dock facilities were built at

Odyssey's complex on the island of Ometepe for their private use only."

"What have you got in mind?" asked Sandecker, as if already reading Pitt's mind.

"I propose Al and I go into the complex and investigate their operation."

Sandecker hesitated. "After your narrow escape from the tunnels, you're pushing your luck."

"We're getting good at breaking and entering."

"Not funny," Sandecker said sharply. "Their security must be very tight. How do you plan to sneak inside?"

"We'll come in from the water."

"Don't you think that they have underwater sensors?"

"Actually," Pitt said pontifically, "I'd be surprised if they didn't."

35

T EN MINUTES AFTER SANDECKER conversed with Pitt, the admiral was staring at Hiram Yaeger in abject incredulity. "Are you sure about this? Your data must be in error."

Yaeger was immovable. "Max is not infallible a hundred percent of the time, but on this one I believe she's right on the mark."

"It's beyond belief," said Gunn, reading over Max's projections.

Sandecker slowly shook his head, jarred by what he read. "You're saying the tunnels were built to divert the South Equatorial Current, which would in turn cause the temperature of the Gulf Stream to drop."

"According to Max's computer model, eight degrees by the time it reaches Europe."

Gunn looked up from the data files. "The effects on European climate would be cataclysmic. The entire continent would go into a deep freeze for eight months out of the year."

"Let us not forget the effect of the Gulf Stream on the east coast of the United States, and the Maritime Provinces of Canada," added Sandecker. "Every state east of the Mississippi and along the Atlantic shore could suffer a cold as bitter as that in Europe."

Gunn said sarcastically. "Now there's a happy thought."

"The Atlantic Drift's warm surface water is controlled by temperature and salinity," Yaeger explained. "As its tropical waters move north, it mixes with the cold water coming down from the Arctic, where it becomes dense and sinks southeast of Greenland. This is called a thermohaline circulation. Then it gradually warms again and rises to the surface as it reaches Europe. The Gulf Stream's sudden drop in temperature could also cause the thermohaline circulation to collapse, a state that would accent the crises and last for several centuries."

"What would be the most immediate results of such an event?" asked Sandecker.

Yaeger spread several papers across Sandecker's desk and began quoting the data. "Death and disruption would run rampant. In the beginning, thousands of homeless people would die from frostbite or hypothermia. Many more thousands might also die when the heating supplies quickly disappear because of the staggeringly high demand. All vital river traffic would come to a standstill, locked in ice. Ports would freeze throughout the Baltic and the North Sea, stranding ships carrying oil and liquefied natural gas used for heating, not to mention millions of tons of food imported from other countries. Most agriculture yields would be cut in half. Food shortages would be magnified because of the shortened growing season. Auto transportation would come to a halt because of freezing road conditions and heavy snowfall and a lack of fuel. Airports and railroads would be paralyzed for weeks at a time. People would be more susceptible to colds, flu and pneumonia. Tourism would vanish overnight. The European economy would go into complete chaos, with no end in sight. And that's only half the story."

"So much for French winemaking and Dutch tulips," Gunn muttered.

"What about the gas sent through the pipelines from the Middle

East and Russia?" said Sandecker. "Can't the flows be increased to alleviate the suffering?"

"A drop in the bucket when you calculate the demand, not to mention the electrical power shortages that would come with severe winter storms. Max estimates at least thirty million homes throughout Europe would be left without heat."

Gunn looked up from taking notes. "You said that was only half the story."

"Further disruption and misery would come with the rising temperatures in the late spring," Yaeger continued. "This terrible scenario will be enhanced by heavy rains and high winds. Violent and massive flooding will be the result. Rivers swelled by massive amounts of melted snow would burst their banks and flood thousands of cities and towns, destroying vital bridges as well as millions of homes. Avalanches and mud slides would bury entire towns and destroy vast stretches of highway. The loss of life following such an appalling cataclysm cannot be imagined."

Gunn and Sandecker remained silent for a few moments. Then Sandecker broke the silence.

"Why?" he asked briefly.

Gunn spoke the single thought on everyone's mind. "What do Specter and the Red Chinese have to gain by such an atrocious scheme?"

Yaeger showed the palms of his hands in a helpless gesture. "Max has yet to come up with an answer."

"Can it be Specter controls the gas coming into Europe?" queried Sandecker.

"We asked the same question and ran profiles on all the major gas producers that supply the continent," replied Yaeger. "The response was negative. Odyssey has no natural gas or oil holdings anywhere in the world. The only minerals in which Specter has an interest is a group consisting of platinum, palladium, iridium and rhodium. For those, he owns the major deposits and producing mines in South Africa, Brazil, Russia and Peru. He'd have a monopoly on the world's reserves if he could gain control of the Hall mine in New Zealand that produces as much as the other countries put together—but the mine's owner, Westmoreland Hall, has refused all offers to sell."

"If I remember my high school chemistry class," Sandecker said slowly, "platinum is used mostly for electrodes like automobile spark plugs and jewelry."

"It's also in high demand in chemistry laboratories because of its high resistance to heat."

"I fail to see a connection between his mining operations and his plot to send Europe back to the glacial age."

"There has to be a rationale," said Gunn. "The return on investment for digging those tunnels would have to astronomical to pay for the excavation. If he doesn't profit from the demand in energy, what can he possibly gain?"

Sandecker turned and stared thoughtfully out his window down at the Potomac River. Then he turned back and looked at Yaeger. "Those pumps, fed by the immense water pressure—could they be used to supply electricity? If so, they'd produce enough energy to power most of Central America."

Yaeger said, "Pitt's report made no mention of generators. He and Giordino would have certainly recognized a power source when they saw one."

Sandecker stared through his authoritative blue eyes at Gunn. "You're aware of the mischief those two want to carry out."

"No, I'm not." Gunn stared back at Sandecker, unintimidated. "I was under the impression that they're on a flight back to Washington."

"There's been a change in plans."

"Oh?"

"They advised me that they were going to make a clandestine inspection of a secret installation Odyssey has built on an island in the middle of Lake Nicaragua."

"Did you give your permission?" Gunn asked, with an astute grin.

"Since when did you know them to take a 'no' answer from *me*?"

"They just might come up with some answers to our dilemma."

"Maybe," Sandecker said grimly. "They also may get themselves killed."

PART FOUR

The Key

BRANWYN MEGALITH

36

THE PRIVATE AND CORPORATE jets began arriving on Branwyn Island fifteen miles south of Basse-Terre, one of the main islands of Guadeloupe in the Caribbean. Exotically designed minibuses with luxurious interiors and painted lavender pulled up to the aircraft to accommodate the passengers. After putting their luggage in the trunk, the drivers transported the travelers to elegant suites in a palatial belowground sanctuary that was only open to private guests of Specter. All those who departed the aircraft were women. None were accompanied by friends or business associates.

They all arrived alone.

The last plane to arrive landed at six o'clock in the evening. It was the familiar Beriev Be-210 of the Specter Corporation, which touched down at six o'clock in the evening. Specter, the only male to make an appearance, lumbered down the boarding steps, his great belly barely squeezing through the door. He was followed by a body carried on a stretcher that was completely covered by a blanket. Specter, wearing his signature white suit, then settled into the rear seat and poured himself a glass of Beaujolais from the bar.

The driver, who had chauffeured Specter on other occasions, was always amazed at how someone so gross could move so agilely. He stood for a moment and watched with curiosity as the form on the stretcher was unceremoniously shoved into the open bed of a pickup truck, without any consideration for the heavy rain that began to fall.

On the south end of the island, a bowl shaped like a sunken cauldron one hundred yards in diameter had been carved into the rock and coral. The concave depression had been hollowed out to a depth of thirty feet, deep enough so no passing boats or ships could observe any activities.

Inside the cauldron, thirty tall shafts of stone thirteen feet high stood evenly spaced three feet apart. It was a copy of the famous mystical monolithic structure known as Stonehenge, which means stone circle. The shafts were six and a half feet wide and three feet thick. Their tapered tops supported ten-and-a-half-foot lintels, shaped to the curve of the circle.

The inner horseshoe-shaped circle known as the Trilithons contained five towering stones with their own lintels. Unlike the hard-grained sandstone of the original structure in England that was built between 2550 and 1600 B.C., these were cut from black lava rock.

The main difference between the old and the new structures was a huge block of marble carved and contoured like a sarcophagus. It was elevated nearly ten feet off the ground within the inner horseshoe profile and reached by steps leading up to a landing that encircled its walls ornately carved with the galloping Horse of Uffington.

At night hidden lights illuminated the interior of the bowl in lavender-colored streams that swirled around the shafts, while a single set of laser beams spaced around the outer circle soared into the nighttime sky. They were turned on briefly early in the evening before blinking out.

A few minutes before midnight, as if by command, the rain stopped. When the lights flashed on again, the floor of the center of the Trilithons was enhanced by thirty women in dresses draped like shawls and rippled with folds. Known as a peplos, from the ancient Greek, the voluminous dresses covered their legs and feet and came in a rainbow of colors with no two the exact same hue. Long red hairpieces adorned their heads as flecks of silver sparkled on their faces, necks and open arms. The silver makeup gave their facial features a masklike effect, making them all appear as if they might have been sisters of the same blood.

They all stood silent, staring at a figure stretched on the block of marble. It was a man. All that could be seen of him was the upper half of his face. His body, chin and mouth were tightly wrapped in black silk. He appeared to be in his late fifties, with a mass of graying hair. The nose and chin were sharp, with suntanned, heavily lined features. His eyes were wide and bulging as they darted around the lights and the tops of the columns. Seemingly adhered to the marble slab, he could not move nor turn his head. His only line of vision was upward, as he stared in terror at the laser beam piercing the black sky above him.

Suddenly, the swirling lights darkened while the lasers around the marble remained on. In a minute the lights spiraled on again. For a moment it seemed that nothing had changed, but then a woman had magically appeared in a gold peplos. Her head was covered by a mass of flame-red hair, long and shiny, that fell in a loose cascade to her hips. The skin on her face, neck and arms had pearl white luster. She was slim, with a body whose shape flared with perfection. With feline grace, she walked up the stairs to the marble block that was now recognized as an altar.

She raised her arms and began to chant: *"O daughters of Odysseus and Circe, may life be taken from those who are not worthy. Intoxicate yourself with wealth and the spoils of men who attempt to enslave us. Seek not men without*

*wealth and power. And when they are found, exploit, dispel their desires, plunder
their treasures and step into their world."*

Then all the women raised their arms and chanted: *"Great is the sisterhood for we are the pillars of the world, great are the daughters of Odysseus
and Circe for their path is glorified."*

The chant was repeated, swelling in volume before dropping almost to whispers as their arms were lowered.

The woman standing before the terrified man on the marble altar
reached beneath the folds of her gown, produced a dagger and raised
it above her head. The other women moved up the steps and surrounded what was about to become a pagan sacrifice. As one, they also
produced daggers and held them high.

The woman who bore the image of a high priestess chanted: *"Here
lies one who should not have been born."*

Then she plunged her dagger into the chest of the horrified man
bound on the altar. Lifting the dagger with blood streaming from the
blade, she stepped aside as the other women came one after the other
and drove their daggers into the helpless man.

The circle of women moved down the steps and stood beneath the
columns, holding the bloody daggers as if presenting them as gifts.
There was an eerie silence for several moments until they all chanted:
"Under the gaze of our gods, we triumph."

Then the laser beams and the swirling rays blinked out, leaving the
pagan temple of murder in the black of the night.

THE FOLLOWING DAY, the business world was stunned by the
news that publishing mogul Westmoreland Hall was presumed
dead after swimming off the reef of his luxurious beach house estate
in Jamaica and vanishing. Hall went for his usual morning swim alone.
He was known to swim beyond the reef into deeper water and allow
the surf to return him to shore though a narrow channel. It is not

known whether Hall drowned, was attacked by a shark or died of natural causes, since his body went undiscovered after an extensive search by Jamaican officials.

His obituary read:

Founder of a mining empire that owned the world's major reserves of platinum and the other five metals in its group in New Zealand, Hall was a hard-driving executive who established his success by taking over the mines when they were on the verge of bankruptcy and turning them into profit makers before borrowing against them for new acquisitions in Canada and Indonesia. A widower who lost his wife in a car accident three years previously, Hall leaves a son, Myron, who is a successful artist, and a daughter, Rowena, who, as executive vice president, will become board chairman and take over the day-to-day management of the conglomerate.

Amazingly, according to most Wall Street economists, stock in Hall Enterprises rose ten points after word spread of his presumed death. In most circumstances when the head of a large corporation dies, the stock falls, but brokers reported heavy buying by several unknown speculators. Most mining experts predict that Rowena Westmoreland will sell her father's holdings to the Odyssey Corporation, since it is known that Odyssey's founder, Mr. Specter, has made an offer above and beyond any other mining conglomerate's bid.

A memorial service will be held for friends and family at Christchurch Cathedral on Wednesday next at 2:00 P.M.

Ten days later an item appeared in the business sections of the world's leading newspapers:

Mr. Specter of the Odyssey Corporation has purchased the Hall Mining Company for an undisclosed sum from the late Westmoreland Hall's family. Chairman and major stockholder Rowena West-

moreland will continue to run day-to-day operations as chief executive officer.

There was no mention that all the processed platinum ore was now being purchased by Ling Ho Limited in Beijing and shipped in Chinese cargo ships to an industrial center on the coast of Fukien Province.

37

THE WIND OFF THE PACIFIC bumped the water on the lake into a mild chop. Though the lake was large, the tide was minimal and the temperature was a mild eighty degrees. The silence over the dark waters was fractured by the harsh whirr of a jet ski's motor. Unseen by human eyes, it raced through the night at a speed of over fifty knots, invisible to radar because of a soft rubber mantle that absorbed the radio wave pulse and stopped the echo from returning to the radar's transmitter.

Pitt steered the Polaris Virage TX with Giordino on the rear seat and a bag full of equipment in the bow storage. Along with their dive gear, they also carried their stolen Odyssey employee jumpsuits, except this time the photos on the IDs matched their faces, with Giordino's features retouched to at least resemble a husky woman. While waiting for their dive gear to be flown in from Washington, they had gone to a photo shop and arranged for their pictures to be taken and reinserted inside the laminated plastic ID holders. The shop's owner charged them a pretty price, but asked no questions.

As they rounded the shoreline below the Madera volcano side of the island, they skirted the isthmus, staying a mile off a sandy beach that stretched between the two mountains. The lights of the complex shone brightly against the black of Mount Concepcion. No blackout here. The Odyssey management felt safe and snug guarded by their army of security agents and array of detection equipment.

Pitt slowed the jet ski as they approached the dock area, where a large COSCO containership was brightly lit under a sea of floodlights. Pitt noted that the cranes were off-loading the cargo containers onto trucks parked beneath the hull. No cargo was going on. He began to think the complex was more than a research and development center. It had to have a connection with the tunnels that ran under it.

Sandecker had finally agreed on the mission in principle. Yaeger and Gunn had filled Pitt and Giordino in on the purpose of the tunnels. It then became imperative in everyone's mind that whatever information they gained inside the complex might be vital for the discovery of Specter's motives for covering Europe in ice.

The Virage TX was painted a charcoal gray that blended into the black water. Contrary to what is shown in the movies where agents sneak around in black skintight suits, dark gray has less visibility under the stars at night. The three-cylinder engine was massaged by NUMA engineers to put out one hundred and seventy horsepower. Noise reduction was also modified to reduce exhaust noise by ninety percent.

Speeding across the black water, the only sounds came from the slap of the bow and the muted hum of the tuned pipe exhaust. They had reached the outer edge of the Isle de Ometepe in half an hour after leaving a deserted wharf south of Granada.

Pitt eased back on the throttle as Giordino studied a basic, hand-held radar detector. "How's it look?" Pitt asked.

"Their beam sweeps past us without pausing, so they must not be reading us."

"We were wise to take the precaution of finishing the trip underwater," Pitt said, tipping his head toward a pair of searchlights that were sweeping the water for five hundred yards off the shore.

"I make it about a quarter of a mile."

"Our depth sounder reads the bottom at only twenty-two feet. We must be out of the main channel."

"Time to abandon ship and get wet," Giordino said, motioning toward a patrol boat that appeared around the end of a long dock.

Already in their light wet suits, they quickly pulled their dive gear and packs from the jet ski's storage areas. The Virage was a stable craft and they could stand while helping each other slip into their oxygen closed-circuit rebreathers, of a type used by the military for shallow-water operations. After quickly going through the predive checking procedures, Giordino slid into the water while Pitt tied the hand grips in a straight position. Then he aimed the jet ski on a course toward the west shore of the lake and set the throttle as he slid off. Neither man took a backward glance at the speeding craft before diving beneath the surface. Though they were using communication equipment, they took no chances of losing each other in the ink-black water. They clipped the ends of a ten-foot line to their weight belts.

Pitt preferred the oxygen closed-circuit rebreather. The semi–closed circuit rebreathers were more efficient for deepwater work, but they left telltale signs of bubbles on the surface. Breathing one hundred percent oxygen, the rebreather was the only true bubble-free diving system, the reason they were used by military divers on covert missions. There could be no detection on the surface because the system eliminated all indications of bubble exhaust. It took specialized training to use the system efficiently without problems, but Pitt and Giordino were no strangers to rebreathers, having used them for twenty years.

Neither man spoke. Giordino trailed behind, tracing Pitt's movement by using a shaded underwater penlight that sent out a thin beam that was next to impossible to spot from the surface. Pitt saw the bottom slope down as they came to the main ship channel. He leveled off, checked his compass and began kicking toward the Odyssey dock. Far into the distance, magnified by the water, he and Giordino could hear the thrash of the patrol boat's twin screws.

Relying on his compass and computer displaying GPS positions, they homed in on the section under the main dock where it met the shoreline. They swam slowly and steadily, seeing the water on the surface become a shade less black as they came closer to the lights beaming over the entire dock area. They could also see the sweep of the searchlights as their yellow shafts streaked across the surface above them.

The water became more transparent, and they began to see the yellow glow turn brighter on the water surface. Another hundred yards and they could make out the faintly shimmering outline of the dock pilings. They skirted around the big COSCO containership, staying far enough away so no idle crewman could see them under the surface. All activity had come to a standstill on the dock. The big cranes became immobile and the warehouses were closed and deserted as the trucks moved away.

Suddenly, Pitt felt the back of his neck tingle and he sensed a movement in the water as a huge shape materialized out of the gloom and swiped Pitt's shoulder with its tail and disappeared. He stiffened and Giordino immediately sensed the rope go slack.

"What is it?" Giordino demanded.

"I think we're being stalked by a carcharhinid."

"A shark?"

"A Lake Nicaragua bull shark, with blunt-nosed snout, big and gray, eight to nine feet."

"Do freshwater sharks bite?"

"Show me one who isn't carnivorous."

Pitt swept the narrow beam of the penlight in a circle, but it failed to pierce the murky water for more than ten feet. "We'd better circle the wagons."

Giordino swiftly picked up on the meaning and swam to Pitt's side and turned until they were back to back, facing in opposite directions to cover three hundred and sixty degrees. As if reading the other's thoughts, they pulled their dive knives from the sheaths attached to their lower legs and held them as if pointing swords.

Their nemesis returned and slowly spiraled around them, moving closer with each circle. Its gray skin was ominously illuminated under the tiny glow of their penlights, a big repulsive beast staring at them from one black eye as large as the rim on a coffee cup, with a wide jaw showing triangular rows of serrated teeth like a snarling dog. It turned sharply and eased past the divers for a closer look, never having seen such strange fish with appendages that did not resemble its usual victims. It had the look of a gluttonous monster trying to make up its mind whether the two weird fish that had intruded into its domain would make a palatable meal. It seemed curious that its prey made no move to dart away.

Pitt knew the sinister murder machine was not quite ready to attack. The mouth was only slightly open and the lips had not pulled away from the hideous teeth. He decided that offense was the best defense and he lunged at the creature, thrusting his knife and making a slashing swipe across the shark's nose, the only tender spot on its taut body.

The shark rolled away, trailing a streak of blood, confused and angered by the sudden show of resistance from what should have been an easy kill. Then it turned, hovered for a few moments, flipped its tail fins and came at them with phenomenal speed in a movement dead silent, straight for the kill.

Pitt had only one trick left in his bag. He shined the beam of the penlight directly into the shark's right eye. The unexpected flash temporarily blinded the killer just enough to induce it to veer and roll to his right, mouth opening in anticipation of biting into flesh and bone. Pitt kicked fiercely, twisting his body to one side as the shark flashed past, using its pectoral fin to push it away. The yawning jaws clamped shut on empty water. Then Pitt lashed out with the knife and gashed the monster in its black lifeless eye.

Two things could have happened. The maddened shark could have attacked without further hesitation, provoked by pain and anger, or it could have swum away, half blinded, giving up the battle for easier prey.

Fortunately, it swam away and did not return.

"That was about as close as we ever came to being a special on a dinner menu," Giordino said, in a vague tone still tinged with tension.

"He would probably have digested me and spit you out for tasting bad," Pitt came back.

"We'll never know whether he enjoyed Italian food."

"Let's get a move on before one of his pals comes nosing around."

They continued on but with greater caution than before, feeling a sense of relief as the lights from the docks now provided them with a good thirty feet of underwater visibility. Finally, they reached the pilings under the dock and swam between them before surfacing and staring up at the wooden planking, where they floated, getting their wind and waiting to see if they had set off any security sensors. After a few minutes, no sounds of approaching security guards were heard from above.

Pitt said, "We'll follow the dock until it reaches the shore before we surface again."

This time Giordino moved off into the lead, with Pitt following. The bottom came up sharply and they were relieved to find a sandy beach free of rocks. Crouching under the dock and shielded from the overhead lights, they removed their dive gear and wet suits, opened their waterproof bags and retrieved their Odyssey jumpsuits and hard hats. Slipping on socks and shoes, they checked their ID badges to see they were attached in the proper position before stepping warily into the open.

A single guard sat in a small house at the edge of a paved road that passed by the entrance to the dock. He was eyeballing a TV channel that was running an old American movie in Spanish. Pitt scanned the area but saw only the single guard.

"Shall we test our presence?" he said to Giordino, face-to-face for the first time since they dove in the water.

"You want to observe his reaction when we walk by?"

"Now or never to see if we can freely move throughout the facility."

They walked casually past the guardhouse. The security guard, wearing the male black jumpsuit, caught their movement and came out onto the road. *"La parada?"* he shouted, a frown on his face.

"La parada?" Giordino repeated.

"It means halt."

"¿Para qué está usted aquí? Usted debe estar en sus cuartos."

"Here's your chance to flash your Spanish," said Giordino, his fingers tightening around the grip of his gun beneath the jumpsuit.

"What Spanish," said Pitt benignly. "I forgot most of what I learned in high school."

"Take a guess. What did he say?"

"He wants to know what are we're doing here. Then he said we're supposed to be in our quarters."

"Not bad." Giordino grinned. He walked up to the guard as if he didn't have a care in the world. *"Yo no hablo el español,"* he said in a high-pitched voice in a sad attempt to mimic a woman.

"Very good," Pitt complimented him in turn.

"I've been to Tijuana." Giordino approached the guard and shrugged helplessly. "We're Canadian."

The guard frowned as he looked at Giordino. If his mind could be read, it would reveal that the woman inside the white uniform jumpsuit was the ugliest he'd ever seen. Then his frown turned to a smile. "Oh, *sí*, Canadians, I speak English." He pronounced it *Englais*.

"I know we're supposed to be in the barracks," said Pitt, smiling back. "We only wanted to take a little walk before going to sleep."

"No, no, that is not allowed, *amigos*," said the guard. "You are not allowed out of your assigned area after eight o'clock."

Pitt threw up his hands. "Sorry, *amigo,* we were talking and didn't notice we had wandered into the wrong area. Now we're lost. Can you
direct us to the barracks?"

The guard came over and shined a flashlight on their badges and
studied them. "You from the dig?"

"*Sí,* we're from the dig. Our superior sent us topside for a few
days' rest."

"I understand, *senor,* but you must return to your quarters. It is reg-
ulations. Just follow the road and turn left at the water tower. Your
building is thirty meters to the left."

"*Gracias, amigo,*" said Pitt. "We're on our way."

Satisfied Pitt and Giordino were not intruders, the guard returned
to his little house.

Giordino said, "Well, we passed the first test."

"Best we hide out somewhere until daylight. Not healthy to wander around here in the dead of night. Too suspicious. The next guard
who stops us might not be so friendly."

They followed the guard's directions until they came to a long row
of buildings. They moved in the shadows through the edge of a grove
of palm trees, studying the entrances to the living quarters for the
employees of Odyssey.

All but the fifth and last building were free of guards. That building had two guards stationed at the entrance, while another two patrolled the perimeter outside a high surrounding fence.

"Whoever lives there must not be popular with Odyssey," said Pitt.
"It looks like a prison."

"The occupants must be held captive."

"Agreed."

"Then we break into one that's open."

Pitt shook his head. "No, we enter this one. I want to talk to those
who are held inside. We may learn more from them about Odyssey's
operation."

"No way we're going to bluff our way in."

"Looks like a small shed next door. Let's move around, keeping the trees as cover, and check it out."

"You never take the easy path," Giordino groaned at seeing that Pitt's face held a remote and thoughtful expression under the glow of the lights lining the street.

"No fun if it's simple," Pitt said seriously.

Like burglars slinking through a residential neighborhood, they moved through the trees, taking advantage of the thin curling trunks until they reached the edge of the grove. Crouched and running, they covered another thirty yards until they reached the rear of the shed. Edging around one corner, they found a side door. Giordino tried the latch. It was open and they slipped inside. Flashing their penlights around the interior, they found that it was an equipment garage that held a street sweeper.

Pitt could see Giordino's teeth spread in a smile in the dim light. "I think we struck the mother lode."

"Are you thinking what I'm thinking?"

"I am," said Pitt. "We start up the sweeper and send it down the street, but with one refinement to get the guard's attention."

"Which is?"

"We set it on fire."

"Your devious mind never ceases to amaze me."

"It's a gift."

In ten minutes, they had siphoned three gallons of gas into a five-gallon can they found in the garage. Pitt climbed into the cab of the street sweeper and turned on the ignition, while Giordino stood ready to swing the doors open. They were both thankful the engine started with a single cough and turned over smoothly without an abundance of exhaust noise. The sweeper had standard four-speed transmission, and he stood outside the open door, ready to shift it into second gear, skipping first so the big vehicle would gain speed faster. Waiting until the last minute to avoid an explosion inside the garage from the gas fumes, he turned the steering wheel of the big vehicle so that it would angle down the road toward a row of parked trucks. Giordino opened the double doors and trotted back to the fuel can. He doused the gas into the empty cab and stood holding the flame starter for an acetylene torch.

"Showtime," he said briefly.

Pitt, standing on the doorframe just outside the cab, jammed the shifter into gear and leaped, as Giordino turned the oxygen and acetylene valves full open and squeezed the handle of the flame starter, sending a two-foot flame bursting from the tip of the torch. There was a loud *whoosh* as a combustion-produced ball of fire enveloped the cab of the sweeper before it accelerated through the doors.

Roaring down the road like a comet, the sweeper, with its brushes spinning wildly and throwing up a cloud of dirt and dust, sped fifty yards before crashing into the first truck and sending it bouncing on all wheels into a palm tree. Then it smashed square into the next truck in the row with a horrendous screech of tearing metal and glass, shoving it into the others, until it finally became jammed and came to a standstill with flames shooting into the sky followed by a swirling cloud of black smoke.

The two guards outside the building stood frozen in shock staring incredulously at the sudden eruption of fire. Finally they were galvanized into action, their first reaction being the obvious conclusion that the driver was still in the cab. They abandoned their posts and went running down the road, followed on their heels by the guards from inside.

Pitt and Giordino took immediate advantage of the commotion focused around the blazing sweeper. Pitt dashed through the gated fence, dove inside the open door of the building and fell on the floor, only to have Giordino, unable to stop his momentum, trip and fall on him.

"You've got to lose weight," Pitt grunted.

Giordino swiftly pulled him to his feet. "Now where, genius?"

Pitt didn't answer but, seeing that it was clear, he took off running down a long hallway. The doors on either side had locked latches. He stopped in front of the third door and turned to Giordino. "This is *your* specialty," he said, stepping aside.

Giordino shot him a testy look, then leaned back and kicked the door half off its hinges. Then he lunged with one shoulder and finished the job. Unable to withstand the muscular Italian's onslaught, the door fell flat on the floor with a loud thud.

Pitt stepped inside and found a man and a woman sitting upright in bed, frozen in shocked silence at the sight of the strangers, their faces expressing icy fear.

"Forgive the intrusion," Pitt said softly, "but we need a place to hide." As he spoke, Giordino was already setting the door back in place.

"Where are you going to take us?" the woman asked in near panic with a heavy German guttural accent as she pulled up the covers around the top of her nightgown. Round, flushed face with wide brown eyes, silver hair pulled back in a bun, she looked like the grandmother she probably was. Though it was buried under a sheet and light blanket, Pitt could see that her body would never fit into a size sixteen dress.

"Noplace. We're not who you think."

"But you're one of them."

"No, ma'am," said Pitt, trying to ease her terror. "We are not employees of Odyssey."

"Then who in God's name are you?" asked the man, slowly recovering. The man in the bed rose in an old-fashioned nightshirt and threw on an equally old-fashioned chenille bathrobe. Just the opposite of what Pitt assumed was his wife, he was quite tall and thin as a yardstick. His thick gray hair stood at least three inches above Pitt's. White facial skin, a sharp pyramid of a nose and tight lips decorated with a pencil-thin mustache defined his face.

"My name is Dirk Pitt. My friend is Al Giordino. We work for the United States government and are here to learn why the existence of this facility is such a well-guarded secret."

"How did you get on the island?" asked the woman.

"From the water," Pitt replied, without detail. "We entered your building after creating a little diversion that drew away the guards." As he spoke, the sound of approaching sirens could be heard echoing down the corridor through the building's still-open front entrance. "I've never known anyone who could ignore watching a good fire."

"Why did you choose our room?"

"Pure chance, nothing more."

"If you will kindly oblige us," said Giordino, "we'd like to spend the night. We'll be gone come the dawn."

The woman studied Giordino, her eyes traveling up and down his white jumpsuit, with a look of suspicion. "You're not a woman."

Giordino responded with a wide smile. "Thankfully, no, but how I came to be in a female Odyssey uniform is a long and boring story."

"Why should we believe you?"

"I can't give you a reason in the world."

"Do you mind telling us why you're confined inside this building?" queried Pitt.

"Forgive us," said the woman, coming back on track. "My husband and I are terribly confused. He is Dr. Claus Lowenhardt, and I am his wife, Dr. Hilda Lowenhardt. We are only locked in at night. During the day we work under heavy guard in the laboratories."

Pitt was amused at the formality of the introductions. "How did you come to be here?"

"We were doing research at the Technical Research Institution in Aachen, Germany, when agents working for a Mr. Specter representing the Odyssey Corporation requested that we come to work for them as consultants. My wife and I were only two out of forty of the top scientists in our field who were lured away from their laboratories by offers of an immense amount of money and promises of funding for our projects after we were finished here and returned home. We were told we were flying to Canada, but they lied. When our plane landed, we found ourselves on this island in the middle of nowhere. Since then, we have all virtually worked as slaves."

"How long ago?"

"Five years."

"What type of research were you forced to conduct?"

"Our academic discipline is in the science of fuel cell energy."

"Is this why this facility was constructed, to conduct experiments on fuel cells?"

Claus Lowenhardt nodded. "Odyssey began construction nearly six years ago."

"What about outside contact?"

"We are not allowed telephone communications with our friends and families," replied Hilda, "only outgoing letters, which are heavily censored."

"Five years is a long time to be away from your loved ones. Why didn't you obstruct the research by slowdowns and sabotage?"

Hilda shook her head solemnly. "Because they threatened a horrible death to anyone who hampered the research."

"And the lives of our families back home as well," added Claus. "We had no choice but to put forth a dedicated effort. We also had a true desire to continue our life's work, to create a clean and efficient energy source for the people of the world."

"One man who had no family was made an example," said Hilda. "They tortured him by night and forced him to work by day. He was found one morning hanging from the light fixture in his room. We all knew he was murdered."

"You believe he was murdered on orders from Odyssey officials?"

"Executed," Lowenhardt corrected him. He smiled grimly and pointed up at the ceiling. "Look for yourself, Mr. Pitt. Would that fixture, which is little more than a wire and lightbulb, support the weight of a man?"

"I see your point," Pitt acknowledged.

"We do what we're told to do," said Hilda quietly, "whatever it takes to prevent harm from coming to our son and two daughters and five grandchildren. The others are in the same boat."

"Have you and your fellow scientists made any progress in developing fuel cell technology?" asked Pitt.

Hilda and Claus turned and faced each other with quizzical expressions. Then Claus said, "Hasn't the world learned of our success?"

"Success?"

"Along with our fellow scientists, we have developed an energy-generating source that combines nitrogen-producing ammonia and oxygen out of the atmosphere to create substantial amounts of electricity at a very low cost per unit, with pure water as its only waste product."

"I thought practical and efficient fuel cells were decades away," said Giordino.

"Fuel cells using hydrogen and oxygen to produce electricity, yes. Oxygen can come from the air. However, hydrogen is not readily available and must be stored as a fuel. But because of our fortunate and almost miraculous breakthrough, we have paved the way to nonpolluting energy that is available to millions of people as we speak."

"You talk as if it is already in production," said Giordino.

"It was perfected and tested with great success over a year ago." Lowenhardt gave him the look of a man staring at a village idiot. "Production began immediately after it was perfected. Surely you're familiar with it."

They could read the expression of bafflement and incomprehension on Pitt's and Giordino's faces as genuine. "That's news to us," said Pitt skeptically. "I'm not aware of a new miracle energy product sitting on store shelves or powering automobiles."

"Nor I," Giordino chimed in.

"We don't understand. We were told that millions of units had already been produced by a manufacturing facility in China."

"Sorry to disappoint you, but your great achievement is still a secret," Pitt said sympathetically. "I can only guess that the Chinese are stockpiling your creation for some inexplicable purpose."

"But what do they have to do with the tunnels?" Giordino muttered, confused at trying to put two and two together.

Pitt sat down in a chair and stared thoughtfully at the design in a throw rug. Finally, he looked up. "The admiral said that Yaeger's computer concluded that the purpose behind the tunnels was to lower the temperature of the Gulf Stream and throw the eastern United States and Europe into eight months of frigid weather." Then he turned to the Lowenhardts. "Your cutting-edge power technology, is it designed for automobiles?"

"Not at the moment. But eventually, with more study and refinement, it will generate enough clean energy to power all vehicles, including aircraft and trains. We've gone beyond the design stage. Currently, we're working out the final phase of engineering before running tests."

"What does the gadget in production accomplish?" asked Pitt.

Claus winced at the word *gadget.* "The Macha is a self-sustaining generator that can provide cost-efficient electrical energy to every home, office, workplace and school in the world. It makes air pollution a nightmare of the past. Now a family home, no matter how large or small, located in the city or in the farthest reaches of the country, can have its own independent source of energy—"

"You call it the Macha?"

"Specter came up with the name himself when he saw the first operational unit. Macha, so he informed us, was the Celtic goddess of cunning, also known as the queen of phantoms."

"The Celts again," muttered Giordino.

"The plot thickens," Pitt said philosophically.

"Guard approaching," warned Giordino at his station by the door. "Sounds like two of them." He leaned his weight against it.

The room became so hushed that the guards' voices became quite audible as they approached down the hallway, checking the doors of the hostage scientists. Their footsteps stopped outside.

The Lowenhardts' eyes took on the look of frightened rabbits hearing the howl of coyotes, until they saw Pitt's and Giordino's automatics appear as if by magic, and they realized these were men who had command of the situation.

"*Este puerta aparece dañada.*"

"He said the door looks damaged," Pitt whispered.

One of the guards jiggled the latch and pushed against the door, but it did not move with Giordino's weight against it.

"*Se parece seguro,*" came another voice.

"It seems secure," Pitt translated.

"*Lo tendremos reparados por la mañana.*"

"They said they'll have it repaired in the morning."

Then the footsteps and voices faded, as they continued on their rounds down the hallway.

Pitt turned and gave the Lowenhardts a long hard look. "We're going to have to leave the island and you must come with us."

"You think that's wise?" Giordino put to him.

"Expedient," said Pitt. "These people are the key to the mystery. Because of what they know, we don't have to take the chance of getting caught while we nose around the facility, nor would we learn a third of what the good doctors know."

"No, no!" Hilda gasped. "We don't dare leave. Once security learns we were missing, the fiends at Odyssey will retaliate and murder our children."

Pitt took her hand and gently squeezed it. "Your family will be protected. I promise you, no harm will be allowed to come to them."

"I'm still not sure," Giordino said, considering the circumstances and possible consequences. "Once we abandoned the jet ski our only plan for escaping the island was to attempt to steal a boat or an airplane, since their security forces would stop any helicopter pickup. That plan won't come easy with a pair of senior citizens in tow."

Pitt turned back to the Lowenhardts. "What you haven't considered is that when your usefulness is over, you and the other hostage scientists will have to be eliminated. Specter cannot risk any of you revealing to the world what went on here."

Total understanding flooded Claus Lowenhardt's face, but he still could not bring himself to fully accept Pitt's words. "Not all of us. It's diabolical. They wouldn't dare kill us all. The outside world would discover the truth."

"Not if a plane carrying you back to your homes mysteriously crashed in the sea. Except for an investigation into the crash, no one would be the wiser about what really happened."

Claus looked at his wife and placed an arm around her shoulders. "I'm afraid Mr. Pitt is right. Specter could not allow any of us to live."

"Once you reveal everything to the news media, Specter would not dare kill the other members of your scientific team. Every law enforcement agency of your respective countries would band together and go after Specter and his Odyssey empire with every international legal means at their disposal. Believe me, leaving now and coming with us is the only way."

"Can you guarantee that you'll get us off the island safely?" asked Hilda hesitantly.

Pitt looked singularly concerned. "I can't promise what I can't predict with certainty. But you will surely die if you remain here."

Claus squeezed his wife's shoulder. "Well, Mother, this looks like our chance to see our loved ones again."

She lifted her head and kissed him on the cheek. "Then we go together."

"They're coming back," announced Giordino, with his ear to the door.

"If you will kindly get dressed," said Pitt to the Lowenhardts, "my friend and I will take care of the guards." Then he turned his back as the scientists began getting their clothes and joined Giordino on the opposite side of the door, Colt .45 drawn and held at the ready.

The seconds ticked off as the guards retraced their steps. Pitt and

Giordino waited patiently until the sound of the guards came outside the door. Then Giordino yanked the broken door inward, sending it crashing to the floor. The security guards were too surprised to offer resistance, as they were pulled into the room and found themselves staring into the muzzles of two very large automatic pistols.

"¡En el piso, rápidamente!" Pitt snapped, ordering them to lie on the floor as Giordino began tearing up the bedsheets. They quickly disarmed, bound and gagged the stunned guards.

Five minutes later, Pitt, with Claus and Hilda behind and Giordino bringing up the rear, passed through the entrance of the unguarded gate in the fence and scurried across the street that was packed with a milling crowd of security personnel and firemen surrounding the still-burning street sweeper, before slipping into the shadows unnoticed.

38

THEY HAD A LONG WAY to go. The hangars at the end of the isthmus airstrip were over a mile across the facility from the Lowenhardts' prison quarters. Besides a satellite photo of the facility for a guide, they now had the assistance of the scientists, who were familiar with the layout of the streets.

Claus Lowenhardt fell back to talk softly to Giordino. "Is your friend truly in control of our situation?"

"Let's just say that Dirk is a man of infinite resource who could talk or extricate himself out of almost any awkward situation."

"You trust him." It was a statement more than a question.

"With my life. I've known him for almost forty years and he hasn't failed me yet."

"Is he an intelligence agent?"

"Hardly." Giordino could not suppress a soft laugh. "Dirk is a marine engineer. He's special projects director for the National Underwater and Marine Agency. I'm his second in command."

"God help us!" Lowenhardt muttered. "If I had known you were not highly trained undercover CIA agents, I would have never come with you and risked my wife's life."

"Your lives couldn't be in the hands of a better man," Giordino assured him, his voice low and hard as concrete.

Pitt moved from one structure to another, trying to stay in the shadows away from the streetlamps and overhead lights on the roofs of the buildings. It was not an easy journey. The facility was brightly lit from one end to the other. Floodlights had been installed on every building, along every street to discourage anyone from trying to escape. Because of the abundance of illumination, Pitt scanned the territory through binoculars rather than his nightscope, continually checking for evidence of guards lurking in the shadows.

"The streets seem unusually empty of patrols," he murmured.

"That's because the guards turn loose the dogs until morning," said Hilda.

Giordino came to an abrupt halt. "You didn't say anything about dogs."

"I wasn't asked," she said blankly.

"I'll bet they're Dobermans," Giordino moaned. "I hate Dobermans."

"We're lucky we got this far," Pitt said frankly. "We'll have to be doubly careful from now on."

"And with us fresh out of meat," Giordino grumbled.

Pitt was about to lower his binoculars when he detected a high chain-link fence with circular barbwire running along the top. He could see that a gate on the road leading to the airstrip was guarded by two men who were clearly exposed by an overhead light. Pitt refocused the lenses and peered again. They were not men but women in blue jumpsuits. Two unleashed dogs nosed the ground in front of the gate. They were Dobermans, and he smiled to himself at Giordino's revulsion of them.

"We have a fence barring the road to the airstrip," he said, passing the binoculars to Giordino.

Giordino peered through the lenses. "Did you notice there is a smaller fence running a few feet in front of the big one?"

"No doubt built to protect the dogs?"

"To keep them from turning crispy-crunchy." Giordino paused and traversed the fence a hundred yards in each direction. "The main fence probably has enough electrical juice running through it to barbecue a buffalo." Giordino paused to check the neighborhood. "And not a vacant street sweeper in sight."

Abruptly, the ground began to move and a low rumbling sound swept the facility. The trees swayed and the windows of the buildings rattled. It was a tremor like the one they experienced inside the lighthouse and on the river. This one lasted longer, over a minute before tapering off. The Dobermans went into a barking frenzy as the guards milled around uneasily. There would be no creeping up on the guards undetected while the dogs were excited and alert.

"We felt an earth tremor earlier," Pitt said to Claus. "Is it coming from the volcano?

"Indirectly," he answered matter-of-factly. "One of the scientists on our research team, Dr. Alfred Honoma, a geophysicist who was lured away from the University of Hawaii, is an expert on volcanoes. In his opinion the tremors have nothing to do with superheated rock ascending through the volcano's fissures. He claims the impending danger is a sudden slip of the volcano's slope that will cause a catastrophic flank collapse."

"How long have you experienced these tremors?" asked Pitt.

"They began a year ago," replied Hilda. "They've increased in frequency until now they come less than an hour apart."

"They've also amplified in intensity," added Claus. "According to Dr. Honoma, some unexplained phenomenon beneath the mountain has caused its surface to shift."

Pitt nodded at Giordino. "The fourth tunnel runs under the base of the volcano."

Giordino merely nodded in agreement.

"Did Honoma have a prediction as to when the shift will occur?" Pitt inquired.

"He thought the final slip might take place at any time."

"What would be the consequences?" Giordino asked.

"If Dr. Honoma is correct," replied Claus, "a devastating flank collapse would unleash a cubic mile of rock, sending it sliding down the mountain slope toward the lake at speeds up to eighty miles an hour."

"That would trigger massive waves once it hit water," said Pitt.

"Yes, the waves could easily wipe out every town and village surrounding the lake."

"What about the Odyssey facility?"

"Since it covers a good part of the volcano's slope, the entire works would be swept away and buried." Claus paused and then he added grimly, "And everybody with it."

"Isn't Odyssey management aware of the threat?"

"They called in their own geologists, who argued that flank collapses are quite rare and only happen somewhere in the world every ten thousand years. My understanding is that word came down from Mr. Specter that there was no threat and to ignore it."

"Specter isn't noted for being considerate of his employees' welfare," said Pitt, recalling the incident on board the *Ocean Wanderer.*

Suddenly, everyone stiffened and stared up into star-peppered sky toward the unmistakable sound of a helicopter coming in from the air terminal. From the floodlights on the ground the lavender color was clearly visible. They all stood immobile, pressed against the wall of a building, as the rotor blades pounded the night air toward them.

"They're looking for us," rasped a frightened Claus Lowenhardt, clutching his wife around her shoulders.

"Not likely," Pitt asserted. "The pilot isn't circling in a search pattern. They're not onto us yet."

The craft flew directly over them, not more than two hundred feet above. Giordino felt as if he could have hit it with a well-thrown rock. Any second the landing lights would come on and target them like rats in a barn under a dozen flashlights. Then Dame Fortune smiled. The pilot didn't flick on his landing lights until the craft had passed safely beyond where they stood. It banked sharply toward the roof of what looked like a glass-walled office building, hovered and then settled.

Pitt took the binoculars from Giordino and trained them on the aircraft as it landed and the rotor blades slowly swung to a stop. The door came open and several figures in lavender jumpsuits crowded around the steps, as a woman stepped down, wearing a gold jumpsuit. He gently rotated the adjustment until he had a sharp definition. He couldn't be absolutely positive, but he would have bet a year's pay that the person who climbed from the helicopter was the woman who called herself Rita Anderson.

His face tightened with anger as he passed the binoculars back to Giordino. "Look closely at the queen in the gold jumpsuit."

Giordino studied the woman closely and watched as she and her retinue walked toward the elevator that led down from the roof. "Our pal from the yacht," he spoke, in a voice low and vicious. "The one who murdered Renee. My kingdom for a sniper rifle."

"Nothing we can do about her," Pitt said regretfully. "Our number one priority is to get the Lowenhardts to Washington in one piece."

"And speaking of one piece, how are we getting past an electric fence, three Dobermans and two heavily armed security guards?"

"Not through," Pitt said quietly, as his mind calculated the odds on a long shot, "but *over*."

The Lowenhardts stood quietly, not quite knowing what to make of the conversation. Giordino followed Pitt's gaze toward the helicopter on the top of the office building a block away, his expression cool and focused. Wordlessly, silently, a plan took root between them. Pitt lifted the binoculars and studied the building.

"The headquarters office of the facility," he said. "It looks unguarded."

"No reason for them to lock people inside. All the workers are loyal employees of Odyssey."

"And no paranoia about unwanted guests entering through the front doors." Pitt tilted the glasses. The pilots followed Rita into the elevator, leaving the helicopter seemingly deserted. "We'll never have a better opportunity."

"I fail to see an opportunity in gaining entrance to a busy office building, bluffing our way past two hundred workers, trespassing to the tenth floor to steal a helicopter without someone suspecting a band of rats in their lair."

"Maybe it would help if I could find you a lavender jumpsuit."

Giordino gave Pitt a look that would have withered a redwood. "I've already gone beyond the call of duty. You'll have to think of something else."

Pitt walked up to the Lowenhardts, who were standing with their arms around each other. They looked apprehensive but not frightened. "We're going to enter the headquarters building and ascend to the roof, where we will appropriate the helicopter," Pitt said. "Stay close to me. If we run into trouble, drop to the floor. We can't have you obstructing our line of fire. Our best hope is to act audacious. Al and I will try to make it look like we're escorting you to a meeting or interrogation or whatever scam works best. Once we reach the roof, hurry into the aircraft quickly and tighten your seat belts. The takeoff might be very rough."

Claus and Hilda solemnly assured him they would follow his instructions. They were in it now up to their ears and had crossed over the point of no return. Pitt had faith in their adhering to his instructions to the letter. They had no choice.

They walked along the edge of the street until they reached the steps leading up to the entrance of the headquarters. A passing truck caught them in its headlights. But the driver took no notice of them. Two women, one in lavender, the other in a white jumpsuit, were standing just outside the portal, smoking cigarettes. This time with Giordino in the lead, who smiled politely, they passed through the big glass door into the lobby. Several women and only one man milled about the lobby in conversation. Few looked their way as Pitt and the others passed, and those who glanced at them did so without suspicion.

Moving along as if it was a common, everyday routine, Giordino hurried the group into an empty elevator before the doors closed. But no sooner had everyone entered, and before he could push the button for the roof exit, than an attractive blond woman in lavender entered, leaned in front of him and pressed the button for the eighth floor.

She turned and studied the Lowenhardts, paused significantly as a look of wariness came to her eyes. "Where are you taking these people?" she demanded in English.

Giordino hesitated, unsure of what tack to take. Undaunted, Pitt stepped beside Giordino and said in broken Spanish, *"Perdónenos para inglés no parlante"* [Forgive us for English nontalking].

The eyes suddenly blazed. "I wasn't speaking to you!" she snapped maliciously. "I was talking to the lady."

Caught in the middle of the exchange, Giordino was afraid of speaking, his voice a sure giveaway that he wasn't feminine. When he spoke, it was a squeaky high pitch that sounded odd and hollow inside the elevator.

"I speak a little *inglés.*"

His answer was a penetrating stare. She studied his face and her eyes widened as she saw his five o'clock shadow. She reached out and rubbed one hand across his cheek. "You're a man!" she blurted. She wheeled and reached out to stop the elevator at the next floor, but Pitt slapped her hand down.

The Odyssey representative looked at Pitt in disbelief. "How dare you?"

He smiled devilishly. "You've made such an impression on me that I'm stealing you away to a better world."

"You're crazy!"

"Like a fox." The elevator stopped on the eighth floor, but Pitt pushed the CLOSE DOOR button. The doors remained shut, the motor hummed and it continued upward to its last stop on the roof above the tenth floor.

"What is going on here?" For the first time she took a good look at the Lowenhardts, who seemed amused by the exchange. Her face clouded. "I know these people. They're supposed to be confined at night in the prison building. Where are you taking them?"

"To the nearest bathroom," Pitt answered nonchalantly.

The woman didn't know whether to stop the elevator or scream. Confused, she fell back on her womanly instinct and opened her mouth to scream. Pitt showed no hesitation in ramming his right fist into her jaw. She went down like a sack of wet flour. Giordino grabbed her under the arms before she hit the floor and pulled her into a corner, where she was out of sight when the doors opened.

"Why didn't you simply gag her?" asked Hilda, shocked at seeing Pitt brutally strike the woman.

"Because she would have bitten my hand, and I didn't feel in a chivalrous mood to let her do it."

Agonizingly, with apparently infinite slowness, the elevator rose the final few feet of its ascent and reached the stop on the tenth floor leading to the roof. After it eased smoothly to a halt, the doors spread apart and they exited.

Right into a group of four uniformed security guards who had been standing out of sight behind a large air-conditioning unit.

THE ATMOSPHERE was one of calm if not an equal level of anxiety in Sandecker's penthouse apartment at the Watergate in Washington. He paced the floor under a trail of blue smoke from one of his mammoth, specially wrapped cigars. Some men might have acted as gentlemen with ladies present rather than enshrouding them with tobacco fumes, but not the admiral. They either accepted his noxious habit or he didn't entertain them. And, despite this liability, single ladies of Washington passed over his doorstep with surprising frequency.

Considered a prestigious catch because he was an unmarried widower with a daughter and three grandchildren who lived in Hong Kong, Sandecker was besieged with dinner invitations. Either fortuitously or unluckily, depending upon how one looked at it, he was constantly introduced to single ladies looking for a husband or a relationship. Amazingly, the admiral was a master at juggling five ladies at the same time, one of the reasons he was a fitness nut.

His lady of the evening, Congresswoman Bertha Garcia, who stepped into the office of her late husband, Marcus, was sitting on the balcony, drinking a glass of fine port while viewing the lights of the capital. Stylishly attired in a short black cocktail dress after attending a party with the admiral, she gazed with amusement at Sandecker's nervousness.

"Why don't you sit down, Jim, before you wear out the carpet?"

He stopped and came over to her, placing a hand against her cheek. "Forgive me for ignoring you, but I've got a situation with two of my people down in Nicaragua." He sat down heavily beside her. "What if I told you that our east coast and Europe were going to suffer severe winters the likes of which we've never seen."

"We can always survive a bad year."

"I'm talking centuries."

She set her glass on a patio table. "Certainly not with global warming."

"With global warming," he said firmly.

The phone rang and he marched in and picked it up from his penthouse office desk.

"Yes?"

"Rudi, Admiral," came Gunn's voice. "Still no word."

"Have they made entry?"

"We've heard nothing since they left on a jet ski across the lake from Granada."

"I don't like it," Sandecker muttered. "We should have heard from them by now."

"We should leave jobs like this to the intelligence agencies," said Gunn.

"I agree, but there was no stopping Dirk and Al."

"They'll make it," Gunn said reassuringly. "They always do."

"Yes," Sandecker said heavily. "But someday the law of averages will catch up and their luck will run out."

39

THE GUARDS WERE as surprised to see the group exit the elevator as Pitt was to see them. Three wore the blue jumpsuits of security guards, the fourth was a woman dressed in green. Pitt guessed she was of a higher rank than the men. Unlike the others, she carried no assault rifle. Her only weapon was a small automatic pistol in a belt holster on her hip. Pitt quickly took the initiative. He walked up to the woman.

"Are you in charge here?" he asked, in a voice calm and authoritative.

The woman, taken back momentarily, stared at him. "I'm in charge. What are you doing here?"

Relieved that she spoke English, he motioned to the Lowenhardts. "We found these two wandering around the fourth floor. Nobody seemed to know how they came to be there. We were told to turn them over to the guards on the roof. That's you."

The woman studied the Lowenhardts, who were looking at Pitt with growing shock and fear in their eyes.

"I know these people. They are scientists who work on the project. They're supposed to be confined to their quarters."

"There was a disturbance, a vehicle caught fire. They must have escaped during the commotion."

The female guard, looking confused, did not question how the Lowenhardts came to be in the headquarters building. "Who told you to bring them to the roof?"

Pitt shrugged. "A lady in a lavender jumpsuit."

The three guards, with their assault rifles held at the ready, appeared to relax. They seemed to buy the story, even if their superior was doubtful. "What are your work positions?" she demanded.

Giordino took a few steps toward the helicopter, turned his head away and looked as if he was admiring it. Pitt stared directly into the woman's eyes. "We work in the tunnels. Our supervisor sent us topside for two days' rest." Out of the corner of one eye he saw Giordino slowly, imperceptibly, move behind the guards.

The story worked before. He hoped it would work again. It did. The woman nodded.

"That doesn't explain why you were in headquarters this time of night."

"We've been ordered back down tomorrow and were instructed to come here and pick up our passes."

He missed on that one. "What passes? I know of no passes issued to tunnel workers. Your identification badges should suffice."

"I only do what I'm told," he said, acting irritated. "Do you want to take charge of these prisoners or not?"

Before she could reply, Giordino had his big gun in one hand. In one lightning motion, he lashed the barrel against one guard's head and then swung it hard against the head of the second guard. The third removed his hands from his rifle when he saw the gaping muzzle of Giordino's .50 caliber automatic aimed between his eyes.

"That's much better," Pitt said quietly. He turned to Giordino and smiled. "A credible piece of work."

Giordino returned a slight grin. "I thought so."

"Take their guns."

The woman's hand crept toward her holstered pistol.

Pitt said, "I wouldn't if I were you."

The female guard's face was a mask of wrath, but she was smart enough to know the odds were against her. She raised her hands as Giordino removed her gun. "Who are you?" she hissed.

"I wish people would stop asking me that." Pitt pointed at the guard still standing. "Remove your uniform. Quickly!"

The guard quickly unzipped the front of his jumpsuit and stepped out of it. Pitt did the same with his black suit. Then he slipped into the blue one.

"Down on the roof next to your men," Pitt ordered the woman and the half-naked guard.

"What are you up to?" Giordino inquired casually.

"Like the airlines, I hate taking off with a half-empty aircraft."

Without further probing, Giordino knew what Pitt had on his mind. He stood in front and over his prisoners so they could see his gun muzzle swing from head to head. He looked at the Lowenhardts. "Time to board," he said firmly.

Obediently and without complaint, the two elderly people climbed into the helicopter, as Pitt walked toward the elevator. A few seconds later, the door closed and he was gone.

INSIDE AN office penthouse on the tenth floor below the roof stretched a magnificent flow of rooms. The lavender suite, as it was appropriately named, was decorated as if swept by a tidal wave of the same color. The enormous ceilings were trimmed around the edges in lavender, with large domes painted in scenes depicting strange religious rituals and dances performed by women in flowing dresses under backgrounds of scenic forests surrounding lakes and mythical mountains. The vast wall-to-wall carpet was lavender flecked with gold, its thickness almost ankle-deep. The furniture was carved from white marble shaped like throne chairs often displayed on a Grecian vase.

They were padded with thick lavender cushions. The chandeliers were coated with a deep iridescent lavender, their crystals surrounding the lights dyed to match. The walls were done in the same universal color, but in a rich velvet. High massive curtains were cut and draped from the same material. Sensual, exotic, decadent, a true dream fantasy, the effect stunned the eye of the viewer far beyond any sight they might have ever imagined.

Two women were seated on a long marble couch, reclined luxuriously in massively thick cushions. An ornately sculptured glass table stood between them with a bucket containing a vintage champagne whose bottle bore a custom lavender label. One of the women was attired in a golden gown, the other was dressed in purple. Their long red hair matched precisely, as if they used the same bottle of dye and same hairstylist. If they had not moved, an observer might have thought they were part of the outrageous decor.

The lady in purple sipped her champagne from a tulip-stemmed glass and said in a voice devoid of inflection: "Our timetable is on schedule. Ten million units of Macha will be ready for retail sale by the first snowfall. After that, our friends in China will have their assembly lines operating at full production. Their new factories will go on line by the end of summer and production will soar to two million units a month."

"Are distribution channels in place?" asked the lady in gold, who was devastatingly beautiful.

"Warehouses either constructed or rented throughout Europe and the northeastern United States are already receiving shipments from China's cargo fleet."

"We were fortunate that Druantia was able to step into her father's shoes and increase our desperate need for platinum."

"Without it we could never have met the demand."

"Have you arrived at a time to open the tunnels?"

The lady in purple nodded. "September tenth is the date calculated by our scientists. They estimated that it will take sixty days to bring down the temperature of the Gulf Stream to where it will cause extreme cold in the northern latitudes."

The lady in gold smiled and poured another glass of champagne. "Then everything is in place."

The other nodded and raised her glass. "To you, Epona, who will soon become the most powerful woman in the history of the world."

"And to you, Flidais, who made it happen."

PITT SURMISED correctly that the main office suite would be on the top floor below the roof. The secretaries and office workers had left hours earlier and the halls were empty when he stepped from the elevator. Wearing the blue coveralls of a security guard, he had no problem walking past two other guards, who paid him scant attention as he passed into the anteroom of the main suite. He found it unguarded so he very quietly pushed open the door and stepped inside, eased the door closed, turned and froze in astonishment, overwhelmed by the tidal wave of the decor.

He heard voices in the next room and slipped between a wall and lavender curtains draped over an arched doorway that were pulled back by gold sashes. He saw the two women lounging in luxury on the couch and scanned the ostentatious suite that would have, in his mind, made the fanciest brothel look like a shack by a railroad track. The occupants were alone. He stepped past the drapes and stood in the middle of the doorway, admiring the beauty of the two women as they continued conversing without turning and finding an intruder in their midst.

"Will you be leaving soon?" Flidais asked Epona.

"In a few days. I have to take care of a little damage control in Washington. A congressional committee is investigating our newly acquired mining operations in Montana. The state's politicians are upset because we're taking all of the iridium ore for our own use and leaving none for sale to U.S. commercial enterprises or their government."

Epona leaned back comfortably in the thick pillows. "And you, my dear friend, what is on your agenda?"

"I've hired an international investigation company to track down the two men who penetrated our security and roamed the tunnels before escaping through the lighthouse ventilator."

"Any idea of their identities?"

"I suspect they were members of the National Underwater and Marine Agency. The same ones I escaped from after they destroyed our yacht."

"You think our efforts for secrecy have been compromised?"

Flidais shook her head. "I don't think so. At least not yet. Our agents have reported no activity by U.S. intelligence agencies to investigate the tunnels. There has been a strange silence. It's as if those devils from NUMA disappeared off the face of the earth."

"We need not be unduly concerned. It's too late for the Americans to stop our operation. And besides, it's doubtful they've discovered the tunnel's true purpose. Only eight more days and they'll be open and pumping the South Equatorial Current into the Pacific."

"I'm hoping the reason for their silence is that they haven't put two and two together and found a threat."

"That would explain their inaction."

"On the other hand," Epona said, thoughtfully, "one would think they'd seek retaliation for the murder of a member of their crew."

"An execution that was a matter of necessity," Flidais assured her.

"I disagree," said Pitt. "Cold-blooded murder is never a matter of necessity."

THERE WAS a stunned moment in time, the champagne glass held between Epona's manicured fingers fell silently to the thick carpet. Both heads whirled around, their long hair snapping around like whips. The long-lashed eyes flashed from surprise to irritation at being interrupted by an unauthorized intrusion by one of their own security personnel. Then came surprise at seeing Pitt's Colt aimed in their direction.

Pitt caught the flick of Epona's eyes toward a small golden remote on the carpet under the glass table. Her foot began slipping toward it. "Not a smart move, dear heart," he said casually.

The foot stopped, her toe inches from one of the buttons. Then she slowly withdrew her foot.

In that instant Flidais recognized Pitt. "You!" she said sharply.

"Hello, Rita, or whatever you call yourself." His eyes swept the room. "You seem to have come up in the world."

The amber-brown eyes glared at him in cold anger. "How did you get in here?"

"Don't you like my designer jumpsuit?" he said, as if modeling at a fashion show. "It's amazing the doors they open."

"Flidais, who is this man?" Epona asked, studying Pitt as one would a specimen in a zoo.

"My name is Dirk Pitt. Your friend and I met off the east coast of Nicaragua. As I recall, she wore a yellow bikini and owned an elegant yacht."

"Which you destroyed," Flidais hissed like a flared cobra.

"I don't recall you giving us a choice."

"What do you want?" inquired Epona, staring at him through jade eyes flecked with gold.

"I think it only fair that Flidais—is that what you call her?—answer for her crimes."

"May I ask what you have in mind?" she asked, staring at him enigmatically.

This woman was a class act, Pitt decided, nothing fazed her, not even the muzzle of his gun. "I'm taking her on a little flight north."

"Just like that."

Pitt nodded. "Just like that."

"And if I refuse," Flidais snarled contemptuously.

"Let's just say you won't enjoy the consequences."

"If I don't do as you say, you'll kill me. Is that it?"

He placed the muzzle of his Colt .45 against the side of her face next to her left eye. "No, I'll simply blow out your eyeballs. You'll live to old age, blind and ugly as sin."

"You're crude and vulgar, like most men," said Epona indignantly. "I'd have expected no less from you."

"It's nice to know I didn't disappoint such an astute and beautiful lady."

"You need not patronize me, Mr. Pitt."

"I'm not patronizing you, Epona, I'm tolerating you." He got to her on that one, he thought, pleased with himself. "Perhaps we'll meet again someday under more enjoyable circumstances."

"Do not count your blessings, Mr. Pitt. I don't see a happy life in your future."

"Funny, you don't look like a gypsy."

He nudged Flidais softly in the back of one shoulder with his gun and followed her from the room. He stopped in the doorway and turned to Epona. "Before I forget, it wouldn't be wise to open the tunnels and divert the South Equatorial Current to send Europe into a deep freeze. I know of a lot of people who might not like it."

He took Flidais by the arm and led her lively but not hurriedly through the arched doorway, down the hallway and into the elevator. Once inside, Flidais stood straight and smoothed her flowing gown. "You're not only boorish, Mr. Pitt, but you're exceedingly stupid as well."

"Oh, how so?"

"You'll never leave the building. There are security personnel on every floor. You don't stand a prayer of passing through the lobby without being apprehended."

"Who said anything about going through the lobby?"

Flidais's eyes widened as the elevator moved up and stopped on the roof. He prodded her out onto the roof as the doors opened. "I don't mean to rush you, but things are about to heat up around here."

She saw the guards lying on the ground with Giordino standing over them, nonchalantly sweeping the barrel of an assault rifle from one head to the other. Then her gaze turned to the idle helicopter and she knew any hope of her security guards intercepting Pitt and his part-ner had flown away on the night air. Seeking a final desperate avenue, her eyes blazed at Pitt. "You can't pilot a helicopter."

"Sorry to disappoint you," Pitt answered in a patient tone. "Both Al and I can fly this bird."

Giordino glanced at Flidais, took in her elegant gown and smiled nastily. "I see you found Rita. You pick her up at a party?"

"A party of two downing expensive vintage champagne. Her name is Flidais. She's coming with us. Keep an eye on her."

"Both eyes," Giordino said icily.

Pitt glanced briefly at Flidais as he entered the helicopter. The glare had gone out of the eyes. The calm and lack of fear had altered to trepidation.

He briefly glanced at the helicopter before he moved swiftly into the cockpit and sat in the pilot's seat. It was an McDonnell-Douglas Explorer model with twin Pratt & Whitney turboshaft engines built by MD Helicopters of Mesa, Arizona. He was pleased to see that it was a rotor craft with an antitorque system that eliminated the tail rotor.

He checked to be sure the fuel shutoff valve was on and took the cyclic and collective friction off. Then, with the pedals and throttles moving smoothly, the circuit breakers in and the mixture to full rich, he turned the master switch on. Next came the ignition, and both en-gines began turning over, eventually reaching idling rpms. Finally, Pitt made certain all warning lights were out.

He leaned out the side window and shouted to Giordino over the whine of the twin turbines. "Jump aboard!"

Giordino was not as polite as Pitt. He literally lifted Flidais off her feet and flung her inside the rotor craft. Then he climbed in and closed the big sliding door. The interior was stylish and elegant with four large leather seats with burled-walnut consoles, one containing a compact office system with computer, fax and a satellite television phone. The console between the opposite seats held a bar with crystal decanters and glasses.

The Lowenhardts sat with seat belts buckled, staring mutely at Flidais who was still sprawled on the floor where Giordino had thrown her. Giordino reached under her arms, pulled her erect and dropped her into a seat, buckling her seat belt. He handed the assault rifle to Claus Lowenhardt.

"If she lifts her little finger, shoot her."

Having no love for his former female captors, Claus relished the opportunity.

"Our agents will be waiting for you when we land in Managua," Flidais said scornfully.

"That's comforting to know."

Giordino turned quickly, entered the cockpit and dropped into the copilot's seat. Pitt glanced at the elevator doors and saw them close. Alerted by the woman in the suite, security guards were waiting for it to descend before they could swarm up to the roof. He reached down and pulled up on the collective, lifting the helicopter into the air. Then he pushed the cyclic forward, the nose dipped and the MD Explorer leaped from the roof of the building. Pitt quickly brought the aircraft up to its top speed of one hundred and eighty-four miles an hour, soaring over the Odyssey facility toward the airstrip stretching between the volcanic mountains. As soon as he reached the slopes of the Madera volcano, he banked the Explorer around the peak and brought it down less than thirty feet above the trees before crossing over the shore above the waters of the lake.

"Not heading for Managua, I hope," said Giordino, putting on his earphones. "Her Royal Highness said her flunkies will be waiting for us."

"I wouldn't be surprised," Pitt said with a wide grin. "That's why we're heading west out over the Pacific before cutting south to San José, Costa Rica."

"Do we have enough fuel?"

"Once we take her to cruising speed, we should make it with a couple of gallons to spare."

Pitt skimmed the surface, staying out of contact with Odyssey's radar systems, before crossing over the spit of land on the west side of the lake. Ten miles out to sea, he turned south and slowly increased altitude as Giordino locked in a course for San José. For the rest of the flight, Giordino kept a wary eye on the fuel gauges.

There was a light overcast, not thick enough for rain but just enough to blot out the stars. Pitt was tired, more worn-out than he could ever remember. He turned over the controls to Giordino and slouched in his seat, closing his eyes and taking a deep breath. There was still one more job to do before he could allow himself the luxury of sleep. He pulled the satellite phone from a waterproof bag and dialed Sandecker's private line.

The admiral's voice came through the earpiece almost immediately. "Yes!"

"We're out," Pitt said wearily.

"About time."

"There was little need for an extended tour."

"Where are you now?"

"In a stolen helicopter on our way to San José, Costa Rica."

Sandecker paused to take it in. "You didn't feel you had to snoop around the facility during the daylight hours?"

"We had a break," said Pitt, fighting to keep from nodding off.

"You collected the data we need?" Sandecker asked impatiently.

"We have everything," replied Pitt. "Through the use of scientists he took as hostages, Specter has perfected fuel cell technology by using nitrogen instead of hydrogen. The Red Chinese are cranking out millions of electrical heat-generating units, which will be distributed and ready for sale when they open the tunnels and the freeze hits the U.S. coast and Europe this winter."

"Are you telling me this crazy scheme is all for the sale of fuel cells?" Sandecker said incredulously.

"You're talking hundreds of billions of dollars, not to mention the power that will come from owning the monopoly. No matter how you slice it, the world economy will be in Specter's pocket when the first snow starts to fall."

"You're certain Specter has perfected the technology when the best minds in the world have yet to make a breakthrough," Sandecker persisted.

"Specter *has* the best minds," Pitt countered. "You'll get the story from two of them who worked on the project."

"They're with you?" Sandecker said with growing anticipation.

"Sitting just behind me along with the woman who murdered Renee Ford."

Sandecker looked like a batter who had hit a home run with his eyes shut. "You have her too?"

"Charter a plane for us in San José and we'll set her in your lap by this time tomorrow."

"I'll put Rudi right on it," said Sandecker, pleasure and excitement evident in his voice. "Come to the office with your party as soon as you land."

There was no reply.

"Dirk, are you still there?"

Pitt had dozed off and was blissfully unaware that he had broken the connection.

40

THE AIR CANADA JET bumped through a thick cloud whose soft white curves showed the first orange tint from the setting sun. As the plane began its slow descent toward Guadeloupe, Summer gazed through her window and watched the deep, dark blue-purple water below turn to light blue and then turquoise as the aircraft flew over the reefs and lagoons. Sitting next to her in the aisle seat, Dirk studied a chart of the waters around the Isles des Saintes, a group of islands to the south of Guadeloupe.

She stared with growing curiosity as the two main islands of Basse-Terre and Grande-Terre merged together in the shape of a butterfly. Basse-Terre formed the western wing and was blanketed with thickly forested hills and mountains. Surrounded by lush ferns, its rain forest contains some of the Caribbean's highest waterfalls, which flow down from the island's loftiest peak, La Soufriere, a smoldering volcano that rises above forty-eight hundred feet. Both islands, with a total land area the size of Luxembourg, were separated by a narrow channel filled with mangroves called the Riviere Salee.

The eastern wing of the butterfly, Grande-Terre was a contrast to Basse-Terre. The island is mostly dominated by flat terrain and rolling hills, much of which is cultivated in sugarcane, the major source for the three distilleries that produce Guadeloupe's fine rums.

Summer's heart rose in anticipation of enjoying some of the island's many black and white sand beaches that were romantically edged with swaying palms. Deep down, she knew it was probably wishful thinking. Once she and Dirk had finished their survey for Odysseus' lost fleet, Admiral Sandecker would no doubt order them home without allowing a few days of rest and enjoyment. She made up her mind to stay, regardless of the consequences of incurring the admiral's wrath.

The plane made a wide circle that took it over Pointe-a-Pitre, the commercial capital of Guadeloupe. She looked down at the red tile roofs mingled with those of corrugated metal. The pleasant town was embellished by a picturesque square in its center surrounded by outdoor shops and cafes. The narrow streets seemed busy and lively, with people heading home for dinner. Few drove cars. Many of them walked while most rode motorcycles and motor scooters. Lights were already beginning to flicker on in the little houses around the port city. Ships were tied to docks, with little fishing boats coming into harbor after a day's catch.

The pilot settled the plane on the landing approach to Guadeloupe's Pole Caraibes Airport. The landing gear thumped as the wheels dropped and locked, and the wing flaps hummed into a downward position. For a brief instant, the last of the setting sun flashed into the windows before the plane settled onto the runway with the usual bounce, protest of tires and shrill whine of the reverse thrust of the turbines as the plane braked before taxiing to the terminal.

Summer always loved early evenings in the tropics. The offshore breezes usually came up and blew away the worst of the day's heat and humidity. She loved the smell of wet vegetation after a rain and the aroma of the ever-present tropical flowers.

"How's your French?" Dirk asked Summer as they descended the boarding stairs from their aircraft at the Guadeloupe airport.

"About as good as your Swahili," she said, looking radiant in a vibrant flowered skirt and matching blouse. "Why do you ask?"

"Only the tourists speak English. The locals speak French or a French-Creole dialect."

"Since neither of us majored in languages in school, we'll just have to use sign language."

Dirk gave his sister a long look and then laughed. He handed her a small book. "Here's an English–French dictionary. I'll lean on you for any translations."

They walked into the terminal and followed the first passengers off the plane to Health and Immigration. The immigration agent looked up at them before he stamped their passports. "In Guadeloupe for business or pleasure?" he asked in fluent English.

Summer wrinkled her pert nose at Dirk. "Pleasure," she replied, flashing what appeared to be a large diamond ring on her left hand. "We're on our honeymoon."

The agent coolly eyed her breasts, nodded and smiled approvingly as he pounded the stamp on blank passport pages. "Enjoy your stay." He said it in a tone that bordered on the unvirtuous.

As soon as they were out of earshot, Dirk asked, "What is this stuff about our being on a honeymoon? And where did you get that ring?"

"I thought acting as newlyweds was a good cover," she answered. "The ring is glass. It cost me all of eight dollars."

"I hope no one takes a close look at it or they'll think I'm the cheapest husband in the world."

They walked into the luggage area, where they had to wait twenty minutes for their bags to arrive. After loading them onto a cart, they cleared customs and moved into the lobby of the terminal. A small crowd of thirty or so people stood waiting to greet friends and relatives. One little man in a white suit with the medium-dark skin of a Creole held a little sign that read: PITT.

"That's us," said Dirk. "This is Summer and I'm Dirk Pitt."

"Charles Moreau." The little man held out his hand. His eyes were as black as ink and he had a nose that looked sharp enough to fight a duel. He came up to Summer's shoulders in a body that was as slim as a sapling. "Your flight was only ten minutes late. That has to be some kind of record." Then he bowed, took Summer's hand and brushed his lips over her knuckles in true continental fashion. "Admiral Sandecker said you were a handsome couple."

"I assume he also told you we are brother and sister."

"He did. Is there a problem?"

Dirk glanced at Summer, who smiled in mock innocence. "Just wanted to be clear on that point."

Summer and Moreau moved through the exit doors while Dirk followed with the baggage cart. An attractive raven-haired woman wearing the traditional Creole dress—a full vividly colored skirt in a madras plaid of orange and yellow, matching headdress and a white lace blouse with petticoat and scarf draped over one shoulder—walked squarely into Dirk from the side. Wise in the ways of travel, he immediately patted the pocket that held his wallet, but it was still in place.

She stood there, massaging her shoulder. "I'm so sorry. It was my fault."

"Are you hurt?" Dirk asked solicitously.

"Now I know what it feels like to run into a tree." Then she looked up at him and smiled openly. "I'm Simone Raizet. Perhaps I'll see you around town."

"Perhaps," Pitt replied, without offering his name.

The woman nodded at Summer. "You have a handsome and charming man."

"He can be on occasion," Summer said with a trace of sarcasm.

The woman then turned and walked into the terminal.

"What do you make of that?" said Pitt, bemused.

"You can't say she wasn't brazen," muttered Summer.

"Most strange," said Moreau. "She gives the impression she lives here. I was born on this island, and I've never laid eyes on her before."

Summer looked vaguely concerned. "If you ask me, the collision was preplanned."

"I agree," said Dirk. "She was after something. I don't know what. But our encounter didn't look accidental."

Moreau led them across the street to the parking lot and stopped at a BMW 525 sedan. He pushed the security lock on his key ring and opened the trunk. Dirk deposited the luggage and they settled into the seats. Moreau pulled out onto the road leading to Pointe-a-Pitre.

"I've reserved a small suite with two rooms for you at the Canella Beach Hotel, one of our most popular hotels, and one where a young couple on a budget might stay. Admiral Sandecker's instructions stated that you were to keep a low profile during your search for treasure."

"Historical treasure," Summer corrected him.

"He's right," said Dirk. "If word leaked that NUMA was on a treasure hunt, we'd be mobbed."

"And thrown off the islands," added Moreau. "Our government has strict laws protecting our underwater heritage."

"If we're successful," said Summer, "your people will inherit an epoch-making discovery."

"All the more reason to keep your expedition secret."

"Are you an old friend of the admiral?"

"I met James many years ago when I was the Guadeloupe consul in New York. Since I've retired, he hires me on occasion for NUMA business in and around this part of the Caribbean."

Moreau drove through the lush green hills down to the harbor and around the city along the southeast shore of Grande-Terre, until he reached the outskirts of the town of Gosier. Then he took a small dirt road that wound around back to the main thoroughfare.

Summer gazed through her window and admired the houses that sat amid lush, beautifully maintained gardens. "Giving us a tour of the country?"

"A taxicab has been hanging on us rather closely since we left the airport," said Moreau. "I wanted to see if he was following us."

Dirk turned in his seat and peered through the rear window. "The green Ford?"

"The same."

Moreau left the residential section and skirted around a steady stream of buses, tourists on motor scooters and the city's fleet of taxis. The driver of the green Ford taxi struggled to keep up, but was hindered by the slow-moving traffic. Moreau expertly threaded his way around two buses that blocked both sides of the road. He made a sharp right turn onto a narrow street that ran between rows of homes whose quaint architectural style was French Colonial. He made another left-hand turn and then another at the next block until he was on the main road again. The taxi swung over a path beside the road around the buses, gained the lost distance and stuck to Moreau's rear bumper like glue.

"It's interested in us, all right," said Dirk.

"Let us see if I can lose him," said Moreau.

He waited until there was a break in the traffic. Then, instead of turning, he shot straight ahead and darted through the traffic onto the street across the main road. The taxi driver was impeded by the stream of motor scooters, cars and buses a good thirty seconds before he could break through and take up the chase.

Turning a corner and temporarily losing sight of the taxi, Moreau swung into the driveway of a house and parked behind a large oleander bush. A few moments later the green taxi swept past the driveway at high speed and was soon lost in a dust cloud. They remained waiting for a few minutes before Moreau backed out of the driveway and joined the traffic rush again on the main road.

"We've lost him, but I'm afraid it may be only temporary."

"Having missed us," mused Dirk, "he may pull the same trick and wait for us."

"I doubt it," said Summer confidently. "My money says he's still on a wild-goose chase."

"You lose." Dirk laughed, pointing through the windshield toward the green Ford that was parked along the side of the road, its driver talking excitedly over a cell phone. "Pull over next to him, Charles."

Coming up behind the taxi slowly, Moreau suddenly pulled around and stopped inches away. Dirk leaned out the window and knocked on the door of the taxi.

"Are you looking for us?"

The startled driver took one look at Dirk's grinning face, dropped the cell phone, jammed his foot on the accelerator and tore off down the palm-lined road toward the town of Sainte-Anne, his wheels spinning in the gravel of the shoulder until they struck the asphalt and shrieked in protest. Moreau pulled the car over and stopped, watching the taxi disappear in the traffic ahead.

"The lady at the airport and now this," Moreau said quietly. "Who can be interested in a pair of representatives from NUMA on a diving expedition?"

"The word *treasure* is a powerful aphrodisiac and spreads like an epidemic," said Summer. "Somehow, word of our intent arrived ahead of us."

Dirk stared thoughtfully into the distance at the point in the road where the taxi had vanished. "We'll know for certain tomorrow who's following in our wake when we sail over to Branwyn Island."

"Are you familiar with Branwyn Island?" Summer asked Moreau.

"Enough to know that it's dangerous to go near it," Moreau said quietly. "It used to be called Isle de Rouge, French for red, because of its reddish volcanic soil. The new owner renamed it. I'm told Branwyn was a Celtic goddess known as the Venus of the Northern Seas and the deity of love and beauty. Conversely, among the more superstitious natives it lives up to its reputation as the island of death."

Dirk was enjoying the warm, scented breeze through his open window. "Because of treacherous reefs or heavy surf?"

"No," answered Moreau, braking so two children in colorful dresses could cross the road. "The person who owns the island does not like trespassers."

"According to our computer department's data search," said Summer, "the owner is a woman by the name of Epona Eliade."

"A very mysterious lady. As far as we know she has never set foot on Basse-Terre or Grande-Terre."

Summer brushed her hair that was becoming stringy from the dampness. "Ms. Eliade must have caretakers if she maintains an elegant home on Branwyn Island."

"Satellite photos show an airfield, a few buildings and an odd circle of tall columns and an elegant house," said Moreau. "It's claimed that fishermen or tourists who tried to land on the island were later found dead. They usually washed up at a beach on Basse-Terre many miles away."

"What about police investigations?"

Moreau slowly shook his head as he switched on his headlights in the growing dusk. "They found no evidence of foul play and could never prove the victims had actually set foot on the island."

"Couldn't local forensic experts determine how the victims died?"

Moreau gave a quick laugh. "The bodies were usually examined by a local doctor, or even a dentist, who happened to be available when and where they came ashore. Due to decomposition any results were speculation. Most all were written off as drownings." Then he added, "And yet, rumors circulated that the victims' hearts had been cut out."

"Sounds morbid," muttered Summer.

"More like distorted rumors," said Dirk.

"All the more reason to stay a safe distance offshore."

"Not possible if we intend to do a subbottom survey of the harbor."

"Just keep a sharp eye out," said Moreau. "I'll give you my cell phone number. If you spot trouble, call me immediately. I'll have a police patrol boat on its way within ten minutes."

Moreau continued down the road for another two miles before turning into the driveway leading to the hotel, and stopped at the entrance. A porter hurried out and opened the car door for Summer.

Dirk came around to the rear of the car and opened the trunk so the porter could take their luggage and bags of dive gear into the hotel and up to their suites.

"You're within walking distance of a variety of restaurants, shops and entertainment clubs," said Moreau. "I'll pick you up at nine o'clock tomorrow morning and take you to the dock, where I've chartered a boat for your search. The subbottom profiler, underwater metal detecter and jet probe that Commander Rudi Gunn airfreighted from Florida is on board and ready for operation. I also had a small compresser mounted on the deck to run your excavation dredge and jet probe."

"You were very thorough," Dirk complimented him.

"We're grateful for your help and courtesy," said Summer as he gallantly kissed her hand.

"And thank you for the interesting ride from the airport," added Dirk, shaking Moreau's hand.

"Not entirely of my doing," Moreau said with a little smile. Then his face clouded. "Please be cautious. There is something going on here that is beyond our grasp. I don't want you to end up like the others."

Dirk and Summer stood in the entrance to the hotel lobby and watched Moreau drive through the front gate. "What do you think of all this?" asked Summer.

"I don't have the vaguest idea," Dirk said slowly. "But I'd give my right arm if Dad and Al were here."

41

THE RECEPTION COMMITTEE was far different than before when Pitt and Giordino exited the jet. No beautiful congress-woman and no elegant classic car. The plane was surrounded by a uniformed security force from a nearby Army base. The cars involved were one black Lincoln Town Car, a turquoise NUMA Navigator and a white unmarked van.

Rudi Gunn was standing beside the Navigator as Pitt and Giordino dropped down the steps and touched the ground. "I wonder if I'm ever going to see a shower and a steak dinner," moaned Giordino, thinking Sandecker had sent Gunn to transport them to NUMA headquarters.

"We have nobody to blame but ourselves for getting into this mess," Pitt sighed.

"Spare me the pitiful groans," said Gunn, smiling. "You'll be glad to know the admiral doesn't want you guys around until tomorrow af-ternoon. A meeting is set up at the White House at two. You'll be de-briefed by the president's advisors."

The Lowenhardts deplaned and came over to Pitt and Giordino.

Hilda stood on her toes and kissed Pitt on both cheeks, as Claus pumped Giordino's hand. "How can we ever thank you?" she said, her voice choking with emotion.

"We owe you more than we can ever repay," Claus said, beaming, as he caught sight of the buildings of Washington.

Pitt put an arm around his shoulder. "You'll be well looked after and I've been assured that your children will be protected and flown here as soon as possible."

"I promise that your people will have our wholehearted coopera- tion. We'll gladly share our total knowledge of nitrogen fuel cell tech- nology with your scientists." He turned. "Right, Hilda?"

"Yes, Claus," she said, smiling. "Our discovery will be a gift to the entire world."

They said their goodbyes as the Lowenhardts were escorted to the Lincoln by an FBI agent for the trip to a safe house in Washington.

Pitt, Giordino and Gunn then watched as Flidais was hustled from the plane by two burly FBI agents, handcuffed to a stretcher and shoved into the van. She glanced at Pitt with a look of absolute loathing. He grinned and waved before the doors were closed. "I'll send cookies to your cell."

Then he and Giordino climbed into the NUMA Navigator, with Gunn acting as chauffeur. Gunn drove across the tarmac to a guard gate, showed his pass and was waved through. He made a left turn onto a tree-lined street and headed for the nearest bridge over the Potomac.

"Now maybe we can settle down and be left alone for a while," Giordino said wistfully, slouching down in the rear seat and half clos- ing his eyes, ignoring the scenic green, fully leafed trees as they marched past. "I could have been home four days ago, wining and din- ing a lovely lady, but no, you insisted we stay and infiltrate Specter's sanctum sanctorum."

"I don't recall having to beg you," Pitt said without apology.

"You caught me in a moment of madness."

"Don't kid yourself. If our information is acted upon quickly, we will have helped save the U.S. and Europe from some very nasty weather."

"Who's to stop Odyssey from opening the tunnels?" said Giordino. "The Nicaraguan government, a U.S. Special Forces team, an empty appeal from the United Nations? The European diplomats will talk themselves into a coma while their countries turn into ice cubes. None will have the guts to bring down the curtain on Odyssey before it's too late to act."

Pitt knew Giordino wasn't far off the mark. "You're probably right, but it's out of our hands now. We gave the warning. We can do no more."

Gunn swung over the bridge toward Alexandria, where Giordino had his condominium. "You certainly made the admiral a happy man. He's the man of the hour at the White House. Your discovery is still under wraps for obvious reasons, but as soon as the president's security advisors come up with a plan to stop Specter and Odyssey's rotten operation, all hell will break loose. Once they get wind of it, the news media will go wild and NUMA will reap the harvest."

"All well and good," muttered Giordino indifferently. "You taking me home first?"

"Since you're the closest," said Gunn. "Then I'll head up the Mount Vernon Highway and drop Dirk off at his hangar."

A few minutes later, a weary Giordino pulled his bags from the rear of the Navigator and trudged up the stairs to his building that had once been a warehouse built during the Civil War and later remodeled into luxury condos. He turned and gave a slight wave before disappearing inside.

After a short drive along the Potomac River, Gunn passed through the gate of Ronald Reagan National Airport and drove along a dirt road to Pitt's old hangar that stood several hundred yards off the end of the runways. Built in the early nineteen thirties to house the aircraft of a long-vanished airline, Pitt had managed to have it declared a historic landmark after buying and refurbishing it as a place to store and maintain his classic car and aircraft collection.

"You picking me up for the meeting?" Pitt asked as he exited the car.

Gunn shook his head and cracked a smile. "I'm not on the guest list. The Secret Service will send a car for you."

Pitt turned and pressed a series of codes into his exotic security system as the Navigator drove up the road, trailing a wisp of dust behind the rear bumper. He opened the door that looked weatherworn with cracked and peeling paint and stepped inside.

The sight never failed to excite him. It was something out of a luxury car dealer's elegant showroom. The entire interior walls, rounded roof and floor were painted a bright white, which enhanced the dazzling display of vivid colors on a fleet of thirty classic automobiles. Besides the Marmon V-16, there was a 1929 Duesenberg, a 1932 Stutz, a 1929 L-29 Cord and a 1936 Pierce-Arrow with a matching factory trailer. Parked together in a row were a 1936 Ford hot rod, Dirk's Meteor sports car and a bright red 1953 J2X Allard. Two aircraft sat in the back of the hangar, an early-nineteen-thirties Ford Trimotor and a World War II Messerschmitt 262 jet. Along one wall stretched a long Pullman car emblazoned with the words MANHATTAN LIMITED across its side. The only objects that seemed out of place were the upper cabin of a sailboat mounted on a rubber raft and a bathtub with an outboard motor mounted on one end.

He climbed up the circular iron steps to his apartment that ran along the north end of the hangar, tiredly carrying his gear bag and suitcase on his shoulders. The interior of the apartment looked like the sales floor of a nautical antique shop. Furniture from old sailing ships, paintings of seascapes and models of ships on shelves built into the walls filled the living room. The floor was from the teak deck of a steamship that ran aground off the island of Kauai in Hawaii.

He unpacked his bag and threw the old clothes in a hamper next to his washer/dryer, took off what he was wearing and dropped them in as well. Thankfully, he stepped into the teakwood shower, turned the water as warm as he could take it and soaped down, vigorously scrubbing his skin until it tingled. When he was through, he toweled off and walked to his bed, settled across the bedspread and instantly fell asleep.

DARKNESS HAD FALLEN when Loren Smith let herself into the hangar with her own key. She came up and looked around the apartment for Pitt, having been alerted to his arrival by Rudi Gunn. She found him lying naked across the bed, deep asleep. Her lips spread into a sensual smile as she leaned over and pulled a bedspread over him.

When Pitt awoke six hours after he dropped off, he could see stars through the overhead skylights. His nostrils also detected the aroma of steak on the stove's grill. He saw the bedspread over his body and smiled to himself, knowing Loren had put it there. He rose and pulled on a pair of khaki shorts and a flowered silk shirt, then slipped into a pair of sandals.

Loren looked lovely in a snug pair of white shorts and a striped silk blouse, her arms and legs tanned from sunning on the deck of her apartment. She gave out a small sigh when Pitt reached around her waist with his arms and squeezed as he nuzzled her neck.

"Not now," she said in mock irritation, "I'm busy."

"How did you know I was dreaming about a steak for the last five days?"

"I don't have to be a psychic to know that's all you ever eat. Now sit down and mash the potatoes."

Pitt did as he was told and sat down at his dining table that was cut, stained and polished from an old ship's cargo hatch. He mashed the potatoes in a bowl and spooned them onto two plates as Loren delivered a porterhouse steak sliced in two. Then she set a Caesar salad on the table and sat down to eat while Pitt opened a cold bottle of Martin Ray Chardonnay.

"I hear you and Al had a rough time of it," she said, cutting her steak.

"A few close scrapes, but nothing that called for medical attention."

She looked into his eyes, violet meeting green. Her face was soft but her manner was intent. "You're getting too old to get into trouble. It's time you slowed down."

"Retire and play golf five days a week at a club? I don't think so."

"You don't have to retire but there are research expeditions you could direct that wouldn't be half as dangerous as some you've been involved with."

He poured her a glass and sat back and watched as she sipped it down. He studied her glamorous features and hair, her delicate ears, her gracefully sculptured nose, the firm chin and high cheekbones. She could have had any man in Washington, from the president's cabinet members to the senators to the congressmen, the wealthy lobbyists and attorneys, the visiting business moguls and foreign dignitaries, but for twenty years, despite several short affairs, she had never loved anyone but Pitt. She'd stray and return to him time after time. She was older now, there were tiny lines around her eyes, and her figure, though firm from exercise, was less accented by rounded curves. Yet, put her in a room with a bevy of beautiful young women, and every male eye would have locked on Loren. She never had to vie with competition.

"Yes, I could stay at home more," he said slowly, never taking his eyes away from her face. "But I would have to have a reason."

As if she hadn't heard, she said, "My term in Congress will be up soon, and you know I've announced that I'm not going to run again."

"Have you thought about what you're going to do when you're on the beach?"

She shook her head slowly. "I've had several offers to head up various organizations, and at least four lobbyists and three legal firms have asked me to join their ranks. But I'd rather retire, do some traveling, write that book on the inside dealings of Congress I've always wanted to write, and spend more time painting."

"You missed your calling," Pitt said, touching her hand from across the table. "Your landscapes are very professional."

"What about you?" she asked, thinking she knew the answer. "Will you and Al be chasing off again, flirting with death and trying to save the oceans of the world?"

"I can't speak for Al, but for me the wars are over. I'm going to grow a white beard and play with my old cars until they push my wheelchair into the nursing home."

She laughed. "Somehow I can't picture that."

"I *was* hoping you might come with me."

She tensed and stared at him through widening eyes. "What are you saying?"

He took her hand and gripped it tightly. "What I'm saying, Loren Smith, is that I think the time has come for me to beg for your hand in marriage."

She stared at him in disbelief. "You wouldn't . . . you couldn't be joking," she said, her voice choking.

"I'm deadly serious," he said, seeing the tears form in her violet eyes. "I love you, I loved you for what seems an eternity, and I want you to be my wife."

She sat there trembling, the iron maiden of the House of Representatives, the lady who never backed down despite the political pressure, the woman who was as strong as or stronger than any man in Washington. Then she took back her hand and held it with the other over her eyes as she sobbed uncontrollably.

He came around the table and embraced her around the shoulders. "I'm sorry, I didn't mean to upset you."

She looked up, tears flooding her eyes. "You fool, don't you know how long I've waited to hear those words?"

Pitt was bewildered. "When the subject came up before, you always said marriage was out of the question because we were already married to our work."

"Do you always believe everything a woman tells you?"

Pitt gently raised her to her feet and kissed her lightly on the lips. "Forgive me for being late as well as stupid. But the question still stands. Will you marry me?"

Loren threw her arms around his neck and flooded his face with kisses. "Yes, you fool," she said in the throes of ecstasy. "Yes, yes, yes!"

42

WHEN HE AWOKE in the morning, Loren had already left for her apartment to shower and change for another day's battle in Congress. He felt a glow remembering her joyful embraces with her arms held tight around him through the night. Though he had a meeting to attend at the White House, he didn't feel in the mood to put on a business suit and play the role of bureaucrat. Besides, his mind was made up to retire so he felt he no longer had to impress presidential advisors. Instead he wore slacks, a golf shirt and a sport coat.

Another black Lincoln, driven by a Secret Service agent, was waiting when he walked from his hangar. The driver, broad-shouldered, but with a fairly substantial belt line, said nothing as he sat behind the wheel, letting Pitt open his own rear door. The journey to Al's condo was conducted in silence.

After Giordino eased into the rear seat next to Pitt, it soon became clear that the driver was not taking the normal route toward the White House. Giordino leaned over the front seat. "Excuse me, pal, but aren't you taking the long way around?"

The driver kept his eyes straight ahead and did not answer.

Giordino turned to Pitt with an expression of circumspection. "A real chatterbox, this guy."

"Ask him where he's taking us."

"How about it?" Giordino spoke directly into the driver's ear. "If not the White House, what's our destination?"

Still no answer. The driver ignored Giordino and steered the car as if he was a robot.

"What do you think?" Giordino muttered. "Should we stick an ice pick in his ear at the next stoplight and hijack the car?"

"How do we know he's actually with the Secret Service?" said Pitt.

The driver's face remained impassive as reflected in the rearview mirror. He reached an arm over his shoulder with his hand displaying his Secret Service identification.

Giordino peered at the ID. "He's genuine. He has to be with a name like Otis McGonigle."

"I'm glad it's not the White House," Pitt said, yawning as if bored. "The people inside are so drab and dreary. And what's worse, they think the country will go to the dogs without them."

"Especially those toadies who protect the president," Giordino added.

"You mean those deadheads who stand around with little radios in their ears wearing sunglasses that went out of fashion thirty years ago?"

"The same."

Still no response, not even a twitch of irritation.

Pitt and Giordino gave up trying to get a rise out of the agent and sat quietly for the rest of the trip. McGonigle stopped at a heavy iron gate. A guard in the uniform of the White House police recognized the driver, stepped into his guardhouse and pressed a switch. The gate swung open and the car rolled down a ramp into a tunnel. Pitt was familiar with the tunnels deep beneath Washington that led into most of the government buildings around the Capitol. Former President

Clinton had often used them during his forays around the city nightspots.

After what Pitt estimated was nearly a mile, McGonigle stopped the car in front of an elevator, got out and opened the rear door.

"Okay, gentlemen, we've arrived."

"He talked," Giordino said, looking around the tunnel. "But how? I don't see his ventriloquist."

"You guys will never get hired at the Comedy Club," muttered McGonigle, refusing to be drawn in. He stood aside as the doors opened. "I'll await your return with bated breath."

"I don't know why, but I like you," Giordino said, slapping the agent on the back as he stepped into the elevator. He failed to see the response as the door closed before the agent could react.

The elevator did not go up, but descended for what seemed a quarter of a mile before it slowed and the doors noiselessly slid open. Here they found an armed Marine standing in dress uniform beside a steel door. He carefully checked Pitt and Giordino, comparing their faces with photographs. Satisfied, he pressed a code on the side of the door and stood aside as it swung open. He merely motioned for them to enter, without speaking.

They found themselves in a long conference room with enough technical communications equipment to support a major war room. TV monitors and visual displays of maps and photographs covered three walls. Sandecker rose from a chair and greeted them.

"Well, you two have really opened a Pandora's box this time."

"I hope the results of our investigation proved useful," said Pitt modestly.

"Useful is a major understatement." He turned as a tall, gray-haired man in a black pin-striped suit with a red tie approached. "I believe you know the president's security advisor, Max Seymour."

Pitt shook the outstretched hand. "I've met him on occasion at my father's Saturday-afternoon barbecues."

"Senator Pitt and I go back a long way," said Seymour warmly. "How is your lovely mother?"

"Except for arthritis, she's doing fine," replied Pitt.

Sandecker quickly made the introductions of the other three men standing around one end of the long table. Jack Martin, White House science advisor; Jim Hecht, assistant director of the CIA; and General Arnold Stack, whose exact job at the Pentagon was never fully revealed. They all sat down as Sandecker asked Pitt to report on what he and Giordino found in the tunnels and at the Odyssey development center on Isle de Ometepe.

After a secretary announced that her recorder was on and receiving, Pitt started off first, trading off every few minutes with Giordino, filling in what the other overlooked. They described the broad spectrum of events and scenes they had witnessed, enhanced by their conclusions. No questions interrupted their report until they wrapped up by telling of their escape off the island with the Lowenhardts and the murderous woman from Odyssey.

The president's men took a few moments to digest the enormity of the looming disaster. Max Seymour looked across the table with an icy smile on his face at Jim Hecht of the CIA. "Seems like your people dropped the ball on this one, Jim."

Hecht shrugged uncomfortably. "No directives were received from the White House to investigate. We saw little cause to send in operatives because our satellite photos showed no indication of a major construction project that could prove detrimental to the security of the United States."

"And the development facility on Ometepe?"

"We checked it," answered Hecht, becoming annoyed with Seymour's questions, "and found it was engaging in alternative power research. Our analysts saw nothing that revealed Odyssey was researching and developing weapons of death or destruction. So we moved on, since our main objective is observing and analyzing the Republic of China's penetration into Central America, in particular, the Canal Zone."

Jack Martin said, "I find it troubling that our best scientific efforts are still years away from producing an efficient fuel cell power system. Not only did Odyssey make an astonishing technical breakthrough, but the Red Chinese are already manufacturing millions of units."

"We can't lead the world in everything, every time," said General Stack. He nodded at Pitt and Giordino. "What you're telling us is that Odyssey lured away a number of the world's leading scientists who were conducting research into fuel cells, took them to the facility in Nicaragua and then coerced them into developing a practical and efficient product."

Pitt nodded. "That is correct."

"I can name at least four of our own scientists who left their research laboratories at universities and quietly disappeared," said Martin.

Hecht looked at Pitt. "Are you certain the Lowenhardts will cooperate and give us the technical data we require to re-create their advance in nitrogen fuel cells?"

"They agreed up and down the line after I promised them that their children would be flown under guard to the United States for a family reunion and protected from now on."

"Good thinking," said Sandecker with a glint in his eyes, "even if you did step beyond your authority."

"It seemed the honorable thing to do," Pitt came back, with a sly grin.

Jack Martin doodled on a notepad. "As soon as they've recovered from their ordeal and are rested, we'll begin interviewing them." He gazed at Pitt across the table. "What did they tell you about the cell's inner workings?"

"Only that after they determined that hydrogen was impractical as a fuel they began experimenting with nitrogen because it makes up seventy-eight percent of Earth's air. By drawing it out of the atmosphere along with oxygen, they ingeniously created a fuel cell that was self-sustaining and powered by natural gases, with only pure water as waste. According to Claus they engineered an ingeniously simple unit with less than eight parts. It was this simplicity that enabled the Chinese to produce so many units so quickly."

General Stack looked grim. "Such huge production numbers in such a short space of time is astonishing."

"Something of that magnitude would have called for a staggering amount of platinum to coat the anodes that separate the gas into protons and electrons," explained Martin.

Hecht replied, "Over the past ten years, Odyssey has accumulated eighty percent of the world's platinum-producing mines. A phenomenon that has cost the auto industry dearly since they rely on platinum for a number of engine parts."

"Once we have the Lowenhardts' blueprint in our hands," said Seymour, "we'll have the same problem of finding enough platinum to match Chinese production."

"They did say they had yet to design a fuel cell to power automobiles," Giordino commented.

Martin said, "By using the Lowenhardts' data and by making an all-out effort, we might get the jump on Odyssey and the Chinese in that field."

"Certainly worth a try," said General Stack, "now that the groundwork has been achieved and the technology laid in our lap."

"Which brings us to a plan about how to deal with Odyssey and the tunnels," continued Stack, his eyes straying across the table to Seymour.

"Sending Special Forces to block a series of tunnels is not the same as sending troops to subdue a dictator who has built up an arsenal of nuclear, biological and chemical weapons like Saddam in Iraq," Seymour spelled out. "I cannot in good conscience advise the president to use force."

"But the results of a terrible freeze above the thirtieth parallel could be just as deadly."

"Max is right," said Martin. "Convincing the rest of the world of the danger would border on the impossible."

"Regardless of how you approach the dilemma," Sandecker said, "those tunnels must be blocked and blocked fast. Once they are opened and millions of gallons of water from the Atlantic is flowing into the Pacific, they'll be much more difficult to destroy."

"How about sending in a small covert team with explosives to do the job?"

"They'd never penetrate Odyssey's security," counseled Giordino.

"You and Dirk made it in and out," said Sandecker.

"We weren't carrying a hundred tons of explosives, which is what it will take to do the job."

Pitt had left his chair and moved around the room, studying the monitors and maps on the walls. He found particular interest in a large satellite photo of the Odyssey R&D facility on Ometepe. He moved in closer and examined the slope of Mount Concepcion and a thought began to form. Finally, he turned and stepped back to the table.

"A B-fifty-two drop of two-thousand-pound penetrating bombs would do it," suggested Stack.

"We can't go around dropping bombs on friendly countries," said Seymour, "despite the threat."

"Then you admit the potential for a deep freeze is a threat to the nation's security," Stack cornered him.

"That part of the equation goes without saying," Seymour said wearily. "What I'm saying is there must be a logical solution that won't make the president and the United States government look like inhuman monsters to the nations of the world."

"And lest we forget," Hecht said with a tight, canny smile, "the political implications and fallout in the next election if we make the wrong decisions."

"There might be another approach," said Pitt slowly, while still looking at the satellite photo. "An approach that would satisfy everyone involved."

"All right, Mr. Pitt," said General Stack dubiously, "how do we destroy the tunnels without sending in the Special Forces or a squadron of bombers?"

Pitt held their attention, every eye was trained on him. "I propose we give the job to Mother Nature."

They all looked at him, waiting for an explanation, their minds beginning to think he may have lost some gray matter. Martin, the scientist, broke the silence.

"Could you please explain?"

"According to geologists, a slope of the Concepcion volcano on Ometepe is slipping. This was no doubt caused by the tunnel excavation under the outer edge of the volcano. When Al and I were in the tunnel closest to its core, we could feel a substantial rise in temperature."

"Well over a hundred degrees," Giordino added.

"The Lowenhardts told us that one of the scientists held hostage, a Dr. Honoma from the University of Hawaii—"

"One of the scientists on our list of the missing," interrupted Martin.

"Dr. Honoma predicted that a sudden slip was possible at any time that would cause the volcano's flank to collapse, with catastrophic results."

"How extensive would be the catastrophic results?" asked the general, not entirely sold on the report.

"The entire Odyssey research center and everybody in it would be buried under millions of tons of rock that would launch a tidal wave around the lake that would wipe out every town and village along the shoreline."

"This certainly isn't a situation we considered," said Hecht.

Seymour gave Pitt a long, considering gaze. "If what you say is true, the mountain will do the job for us and destroy the tunnels."

"That's one scenario."

"Then all we have to do is sit and wait."

"Geologists haven't witnessed enough volcanic slope collapses to form a timetable. The wait might last a few days or a few years. Then it would be too late to avert the freeze."

"We can't just sit on our hands," Stack spoke in a hard tone, "and watch helplessly as the tunnels go into operation."

"We *could* sit on our hands," said Pitt, "but there is another way."

"Kindly tell us what you've got in mind," Sandecker demanded impatiently.

"Inform the Nicaraguan government that our scientists have monitored the slippage on Concepcion volcano by satellite, and its slope is ready to collapse at any hour. Scare the hell out of them. Describe a possible death toll in the thousands, then feed them the bait."

Seymour looked confused. "Bait?"

"We offer to provide massive aid in helping the people inside the facility and the inhabitants around Lake Nicaragua to evacuate the area and head for high ground. Once they are free and clear, you can drop a bomb into the side of the volcano from fifty thousand feet without anybody being the wiser, set off the slide and destroy the tunnels."

Sandecker leaned back in his chair and stared thoughtfully at the surface of the table. "It sounds too simple, too elementary for such an enormous event."

"From what I know of the area," said Martin, "Mount Concepcion is still active. A bomb might set off an eruption."

"Dropping the bomb down the volcano's crater might induce an eruption," said Pitt. "But we should be safe if we guide it to explode below the base of the volcano's slope."

For the first time, General Stack smiled. "I believe Mr. Pitt has something. The simplicity is what makes it logical. I propose we investigate the possibilities."

"What about the workers below in the tunnels?" asked Seymour. "They wouldn't have a chance of escaping."

"Not to worry," replied Giordino. "They would have left a good twenty-four hours before the tunnels were to be opened to the sea."

"We can't waste time," Pitt cautioned. "I overheard the two women in Odyssey's headquarters say they were going to open the tunnels in eight days. That was three days ago. We're now down to five."

Hecht peered over a pair of reading glasses at Seymour. "It's up to you, Max, to get the ball rolling. We'll need the president's approval to proceed."

"I'll have that within the hour," Seymour said confidently. "My next job is to convince Secretary of State Hampton to launch immediate negotiations with the Nicaraguan officials to allow our rescue force to enter the country." He glanced at Stack. "And you, General, I'll rely on you to set up and direct the evacuation." Then it was Jack Martin's turn. "Jack, it will be your job to put the fear of God in the minds of the Nicaraguan government that the catastrophe is very real and imminent."

"I'll help on that score," offered Sandecker. "I'm very close with two of the country's ocean scientists."

Last, Seymour stared at Pitt and Giordino. "We owe you gentlemen a great debt. I only wish I knew how to repay it."

"There is something," Pitt said, grinning, exchanging looks with Giordino. "There is this Secret Service agent we know by the name of Otis McGonigle. Al and I would like to see him promoted."

Seymour shrugged. "I think I can arrange that. Any particular reason you've selected him?"

"We have great rapport," Giordino answered. "He's a credit to the service."

"There is one other favor," said Pitt, looking at Hecht. "I'd like to see your file on Specter and the Odyssey conglomerate."

Hecht nodded. "I'll have one of my couriers bring it to NUMA headquarters. You think there is anything in it that may prove useful to this situation?"

43

Moreau, dressed in white shorts, white open shirt and high kneesocks, was waiting for Dirk and Summer at precisely nine o'clock as they exited the lobby of the hotel with the duffel bags containing their dive gear. The doorman set their bags in the trunk and they all climbed into the 525 BMW under a light rain deposited by a single cloud in an otherwise clear blue sky. The wind was gentle and barely fluttered the fronds of the palm trees.

The drive to the wharf where Moreau had arranged for their chartered boat to be moored was a short two miles down a winding road to the water. He pulled onto a narrow stone jetty that extended from the shore over water that altered from a yellow-green to a blue-green as it deepened. He stopped above a boat that was nestled against the dock like a duckling to its mother, fenders like feathers bumping from stone to fiberglass hull as she dipped in the gentle waves flowing in from the lagoon. The name in gold letters across her stern read: DEAR HEART.

She was a pretty little sailboat, a masthead sloop with her mainsail and jib going to the top of the mast. Twenty-six feet in length with a nine-foot beam, her draft was only a few inches over four feet. She had three hundred and thirty-one square feet of sail area and a small ten-horsepower auxiliary diesel engine. Her cabin comfortably slept two with a head, shower and a small galley. As Moreau had promised, a Fisher metal detector and a Klein subbottom profiler were mounted and ready for operation in the cockpit. Dirk dropped down a ladder to the deck and caught the bags as they were dropped by Moreau, before carrying them down to the cabin.

"A safe voyage," said Moreau to Summer. "I shall keep my cell phone on my person at all times. Please call if you encounter trouble."

"We shall," said Summer confidently. Then she slipped lithely down the ladder and joined Dirk as he started the little diesel. At his signal, Moreau cast off the lines and stood on the dock, an expression of dire concern on his face as the little boat's diesel engine knocked across the lagoon and out into the sea.

Once they cleared the last buoy, Dirk ran the mainsail and jib up the mast, with Summer at the wheel. The canvas was crimson red against the blue sky. It flapped back and forth until set by the wind. The sail puffed out and the boat began to slip smartly across the growing swells rolling from offshore. Dirk looked along the deck. Everything was scrubbed and bright. *Dear Heart* looked to be less than a year old, her brass work and chrome gleamed under the sun, and her deck looked well-scrubbed.

She was a sleek and smart sailer, slipping through the water and taking the swells like a cat running across a lawn. A random gust from a passing squall chopped the blue water and flecked the crests of the waves with foam. Then they were out of it and into smooth seas and dry air again. Beyond her bowsprit the sea stretched like a giant carpet.

"How far to Branwyn?" asked Summer, deftly heeling *Dear Heart* over on her beam to gain another knot in speed as the water seethed past her lee rail.

"About twenty-three miles," replied Dirk. "Put her on a heading due south. No need for a detailed course. The island has a distinctive light tower on the eastern end."

Dirk removed his shirt and trimmed the sail in his shorts. Summer had slipped off her dress and changed into a green bikini with floral designs. Her hands were poised and steady on the wheel and she steered the boat over the crests and troughs of the waves with a deft touch, keeping one eye on the islands looming on the horizon and the other on the compass.

Her flowing red hair blew free behind her head and she had the look of a sailor who was going on a day trip from Newport Beach to Catalina Island. After an hour, she lifted a pair of binoculars to her eyes with one hand and stared into the distance. "I think I see the light tower," she said, pointing.

Dirk followed her extended arm and finger. He could not quite make out the tower, but a smudge across the horizon line soon became the low shape of an island. "That will be Branwyn. Steer straight toward it. The harbor lies on her south shore."

A school of flying fish burst from the water in front of the bow and flashed away in all directions. Some leaped alongside the boat as if hoping for food to be thrown over. Then they were replaced by five dolphins, who cavorted around the boat like clowns who wanted applause.

Now the island showed distinctly only three miles distant. The light tower was clearly visible, as was the three-story house on the nearest beach. Dirk picked up the binoculars and peered at the house. No human was visible and the windows looked shuttered. There was a dock running from a sandy beach, but no boat was moored alongside.

They changed places. Dirk took the wheel while Summer went up to the bow, hung on to the rigging and gazed at the island. It was ugly, as islands went. No thick underbrush filled with tropical flowers, no palm trees arched over the beach. Most islands have their own smell. The aroma of moldy vegetation, tropical plants and the scent of its people and their cooking, the pungent smell of smoke from burned fields mixed with that of copra and coconut oil. This island had an essence of death about it, as if it reeked of evil. Her ears picked up the distant rumble of surf as it struck a reef surrounding a lagoon in front of the house. Now she could see a low building on the end of a long runway that must have served as a hangar. But like Dirk, she saw no sign of life. Branwyn was like an abandoned graveyard.

Dirk kept well off the reef while keeping a wary eye over the side at the water that was as clear as water in a bathroom sink. The bottom came into view, a smooth sandy bottom clear of coral. He glanced at the echo sounder every few seconds to make sure the seabed didn't take a sudden rise toward the keel. With a firm hand on the wheel, he steered around the island until he came up on the southern end. He consulted his chart and made a slight course change before he turned and entered the channel as determined by the echo sounder. The rolling waves of the sea turned choppy here, as he sailed through a hundred-yard gap in the outer reef.

It was a tricky entrance. The current was pushing him to port. He thought that Odysseus and his crews must have found entering the harbor duck soup for mariners who had crossed the Atlantic Ocean. Their advantage in navigating unruly waters was that they could throw out their oars and row. Dirk could have started the engine, but like a pilot with an aircraft that could land by autopilot, he preferred to use his own skills and take her in himself.

Once through the straits, the water calmed and he watched the bottom slowly pass under the keel. He turned the wheel back over to Summer and dropped the sails. Then he started the little diesel and began inspecting the interior of the harbor.

It was small, no more than half a mile in length and half again as much in width. While Summer leaned over the side and inspected the bottom for any unusual anomalies, he leisurely cruised back and forth across the harbor, trying to get a feel for the current and imagining himself on the deck of one of Odysseus' ships, trying to predict where the ancient mariners might have anchored so many centuries ago.

Finally, he settled in an area that was sheltered from the prevailing winds by a rise on the island, a sandy mound that rose nearly a hundred feet above the shoreline. He shut off the engine and dropped the bow anchor by flicking a switch in the cockpit that lowered it by a winch.

"This looks about as good a place as any to go over the side and inspect the bottom."

"It looks flat as a dining room floor," said Summer. "I saw no humps or contours. It stands to reason that wood from a Celtic shipwreck would have rotted away thousands of years ago. Any pieces that survived have to be buried."

"Let's dive. I'll test the consistency of the sand and silt. You swim around and do a visual inspection."

After they put on their dive gear, Dirk checked the anchor to be sure it was snug on the bottom and wouldn't break loose and allow the boat to drift away. Not that it would go far in the harbor. Without the need for wet suits to protect their bodies from cold water temperatures or sharp coral, they went over the side in ten feet of water in only their bathing suits. The water was almost as clear as glass. Visibility was nearly two hundred feet, the temperature warm in the middle eighties, perfect diving conditions.

Forty minutes later, Dirk climbed up the boarding ladder to the deck and removed his air tank and weight belt. He had run a metal probe beneath the surface of the sand, checking for a harder clay layer beneath but found fifteen feet of soft sand before striking bedrock. He sat there for a few minutes, watching Summer's air bubbles travel around the boat. Soon, she was climbing aboard and paused on the boarding ladder to carefully set a coral-encrusted object on the deck. Then she stood with water trickling down her body onto the teak deck as she slipped out of her dive gear.

"What have you got?" asked Dirk.

"I don't know, but it feels too heavy for a rock. I found it a hundred yards offshore, protruding out of the sand."

Dirk scanned the shoreline, still seemingly deserted. He had a strange feeling in the pit of his stomach, as if they were being watched.

He picked up the object and gently chipped away the encrustation with his dive knife. Soon the object took on the look of a bird with outstretched wings.

"Looks like an eagle or swan," he said. Then the tip of his knife cut a small scratch that showed silver. "The reason it's heavy is because it's cast out of lead."

Summer took it in her hands and stared at the wings and the beaked head that was turned to the right. "Could it be ancient Celt?"

"The fact that it's sculpted out of lead is a good sign. Dr. Chisholm told me that, besides tin, one of the main attractions of Cornwall was its lead mines. Did you mark the site where you found it?"

She nodded. "I left my probe in the sand with a little orange flag on it."

"How far out?"

"About fifty feet in that direction," she said, pointing.

"Okay, before we dredge or probe with the water jet, we'll run over your site with the metal detector. The side-scan sonar won't be of much use if all the ship wreckage is buried."

"Maybe we should have had Rudi send a magnetometer."

Dirk smiled. "A magnetometer detects the magnetic field of iron or steel. Odysseus sailed long before the Iron Age appeared. A metal detector will read iron besides most other metals, including gold and bronze."

Summer turned on the Fisher Pulse 10 detector as Dirk connected the cable from the meter and audio readouts to the tow fish encasing the sensor. Then he lowered the tow fish over the side, leaving just enough cable so that it wouldn't drag on the bottom at slow surveying speed. His final task was to raise the anchor.

"Ready?" he asked.

"All set," answered Summer.

Turning over the diesel engine, Dirk began making closely spaced survey lines over the target area, mowing the lawn until they struck an anomaly. After only fifteen minutes, the needle on the meter began to zig and zag in unison with an increased buzzing sound over Summer's earphones.

"We're coming up on something," she announced.

Then came a slight zip in sound and a brief swing of the needle as they passed over Summer's metal probe that was sticking out of the bottom.

"Get a good reading?" asked Dirk.

Summer was about to answer in the negative when the needle began wildly sweeping back and forth, indicating a metallic object or objects passing under the keel. "We have a pretty good mass down there. What direction are we running?"

"East to west," replied Dirk, marking the target coordinates from his global positioning instrument.

"Run over the site again, but this time from north to south."

Dirk did as he was told, passing beyond the target for a hundred yards before swinging *Dear Heart* on a ninety-degree turn heading north to south. Again the meter and audio sound went wild. Summer penciled the meter readings in a notebook and looked up at Dirk standing at the wheel.

"The target is linear, about fifty feet in length with a broad dipolar signature. It looks to have a minimal but dispersed mass, similar to what you'd expect from a broken-up sailing vessel."

"It seems to be in the expected range of an old wreck. We'd better check it out."

"How deep is the water?"

"Only ten feet."

Dirk eased the boat around again, shut down the engine and let the *Dear Heart* drift with the current. When the GPS numbers began to match those of the anomaly, he dropped the anchor. Then he fired up the compressor.

They put on their dive gear and dropped into the water from opposite sides of the boat. Dirk turned the valve for the water jet and pushed it into the sand in the manner of kids pushing the nozzle of a hose into the ground to make a hole. After five attempts and feeling nothing solid, he suddenly felt the tip of the probe strike a hard object three feet beneath the surface of the sandy bottom. Several more probes later and he had laid out a grid, with Summer's metal shaft sticking up on an outside corner.

"Something down there, all right," he said, spitting out his mouthpiece as they surfaced. "About the right size for an ancient ship."

"Could be anything," said Summer sensibly, "from the wreck of an old fishing boat to trash dumped off a barge."

"We'll know as soon as we dig a hole with the induction dredge."

They swam back to the boat, attached the hose to the dredge and dropped it into the water. Dirk volunteered for the dirty job of excavation while Summer stayed aboard to watch the compressor.

He pulled the hose after him that was attached to a metal pipe that sucked the sand from the bottom and shot it out of a second hose that he laid several feet away to scatter the muck. The dredge acted like a vacuum cleaner as it burrowed into the bottom. The sand was soft, and in less than twenty minutes he had dug a crater four feet across and three feet deep. Then at slightly less than four feet he uncovered a round object, which he identified as an ancient terra-cotta oil jug, like one Dr. Boyd showed in photos during the conference at NUMA. He very carefully sucked the sand away from it until he could lift and set it outside the crater. Then he returned to his work.

Next came a terra-cotta drinking cup. Then two more. These were followed by the hilt and badly eroded blade of a sword. He was about to quit and bring his trove to the surface, when he removed the overburden from a round object in the shape of a dome, with two protrusions sprouting from it. As soon as he'd uncovered fifty percent of it, his heartbeat abruptly increased from sixty beats to a hundred. He recognized what Homer had described in his works as a Bronze Age helmet with horns.

Dirk finished removing the ancient artifact from its resting place of over three thousand years and gently laid it in the yellow sand beside the other discoveries. Standing in the crater amid the swirling sand and working the dredge was tiring work. He had been down nearly fifty minutes and found what he came for, evidence that Odysseus' fleet had come to grief in the West Indies and not the Mediterranean. His air was about gone, and though he could have sucked the air tank dry and easily reached the surface only ten feet away by exhaling a single breath, it was time to take a break. The next step was to bring the artifacts safely aboard *Dear Heart*. Holding the helmet as though it was a newborn baby, he ascended.

Summer was waiting at the boarding ladder to take his weight belt and air tank. He lifted the helmet out of the water and carefully handed it to her. "Take it," he said. "But treat it gently. It's badly eroded." Then, before she could comment, he jackknifed and dove to retrieve the other artifacts.

As he climbed on the boat, Summer had emptied their ice chest of drinks and was immersing the artifacts in salt water to preserve them. "Cool," she repeated three times. "I can't believe what I'm seeing. A helmet, an honest-to-goodness ancient bronze helmet."

"We were exceedingly lucky," said Dirk, "to find them so early in the game."

"Then these *are* from Odysseus' fleet."

"We won't know for sure until experts like Dr. Boyd and Dr. Chisholm can make an identification. Fortunately, they were buried in the silt, which preserved them all these years."

After a light lunch and relaxing for another hour, while Summer gently cleaned some of the outer layers of marine concretion without damaging the artifacts, Dirk went back down to operate the dredge.

This trip he found four copper ingots and one ingot of tin. They were oddly shaped with concave edges, a fair indication that they came from the Bronze Age. Next he uncovered a stone hammer. At four and a half feet, he struck fragmentary wooden planks and beams. One section of beam measured two feet long by five inches thick. Maybe, just maybe, Dirk thought, a dendrochronology lab would be able to

date the growth rings from the tree it was cut from. By the time he carried the artifacts to the surface and hauled in the dredge, it was late in
the afternoon.

He found Summer gazing at a magnificent sunset with clouds
painted red-orange from the enlarged ball of the sun as it fell toward
the horizon. She helped him off with his gear. "I'll fix dinner if you'll
open a bottle of wine."

"How about a little cocktail to celebrate?" Dirk said, smiling. "I
bought a bottle of good Guadeloupe rum at the hotel. We have gin-
ger ale, I'll make rum collinses."

"They'll have to be room temperature. I threw out the ice from the
chest when you brought aboard the first artifacts so I could use it as
a preservation tank."

"Now that we have a productive site with artifacts," said Dirk, "I
think that tomorrow we'll search and survey for the other ships in
Odysseus' fleet."

Summer looked wistfully at the water that was turning to a dark blue
as the sun vanished into the sea. "I wonder how much treasure is
down there."

"There may not be any."

She saw the doubt in his eyes. "What makes you say that?"

"I can't be certain, but I believe the site I worked had been
disturbed."

"Disturbed?" she said skeptically. "Disturbed by whom?"

As Dirk spoke, he stared apprehensively at the buildings on the island. "It seemed to me the artifacts had been moved about by human
hands rather than by tides and shifting sand. It was almost as if they
had been stacked on top of one another in a pile that was foreign to
nature."

"We'll worry about it tomorrow," Summer said, turning from the
magnificent twilight. "I'm starved and thirsty. Get busy on those rum
collinses."

It was after dark when Summer finished heating conch soup and boiling a pair of lobsters that she had caught during her dive. For dessert she served bananas Foster. Then they lay on the deck, stared at the stars and talked until nearly midnight, listening to the water slap lightly against *Dear Heart*'s hull.

As twin brother and sister, Dirk and Summer were very close, yet, unlike identical twins, they went their separate ways when not on the job. Summer was dating a young career diplomat with the State Department to whom her grandfather, the senator, had introduced her. Dirk pretty much played the field, not forming any close attachment and preferring a variety of girls as different in looks as they were in personality and taste. Though cut from the same cloth as his father, Dirk didn't share all the same interests. True, they both loved old cars and aircraft and had a passion for the sea, but there any similarity ended. Dirk liked to race motorcycles cross-country and enter in powerboat races. He was driven to compete on his own skills. On the other hand, his father was rarely competitive in a solitary sense, choosing to take part in sports that called for a team effort. Where young Dirk entered individual competition in track-and-field events at the University of Hawaii, Dirk the elder played football, becoming a star quarterback at the Air Force Academy.

Finally, after exhausting all conversation on Odysseus and his voyage, they decided it was time to turn in. Summer went below and slept in one of the berths while Dirk elected to sleep up on deck on the cushions in the cockpit under the open sky.

At four in the morning, the sea was black as obsidian. A light rain came that blotted out the stars. One could have walked off the deck into the water and never known it until he felt the splash. Dirk pulled an oilcloth over him and contentedly returned to dreamland.

He did not come awake at the sound of a boat engine, because there was no boat and no engine. They came from the water, silently, like ghosts flying around tombstones on Halloween night. There were four of them, three men and one woman. Dirk did not hear the gentle touch of feet on the boarding ladder that he had neglected to pull up. Without realizing it, he made it easy for them to creep on board.

Some people wakened in the night by intruders react in different ways. Dirk had no time to react. Unlike his father, he had yet to learn not to trust in luck or fate and always to follow the old Boy Scout motto: Be prepared. Before he knew strangers were on *Dear Heart,* the oilcloth was pulled up around his head, and a club or a baseball bat or a truncheon, he never knew, came down on the back of his head and sent him far beyond dreamland, falling into a deep black pit that never seemed to end.

44

T HE PREPARATIONS TO EVACUATE Isle de Ometepe came down to the wire. It took four days for Secretary of State George Hampton to convince Nicaraguan president Raul Ortiz that the American intentions were purely humanitarian. He promised that once the evacuation was completed, all American forces would leave the country. Jack Martin and Admiral Sandecker worked on Nicaraguan scientists who, once briefed on the looming disaster, lent their full support to the operation.

As expected, local government officials who were in Specter's pockets because of bribes, fought the intrusion. Those close to the Red Chinese also had their marching orders and put up a fight. But as Martin proposed at the conference, he and Sandecker put the fear of God into the leaders of the country by describing the potential catastrophe and the estimated number of dead within a mile of the lake. All opposition was quickly drowned in a river of panic.

Working closely with General Juan Morega, chief of the Nicaraguan armed forces, General Stack had all elements of his special rescue force in place. Once permission was given, he moved quickly. All boats around the lake were commandeered to evacuate residents of towns and villages that had no major roads available by which to flee. Trucks and U.S. Army helicopters carried the rest to high ground. At the same time a special fighting force was assembled to assault the Odyssey facility.

No one doubted that Odyssey security would put up a fight to keep their covert project and scientists who were held in illegal captivity an ongoing secret. There was also the fear that Specter would murder and dispose of the scientists' bodies so no trace was left of their existence. General Stack was sympathetic, but the possibility of thousands of deaths and trillions of dollars lost in shattered economies outweighed twenty or thirty lives. He gave orders that the facility and its workers be evacuated as swiftly as possible, including the scientists if they were still on the island.

He put Pitt under the command of Lieutenant Colonel Bonaparte Nash, called Bony by those close to him. A member of a Marine recon team, Nash welcomed Pitt and Giordino at the helicopter evacuation team's temporary base across the lake at the small city of San Jorge on the western shore. Blond hair cropped short, a body tight from muscles built from long hours of exercise, he had a round, soft face with friendly blue eyes that betrayed the toughness that lurked beneath.

"Real good to meet you, Mr. Pitt, Mr. Giordino. I was briefed on your qualifications as members of NUMA. Quite impressive. I trust you can lead me and my men to the building where the scientists are kept prisoner."

"We can," Pitt assured him.

"But as I understand it, you were only there once."

"If we found it at night," said Giordino testily, "we can find it in broad daylight."

Nash laid out a large satellite photo of the facility on a small table. "I have five CH-forty-seven Chinook helicopters, each carrying thirty men. My plan is to land one at the air terminal, the second at the docks, a third alongside the building you described as the security headquarters and a fourth in a park area between a row of warehouses.

You two will come along with me in the fifth to make certain we have the right building where the scientists are held."

"If I might make a suggestion," offered Pitt. He pulled a pen from the breast pocket of his flowered shirt and tapped it on a building beside a palm-lined street. "This is the main headquarters building. You can land on the roof and seize the top executives of Odyssey before they have time to escape in their own helicopter."

"How do you know this?" Nash inquired thoughtfully.

"Al and I stole a copter from the roof when we evaded capture six days ago."

"They have at least ten security guards in the building that your men will have to deal with," said Giordino.

Nash looked at them with growing respect, but still not certain whether to fully believe them.

"There were security guards when you escaped?"

Pitt saw Nash's reservation. "Yes, four of them."

Giordino picked up on it too. "Overpowering them was like taking candy from a baby."

"I was told you guys were marine engineers," said Nash, confused.

"We do that too," Giordino said glibly.

"Okay, if you say so." Nash gave a slight disconcerted shake of his head. "Now, then, I can't issue you any weapons. You'll be along for the ride as guides. You'll leave any fighting to me and my men."

Pitt and Giordino glanced at each other with a twinkle in their eyes. Pitt's .45 and Giordino's .50 caliber auto were concealed in the back of the waistband behind their pants under loose tropical shirts.

"If we get into trouble," said Giordino. "We'll throw rocks until your men rescue us."

Nash wasn't sure if he liked these two wisecracking men. He held up his wrist and studied his watch. "We take off in ten minutes. You'll ride with me. After we land, you make certain we've got the right building. We can't lose a minute wandering around lost after we land, if we're to save the hostages before Odyssey guards execute them."

Pitt nodded. "Fair enough."

In precisely ten minutes he and Giordino were buckled into their seats inside the big Chinook transport helicopter with Lieutenant Colonel Nash. They were accompanied by thirty big, silent purposeful-looking men dressed in camouflaged combat fatigues with armored vests, huge guns that looked like arms out of a science fiction movie, and an assortment of rocket launchers.

"Tough bunch," Giordino said admiringly.

"I'm glad they're on our side," Pitt agreed.

The pilot lifted the helicopter off the ground and took off across the beach over the lake. It was a short hop of fifteen miles to the Odyssey center. The entire operation was based on surprise. Colonel Nash's plan of operation was to subdue the guards, rescue the hostages and then evacuate the hundreds of workers in boats that were already on their way around the lake to Ometepe. Soon as the last person was off the island and safely ashore on high ground, Nash was to give the signal to the pilot of a B-52 bomber circling at sixty thousand feet to drop a massive ground-penetrating concussion bomb on the base of the mountain, unleashing a flank avalanche that would collapse the tunnels and sweep the research and development facility into the lake.

It seemed to Pitt that they had no sooner taken off than the helicopter stopped, hovered for a few seconds and set down. Nash and his men leaped from the seats through the open hatch and shouted for the security guards at the fenced gate to the hostage quarters to throw down their arms.

The other four copters had landed and received sporadic fire from a few security guards who had no idea they were up against an elite force. Seeing that resistance was hopeless, they quickly surrendered as fast as they could drop their weapons and raise their hands. They had not been hired to fight professional forces, only to protect the facility, and none had a death wish.

Pitt, with Giordino right on his heels, rushed through the gate and burst in the front door of the building ahead of Nash and his men. The guards inside, although hearing shots elsewhere on the facility, were stunned to find themselves looking down the muzzles of two very large automatic pistols before they had a chance to realize what was happening. They froze not so much in shock as in fear.

Nash was more than surprised to see Pitt and Giordino with weapons, he was madder than hell. "Give me those guns!" he demanded.

He was ignored, as Pitt and Giordino began kicking in the doors to the rooms. The first, second, third and fourth. They were all empty. Pitt rushed back to the guards that were being escorted from the building by Nash's team. He grabbed the nearest guard and jammed the Colt against the man's nose, flattening it.

"English!"

"No, *senor.*"

"*¿Dónde están los científicos?*"

The guard's eyes widened as they crossed and focused on the muzzle mashing his nose. "*Ellos fueron tomados lejos a la darsena y colocados en el transbordador.*"

"What's going on?" Nash demanded. "Where are the hostages?"

Pitt pulled the Colt back from the man's nose as it began to bleed. "I asked him where the scientists were. He said they were taken to the docks and put on a ferry."

"It looks as if they're transporting them out onto the lake before sinking the ferry with everyone on it," said Giordino grimly.

Pitt looked at Nash. "We'll need your men and a copter to go after them before the Odyssey guards can scuttle the ferry."

Nash shook his head. "Sorry, no can do. My orders are to secure the base and evacuate all personnel. I can't spare any men or a helicopter."

"But these people are vital to our national interest," Pitt argued. "They hold the key to fuel cell technology."

Nash's face was hard as stone. "My orders stand."

"Then loan us a grenade launcher and we'll go after the ferry ourselves."

"You know I can't issue weapons to civilians."

"You're a big help," snapped Giordino. "We haven't time to waste debating with a hard nose." Giordino nodded toward a golf cart like the one he drove in the tunnels. "If we can't stop them on the dock, maybe we can grab one of Odyssey's patrol boats."

Pitt threw Nash a look of disgust and then he and Giordino ran for the cart. Eight minutes later, with Giordino at the wheel, they sped onto the dock. An agonized look swept Pitt's face as he saw an old ferryboat pulling out into the lake, followed by a patrol boat.

"Too late," groaned Giordino. "They've taken along a patrol boat to remove the guards after they blow out the bottom of the barge."

Pitt ran to the opposite side of the dock and spotted a small outboard tied to a piling no more than twenty yards away. "Come on, the *Good Ship Lollipop* awaits." Then he took off, running toward the boat.

It was an eighteen-foot Boston Whaler with a one-hundred-and-fifty-horsepower Mercury motor. Pitt started the motor while Giordino cast off the lines. Giordino had barely thrown the lines onto the dock when Pitt shoved the throttle to its top and the little Whaler leaped over the water as if kicked in the stern and took off after the wakes of the ferry and patrol boat.

"What do we do when we reach them?" Giordino yelled over the roar of the motor.

"I'll think of something when the time comes," Pitt shouted back.

Giordino eyed the rapidly closing distance between the vessels. "You'd better come up with something quick. They have assault rifles against our popguns, and the patrol boat has a nasty cannon on its bow."

"Try this," Pitt said loudly. "I'm going to swing around and come in with the ferry between us and the patrol boat. That will neutralize its field of fire. Then we come alongside the ferry and jump on board."

"I've heard of worse schemes," Giordino said glumly, "but not in the last ten years."

"It looks like two, maybe three, guards on the upper deck next to the wheelhouse. Take my Colt and play two-gun desperado. If you intimidate them, maybe they'll throw up their hands and surrender."

"I won't hold my breath."

Pitt cranked the wheel and spun the Whaler in a broad arc, circling around the ferry before the crew of the patrol boat could bring their bow gun to bear. The boat bounced over the crest of a small wave from the ferry's wake and dropped into the trough as a barrage of bullets flew harmlessly overhead. Giordino replied by squeezing both triggers as fast as his fingers could pull. The hail of bullets caught the guards by surprise. One dropped to the deck with a bullet in the leg. Another spun around, clutching his shoulder, while the third dropped his weapon and raised his hands.

"See," said Pitt, "I told you so."

"Sure, after I put two of them out of action."

Twenty yards from the ferry Pitt eased back on the throttle and gave the wheel a light twist to starboard. With a deft touch from years of practice, he slipped the Whaler along the ferry's hull with barely a bump. Giordino beat him on board and was disarming the guards as Pitt leaped onto the deck. "I inserted a full clip." He threw Pitt his .50 caliber automatic. "Take it!"

Pitt grabbed it and dropped through an open hatch and scrambled down the ladder below. His feet no sooner landed on the deck of a corridor than a rumble came from the engine room that shook the ferry. One of the guards had set off the detonators and the resulting explosion blasted a hole in the bilge of the hull. Pitt was knocked off his feet, but recovered instantly and ran through the central corridor, kicking in doors as he went.

"Out, get out quick!" he shouted to the frightened scientists who had been locked inside. "This boat is going to sink!" He began herding them toward the ladder leading topside. He stopped a man with gray hair and beard. "Are there any more of you?"

"They locked some of us in a storeroom at the end of the hallway."

Almost before the scientist got the words out, Pitt rushed to the storeroom door. Already the water was sloshing around his ankles. This door was too solidly built for him to kick in. "Stand back from the door!" he shouted. Then he aimed Giordino's hand cannon at the latch and fired. The big shell shattered the bolt, allowing Pitt to shove the door open with his shoulder. Nearly ten people stood stunned inside, six men and four women. "Everybody move, now! Abandon ship before she goes down!"

After he pushed the last of the scientists up the ladder and was about to follow, a second, larger blast hurled him backward against a bulkhead. The impact drove the breath from his lungs and left him gasping for air as a bump mushroomed on the back of his head. Then he momentarily blacked out. When he recovered his senses two minutes later, he found himself sitting in water that had risen to his chest. Painfully, he pushed himself to his feet and struggled up the ladder one step at a time.

There was less than a minute left before the ferry plunged to the bottom of the lake bed. He heard a strange thumping sound over the rush of the rising water. What of the people he had saved and drove up to the deck? Had they drowned? Had the guns of the patrol boat shot them them like fish in a barrel with its cannon? And what of Al? Was he there to help the survivors? Still dazed from his collision with the bulkhead, he reached down inside himself for the last of his strength and pulled his shoulders and chest over the edge of the ferry's deck.

The stern of the ferry was about to go under, the water rolling up the deck and flooding into the open hatch. The thumping sound in his ears came louder and he looked up to see Giordino hanging on to a sling, seemingly floating in midair. Then Pitt saw the helicopter. Thank God Nash had a change of heart, he thought in his fogged mind.

He grabbed Giordino around the waist as strong muscular arms gripped him under his shoulders. The ferry slipped away beneath his feet and sank below the waves, just as he was hauled into the air.

"The scientists?" he gasped to Giordino. He saw none in the water.

"Lifted on board the copter," Giordino shouted above the wind and rotor noise. "The guards gave up when Nash and his team showed up and fled in the patrol boat."

"Is everybody off the island?" he asked Nash, who came over and knelt beside him.

"We even evacuated the stray cats and dogs," Nash said with a satisfied grin. "We pulled off the operation ahead of schedule and then came after you. When you didn't surface with the rest of the people, we thought you were a goner, all except Al here. Before I could stop him, he'd dropped down on the lift cable to the ferry deck. Only then did we see you appear out of the hatch."

"Lucky for me you arrived at an opportune moment."

"How long before the finale?" asked Giordino.

"As soon as we evacuated everyone from Ometepe to shore, they were transported by truck and buses to high ground, along with all the residents living within two miles of the lake." Nash paused to read the time on his wristwatch. "I estimate it will take another thirty-five minutes before they reach complete safety. When I receive word all is well, I'll send the signal to the pilot to drop his bomb."

"Did your teams meet up with a small army of uniformed women who put up a resistance?" Pitt inquired.

Nash gave him an odd look and grinned. "Wearing funny-colored jumpsuits?"

"Lavender and green?"

"They fought like Amazons," answered Nash in leftover disbelief. "Three of my men were wounded when they temporarily refrained from shooting at women who were shooting at them. We had no choice but to return fire."

Giordino stared down at the headquarters building as the helicopter passed over the facility. The windows were shattered and smoke was rolling from the tenth floor. "How many did you take down?"

"We counted at least nine bodies." Nash looked mystified. "Most of the women were knockouts, really beautiful. My men took it hard. I don't doubt some will suffer psychological problems when they return to home. They weren't trained to fire on civilian women."

"One of them didn't happen to be wearing a gold jumpsuit?" Pitt asked.

Nash thought a moment and then shook his head. "No, I didn't see anyone fitting that description." There was a pause. "Did she have red hair?"

"Yes, her hair was red."

"So were all those who died, the same red tint on all of them. They fought like crazy fanatics. It was unreal."

T HE HELICOPTER remained on station over the island. Nash received word that the evacuation was successfully completed almost to the minute of his estimate. Without a second's hesitation, he issued the clearance for the B-52 to drop the bomb.

The bomber was so high in the sky, they could not see it or detect the bomb as it fell from sixty thousand feet. Nor did they see the bomb strike the volcano's slope above the Odyssey facility and penetrate deep below the surface. Seconds later, a great rumble came from the slope of Mount Concepcion. The detonation seemed more like a huge thud than the sharp boom of a bomb exploding on impact with the ground. This was quickly followed by a new sound like rolling thunder, as the slope of the volcano let loose its grip on the cone and began collapsing, picking up speed as it shot downward until it reached an incredible eighty miles an hour.

From the air it looked as if the entire research and development complex with all its buildings, docks and aircraft terminal was sliding under the lake's surface like a monstrous coin thrown by a giant hand. Clouds of debris and dust burst into the sky as an enormous wave built and rose over two hundred feet high. Then the crest curled and swept across the lake at astonishing speed, eventually crashing against the shorelines and inundating everything that stood in its path, before finally dying at its highest penetration and receding almost reluctantly back into the lake bed.

In the time it took to turn two pages in a book, the great research center created by Specter, his female directors and his Odyssey empire had vanished, along with the tunnels that were crushed flat.

The South Equatorial Current would not be diverted into the Atlantic Ocean. The Gulf Stream would flow as it had for a million years, and there would be no deep freeze across Europe and North America until the next ice age.

45

THE LAYER OF BLACK HAZE began to merge with a bright white glow. The stars that had soared inside his head faded to a scant few as Dirk slowly returned to consciousness. He felt cold from the damp. Stunned by a sea of pain inside his head, he rose up on his elbows and looked around him.

He found himself in a small rectangular room, no more than five by three feet. The ceiling, floor and three walls were solid concrete. The fourth wall was filled by a rusty iron door. There was no handle on the inside. A small window no larger than a pie plate was embedded in the roof of his cell. Light filtered through it and dimly lit his tiny gray world. There was no bunk or blanket, only a hole in the floor for sanitation.

He never experienced a hangover to match the throb inside his head. There was a knot above the left ear that felt as big as a computer mouse. Rising to his feet was a major effort. If nothing else but to satisfy his curiosity, he pushed on the door. He might as well have tried to knock over an oak tree. All he wore when he went to sleep on the boat were a pair of shorts and a T-shirt. Looking down, he saw that his shirt and shorts were gone and he was wearing a white silk bathrobe. It seemed so out of place with his surroundings that he could not begin to imagine its significance.

Then his thoughts turned to Summer. What had happened to her? Where was she? He could remember nothing except watching a half-moon rise over the sea before falling asleep on the boat. The ache in his head began to subside slightly. He came to realize that someone must have clubbed him on the head, then carried him ashore and put him in this cell. But what of Summer. What had happened to her? Desperation began to seep into his mind. His situation looked hopeless. He could do nothing trapped in a concrete box. Escape seemed impossible.

It was sometime late in the afternoon when Dirk heard a sound outside his cell. There came the click of a lock turning and the door swung outward. A woman with blond hair, blue eyes and wearing a green jumpsuit stood with a large automatic pistol in her hand, aimed squarely at his chest.

"You will come with me," she said softly, without the slightest harsh quality.

In another setting Dirk would have found her quite attractive, but here, she seemed as nasty as the Wicked Witch of the West. "Where to?" he asked.

She prodded him in the back with the muzzle of her gun without replying. He was marched down a long corridor past several iron doors. Dirk wondered if Summer was behind one of them. They came to a stairway at the end and he began climbing without being told. At the top, they passed through a door into a marble-floored entry with walls embedded with millions of pieces of mosaic gold tile. The chairs were covered in lavender-dyed leather and the tables with inlaid lavender-stained wood. He thought it gaudy and overdone.

The female guard escorted him to a huge pair of gold-gilded doors, knocked and then stood aside as they were opened from within. She motioned for him to enter.

Dirk was stunned at the sight of four beautiful women with flow-

ing red hair in lavender and gold gowns sitting around a long conference table carved from a solid block of red coral. Summer was also
sitting at the table, but attired in a white gown. He rushed over to her
and grasped her by the shoulders.

"Are you all right?"

She turned slowly and looked up at him as if in a trance. "All right?
Yes, I'm all right."

He could see that she was heavily drugged. "What have they done
to you?"

"Please sit down, Mr. Pitt," ordered the woman seated at the head
of the table, who was attired in a gold gown. When she spoke, her
voice was quiet and musical, but touched with arrogance.

Dirk sensed a movement behind him. The guard had withdrawn
from the room and closed the door. For a brief instant, he thought that
even though the women outnumbered him, he could do enough damage to incapacitate them and make a run for it with Summer, but he
could see that she was so heavily sedated that she couldn't run anywhere. He slowly pulled out a chair at the opposite end of the table
and sat down. "Can I inquire as to your intentions regarding my sister and me?"

"You may," said the woman obviously in charge. Then she ignored
him and turned to the woman on her right. "You searched their boat?"

"Yes, Epona. We found dive gear and underwater detection
equipment."

"I apologize for any intrusion," said Dirk, "but we thought the island was deserted."

Epona stared at him, her eyes hard and cold. "We have ways of dealing with trespassers."

"We were on an archaeological expedition to find ancient shipwrecks. Nothing more."

She glanced at Summer, then back to Dirk. "We know what you
were searching for. Your sister was most cooperative in providing us
with a full report."

"After you drugged her," said Dirk, maddened within an inch of coming across the table after the woman.

It was as if she read his mind. "Do not think of resisting, Mr. Pitt. My guards will respond in an instant."

Dirk forced himself to relax and act indifferent. "So what did Summer tell you?"

"That you and she work for the National Underwater and Marine Agency and that you were here looking for Odysseus' lost fleet that Homer described as being sunk by the Laestrygonians."

"You have read Homer."

"I live and breathe Homer the Celt, not Homer the Greek."

"Then you know the true story of Troy and of Odysseus' voyage across the ocean."

"The reason my sisters and I are here. Ten years ago, through long years of research, we concluded that it was the Celts and not the Greeks who fought the Trojans, and not for the love of Helen but the tin deposits in Cornwall to make bronze. Like you, we retraced Odysseus' wake across the Atlantic. You might be interested in learning that his fleet was not destroyed by huge rocks thrown by the Laestrygonians, but was destroyed by a hurricane."

"And the treasure from his lost fleet?"

"Salvaged eight years ago and used to build our Odyssey financial empire."

Dirk sat quite still, but his hands were trembling out of sight under the table. A warning light blinked on inside his head. These women might allow Summer to live, but he doubted they would let him see another sunrise. "May I ask what the treasure consisted of?"

Epona shrugged. "I see no reason to conceal the results. There is no mystery to our achievement. Our salvage teams recovered over two tons of golden objects, plates, sculptures and other decorative Celtic objects. They were masters of intricate metalworking. These, along with thousands of other ancient artifacts, we sold on the open market around the world, netting just over seven hundred million dollars."

"Wasn't that risky?" asked Dirk. "The French, who own Guadeloupe, the Greeks and the nations of Europe that were once ruled by the Celts, didn't they step in and demand ownership of the treasures?"

"The secret was well-kept. All the buyers of the artifacts wished to remain anonymous and all the transactions were discreetly completed, including the gold, which was placed in depositories in China."

"You mean the People's Republic of China, of course."

"Of course."

"What about the salvage operators and their divers? They would have expected a share of the spoils, and keeping them quiet would not have been easy."

"They received nothing," said Epona, with a sardonic inflection, "and the secret died with them."

The innuendo was not lost on Dirk. "You murdered them?" He said it as if it was a fact rather than an assumption.

"Let's simply say, they joined Odysseus' crews who were lost," she hesitated and then smiled enigmatically. "Nobody who ever came to this island lived to tell of it. Even tourists who anchored their boat in the harbor or simple fishermen who became too curious. They could not tell what they have seen."

"So far I haven't seen anything worth dying for."

"And you won't."

Dirk felt a moment of uneasiness. "Why the fiendishness? Why murder innocent people? Where are you sociopaths coming from, and what do you hope to accomplish?"

There was just the slightest edge of anger in Epona's voice. "You are quite correct, Mr. Pitt. My sisters and I are all sociopaths. We conduct our lives and our fortunes without emotion. That is why we have come so far and accomplished so much in such a few short years. If left to their own devices, sociopaths could rule the world. They are not possessed by morality, nor influenced or hindered by ethics. Complete absence of sentiment makes it easier to achieve their goals. Sociopaths enjoy the highest level of genius and nothing else matters. Yes, Mr. Pitt, I am a sociopath and so is our sisterhood of goddesses."

"The sisterhood of goddesses," Dirk repeated very slowly, accenting each word. "So you have elevated yourselves to deities. Being mortal isn't good enough for you."

"The great leaders of the past were all sociopaths and a few came very close to ruling the world."

"Like Hitler, Stalin, Attila the Hun and Napoleon. The mental institutions are overflowing with inmates who have dreams of grandeur."

"They all failed because they overestimated their power. We do not intend to make that mistake."

Dirk looked around the table at the beautiful women. It did not go unnoticed that his sister's red hair matched theirs as well. "Despite the fact you have the same hair color, you can't all be blood siblings."

"No, we are not actually related."

"When you say *we*, who do you include?"

"The women of the sisterhood. *We*, Mr. Pitt, are of the Druid religion. We follow the long-lost teachings of the Celtic Druids handed down through the centuries."

"The ancient Druids were more myth than fact."

Irritation flickered at the corners of Epona's lips. "They have existed for five thousand years."

"They're only the stuff of which legends are made. No records of their religion and rituals existed until one hundred years before Christ."

"No written records, but their knowledge and spheres of power were handed down by word of mouth through hundreds of generations. The Druids originated in the ancient Celtic tribes. Circled around the campfires at night, they offered their people dreams of happiness amid the day-to-day toil to stay alive. They conceived their mysticism, philosophy and perception. They became gifted at creating a religion that inspired and enlightened the Celtic world. They acted as doctors, magicians, seers, mystics, advisors and, perhaps most important, they became teachers who aroused a desire for learning. Because of them, a higher intelligence began to spread throughout the Western world. To become a Druid, young men and women studied up to twenty years until they became walking encyclopedias. Diogenes the Greek said the Druids were the world's wisest philosophers. Many Druids were women who became goddesses and were worshiped throughout Celtic culture."

Dirk shrugged. "Druidism was a pathetic illusion. It was also evil. They held human sacrifice then, and today you conduct murder and go about your business as if the people you killed never existed. Druidism died centuries ago and you won't accept it."

"Like most men, you have stone for a brain. Druidism, though ancient in concept, is as relevant and alive today as it was five thousand years ago. What you don't realize, Mr. Pitt, is that we are experiencing a Renaissance. Because Druidism has a timeless wisdom and is spiritual and charismatic, it has been reborn around the world."

"Does it still include human sacrifice?"

"If the ritual calls for it."

Dirk was repulsed by the thought that these women could actually believe in and take part in religious sacrifice as an excuse for murder. He began to see that if he couldn't take Summer and flee the island, the same fate was likely in store for them. He stared at the polished surface of the table, composing himself, and noted there was a long metal curtain rod that would make a good weapon.

Epona paused. "By adhering to the principles of Druidism, my sisters and I have helped raised a formidable business that reaches around the world in real estate, construction and development, fields that men traditionally dominate, but we found that collectively we could outsmart them at every turn. Yes, we built an empire, one so powerful that soon we will control the economy of most of the Western world through our development of fuel cell technology."

"Technology can be duplicated in time. No one, not even your empire, can hold a monopoly for long. There are too many great scientific minds and the money to back them to improve your model."

Epona spoke equably. "They have all been left at the starting gate. Once our operation is up and running, it will be too late."

"I'm afraid I don't know what you're talking about. What operation?"

"Your friends at NUMA know."

Dirk was only half listening. He was intrigued by the fact that none of the other women around the table spoke. They sat there like figures in a wax museum. He studied them to see if they were drugged, but saw no indication. He began to realize that they were under the total spell of Epona. It looked as if they were brainwashed.

"They apparently didn't bother to inform me. I know nothing of this operation you speak of."

"Under my direction, Mr. Specter . . ." She paused. "Do you know of him?"

"Only what I've read in the newspapers," Dirk lied. "He's some kind of wealthy eccentric, like Howard Hughes."

"Mr. Specter is also the genius behind Odyssey's success. What we have accomplished is due to his superior intelligence."

"I had the impression you were the brains of the outfit."

"My sisters and I carry out Mr. Specter's directives."

A knock came at the door and a woman in the green jumpsuit entered, walked around the table and handed a piece of paper to Epona before leaving the room. Epona studied the message and her expression crumpled from arrogance to horror. She looked as if she had been struck and a hand flew to her mouth. Finally, as though in a daze, she announced in a voice choked with emotion, "This is from our office in Managua. Our Ometepe research center and the tunnels have been destroyed by a collapse of the Concepcion volcano."

The news was received in utter anguish and astonishment. "It's gone, all gone?" asked one of the women in total disbelief.

Epona slowly nodded. "It's been confirmed. The center now lies at the bottom of Lake Nicaragua."

"Was everyone killed?" asked another. "Were there no survivors?"

"The workers were all saved by a fleet of boats around the lake and helicopters from United States Special Forces that attacked our headquarters. Our sisters, who heroically defended our headquarters building, were all killed."

Epona rose and moved away from her chair. She took Summer by the arm and pulled her to her feet. Then the two of them walked haltingly toward the door as if one was in a dream and the other a nightmare. Epona turned, the red-contoured lips spread in a leer. Her head tilted toward Dirk a fraction.

"Enjoy your last few hours on Earth, Mr. Pitt."

Then the door opened, the guard walked in and pressed the muzzle of her gun against Dirk's temple as he came to his feet, knocking over the chair, and made a move toward Epona with murder in his eyes. He stopped dead in his tracks, raging with frustration.

"And bid farewell to your sister. You won't be enjoying her company again."

Then she placed her arm around Summer and led her from the room.

46

THE SUN BLAZED DOWN on the asphalt outside the private
aircraft terminal of the Managua International Airport as Pitt
and Giordino stood under a covered patio and watched the NUMA ·
Citation jet land. The pilot took it down to the last turnout and taxied back to the terminal. As soon as the plane came to a halt, the door
was opened from the inside and Rudi Gunn stepped to the ground.

"Oh, no," Giordino groaned. "I can smell it in the air. We're not
going home."

Gunn did not walk toward them but motioned for them to approach the plane. As they neared, he said, "Climb aboard, we haven't
time to spare."

Without comment Pitt and Giordino threw their bags into the cargo
compartment. They had no sooner sat down and snapped their seat-
belt buckles than the turbines roared and the plane was speeding down
the runway and rising into the air.

"Don't tell me," said Giordino dryly, "we're going to spend eternity
in Nicaragua."

"Why the rush?" Pitt asked Gunn.

"Dirk and Summer have disappeared," Gunn said without prelude.

"Disappeared," said Pitt, with a sudden flash of apprehension in his eyes. "Where?"

"Guadeloupe. The admiral sent them to an offshore island to search for the remains of Odysseus' fleet of ships thought to be destroyed there during his voyage from Troy."

"Go on."

"Mr. Charles Moreau, who is our representative for that part of the Caribbean, called last night and said that all communication with your son and daughter had ceased. Repeated attempts to contact them proved fruitless."

"Was there a storm?"

Gunn shook his head. "The weather was ideal. Moreau rented a plane and flew over Branwyn Island, where Dirk and Summer were headed. Their boat had vanished and there was no sign of them on or around the island."

Pitt felt as if a great weight was pressing against his chest. The appalling possibility that his children might be injured or dead was barred from his mind. For a moment he was incapable of believing harm had come to them. But then he looked into the face of the usually taciturn Giordino and saw a look of deep concern.

"We're headed there now," Pitt said, as if it was a point of fact.

Gunn nodded. "We'll land at the airport in Guadeloupe. Moreau has arranged for a helicopter to take us directly to Branwyn."

"Any speculation as to what might have happened to them?" asked Giordino.

"All we know is what Moreau has told us."

"What of this island? Are there inhabitants? A fishing village?"

A grave expression spread across Gunn's face. "The island is privately owned."

"By whom?"

"A woman by the name of Epona Eliade."

Surprise showed in Pitt's opaline green eyes. "Epona, yes, of course, it would be her."

"Hiram Yaeger ran an extensive check on her. She's at the top level of Odyssey and is reported to be Specter's right hand." He stopped and gazed at Pitt. "You know her?"

"We met briefly when Al and I rescued the Lowenhardts and snatched Flidais. It looked as though she was high in the Odyssey hierarchy. I understand she wasn't killed during the fighting at Odyssey's research center."

"Apparently she slipped through the net before the center was destroyed. Admiral Sandecker asked the CIA to trace her. One of their agents reported that her private plane was detected by satellite on a landing approach to the airfield on Branwyn Island."

Pitt was holding in his fear with difficulty. Then he said in quiet certainty, with unshakable conviction in his voice, "If Epona is responsible for any harm that might come to Dirk or Summer, she'll never live to collect her retirement pay."

DUSK HAD TURNED to dark when the NUMA jet landed in Guadeloupe and taxied to a private hangar. Moreau was standing beside the ground crew as Pitt, Giordino and Gunn exited the plane. He introduced himself and quickly escorted them less than a hundred feet to a waiting helicopter.

"An old Bell JetRanger," said Giordino, admiring the beautifully restored old helicopter. "I haven't seen one of those in a while."

"It's used for tourist sight-seeing," explained Moreau. "It was all I could arrange on short notice."

"She'll do just fine," said Pitt.

He threw his duffel bag inside and entered the craft, moving to the cockpit, where he conversed briefly with the pilot, a man in his early sixties with many thousands of hours in the air in two dozen different types of aircraft. After he lost his wife to cancer and retired as chief pilot on a major airline, Gordy Shepard had come to Guadeloupe and taken a part-time job flying tourists around the islands. His hair was a neatly brushed bush of gray that complemented his black eyes.

"That's a maneuver I haven't attempted in a long time," said Shepard, after hearing Pitt's instructions. "But I think I can handle it for you."

"If not," Pitt said with a taut grin, "my friend and I will hit the water with the force of cannonballs."

Outside, Gunn thanked Moreau and closed the door as the rotor blades began to slowly revolve, increasing their beat until the pilot lifted the craft off the ground.

It took less than fifteen minutes to cover the twenty-seven miles from the airport to the island. At Pitt's request, once they were over water, the pilot flew without lights. Flying above the sea at night was like sitting blindfolded in a closet sealed with duct tape. Using the light beacon on the island as a guide, Shepard flew an unerring straight line for the south shore.

Back in the passenger compartment, Pitt and Giordino opened the duffel bag and put on wet suits and nothing else except hard rubber boots. They carried no scuba gear, fins or masks, only weight belts to compensate for the buoyancy of the neoprene wet suits. The only equipment Pitt took was his satellite phone inside a small waterproof bag tightly belted to his stomach. Then they moved to the rear of the compartment and opened the cargo hatch.

Pitt nodded at Gunn. "Okay, Rudi, I'll call in case we need a quick getaway."

Gunn held up his phone and grinned. "It shall remain glued to my hand until you tell me to evacuate you, Al and the kids off the island."

Though he didn't fully share Gunn's optimism, he was grateful for the show of confidence. He lifted a phone from a vertical base on the bulkhead and called the pilot. "All set back here."

"Stand ready," instructed Shepard. "We'll be coming up over the harbor in three minutes. You sure you've got enough water depth for your dive?"

"Jump," Pitt corrected him. "If you programmed the correct GPS coordinates and stop on them, we should have enough water to cushion us from striking the bottom."

"I'll do my best," acknowledged Shepard. "Then your friend, Mr. Gunn, and I will make it look like we're flying on toward another nearby island before circling back and waiting for your call to come and get you."

"You know the drill."

"I wish you boys luck," Shepard said over the phone, as he closed communications to the passenger compartment. Then he straightened in his seat with both hands and feet on the controls and focused his mind on the maneuver coming up.

The island looked dark, as if it was deserted, the only light was the beacon above its metal frame. Pitt could just vaguely distinguish the faint outline of the buildings and the Stonehenge replica in the middle of the island on a slight rise. It would be a tricky approach, but Shepard seemed as calm as a mobster in a box seat at the Kentucky Derby, knowing the fastest horse was about to throw the race because he paid off the jockey.

Shepard brought the old Bell JetRanger in from the sea right up the center of the channel into the harbor. In the rear, Pitt and Giordino stood poised in the cargo door. The airspeed was nearly a hundred and twenty miles an hour when Shepard's hands and feet danced over the controls and the helicopter stood on its tail and came to an abrupt stop, twisting to starboard and allowing Pitt and Giordino to jump unobstructed through the door into the darkness. Then Shepard pushed the helicopter forward and picked up speed again, banking around the island and heading out to sea. The entire maneuver went off flawlessly. To anyone observing on the island, it hardly looked like the helicopter came to a stop.

Holding their breath, Pitt and Giordino dropped thirty feet before striking the water. Despite their attempts to fall cleanly feet first, the sudden tilt of the helicopter prevented a smooth jump. They found themselves tumbling through the air and doubled up with arms clasped around their knees to prevent smashing into the solid wall of liquid in a flat position that could have badly injured them or at least knocked the wind out of their lungs and rendered them unconscious. The neoprene wet suits absorbed most of the harsh impact, as they struck the surface and plunged nearly ten feet into the deep before losing all momentum.

Feeling like they'd run a gauntlet through sadists beating on them with flat boards, they stroked to the surface just in time to see a pair of searchlights flash on and sweep the water until they found their target and lit up the helicopter like a Christmas tree ornament. Shepard was an old pro who had flown in Vietnam. He anticipated what would happen next. He suddenly dipped the helicopter toward the sea in a steep dive just as a hail of automatic-rifle fire split the night and sprayed the area a good hundred feet behind the tail rotor. Then he spun the aircraft wildly and clawed for altitude. Again the gunfire went wide.

Shepard knew his antics wouldn't keep the wolves from his door much longer, not with the searchlights clinging to him like leeches. Second-guessing the gunmen on the island, he brought the Bell to a quick stop and hovered for a split second. The gunmen, having learned their lesson, led the helicopter and fired at its intended path, but Shepard had conned them again. The trajectory of their fire tore through the air fifty feet in front of the cockpit.

Incredibly, Shepard had gained over half a mile on the gunners and swooped away as the parting shots stitched the fuselage, worked their way toward the cockpit and shattered the windshield. A bullet struck Shepard's arm and passed through his biceps without hitting bone. Gunn had flung himself down and forward and took a small crease on the top of his head that would have removed half his skull if he hadn't ducked.

In the water, Pitt watched with growing relief as the helicopter flew beyond the range of the island's gunners and vanished into the darkness. Not knowing if Gunn or Shepard had been injured, he knew that they could not return as long as concentrated fire swept the skies above the island.

"They can't return until we take out the searchlights," said Giordino, floating on his back as leisurely as if he was in the pool at his condo.

"We'll worry about that little problem after we find out what happened to Dirk and Summer." Pitt stared at the island, his voice firm with the confidence of a man who was gazing at something unseen by others. Then he saw the searchlights lower their beams and begin sweeping over the waters of the harbor.

They dove under, not wasting a breath on warning the other, knowing their instincts were tightly bonded over the years. Pitt rolled over on his back at ten feet and stared up at the surface, seeing the glow of the brilliant light flash over the surface with the brightness of the sun. Only when the lights moved off did they surface and catch a breath. They had been down over a minute, but neither gasped for air, having practiced the art of holding their breath for deep dives without breathing equipment.

When the light beams above danced away, they surfaced, took a breath and dove again. Warily watching the movements of the searchlight and timing its sweep to gain air, they began stroking toward shore that was little more than a hundred yards away. At last the lights blinked out and they could resume swimming on the surface. Ten minutes later their feet touched sand. They rose to their feet, dropped their weight belts and crept into the shadows beneath a bank of rocks, resting for a few moments while appraising the situation.

"Where to?" asked Giordino in a whisper.

"We've landed south of the house and about two hundred yards east of the Stonehenge replica," Pitt replied quietly.

"A folly," said Giordino.

"What?"

"Fake castles and facsimile ancient structures are called follies. Remember?"

"It's burned in my brain," Pitt muttered. "Come on. Let's scout around, find and sabotage the searchlights. It won't do to have them expose us like a pair of rabbits."

It took them another eight minutes to locate the twin searchlights. They almost stumbled on them in the dark. The only thing that saved them from being discovered by the guards manning the lights was their black wet suits, which made them almost invisible in the night. They discerned the outlines of one man lounging on his back in the sand while another peered out to sea with night glasses. Not expecting intruders from their rear creeping onto the raised stand mounting the lights from behind, they were not alert.

Giordino came out of the darkness silently, but the squeak of his rubber-soled boots gave him away and the man with the night glasses spun around in time to see a shadow coming at him out of the night. He grabbed an automatic rifle propped on its butt against the light mount and swung the muzzle toward Giordino. He never pulled the trigger. Pitt had come up from the opposite side five steps ahead of his friend. He snatched the rifle out of the guard's hands and clubbed him over the head with the stock. Then Giordino was on the guard relaxing on the ground, knocking him unconscious with a well-delivered fist to the side of the jaw.

"Doesn't it give you a comfortable feeling to know we're armed?" said Giordino buoyantly, as he disarmed the guards and handed Pitt one of the rifles.

Pitt didn't bother to reply, as he unlatched the lenses of the searchlights, swung them open and lightly, with the slightest of sound, smashed the filaments. "Let's check the house next. Then your folly."

There was no moon, but they took no chances and moved slowly, cautiously, barely seeing the ground beneath their feet. The hard rubber boots protected their feet from the sharp coral that lay between patches of smooth sand. They found a frond under a palm tree and dragged it behind to obscure their footprints. If they couldn't get off the island before daylight, they would have to find a place to hide out until Moreau and Gunn could arrange a rescue.

The house was a large colonial structure with a wide veranda running around the entire building. They crept onto the veranda, moving silently in their rubber-soled boots. A single light could be seen through a crack in the boards over the windows, put there to protect them from the ravages of a hurricane-inspired gale. Pitt moved on his hands and knees to the window and peered through the crack. The room on the other side was bare of furniture. The interior had the look of a house that hadn't been lived in for years.

Unable to see a need for further stealth, Pitt stood and said to Giordino in a normal tone, "This place is abandoned and has been for a long time."

The expression of puzzlement on Giordino's face was not visible in the darkness. "That doesn't make sense. The owner of an exotic island in the West Indies who never stays in the only house. What is the purpose of owning such a spot?"

"Moreau said aircraft and people came in and out during certain times of the year. They must have some other place for guests to stay."

"It would have to be underground," said Giordino. "The only surface structures are the house, the folly and a small aircraft maintenance hangar."

"Then why the armed reception committee?" mused Pitt. "What is Epona trying to hide?"

He was answered by the abrupt sound of strange music, followed by an array of colored lights that flashed on and around the Stonehenge folly.

THE DOOR to Dirk's cell clanged as it was thrown open against its stop. The afternoon heat lingered and the small airspace was still sweltering hot. The female guard motioned him out into the hallway with the muzzle of her rifle. Dirk felt a sudden cold, as if he had stepped into a refrigerator. Goose bumps ran down his arms and across his back. He knew it was useless to question the guard. She would tell him nothing of interest.

They did not enter the exotically decorated room, but passed through a door and stepped into a long concrete corridor that appeared to stretch into infinity. They walked for what seemed almost an entire mile before coming to a circular staircase that wound upward for what Dirk estimated as four stories. At the top, a landing led through a stone arch to a large thronelike chair that sat dimly illuminated by a golden light. Two women in blue gowns stepped out of the darkness and chained him to rings clamped into the chair. One of them tied a black silk gag over his mouth. Then all three women faded back into the darkness.

Suddenly, an array of lavender-colored lights flashed on and swirled around the interior of a concave stone amphitheater bowl built without seats for an audience. Next a set of laser beams lit the black sky, illuminating a series of columns spaced around the bowl and a larger outer ring of black lava columns. Only then did Dirk see a huge block of black stone shaped like a sarcophagus. He tensed and threw himself forward, only to be stopped by the chains as he identified it as some kind of altar used for sacrificial rituals. Sheer horror widened his eyes above the gag as he recognized Summer in a white gown spread-eagled on top of the great black stone, as if somehow bound to the hard surface. A cold fear ran through him as he struggled like a madman in a futile attempt to break his chains or pull them from their rings. Despite a strength enhanced by adrenaline, his efforts were in vain. No humans numbering less than four Arnold Schwarzeneggers could have broken the links of the chains or pulled them out of the stone chair. Still, he fought until he hadn't the strength to struggle any longer.

The lights suddenly blinked out and the odd sounds of Celtic music echoed among the upright stones. Ten minutes later they flashed on again, revealing the thirty women in their colorful flowing gowns. Their red hair gleamed under the lights and the silver flecks on their skin twinkled like stars. Then the lights spiraled as they had many times before as Epona appeared in her golden peplos gown. She stepped up to the black sacrificial altar, raised her hand and began to chant, *"O daughters of Odysseus and Circe, may life be taken from those who are not worthy."*

Epona's voice droned on, pausing as the other women raised their arms and chanted in unison. As before, the chant was repeated, becoming louder before dropping off to inaudible whispers as they lowered their arms.

Dirk could see that Summer was oblivious to her surroundings. She stared at Epona and the columns rising around the altar, not seeing them. There was no fear in her eyes. She was so heavily drugged that she had no concept of the threat on her life.

Epona reached inside the folds of her gown and raised the ceremonial dagger above her head. The other women came up the steps and surrounded their goddess, also producing daggers held above their heads.

Dirk's green eyes were stricken, they were the eyes of someone who knows his world will soon be shrouded in tragedy. He screamed in anguish, but the sound of his voice was muted by the gag.

Epona then uttered the death chant: *"Here lies one who should not have been born."*

Her knife and the knives of the others glinted under the swirling lights.

47

IN THE SPLIT SECOND before she and the others could plunge their daggers into Summer's helpless body, two phantoms encased entirely in black materialized as if by magic in front of the altar. The tall figure grabbed Epona's upraised wrist, twisted it and forced her to her knees, to the utter shock of the women surrounding Summer.

"Not tonight," said Pitt. "The show is over."

Giordino moved like a cat around the altar, swinging the barrel of his gun from one woman to another in case they had any ideas of interfering. "Stand back!" he ordered harshly. "Drop your knives and move to the edge of the steps."

Keeping the muzzle of his rifle pressed against Epona's breast with one hand, Pitt coolly went about freeing Summer, who was bound to the altar by a single strap across her stomach.

Confused and fearful, the red-haired women slowly backed away from the altar and grouped together, as if impelled by an instinctive urge of protection. Giordino wasn't fooled for an instant. Their sisters had fought the Special Forces on Ometepe like tigers. His muscles tensed as he saw they made no move to drop their daggers, and began moving in a circle around him. Giordino knew this wasn't the time for niceties, such as asking them again to drop their daggers. He took careful aim, squeezed the trigger of his rifle and shot off the left earring of the woman who looked as if she carried the weight of authority.

Now Giordino stiffened when he saw the woman seemed incapable of pain or emotion. No hand lifted to feel the pain and the trickle of blood from her earlobe. She merely fixed Giordino with a fixed look of rage.

He snapped over his shoulder at Pitt, who was busily trying to unbuckle the strap binding Summer to the top of the stone. "I need some help. These crazy females are acting like they're about to charge."

"That's only the half of it. The island's security guards will come running when they get wise that all is not well."

Pitt looked up and saw the thirty women begin moving back toward the altar. It went against all his breeding and upbringing to unmercifully shoot a woman, but there was more than their own lives at stake. His children would die too if they didn't stop thirty hard-core members of the sisterhood from rushing them with slashing knives. It was as if a pack of wolves were circling a pair of lions. With guns against knives, one against five still gave the men an advantage, but a mass rush of fifteen against one was too one-sided.

Pitt stopped in the act of freeing a drugged Summer. In the same instant, Epona jerked her wrist out of Pitt's grip, slicing a deep cut in his palm with a razor-sharp ring. He grabbed her hand and glanced at the ring that gashed his hand. It held a tanzanite stone cut in the design of the Uffington horse. He disregarded the stabbing pain and pushed her away. Then he brought up his rifle.

Unable to murder but at least maim to keep his closest friend and children from a bloody death, he calmly fired off four shots that struck the nearest women in the feet. All four went down with cries of pain and shock. The others hesitated, but hyped-up with anger and fanaticism they began to press forward, making threatening motions with the daggers.

No more mentally geared to kill a woman than Pitt, Giordino slowly, methodically, took Pitt's cue and began shooting the women in the feet, downing five of them who crumpled in a heap together.

"Stop!" Pitt shouted. "Or we will shoot to kill."

Those still unscathed paused and looked down at their sisters writhing at their feet. One of them, who was dressed in a silver gown, raised her dagger high over her head and let it drop with a clang onto the stone floor. Slowly, one by one, the others followed suit until they all stood with empty hands outstretched.

"Tend to your wounded!"

Quickly, Pitt finished releasing Summer, as Giordino covered the women and kept an eye out for any alerted guards. He cursed himself at finding that Epona had escaped and vanished during the melee. Seeing Summer was in no condition to walk on her own, Pitt threw her over his shoulder and made his way to the throne, where he rapidly pried apart the rings holding Dirk's chains with the barrel of his weapon.

After pulling his gag off, Dirk gasped, "Dad, where in God's name did you and Al come from?"

"I guess you could say we dropped from the sky," said Pitt, happily embracing his son.

"You cut it close. Another few seconds and . . ." His voice trailed off at the grim thought.

"Now we have to figure a way out of here." Then Pitt stared into Summer's glazed eyes. "Is she all right?" he asked Dirk.

"Those Druid witches drugged her to the gills."

Pitt wished that he still had Epona clutched in his hands. But there was no sign of her. She had deserted her sisters and disappeared into the darkness beyond the ritual stones. He removed the satellite phone from the pack around his waist and dialed a number. After a long pause, Gunn's voice came over the receiver. "Dirk?"

"What's your status?" asked Pitt. "It looked as if you took hits."

"Shepard took a bullet through his upper arm, but it was a clean wound and I bandaged it up the best I could."

"Can he still fly?"

"He's a tough old dog. Too mad not to fly."

"How about you?"

"One bounced off my head," Gunn answered buoyantly, "but I suspect the bullet took the worst of it."

"Are you airborne?"

"Yes, about three miles north of the island." Then Gunn asked hesitantly, "Dirk and Summer?"

"Safe and sound."

"Thank God for that. Are you ready to be picked up?"

"Come and get us."

"Can you tell me what you found?"

"Answers to questions come later."

Pitt switched off the phone and looked down at Summer, who was being brought back to reality by Giordino and Dirk as they walked her back and forth to get her circulation restored. While waiting for the helicopter, he walked around the sacrificial block, watching for any sign of Epona's security guards, but none appeared. Then the lights around the stones blinked out and his world turned black as silence settled over the pagan amphitheater.

By the time Gunn and Shepard reappeared, the roar of jet engines could be heard on the island's airstrip as several planes took off, one almost on the tail of the one in front. Confident now there was no danger from guards appearing out of the night, Pitt informed Shepard that he could turn on his landing lights when they arrived to lift them up. When the helicopter arrived and hovered briefly before descending, Pitt could see they were alone inside the bowl of the ritual stones. All the women had vanished. He looked up into a cloudless sky carpeted with a million stars, wondering what destination Epona was headed for. What were her plans now that her freakish operation that would have caused undue suffering to millions of people lay in ruins beneath Lake Nicaragua?

She would be a wanted woman now that it was known she had conducted criminal acts for her boss, Specter. International law enforcement agencies would be on her trail. Every aspect of Odyssey's operations would be investigated. Lawsuits would fill courts in Europe and America. Whether Odyssey could survive the scrutiny was doubtful. And what of Specter? What was his role in the scheme? He was the man at the top, so he had to be responsible. What force governed the relationship between Specter and Epona? The questions spun in Pitt's mind without answers.

The enigma would have to be solved by others, he thought. His role, and that of Giordino, was thankfully finished. He turned his thoughts to more mundane matters, like his own future. He looked up as Giordino came over and stood next to him.

"This may be a strange time to bring this up," said Giordino almost as if he was meditating. "But I've been giving it a lot of thought, especially during the past ten days. I've come to the conclusion that I'm getting too old to be chasing around the oceans and getting involved with Sandecker's crazy ventures. I'm tired of madcap exploits and wild escapades or expeditions that come within inches of halting my productive love life. I can't do all the things I used to do. My joints ache and my sore muscles take twice as long to heal."

Pitt looked at him and smiled. "So what's your point?"

"The admiral has a choice. I can either be put out to pasture and find a cushy job with an ocean engineering company or he can put me in charge of NUMA's underwater technical equipment department. Any job where I don't have to be maimed or shot at."

Pitt turned and stared for a long moment over the restless black sea. Then he gazed at Dirk and Summer, as his son helped his daughter to board the aircraft. They were his future.

"You know," he said finally. "You've been reading my mind."

PART FIVE

Exposed

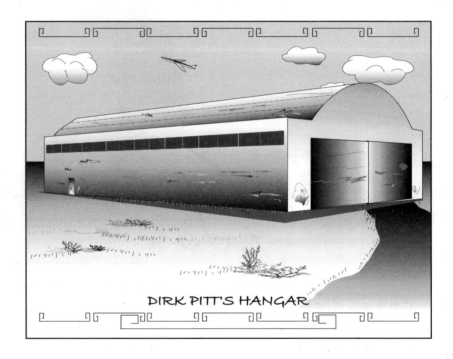

DIRK PITT'S HANGAR

48

A T NINE O'CLOCK in the morning, three days after he and
his offspring returned to his hangar, Pitt adjusted the tie to his
sincere suit, as he called it, his one and only tailored black pin-striped
suit with vest. Then he buttoned the vest and set an antique gold
pocket watch in one pocket, draping a gold chain through a button-
hole with the weighted end going into a pocket on the opposite side.
It was not often he wore the suit, but this was a very special day.

Specter had been apprehended by Federal marshals when his pilot
made the mistake of landing in San Juan, Puerto Rico, for fuel during
a flight to Montreal. He was served with a subpoena to appear and tes-
tify before a congressional committee that was investigating his shady
mining operations within United States territory. The marshals took
him into custody and transported him to Washington so there was no
way he could flee to another country. Because his attempted operation
to freeze North America and Europe took place outside the nation's
jurisdiction in a foreign country, he was exempt from Federal prose-

cution. If anything, the committee had its hands tied. There was little hope of a legal victory. The most they could accomplish was to expose Specter's dealings and hamstring any of his future operations inside the United States.

Epona, however, had escaped the net and her whereabouts were totally unknown. She was another matter the committee planned to question Specter about.

Pitt made one last check in an antique upright mirror that had come from the first-class stateroom of an old steamship. His only departure from the rest of the Washington herd was a gray-and-white paisley tie. His thick black curly hair was neatly brushed and his green eyes were clear with their usual twinkle, despite the lack of sleep from an all-night tryst with Loren. He walked over to his desk and picked up the knife he'd taken from Epona on Branwyn Island. The hilt was encrusted with rubies and emeralds, the blade was thin and sharpened on both sides. He slipped it into the inside breast pocket of his coat.

He stepped down his ornate iron circular staircase to the floor filled with old land and air vehicles. A NUMA Navigator SUV stood in front of the main door. It was a big car to drive the busy streets of the capital, but he found it responsive and enjoyed the comfortable ride. The NUMA name and color also provided him with a government vehicle that provided parking places not available for personal cars.

He drove over the bridge into the core of the city and parked in a government-only parking area two blocks from the Capitol Building. Once he climbed the great staircase and entered under the dome, he followed Loren's instructions to the meeting room where the investigation was being held. Not wishing to pass through the doors open to journalists and the public, he walked through the corridors until he came to a Capitol security guard who stood beside the door reserved for the House of Representatives' committee, their aides and lawyers.

Pitt gave the guard a slip of paper and asked him to give it to Congresswoman Loren Smith.

"I'm not supposed to do that," protested the guard in a gray uniform.

"It's extremely urgent," said Pitt in an authoritative voice. "I have a pivotal piece of evidence for her and the committee."

Pitt displayed his NUMA credentials to show the guard he was not someone who had walked in off the street. The guard compared the photo on the ID with his face, nodded, took the note and stepped into the committee room.

Ten minutes later, when there was a break in the questioning, Loren came through the door. "What's this all about?" she asked, her perfectly shaped brows raised.

"I have to get in the room."

She looked at him, confused. "You could have come through the public doors."

"I have an item which will expose Specter for what he is."

"Give it to me, and I'll present it to the committee."

He shook his head. "No can do. I have to present it myself."

"I can't let you do that," she countered. "You're not on the list of witnesses."

"Make an exception," he persisted. "Ask the chairman."

She stared into the eyes she knew so well, looking for something but not finding it. "Dirk, I simply can't do that. You've got to tell me what it is you're doing."

The guard was standing nearby, listening to the conversation. The door, normally locked, was standing slightly ajar. Pitt took Loren by the shoulders, turned her around in one swift motion and pushed her into the guard. Before they could stop him, he was through the door and walking rapidly along the aisle between the seated representatives and their aides. No one made any attempt to protest or restrain him from coming down the short stairway to the witness and audience floor. He stopped in front of the table where Specter was seated, surrounded by his high-priced attorneys.

2222222222

Congressman Christopher Dunn of Montana pounded his gavel and called out, "You, sir, are interrupting a very important investigation. I must ask you to leave immediately or I will have the guards escort you out."

"If you will indulge me, Congressman, I will set your investigation onto an entirely different track."

Dunn motioned toward the guard who had chased Pitt into the room. "Remove him!"

Pitt pulled the knife from under this coat and extended it out toward the guard, who stopped dead in his tracks. Slowly, the guard began to reach for his gun, but hesitated when Pitt moved the knife within an inch of his chest.

"Indulge me," he repeated. "Believe me, Congressman, it will be well worth your time to hear me out."

"Who are you, sir?" Dunn demanded.

"My name is Dirk Pitt. I am the son of Senator George Pitt."

Dunn mulled that over for a moment, then nodded at the guard. "Hold on. I want to hear what Mr. Pitt has to say." Then he looked at Pitt. "Drop that knife. Then I'll give you exactly one minute to state your case. You'd better make it good or you'll be behind bars within the next hour."

"You'd arrest the son of an esteemed senator?" asked Pitt facetiously.

"He's a Republican," said Dunn with a crafty grin. "I'm a Democrat."

"Thank you, Congressman." Pitt laid the ornate knife on the table and moved until he was standing opposite Specter, who sat in silent calm, dressed in his white suit with his customary scarf draped around his lower face beneath dark sunglasses. "Will you please stand up, Mr. Specter?"

One of Specter's attorneys leaned over and spoke into the table's microphone. "I must protest most vigorously, Congressman Dunn, against this man who has no business in this room. Mr. Specter is under no legal obligation to acknowledge him."

"Is Specter afraid?" said Pitt tauntingly. "Is he frightened? Is he a coward?" Pitt paused and stared at Specter provokingly.

Specter took the bait. He was too arrogant to ignore Pitt's insults. He put his hand on his attorney's arm to restrain him and slowly heaved his huge bulk up from his chair, until he stood, face unseen, the consummate riddle in an enigma.

Pitt smiled and gave a slight bow, as if in relaxed satisfaction.

Suddenly, before anybody realized what he was doing, he snatched up the knife and slashed the blade across Specter's stomach, slicing through the white suit up to the hilt.

Shouts from the men and screams from the women erupted and reverberated throughout the room. The security guard lunged toward Pitt, who stood ready and stepped aside, tripping the guard and sending him spilling onto the floor. Then he plunged the knife blade into the table in front of Specter and stood back, his expression one of extreme gratification.

Loren, who had leaped to her feet, shouting at Pitt, abruptly went silent. She was one of the first to see that Specter was not bleeding.

Blood and intestines should have flooded onto the surface of the table, but the white suit was unstained with crimson. Soon the hundred or more people who had come to their feet in shock began to notice the same phenomenon.

His face pale, Congressman Dunn stared down at Specter, pounding his gavel like a madman. "What is going on here?" he shouted.

No one interfered as Pitt stepped around the table, pulled off Specter's sunglasses and casually flipped them onto the floor. Then he reached up and pulled off Specter's hat and scarf and threw them on the table.

Everyone in the room gasped at seeing a great mass of red hair fall down around Specter's shoulders.

Pitt approached Congressman Dunn. "Sir, permit me to introduce Ms. Epona Eliade, also known as Specter, the founder of the Odyssey empire."

"Is this true?" said a confused Dunn, coming to his feet. "Is this woman really Specter and not a disguised double?"

"She is the genuine article," Pitt assured him. Then he turned to Epona. "Strange as it sounds, I've missed you," he said, with a voice heavy with sarcasm.

She should have trembled like a mouse filled with fear at the sight of a snake. But she stood tall and did not answer Pitt. She didn't have to. Her eyes flashed, lips tightened, as her face filled with enough hate and contempt to launch a revolution. Then something totally inconceivable happened in the next macabre moment. The look of anger faded from the eyes and tightened lips as abruptly as they appeared. Slowly, very slowly, Epona began removing the knife-slashed white suit until she stood incredibly serene and beautiful in only a white form-fitting silk dress that fell off the shoulders and stopped just below the hips, her red hair cascading past her bare shoulders.

It was a vision that the hearing room and the stunned audience would never witness again.

"You have won, Mr. Pitt," she said, in a soft voice with just a trace of huskiness. "Do you feel triumphant? Do you believe you have accomplished a miracle?"

Pitt shook his head slowly. "Triumphant, no, and certainly no miracle. Gratified, yes. Your outrageous attempt to demoralize the lives of millions of people was despicable. You could have given your great advance in fuel cell technology to the world, and your tunnels under Nicaragua would have provided untold opportunities to reduce the time and cost of shipping cargo through the Panama Canal. Instead, you banded with a foreign nation to gain nothing more than wealth and power."

He could see that she was the mistress of her emotions, and harbored no debate. She smiled a smile that seemed to portend something. No one in that room that day would forget the exotic, compelling creature who exuded a feminine magnetism that was indescribable.

"Pretty words, Mr. Pitt. But meaningless. Except for you, I might have changed the course of world history. That was the goal, the ultimate achievement."

"Few will grieve that you failed," Pitt said with a cold edge in his tone.

Only then did Pitt see the faint look of despair in her captivating eyes. She pulled herself erect and faced the congressional committee.

"Do with me what you wish, but be advised, it will be no small battle to convict me of any crime."

Dunn pointed his gavel at two men seated in the back of the room. "Will the Federal marshals please step forward and take this woman into custody?"

Epona's lawyers immediately leaped to their feet, protesting that it was not in Dunn's power as a congressman to arrest anyone. He glared at them.

"This person has committed a crime in committing fraud in front of this committee. She shall be held until such time as the Attorney General's Office has a chance to review her criminal actions and take the proper legal action."

As the marshals took Epona by the arm and began leading her from the hearing room, she stopped in front of Pitt and stared at him with an expression that was sardonic but oddly lacking anger. "My friends across the sea will never allow me to be prosecuted. We will cross paths again, Mr. Pitt. Nothing ends here. The next time we meet, you will fall into my web, make no mistake."

Pitt brushed aside his wrath and gave her a cool and enigmatic smile. "Next time?" He posed it as a question. "I don't think so, Epona. You're not my type."

The lips went taut with anger again. Her skin noticeably paled and her eyes lost their luster, as the marshals hustled her out a side door. Pitt could not help but admire her beauty. Few women could have made a dramatic exit after a fall from heights with such style and grace. Deep down, his stomach twisted with the thought that he would indeed cross paths with her another day.

Loren came down onto the witness floor and unashamedly hugged Pitt. "You crazy fool. You might have been shot."

"Forgive the theatrics, but I figured now was the time and this was the place to expose the witch."

"Why didn't you tell me?"

"Because, if I was wrong, I didn't want you involved."

"You weren't sure?" she asked in surprise.

"I knew I was on solid ground, but not absolutely positive."

"What put you onto her?"

"At first I was only working on a hunch. When I came here today, I was still only sixty percent certain. But once I came face-to-face with Specter, it seemed obvious to me that even sitting in his chair, the bulk of his weight wasn't distributed like a man who weighed four hundred pounds." Pitt held up his hand and displayed the scar on his palm. "Then I recognized the ring on the index finger of the right hand that Epona used to cut me on Branwyn Island. That clinched it."

Dunn was shouting for order in an attempt to bring the proceedings back on track. Not caring what anybody in the committee room thought, Loren gave Pitt a light kiss on the cheek.

"I must get back to work. You've opened a can of worms that has changed the entire course of the investigation."

Pitt began to move away, as if he was leaving, but turned and took Loren's hand. "Will a week from Sunday work for you?"

"What's happening a week from Sunday?" she asked innocently.

His lips spread in the devilish grin she knew so well. "That's the day of our wedding. I reserved the Washington Cathedral."

Then he left the Colorado congresswoman standing there with a dazed look in her gray eyes, and walked from the room.

49

N O WAY WAS LOREN buying into a wedding only ten days away. She insisted the nuptials be held one month later, which gave her barely enough time to plan the event, reserve a place for the ceremony, have a seamstress fit her with her mother's wedding dress and arrange for the reception, which would take place amid Pitt's old cars in his hangar.

The ceremony took place at the Washington National Cathedral that sits on Mount Saint Alban, a hill that dominates the capital city skyline. Officially called the Cathedral Church of Saint Peter and Saint Paul, it took from 1907 until 1990 to complete it. The first stone was laid in the presence of Theodore Roosevelt. Shaped like the letter *T,* two towers stand on each side of the entrance at the bottom of the *T.* The third, the bell tower containing the bells, soars more than three hundred feet. The cathedral was built with the same architectural design as those in Europe eight hundred years ago. It is considered the last pure Gothic architecture in the world.

Inside, there are two hundred and fifteen windows, many with stained glass that filter the sunlight as it enters the walls and tints the floor with their designs. Some feature floral patterns, others have religious images or tales from American history. The most striking window is the Space Window, a striking work that contains an actual piece of lunar rock.

Close to five hundred friends and family attended the event. Loren's father and mother came from their ranch in western Colorado, along with her two brothers and two sisters. Pitt's father, Senator George Pitt, and his mother, Barbara, were there, beaming now that their wild son was finally settling down with a woman they both loved and admired. The NUMA gang turned out: Admiral Sandecker, actually looking like he was enjoying himself; Hiram Yaeger, with his wife and daughters; Rudi Gunn; Zerri Pochinsky, Pitt's longtime secretary; and a score of other people whom Pitt had worked with during his many years with NUMA. St. Julien Perlmutter was there, taking up nearly three places on the bench seats.

A large number of Washington's elite were in the audience, senators, congressmen, bureaucrats, statesmen and even the president and his wife, who were in residence and able to attend.

Loren's bridesmaids were her sisters. Her matron of honor was her secretary, Marilyn Trask, who had been at Loren's side from the time she first ran for Congress. Summer Pitt, her soon-to-be daughter-in-law, was also a bridesmaid. Pitt's best man was his old sidekick, Al Giordino, and his ushers were his son Dirk, Rudi Gunn and Loren's brothers.

Loren wore her mother's 1950s-vintage wedding gown: a combination of white lace and satin with a deep V neckline; embroidered bodice; long, fitted sleeves of white lace; and a very full three-layered satin skirt that was worn with a hoop to achieve a dramatic effect. Dirk and his team looked resplendent in white tie and tails.

The cathedral choral choir sang as the guests were seated. Then they became still as the organ began playing the traditional wedding march.

Every head turned and stared up the aisle. At the altar, Pitt and his friends stood in a line and gazed toward the back of the church as the bridesmaids, led by Summer, began walking down the aisle.

Loren, looking radiant as she held the arm of her father, smiled and smiled as she locked eyes with Pitt.

When they reached the altar, Mr. Smith stepped aside and Pitt took Loren's arm. The ceremony was officiated by Reverend Willard Shelton, a friend of Loren's family. The rite was traditional, with no original odes of undying love given by bride and groom.

Afterward, as they walked up the aisle to the entrance of the church, Giordino ran out a side exit and brought the car around to the cathedral steps just as Pitt and Loren walked out into a beautiful afternoon with white clouds sailing majestically across the sky. She turned around and threw her bridal bouquet and it was caught by Hiram Yaegar's eldest daughter, who laughed, blushed as red as a valentine and broke into a fit of giggles.

Giordino was waiting in the driver's seat of the rose-colored Marmon V-16, as Pitt opened the door for Loren and helped her inside by folding her wedding gown. No longer accepted, rice was replaced with birdseed that rained down upon them as they waved to the crowd. Giordino eased the gearshift into first and the big car pulled away from the steps of the cathedral. He drove through the gardens onto Wisconsin Avenue and turned toward the Potomac River and Pitt's hangar, where the reception would be held. The rear divider window between the driver's seat and the passengers was rolled up and Giordino could not hear what Loren and Pitt were saying.

"Well, the evil deed is done," Pitt said, laughing.

Loren punched him in the arm. "Evil deed, is that what you call our beautiful wedding?"

He held her hand and looked at the ring he had slipped on her third finger. It held a three-carat ruby surrounded by small emeralds. After the Shockwave exploits, he was savvy enough to know that rubies and emeralds were fifty times more rare than diamonds, which in reality were a glut on the world market. "First I'm confronted with two grown children I never knew I had, and now I have a wife to cherish."

"I like the word *cherish*," she said softly, throwing her arms around his neck and kissing him forcibly on the mouth.

When he finally eased her back, he whispered, "Let's wait for the honeymoon before we get carried away."

She laughed and kissed him again. "You never told me where you were taking me. You kept it a big surprise."

"I chartered a small sailing yacht in Greece. We're going to sail around the Mediterranean."

"Sounds wonderful."

"Think a Colorado cowgirl can learn to raise sails and navigate?"

"Just watch me."

They soon arrived at Pitt's hangar. Giordino used the remote to turn off the security alarms and open the main door. Then he drove the Marmon onto the main floor. Pitt and Loren stepped from the car and climbed the stairway to his apartment, where they changed into more casual clothes for the reception.

St. Julien charged into the hangar like a maddened hippopotamus and began shouting orders to the caterers. He dabbed sweat from his brow brought on by the warm, humid Indian summer day and admonished the maître d' of Le Curcel, the Michelin three-star restaurant he had hired to cater the reception. "These oysters you expect to serve are the size of peanuts. They simply won't do."

"I shall have them replaced immediately," the maître d' promised before rushing away.

Soon the guests began arriving and were served a California estate champagne while seated at tables throughout the hangar. They began dabbling in the gourmet delicacies from several buffet tables laid around the ornate antique bathtub with an outboard motor that Pitt had used to escape Cuba many years earlier. The buffet table featured polished silver chafing dishes and iced platters kept filled with every variety of food that could be pulled from the sea, including abalone and sea urchin.

Perlmutter did himself proud by creating a menu that most likely would never be duplicated again.

When Admiral Sandecker arrived, he asked to see Pitt alone. He was shown into one of the staterooms of the Manhattan Limited Pullman car that Pitt used as an office. After Pitt closed the door and they sat down, Sandecker lit up one of his battleship cigars and blew a blue haze toward the paneled ceiling.

"You know that Vice President Holden is in poor health," the admiral began.

"I've heard rumors."

"The situation is much worse. Holden isn't expected to live out the month."

"I'm sorry to hear that," said Pitt. "My father has known him for thirty years. He's a good man."

Sandecker looked at Pitt to see his reaction. "The president has asked me to be his running mate in the next election."

Pitt's heavy black brows knitted together. "The president is a shoo-in to win. Somehow, I can't picture you as a vice president."

Sandecker shrugged. "It's an easier job than I have now."

"Yes, but NUMA is your life."

"I'm not getting younger and I'm burned out after twenty-five years in the same job. It's time for a change. Besides, I'm not the type to sit as a do-nothing vice president. You've known me long enough to know I'll shake the government by the throat."

Pitt laughed. "I know you won't hide in a closet in the White House or remain silent on issues."

"Especially environmental issues pertaining to the seas," Sandecker elaborated. "When you think about it, I can do more good for NUMA from the White House than I can in my fancy office across the river."

"Who takes over as head of NUMA?" asked Pitt. "Rudi Gunn?"

Sandecker shook his head. "No, Rudi doesn't want the job. He feels more comfortable as second in command."

"Then who do you plan to tap?"

A sly smile spread Sandecker's thin lips. "You," he replied briefly.

At first the word *you* flew over Pitt's head, and then it sank in. "Me? You can't be serious."

"I can't think of a more qualified person to take the reins."

Pitt came to his feet and paced the room. "No, no, I'm not an administrator."

"Gunn and his team can handle the day-to-day business," explained Sandecker. "With your background of achievement, you'd be the perfect choice to act as NUMA's chief spokesman."

The enormity of the decision was not lost on Pitt. "I've got to think about this."

Sandecker came to his feet and walked to the door. "Think about it during your honeymoon. We'll discuss it when you and Loren return."

"I've got to discuss it with her first, now that we're married."

"We've already talked. She's in favor."

Pitt fixed the admiral with an iron stare. "You old devil."

"Yes," said Sandecker cheerfully. "I am that."

Pitt returned to the reception and mingled with the guests, posing for pictures with Loren and their parents. He was talking with his mother when Dirk came up and tapped Pitt on the shoulder.

"Dad, there's a man at the door who wants to see you."

Pitt excused himself and walked through the rows of old cars and the throng of friends and guests. When he reached the door, he found an older man, around seventy with white hair and beard. He stood almost the same height as Pitt, and though his eyes were not as green they had a similar twinkle.

"Can I help you?" asked Pitt.

"Yes, I contacted you some time ago about coming by and viewing your car collection. We parked next to each other at a concourse a few years ago."

"Of course, I displayed my Stutz and you had a Hispano Suiza."

"Yes, that's right." The man looked behind Pitt at the festivities. "It seems I've come at a bad time."

"No, no," said Pitt in a happy mood. "It's my wedding day. You're welcome to join the party."

"That's very gracious of you."

"I'm sorry, I've forgotten your name."

The old man looked at him and smiled. "Cussler, Clive Cussler."

Pitt studied Cussler pensively for a long moment. "Strange," he said in a vague tone, "I get the feeling I've known you for a long time."

"Perhaps in another dimension."

Pitt put his arm around Cussler's shoulders. "Come on in, Clive, before my guests drink up all the champagne."

Together, they stepped into the hangar and closed the door.